SILENT PARTNERS

Margaret Wiermanski

Silent Partners

Margaret Wiermanski

Editing by **Booktique Editing**
Proofing by **Booktique Editing**
Book design by Swish Design & Editing
Cover design by Kate DeGroot and Jodi Welter
Published by Aether Analytics, LLC
Cover Image Copyright 2020
All Rights Reserved

Table of Contents

Prologue

Since high school, I have consistently worked in the Chicago and New York floor trading community. My specialization is not with the big Wall Street firms. After college, I did a brief stint at a Big Eight accounting firm, now known as The Big Four. In those days, there were a lot of people with decades of experience with stocks and traditional futures, but I grew up with options and financial futures, which were relatively new. Derivatives are as much of my family's lifeblood as local Chicago politics. I knew the language, the players, and could actually understand trading sheets. As a consequence, at the ripe old age of twenty-six, I was the expert on anything pertaining to options and financial futures in the Chicago office of the world's largest accounting and financial services consulting firm.

For the next ten years, I worked mostly with groups that had operations on an exchange floor. At three of the firms, my role was to stage them for either a total acquisition or an external investor, besides establishing and managing the financial management, compliance, and general administration functions. Traders don't put much stock into those functions until it affects the valuation of their firm. In fact, they usually think it is a plot subverted by some socialist, full employment act conspiracy to require and enforce those disciplines. It is a total mystery to most alpha traders why their trading sheets are not sufficient and why the SEC, CFTC, investors, etc. adhere to a pesky GAAP accounting reporting standard.

I am forty-seven years old and have been working at a clearing firm, Lough Key Clearing Services, founded by my grandfather, passed down to my uncle and now largely owned and managed by my first cousin, William Keagan. A clearing firm is like a bank for traders that not only provides cash to pay for their trades and margin requirements but also is where their positions are maintained like Merrill Lynch or Fidelity for a retail investor.

We are obviously professionally Irish, except me. It is at the suggestion of my cousin, William Keagan, or Billy, that I write this book. I am suffering from a bad case of 'Empty Nest Syndrome'. My husband has been missing in action for two years in the Middle East, which is another story, and one I don't want to think about. My twenty-two-year-old son, Cahill, graduated early from the University of Michigan and is now in a financial engineering master's program at the University of Edinburgh. Ellie Rose, my nineteen-year-old daughter, is attending Georgetown University and is under the misimpression she can change the world.

I live in a three-flat greystone in Oak Park, Illinois, the first suburb west of the city. We owned it as an investment, rental property, and until about a year ago, my family resided in a large brick bungalow in River Forest. I can't stand the quiet, so now I rent the bungalow out and live in one of the apartments with my two sets of geriatric tenants and my dog, Fred, a 215-pound English Mastiff.

Billy describes me as the proverbial fly-on-wall during interesting times. He is right, but I think of myself more like a narrator in a contemporary Damon Runyon story. I work in a neighborhood populated by math whiz characters and a few miscreants who make a living responding to economic events. I am an observer and a facilitator, but not an instigator or even interesting on my own. In spite of my best efforts, I get caught in the undertow of the misadventures of my clients, friends, and family. I wouldn't have it any other way.

Chapter 1

I always hate the first Monday after we switch the clocks ahead an hour in March. An hour is a big difference to people who start work at six thirty in the morning. I was treating myself to a late start and was hoping for a quiet day to catch up after closing the audit last Friday, but that was not in my stars today. There were two men in suits standing by the reception desk. Guests at seven fifteen are rare, just like men in suits at a trading company in Chicago.

Jason, one of the trading clerks, was sitting at the reception desk with a phone in his hand. His day starts at five thirty in the morning, which explains why he always looks overly caffeinated. Today was worse because his eyes looked ready to pop out of his head.

"Police, asking for you." He pointed at the two men.

I would never have pegged them to be policemen, but I probably watch too much TV. The taller one was African American and looked like a nice person and probably played football in college. He had a friendly gruffness, wore at least a size fourteen shoe, and clearly a client of the Big & Tall Department of Men's Warehouse. His navy-blue suit with white shirt and red tie looked like his work uniform and not a reflection of his after-hours wardrobe.

"I'm Detective Williams, and this is Detective Guzman. Are you Laney Daye?" He extended his hand to me.

"What's wrong, is somebody hurt?" My immediate reaction was alarm.

"This has nothing to do with your family, or at least I don't think so. Is there a place where we can sit down and talk?" Detective Williams responded.

"Um, sure. We can step into the conference room." I pointed through the open door to a large table and chairs with a view of the south side of the Loop overlooking the Rock Island commuter train tracks.

I turned to Jason. "Is Billy around?"

Jason shook his head. "Not yet. I just called him, and he's on his way up from Ceres."

"Thanks. Listen, can you please not spread this around until we know what this is about?" I asked just like I thought there was an actual chance he would comply.

Relieved, but puzzled, I walked the few steps to the conference room and stepped aside to let them enter first. Out of habit, I asked them if they wanted coffee or water. Both shook their heads no.

Detective Guzman quietly closed the door, and Detective Williams asked me to have a seat. "Can you please tell us how you're acquainted with Benjamin Stein? He died yesterday."

In spite of seeing almost this same scene in countless crime dramas, I was dazed by the question. "I don't know how to answer that. I have known him for over twenty years, but we don't socialize or have the same friends. He's somebody who's always around, and we both more or less grew up professionally around the exchanges, but that isn't like I know him. I'm assuming you being here means he didn't die in his sleep. I can't imagine why you want to talk to me about him. How did he die?"

Billy Keagan stepped in. He is what my grandmother calls 'Dark Irish' meaning jet-black hair with a fair complexion and deep blue eyes. He keeps in shape and is always well-dressed, which, for a trading company, means button-down shirt and slacks straight from the dry cleaner. Billy is gifted with professional charm and habitually takes over most situations.

"Hey, what's up, Laney?"

"All I know is Benny died yesterday. These two are police detectives, Mr. Williams and Mr. Guzman," I said, pointing in their direction.

"Excuse me, you are?" asked Detective Guzman. He gave the impression of quiet calm. That may be due to being dressed in warm shades of tan, lots of dark hair combed back, friendly brown eyes, and a really nice smile.

"Oh, sorry. Bill Keagan, the Managing Partner of the firm. What can we do for you this morning?" he asked while walking up to shake hands.

Detective Williams responded by explaining that Benjamin Stein was shot sometime the day before, and they wanted to talk to me because there was a note on his desk to ask me questions that seem to have to do with banking.

"Please get Oscar to come in now," I requested, turning to Bill. My stomach lurched. I had a very bad feeling, and my notions are usually right, especially with anything involving Benny Stein.

Billy gave me his look meaning WTH.

"Who's Oscar?" Detective Williams asked while Billy was texting.

"Oscar Marquis is the firm's General Counsel. I'd feel a lot better if he participated." I could see neither of the detectives liked the idea. "I'm overly cautious by nature, and you coming here and mentioning Benny wanting to discuss banking makes me nervous. I have never been interviewed by the police before." To make the point, I started scratching my left palm with my right hand.

"Why don't we start out with some basic information. There's no need to be nervous. Let's begin with something simple. Please confirm your name and start out explaining what do you do here and what was Mr. Stein's relationship with you and your firm?" Detective Williams asked quietly.

Billy nodded okay, and I started.

"My name is Elaine Daye, and Benny was a clearing client of Lough Key Clearing Services for many years. He used to be a big pit trader, but lately, he hadn't been doing much in any trading accounts here. From what I gathered, he was mostly active in his personal trading account at IB. A few months back, he leased a cheap seat for a few hundred bucks a month just to give him access to the floor and building. Starting at around nine thirty or ten in the morning, he spent his time trolling what remains of the floor, the cigar shop, Ceres, the restaurant and bar in the lobby, and the rest of the Board building for people to talk to. I was a favorite to bother with stupid questions and adolescent comments."

"Did you discuss business or anything personal? What was a typical conversation?" Detective Williams interrupted. I sighed.

"Lately, they really were stupid. He'd ask questions like do breast implants qualify as a tax-deductible medical expense. At least twice a week he'd make some off-color comment about daydreaming, which, in his mind, was a clever pun based on my last name. He was just a pest. He never shut up, but our conversations lately were mostly time-wasters because he was bored."

"You never had any professional interactions with him?"

I shook my head no. "I did years ago, but these past couple of years, he has been an independent trader who clears here, and I only speak with him in passing."

"What was your prior business association about? Did you do business with or for him?"

Again, I shook my head no and looked at Billy.

"Shortly after Y2K, a bunch of local option trading firms were acquired by banks that had or wanted options trading operations on the exchange floors. Many were bought at fire-sale prices because of the deep losses so many took, and the business model changed to require expensive infrastructure. I was an outside auditor for such a firm where Benny was a partner, that sold to a Canadian bank. A couple of years later, the traders who sold out to the bank were suing for breach of contract on deferred compensation subject to an earn-out, and the bank countersued alleging the traders of mismarking their trading inventory. I wound up being deposed by both sides and almost had to go to court to testify as an expert witness. You remember what a mess that was, Billy?"

Billy nodded. "Yeah, I do remember. Benny was one of the traders in the middle of that fray. Did you have to deal with him much?"

"Sort of. He'd call all the time trying to engage me to listen to his version of events, and he sat through a couple of my depositions." I turned toward the policemen. "That's how we initially bonded in Benny's mind. He thought my testimony supported their position. I have not had any interaction with him since outside of him being a client here who likes being a nuisance."

"So why do you want lawyers and the head man here to participate?" Detective Williams asked.

I shook my head, and said I wanted to wait. Bill was shooting me more WTH glares, and I became aware of how intensely Detective Guzman was observing me.

"Why did you put up with him? Was he that good of a client? There're laws now against workplace harassment," Detective Williams

"No, Benny wasn't like that. He was harmless and didn't bother the younger girls. In fact, he was really sweet, in his way, to any female he thought of as a nice girl, and nobody was nicer to pregnant women. He used to be a big trader, and I think his father is a friend of Billy's father, who's a founding partner. With me, he was like a pesky cousin trying to get a rise out of me. If he didn't go away after the second time, I told him to shut up he knew I'd charge his account five hundred dollars for wasting my time. It's as dumb as it sounds but harmless." Detective Williams noticed Billy smirking. "Do you have something to add?" he asked, turning toward him.

"You have to understand that everybody knew Benny, and he was viewed mostly as a local character. You couldn't believe half of what he said, and he didn't expect anybody to. He never kept his stories straight, but they were all about big scores of one sort or another. He spent most of his time putting on a show. He'd do things like having his driver illegally park his white Beamer on Van Buren behind the

Board building with 'THE MAN' vanity plates. He never outgrew being the class clown."

"Why did people tolerate him?"

"First, he was always good for picking up the tab. Secondly, there're a lot of people who find his humor funny. He'd do things like order Carson's ribs or Shrine's steak sandwiches for his entire pit every expiration Friday. He'd even order enough for the floor staff who would fine him every month for bringing food down on the exchange trading floor. The other thing is he had a very long run as a successful trader and was very generous to a lot of people," Billy responded.

"Had?"

I shook my head. "No business until Oscar gets here."

"What do you do here?" Detective Guzman looked up from his tablet and asked.

"I'm the COO and in charge of the finance, compliance, and general admin functions of the firm, which mostly run by themselves. My daily focus is on clearing corporation deposit requirements and balances and all of the banking. We're clearing members at all the US futures exchanges and a couple in Europe. Basically, I keep track of all of the firm's deposits and make sure we're efficient with our cash. I'm an accountant, and I also do a lot of the research on how to structure the company for new business lines."

An older, lanky gentleman stepped in straight from the elevator. His suit was obviously expensive. His old-fashion tasseled loafers, gray clipped hair, and wireless-frame glasses completed the image of a successful corporate attorney. He is my friend and the wisest man I know, Oscar Marquis.

"Hello, gentlemen! To what do we owe the pleasure?" greeted Oscar.

He nodded toward me. "Laney?"

Relieved, but speaking too fast, I answered.

"So far all we know is Benny Stein was shot yesterday, and these two policemen are here because Benny made some note to speak to me about banking. Oscar, Benny was

12

badgering me with questions last week, and he and I had our monthly standoff on what types of expenses could be taken out of a trading account. I blew him off because we were busy getting the yearly audit closed but did agree to let him buy me lunch in the office today to ask his questions. I was planning on speaking to you if it seemed more-than-usual Benny nonsense. I asked for you to come because I started to get a feeling that something wasn't right with him, and I wonder if whatever happened to him explains why he has been less needy and more business-like lately."

"Okay. Calm down. Do you know anything for a fact about his finances, business, other relationships, or what Benny has been up to lately?" Oscar asked.

"No, which is why I want you here. I'm not sure what to say for that reason."

Detective Williams stopped Oscar from speaking to me. "Now that your lawyer is here, let's start over. This isn't a formal statement, counselor, just some beginning background information. Ms. Daye, why don't you share with us your recent interactions with Mr. Stein?"

Oscar nodded his consent and moved to sit at the head of the table. Bill kept vigilance standing at the window, so I began.

"The first thing is that I think Benny was feeling old and was lonely. He worked very hard since at least the eighties to embody the mythical version of a Chicago pit trader, down to the phony wise-guy accent and Andrew Dice Clay clothes and humor. But that isn't edgy cool anymore. There aren't too many guys around who want to see his picture with Dennis Rodman at a strip club in Detroit. Benny was totally shut down the other week when one of the younger guys told him he was in kindergarten when the Bulls were last hot, and it might be a cool story if Benny was with Patrick Kane.

"To understand Benny lately, you first have to appreciate how shutting down the trading floors and everything moving upstairs to computerized trading further displaced him. It isn't as social, and the career path for college grads going into trading isn't starting out as a clerk and near-slave of a trader for the chance of learning how to trade in the pits and being staked some starting capital. The younger traders are mostly engineers with impressive grade point averages from good schools and aren't going to take crap from a guy like Benny. They make good money right out of school, don't have to start out running errands and collecting trading cards, and can pay for their own drinks, which they would rather have not in the company of a guy almost their dad's age. Worse for him, they sit at desks in offices that he can't enter and are more analytical in how they approach and discuss trading.

"Around Christmas, he told me he was going to move. I thought he just had a bad case of the holiday blues. His master plan was to go to Florida because he'd be one of the few able-bodied men under the age of one hundred. He thought it would be easier for him to pick up a different waitress every night. He didn't answer when I asked him about his girlfriend who I have not seen in months.

"It was about then that he started talking about trading an account or fund for a European bank. On New Year's Eve, he brought three shady-looking guys in the office to open a corporate trading account. They left once I made it clear we adhere to the European protocol that all company principals have to present themselves with certified Letters of Authorization and passports plus submit appropriate Articles of Organization and Certificates in Good Standing from wherever the company headquarters are located, and we also require a US agent. Since then, Benny has asked me a lot of questions about tax havens, setting up companies in the Netherland Antilles, and other odd questions centered on tax evasion. I didn't take him seriously.

"Late January, he deposited 2.4 million dollars into his trading account, which is a limited liability company. I called him in and asked him where he got the money. He told me that it was his, and it was going to be his capital contribution to some European trading operation. Supposedly, he or this group had hired lawyers to restructure Benny's company, so they could be owners. The check was a personal check drawn from his account at the Lake Shore Bank, located in the lobby of this building. I called one of the bankers I know there with Benny in the office to confirm they were satisfied with its origins and had done the Anti-Money Laundering [AML] due diligence. I never got an answer as to why he couldn't wait until whatever company or partnership was legally established, but he clearly thought it was imminent.

"In February, he wanted to make withdrawals from his account with us for things like his rent, driver, car lease, and credit card. He had this notion that since he rented at Presidential Towers, the name on the rent checks could pass as an office lease, and he could also claim the other expenses were for business. His scheme was to make them appear to be valid business expenses if they were paid from a trading account. I told him no, we aren't going to do that but would send a wire to his or a business bank account enough for him to pay his bills. He didn't like that or that only the first wire a month would be free, and each subsequent one would be twenty dollars. We had that same conversation multiple times.

"Last week, he was being polite and acting like a normal person. He said he really needed advice and promised not to take up much of my time and would bring me lunch from my favorite sushi restaurant. Truthfully, what I considered most odd was that Benny was willing to walk two blocks to get a box lunch. I never did discuss the matter further and have no idea of any of the specifics."

I felt sick when I finished, and the four sets of eyes staring at me didn't help. The two detectives were watching us and waiting to see who would take the lead. I could tell that Oscar was calibrating the situation but had not yet made up his mind whether to shut me up.

Bill took the hint. "Lane, why didn't you say anything to us?"

"What was there to say? Benny is being a blowhard, annoying, he's bored, and bothering people? Before today, how would this be any different than any of his stories?"

"Like what?" asked Detective Williams.

"He had dozens like about partnering with a Russian syndicate in some internet gambling site or being invited by the Symmetry Trading partners to invest in a hockey team. Lately, he has been all about being a market maker in Bitcoins, the virtual currency."

"She's right. The more ignored he was, the more outrageous his stories became," Billy added, nodding.

"So why did he keep coming to you if you didn't encourage him?" Detective Guzman asked.

"Well, I guess it was out of habit. For years, his routine was to go to the floor, trade the opening of whatever he was trading at the time for an hour or so, and then come upstairs. He'd then walk around the entire office looking for an audience or victim. At lunchtime, he'd either go out or return in time to trade the close or leave for the day, depending on market conditions. He usually traded products that close shortly after one or two o'clock, and then he'd go workout. As he got older and less of a trading rock star, he couldn't command male camaraderie like he desired, so he reverted to being a bigger pest. I put up with a small amount of his BS because I have seen him do many kind things for people really down on their luck, and I felt sorry for him."

"Nice life. How good of a trader was he? Was it possible for him to have 2.4 million dollars sitting in an account like that?" Detective Williams asked.

Billy walked away from the window to answer. "Yes. He actually was pretty smart. He graduated with honors as an accountant and finance major from Penn State. He later would audit a lot of financial engineering graduate classes at the University of Chicago. He never got an MBA as he didn't care about the grades. He just wanted the information. For somewhere around for twenty years, he was a consistent seven-figure producer without taking much risk."

"What does that mean?" questioned Detective Guzman.

"It means that for around twenty years, he made more than a million dollars each year, sometimes several, but without taking crazy chances and counting on blind luck, and he didn't require much capital to back him."

"So, what happened to him?" prompted Detective Guzman.

"His run ended with the increased cost of doing business due to everything going electronic at a time when profit margins shrank. To achieve the same net income, you need a group effort on many levels and a significant investment in technology and highly compensated programmers with high-end math skills. That isn't possible for a sole prop trader, and Benny wasn't a person who worked well with others at a peer level."

"I want to return to the three men you mentioned meeting on New Year's Eve. Do you know who they were? Why didn't you like them?" Detective Williams asked, turning to me.

I shook my head. "No, I never found out who they really were. One was short, about forty, and he looked like he was trying too hard to appear like he was from the Caribbean. He had a cream color linen suit on in December in Chicago, and his tan was too orange like it came from a bottle. His hair was highlighted with blond streaks and looked too done for a man or at least one from Chicago. His business card looked equally fake. It was expensive paper stock with gold, raised print but no firm name, no logo, and only a PO Box in the Cayman Islands. The card had his name as James William Henry Carrington III, which is consistent with his exaggerated Boston, Ivy League accent. I remember it because it was so implausible. He was trying to pass himself off as some sort of international financier from a European hedge fund that required strict confidentiality.

"The second guy was short, too, only weedy. He wasn't going for the GQ look and was pretty scruffy. His hair was too long but looked naturally bleached blond from the sun, but his tan was real. He wore European style jeans, a leather jacket, clogs, smelled like an ashtray, and carried a large, buckskin leather bag. He was introduced as the idea or concept guy and purported to be a consultant for the hedge fund. He never gave me a card and didn't say much, but he seemed to be the most interested in reading me. I got the impression he thought James William was trying too hard with his pitch. I can't identify his accent other than it was probably not one of the romance languages, and I don't think it was German.

"The third man was exotic-looking and hard to place. He could be from Bosnia, Turkey, or otherwise Middle Eastern, but I don't think he was Latin. He was tall, very handsome, and perfectly tailored with striking elegance like the real deal from Bond Street in London. He had large gold cufflinks and what I took as a multi-thousand-dollar watch. I couldn't place his accent other than thinking he was educated in the UK or someplace where his English was taught by a Brit. He clearly took for granted his irresistible charm on women. He was the one who supposedly worked for the bank or bank hedge fund that was looking for alternative investments. He also didn't provide a business card. His main contribution was smiling meaningfully at me and complimenting Benny and his wise choice for a clearing firm with such a long-standing reputation of excellence.

"I got the feeling they intentionally picked New Year's Eve because the two of you were known to be out. My sense is that the plan was to overwhelm me with charisma and get me to believe their story and compelling sense of urgency in opening a trading account in a company name without having any bona fides. Looking back, Benny didn't seem surprised at the outcome and didn't say much. It ended with the tall one not being able to contain his anger at Benny or me, and the other two following him out like disappointed boy scouts."

"Lane! Why didn't you mention this to Oscar or me?" Billy asked.

"Well, I guess it wasn't that good of a story a week later when you were back, and we were both so busy. Besides, at the end of the day, what was the big take away? Benny tried another con, and I bounced him. So what? As I said, I was planning on discussing it with at least Oscar if I felt there was reason to be concerned about Benny after we were to speak today."

"Okay, folks. Let's take a step back. Ms. Daye, how were you introduced to the three of them, did you get any names?" Detective Williams interrupted.

"I know this scenario and me are sounding more stupid by the minute. I also sound like I have an overactive imagination and read too many John Grisham books. You have to understand that at the time, I thought this was more about Benny hanging out with sketchy people, which, in my opinion, he did frequently, and was another exaggerated claim of untold millions. I didn't care what their names were, and I wouldn't have remembered John William Henry Carrington III if it didn't strike me as funny. He said his name almost like he was singing a song. I really don't recall ever being told what the skinny blond man's name was. When I was introduced to the tall one, I was more entertained by his performance. I think his name was something like Nivar, but I'm notorious for being very bad with names." Now I felt really sick, shaking my head.

"Do you recall if Nivar is a first or last name?" asked Detective Williams.

"No."

"Do you recall what bank he represented?"

"It had a vague name like EuroCredit Bank. I never heard of it before, which is another reason why I thought this was a scam."

"Were you told when they came to town or this country? Do you know where they stayed or who else they may have met? Was there anything at all, even the name of a restaurant or bar they went to?" Detective Guzman asked.

"No."

"But..." Billy added, "Benny was a creature of habit and tended to frequent the same places, depending on the company he was keeping. Do you think that would help?"

"You can't tell, but maybe we can find out a name from a credit card? Would Mr. Stein be such a regular that staff would know him?" Detective Williams asked.

"Oh yeah," responded Billy. "You couldn't miss Benny when he was in entertainment mode. For one thing, he often preferred a white stretch over his BMW at night. The parking valets would remember that."

Detective Williams turned to Detective Guzman. "We can probably work backward from his credit card statements."

"Maybe not," Billy said, and I nodded in agreement. He elaborated. "Benny liked paying in cash. He loved displaying large bills in a money clip."

"The few times I thought about it, I wondered why because of the various reward programs offered by credit card companies, and Benny loved getting something for nothing. It never made sense to me. At one time, I decided he must be doctoring receipts for tax purposes, which wouldn't be possible if the receipts had to tally to a credit card statement," I added.

Detective Williams was getting visibly impatient. "So, you routinely let a guy hang around your office who isn't conducting business, discuss financial fraud, and bring in questionable associates. You really have no idea what they were intending on doing with an account at your firm?

Oscar cleared his throat. "Excuse me, but I think we need to establish the salient points here. Ms. Daye followed firm policies, and as a consequence, Lough Key and its staff complied with all applicable laws and regulations. It isn't Ms. Daye's role to ensure that our clients prepare their tax returns properly. Ms. Daye did all she could not to aid and abet any possible tax fraud Mr. Stein may have been contemplating. Also note, we don't know for a fact how seriously he may have been actually considering such an action. I view the rapport between Ms. Daye and Mr. Stein as nothing more than her demonstrating a little humanity to someone a bit eccentric or down on his luck. I'm sure you two have seen and done something similar many times in your line of work."

He turned to me. "Is there anything else you can add?"

I shook my head no. "If I were to guess, I'd say whatever it was in play had something to do with Bitcoins. Benny came into the office a few days later with a story about having drinks during an afternoon with those three men at the JW Marriott over on Adams. He said the short guy in jeans did business with three random people he met through a chat room or maybe a phone app to exchange Bitcoins for actual currency. He was enamored by the bid-ask spread of the transactions."

"He never said anything about that to me. I'm really surprised. I didn't think Benny spared me from his tall tales. When did this take place?" Billy asked.

"I may have provoked it. New Year's Eve came on a Thursday, and we were all crazy to get through the close, and I just wanted him and the rest of them out. When I saw him the next week, I shared with him my reservations. His response was something like he knows he can count on me to watch his back. I thought I did my good deed and was done.

"When he deposited the 2.4 million dollars, I told him I saw no reason why he had to contribute such a sum before they had any basic documentation or their capital. He then told me about the huge profit potential of Bitcoins and how those men have a relationship with a Russian hedge fund that's the world's biggest Bitcoin market maker. He was thrilled that he found a trading vehicle with huge spreads, which is when he told me the story. His role was to hedge with regular exchange-traded currency futures and options. He wanted to get started because he'd be switching from whatever he was trading previously."

Looking at Detective Williams, I continued with my thoughts.

"I did ask him if he saw the people involved with these transactions. Benny told me two were Asians he took for tourists and one was an Italian-looking young man wearing a lot of bling who pulled up in a Cadillac Escalade in front of the hotel. That transaction took place on the curb. Benny was very proud he anticipated my question about drug dealing and said the Italian guy sold limited-edition athletic shoes that sell for big money to collectors. The story goes that this shoe dealer delivered authentic goods to buyers, who subsequently claim the shoes were not legit. The buyers complained to whatever website they bought them from, I'm assuming eBay, which resulted in the shoe dealer being out his product and the website charging him back for the cash. Bitcoin transactions are not reversible, which eliminates this problem.

"And, yes, I did tell him that I still thought the whole setup was suspicious, and I didn't have a good feeling about his friends. They should know better than trying to pull the stunt they did in my office if they really do work for a legitimate bank. I advised him to consult an attorney, and not his brother or Larry Katz if he was still serious about partnering with them. He should go to a major law firm with a banking practice to first obtain references. Benny laughed at me and told me again how good I am at watching his back."

Detective Guzman was listening and taking notes. I paused. "What are Bitcoins? I think I read they are like money you can buy things with online that can't be traced," he asked.

Billy and I looked at each other, and I shrugged. Billy decided to respond.

"Bitcoins are a form of international currency often called digital or cryptocurrencies that aren't backed or issued by a country. There're probably hundreds of them, but Bitcoin is one of the most known and used in the US. Think about them like baseball cards. They have a value that's determined by the market or sub-group of people who come to an agreement of how much a card is worth in terms of a national currency like US dollars. The mechanical difference is you can actually hold a baseball card because it's a physical object. Bitcoins and other cryptocurrencies are like an account balance for notional credit. It's sort of like a prepaid credit or debit card, but they are contained in a digital wallet on your phone or other computerized device. It's conceptually similar to ApplePay, but way more complicated. They are very controversial.

"There're legitimate reasons to use Bitcoins, especially if you come from a country that doesn't have a currency of its own or one with a limited ability to exchange it for other currencies or goods and services. There're many countries that don't have established banking structures like First World nations. This is also a way to prevent your cash assets from being commandeered should your country experience a regime change or if assets from your country are frozen. Africa has many countries like that.

"Another motive to use them is some countries charge a tax for taking money out of that country or for converting more global currencies like US dollars and euros into the local currency. Bitcoins are a way to avoid that penalty. Brazil is an example. I think it charges a six percent tax to convert US dollars into Reals, its currency which you need to conduct business there. Digital currencies are a popular work-around for people from China and India to conduct business, particularly in real estate in other countries.

"There's a lot of controversy surrounding Bitcoins and the like as the preferred currency for terrorists, drug dealers, and anybody who wants to launder money or avoid taxes. In spite of that, reputable financial institutions are working on how to provide more structure and transparency with the goal of creating more stability and legitimacy in their ownership. There's even a school of thought that predicts global currency equivalents not issued by a government will replace traditional forms of money. The thinking is they will be more stable and efficient in a truly global economy because they won't be subject to many forms of conversion risk and transaction fees."

Latesha opened the conference room door and slammed it shut. She is the Office Manager and usually even-tempered.

She is a tall, impeccably groomed black woman and not the type ever to be intimidated. "Larry Katz is in the hallway and screaming at me to buzz him into the office *now*. He's yelling trash about injunctions, lawsuits, calling the Feds but seems actually serious. Can I call security?"

"Yes, and right away," I said.

I turned to Oscar. "I know that isn't your preference, but you've never seen him in full swing. Billy, I don't know if you would be more effective with him."

"No, just call security and tell them they may want to bring a couple of the beat police officers. Latesha, did he give any indication what he wants?"

She shook her head no. "I just know he'll try to force his way in the next time somebody enters or leaves the office, and this is a busy time of day. What do I tell the office?"

"Send an email asking everybody who can to avoid that door and ask a couple of the Eurodollar guys to block him if he does try to push his way in. He'll be impossible to remove if he gets on this side of the door," Billy responded.

Latesha nodded and left giving Billy a meaningful glare.

"Is this a typical thing? Who's he, and why aren't one of you going out there to handle the situation?" Detective Williams asked.

"Because it's a very bad sign and a safe bet we're in for more trouble," I said. "I wouldn't be surprised if this has something to do with Benny."

"And why do you think that?" Oscar asked.

"First, please explain how you know him," requested Detective Williams.

Billy and I looked at each other, so I took the lead. "It's a long story about who and what Larry Katz is. Local legend has it that he overtly cultivates a reputation for circumventing rules. His alleged expertise is in corporate law and tax loopholes. I saw the two of them together lately in the lobby and having breakfast at Ceres. I didn't think twice about it before, but this is too much of a coincidence."

I actually bent over and crossed my arms over my stomach. I am not a timid person. During my twenty years working at Chicago trading exchanges, I have been aggressively interviewed by the FBI, deposed by the SEC and CFTC, and was raised to be totally immune to noise since my father was a field artillery officer in the army who could yell over howitzers. I can hold my own with any group of traders in any pit. I also work a lot of community service in neighborhoods run by gangs where gunshots are an everyday occurrence.

Larry Katz is the vilest person I ever encountered. He looks and dresses like a fifteen-year-old stoner with the same slouching posture and messed-up 'meth teeth.' He smells like someone who chronically smokes dope and doesn't bathe or wash his clothes, but his odor reminds me of the sulfuric smell of the devil. What disturbs me most about him are his eyes. They are taunting and intelligent. Anything I heard involving him never had a happy ending.

By now, we could hear yelling in the reception area outside the conference room. Billy got up and said he would handle it. I took that as a sign to stay put. Oscar was giving me meaningful stares.

"Do you know any factual link between Katz and Benny other than geographic proximity and being acquainted?"

"Not really. I'm under the impression his brother or someone at his firm did most of Benny's legal work, but Benny did enjoy sharing his opinion of Larry's various twists on legal interpretations. Benny talked like Larry's disbarment was a positive reflection on his skill set but to your point... I don't know anything specific that's a fact."

Oscar nodded his approval that I had taken his hint and turned to the detectives. "I suggest your best resource on Mr. Stein's legal and financial affairs may be his brother. Lane, do you have his contact information?"

Billy returned to the conference room but remained standing by the door. "Latesha had enough. She expedited Larry's departure by pointing a can of what she claimed was pepper spray and told him she'd love to bathe his eyes in it and had called security. He's gone, but I suspect not for long. What's really interesting is he claims he has a stake in Benny's trading account, and he does not want his rights being usurped."

Billy looked at the detectives. "How public is it that Benny was killed yesterday? I wouldn't have missed it if it were mentioned in the local news."

The two detectives looked across the table at each other, and Detective Guzman shook his head. "Good question," Detective Williams acknowledged.

"What general background can you three share regarding Larry Katz? We get, counselor, your reluctance to discuss anything anecdotal. I'm hoping for a little background color. I am curious how Mr. Katz can be connected and what you know about his professional activities," he followed, looking directly at Oscar.

I shook my head to indicate I didn't want to start. After five long seconds, Billy started. "Well, Larry is hard to describe, and I don't think any of us here really know what's fact or myth. I don't think a Google search will do him justice because a lot of misdeeds attributed to him are below the surface. I have run into him a handful of times over the years but have fortunately never been involved in any of his business situations. I get the impression he's a professional deviate. He could be successful in legitimate enterprises, but he likes trying to outsmart the system, however he defines it.

"To give you an example, a few years back his then accountant told me that Larry registered as a reverend, like the kind of license anybody can get from those ads in the back of the *Rolling Stone Magazine*. He set up a church complete with an IRS 501c-3 registration as a tax-exempt non-profit charity. The name of the church was long, but I recall the last two words in it were 'saved souls.' Larry placed ads in publications that appealed to religious fundamentalists. The ads promised that for seven dollars, his church would hold your soul in escrow. The owner of the soul could rape, steal, and murder without consequence in the afterlife because the soul was placed in safekeeping with the church and would be reunited when the owner died and apparently unblemished by sin.

"Larry actually did take out a safety box in a bank where the souls were supposedly deposited. According to the accountant, Larry made around 40K a year, tax-free, saving souls. What was so clever and amusing to him was that seven dollars isn't a big enough sum to warrant any criminal charges, and he thought he had the perfect retort to the question, how many angels can fit on the head of a pin? His accountant surmised that people bought them for gag gifts like for guys going to a bachelor party.

"However, not all of his exploits are rumored to be harmless. You may want to check what his real involvement was a couple of years back selling short regional bank stocks. Everyone involved with the local stock clearing corporation heard some version of how Larry was selling short more shares than were ever issued on little banks that had their shares traded publicly. It caused all kinds of settlement problems because there would never be enough shares to deliver to the people who bought them, and some of the banks filed a lawsuit alleging he was manipulating the price of their shares and artificially forcing them down way below fair value. The result was that the clearing corporation almost defaulted, and this situation is a case study example of why there're now so many rules with stiff consequences regarding short selling.

"I know this doesn't sound on point for your investigation, but it gives you an idea of why he's associated with financial malfeasance. I really don't know anything about Larry firsthand, and I'd never knowingly permit him to be associated with any account here."

During Billy's narrative, Detective Guzman took notes, but Detective Williams listened with a stony expression.

"Why are you so shook up? Are you worried about him being violent or another form of retribution?" Detective Williams looked at me.

"A little," I answered. "Years ago, he insinuated he'd put out some kind of contract on me. At the time, I laughed it off and called his bluff."

I noticed the surprised response of the two detectives. "I started as an auditor of clearing firms. At the time, I was very pregnant but was called in by an exchange to help out closing down a firm that was in net capital violation because it was letting Larry price and set the margin for a vast portfolio of junk bonds. He came up to me and told me he knew people who could easily take me out. I was raised in North Oak Park, River Forest among many Italian families. I wasn't worried because people who really are mob connected never admit it. I told him I lived down the street from John Buglioni and am best friends with the Gloriosos and Durantes, with whom I was having dinner. I asked if I should send his regards or otherwise forward his comments. It shut him up, but I think because he didn't scare me, and he didn't know what to do next and not because he believed me.

"There're a couple of stories about people associated with him who have committed suicide or had random accidents. I suspect he circulates them himself. I wouldn't describe my aversion to him as fearful in a physical sense, but I'm afraid of the serious trouble that follows in his wake."

Latesha entered the conference room again, and shut the door behind her. "It gets more interesting by the minute. Paul Stein has called at least five times insisting on speaking to you, Bill. He just hung up on me and told me he's coming over to see you in person and to make sure you'll be available to meet with him. Do I let him in?"

"Has the family been notified?" Billy spoke to the detectives.

"Not prior to when we left the station to come over here. It still had not been determined who to contact," Detective Williams responded.

Bill looked at Latesha. "Do people in the office generally know that Benny died?"

Latesha nodded. "Yes, word has it that everybody living in Presidential Towers knew yesterday. From what I heard, there was a lot of police activity parked outside on the Madison Street entrance, which would be hard to miss. By now, nearly everybody downtown knows you three are in here with policemen regarding Benny."

"Okay. Please put all our calls through to the general voicemail and screen them. We might get a few calls from the press, but I'm more concerned about who else will be contacting us regarding Benny."

"Do you want a list, or is that overkill?" Billy asked the detectives.

"You read my mind, thanks. Just in case, can you not erase them until we go over the list?"

Detective Williams said.

Latesha nodded. "What do I do when Paul shows up?"

"Is it okay if we meet with him here?" Detective Williams asked.

"Sure." Billy chuckled.

"I'd like to call our outside counsel to find out where we stand in this type of situation. Bill, Lane, I'd prefer you not to participate in any further discussions, especially with Paul," Oscar injected.

"So, the answer is to let him in but straight here." Latesha left after Oscar and Billy nodded.

"Look, we have a few more questions that shouldn't put you in any legal peril but would help us out. Do any of you know what Paul Stein's relationship is to Benjamin Stein, and do you know who his close family is, and who's the girlfriend you mentioned earlier?" Detective Williams asked.

Oscar nodded and looked at Billy to answer. "Paul is his older brother. He's an attorney specializing in commercial real estate. Their father passed away over ten years ago. Their mother is Beverly Stein, and I don't think she ever remarried. They have a sister, Sharon, who was seriously injured in a water-skiing accident a few years ago. I'm under the impression she lives with her mother because her injuries were permanently disabling. I don't know much more about the family other than they live or did live in Glenview. I don't know anything else for certain regarding Benny's personal life."

Detective Guzman looked up from his notebook at me. "You mentioned a girlfriend, but that incident sounds like it happened a long time ago. Can you add anything?"

I did not like where this was going, especially since it was my fault I mentioned a girlfriend. "What now? I don't know anything for a fact. I really didn't know Benny on a personal level," I asked Oscar.

A loud buzz emitted from the conference table speakerphone. "That must mean Paul is here. We'll step out now. I'll ask Latesha to inform me when you have finished your business with Paul Stein. I hope to speak to our attorney by then to confirm how we may assist you further," Oscar said.

At that moment, a flushed, short man with dark hair exploded into the room. "Bill, Bill, I need to talk to you now. You need to liquidate Benny's accounts and release all funds to me today, tomorrow morning at the latest!"

"Paul Stein, how nice of you to stop by. May I introduce Detectives Williams and Guzman from the Chicago Police Department? They were just asking about your brother." He touched Paul's shoulder. "We're all sorry and shocked to hear about your loss. We'll certainly do what we can to offer you and your family any assistance. I trust you would prefer to have your interview with the police conducted in privacy," Oscar said as if we were all at a neighborhood party.

Taking that as our cue to leave, the three of us filed out of the conference room, and Oscar shut the door.

Chapter 2

We walked a few steps into the lobby. Oscar stopped and told us to meet him in his office in a half hour. He was hoping to speak to Scott Simon, our outside attorney with Finnerty & Fitzpatrick, to have somebody from litigation who also has criminal law expertise to advise us. He was absorbed with the list he was compiling in his head and not approachable for conversation.

Billy told me he was checking with someone he knew who covers breaking crime news with a local television station. He was hoping to find out more of what the police knew so far. I wanted to make a clever remark about how like Archie Goodwin he is but stopped. In my world, people don't have murdered clients or police detectives in the office for interviews and don't really know a reporter they can call for inside scoops.

Responding in kind, I went to my office and started pulling up Benny's account statements for the past year. Latesha came into my office and sat down but left the door open. She is about my age but hasn't aged in the past ten years or so. She wears her hair in long braids collected in a coil at the nape of her neck. She favors Caribbean bright sleeveless dresses, long or short, with jackets or cardigans in the cooler weather. I am still not clear on where she is from. Her skin tone is dark like a Jamaican, but she speaks with a slightly Latin accent. I can't tell if it is from Cuba or Puerto Rico. All she shares is that she moved to Chicago with her parents when she was ten. She has no patience for anybody who does not behave with manners or class, especially younger African Americans.

Latesha has a regal air and treats all of us like beloved minions. She takes advantage of the fact that most of the traders are white and from the suburbs or affluent city families and don't know how to respond to any of her mandates. When we had offices in the Board of Trade, we were the only group that had any services from the building management. Part of her charm is that she really will do something outrageous to make her point. She is the master of using social media to entice cooperation.

She even took on the Board of Trade building management. It was unresponsive to our complaints about cockroaches so large you could leash them and the mice racing around the office and even across people's feet. Latesha mentioned how she just might need to post videos of our offices on YouTube featuring mice happily trotting down the halls and around walkways and the roaches in the ladies' room in locations that clearly are in the Board of Trade building. This was when the building management was marketing to electronic, non-floor-based trading firms and didn't need to be located at or near the Board. We've had no problems since, but we understand our neighbors on other floors do not have the same level of attention from the building management.

Latesha handed me a large cup of scalding hot black tea. "Larry will be back, I feel it. He only left because Joe Kawolzinski came off the Eurodollar desk wearing his University of Michigan football jersey and looked like he wanted to hurt someone real bad."

Like a lot of firms that still have floor traders, we intentionally recruit guys who played college basketball and football from good schools. It has been a successful strategy, and contrary to stereotypes, many of them are pretty smart. Joe is at least three hundred pounds and played defensive line for the Wolverines, yet still graduated with a degree in financial engineering in four years. Today is the kickoff day for the pre-game festivities for the Big Ten Basketball Conference, which explains why he is wearing his college gear. It will be a week full of trash-talking and various kinds of statistically based gambling games on the outcome because so many people in the firm are alums from the Big Ten

Conference, with the biggest concentration being the Illini from the University of Illinois and Wolverines from the University of Michigan.

I held the cup with both hands to absorb its warmth and leaned back in my chair, resting my head against it. A chill raced through my entire body, and it was not because the knit jacket and long-sleeve sweater I was wearing weren't adequate for the weather. I needed a minute to think. We needed to get ahead of whatever was coming.

"Okay, let's start with a list. First, ask Raj from the Help Desk to walk over with you to see Linda and Kevin in Compliance. If both aren't there, start with whoever is. Once you're together, ask Raj to print out four sets of a report or audit of Benny's network activity. Have him make an electronic file on the Compliance drive. For the past six months, we want to see every website he visited, confirm no files from the network were sent to any external location, his activity within our network, any work product he may have produced like spreadsheets, and a list of all email addresses, incoming and outgoing. Have Compliance document the extent he was flagged on any monitoring they do of electronic communication. Please tell them Billy or I would ask ourselves, but we don't have time right now, and I don't want to send an email with this request. Let them know this is in anticipation of the police asking for this type of information. Go ahead and tell them the full recap of what happened this morning. Under no circumstances are they to communicate anything related to this request in an email.

"Second item, send an email to the office announcing an update of today's events will be provided in the trading room near the south facing windows at three thirty, after the equity CBOE index options close, so everybody should be able to attend.

"Since you don't have access to the drive with client trading sheets, I'll be sending you a PDF of Benny's monthly statements for the past two years and his daily activity confirmation for the first few days of this month. Please print four copies and send one electronic file for Compliance to save with Benny's network audit. Have them make sure that Benny didn't have a company cell phone or any other company-owned or supported device. He shouldn't, but we need to confirm."

"What do you think is going to happen? Are you really concerned, or are you preparing for a worst-case scenario?"

I felt another chill and leaned back against my chair again. "I don't know. I'm spooked by Larry's visit this morning and his assertion that he has some claim on Benny's trading account. He's a professional bullshit artist, but there must be something behind it. I'm also alarmed that Paul rushed over in a panic to cash out that account. Think about it, his first concern should be Shiva and funeral arrangements, not getting his hands on the cash tomorrow morning. He'd only do that if he's worried he won't be able to get at it. There must be a reason why, and I'm wondering if it has something to do with Larry Katz. Add that to the field day the press can have with Benny and whatever he was up to, which means Lough Key can be dragged into a sensationalized mess."

"So why don't you want email follow-up? Are you worried they will find something bad?"

"No... it's just so easy for cryptic email statements to be taken out of context. Oscar is clearly worried about litigation, which means all of Benny's activity and files may be combed through by people with a motive to put a bad light on innocuous data points. For example, us looking into Benny's files outside of the scope of our regular monitoring can look like we're worried something is amiss, or we don't have sufficient network security and monitoring procedures in place. I have full confidence that the compliance and network teams do their jobs well. However, it's possible he corresponded by email to a person the police determine is interesting in this case, which does not mean those messages should have been flagged by Compliance. I'm just guessing that the police will want that information and may question us about it. We should be prepared for any scenario. Frankly, things are about to suck big time."

My phone lit up with a text from Oscar asking where Billy and I are. I looked at Latesha. "And it all starts now. The games have begun."

Oscar's office isn't much different than all corner offices in Chicago trading companies. There are the mandatory lithographs—one of the Board of Trade, the Chicago skyline, and the New York Stock Exchange. He has a standard-issue wooden desk and credenza with golf trophies and diplomas scattered about and cute pictures of his wife and two kids. What is nice about Oscar's office is his view of Lake Michigan with Buckingham Fountain. The sunrise is spectacular from his office because it faces east if you like getting in early enough to see the sun rise.

Billy was pacing behind the two guest chairs that face Oscar's office and was in mid-sentence. "... I texted Mike in Risk to check out what positions Benny had opened. Benny went home flat and had closed out all of his positions before he left yesterday. He hadn't been trading much, anyway. It looked like he wasn't building up a position or trading a strategy but was testing a new front-end trading system. I also had Membership terminate his membership and make sure no trades can be initiated in his account. Mike froze the account so no cash can be withdrawn electronically with Benny's passwords. Nothing can be moved without Laney's or my signature.

"I was lucky enough to get Jeff Davies from WGN. Because WGN shares a lot of reporting resources with the *Trib*, he has a contact over there who covers shootings, fires, and the like in the city. Jeff confirmed that Benny was shot yesterday by a nine-millimeter gun, later in the afternoon, probably with a Glock 19, something commonly sold retail for home and personal defense that conforms to the conceal-and-carry limitations. The gun is now assumed to be Benny's or at least bought by him because a Glock 19 is registered to him, but that's still subject to confirmation. There were no signs of forced entry or any struggle. Robbery does not appear to be a motive because he had his wallet and an expensive watch on him plus expensive gold bling chains. Benny was shot three times in the face from only a few feet. The thinking is the shooter isn't a professional but somebody he knew well. There are no security cameras in the halls. His floor is rented to mostly corporate clients which begs the question of why Benny was on that floor. It probably had to do with Benny's apartment being fully furnished with maid service and renewable every three months. Nobody heard anything, but it may be because his neighbors were not around at that time.

"His body was discovered yesterday because his driver got mad when Benny didn't respond. Benny booked the driver and the stretch for the entire night. When he didn't pick up, the driver asked the maid to come by with the key. I don't know the connection between the two, but the driver's story is he didn't want to be out a night's worth of revenue if Benny passed out for the night. Again, I'm only repeating and not sure why Benny didn't have to pay anyway or why he felt compelled to check on Benny's well-being. From subsequent events, one can conclude the driver wanted to double-dip and charge Benny a cancellation fee plus book other fares for the night. The police were called at about eight last night, but only the maid waited for the police to show up. The driver was interviewed around midnight with the same story. He left to work immediately after the call and didn't care the police were threatening him with leaving the scene."

Oscar nodded and indicated I was up next. I recapped my discussion with Latesha, including the precaution to have no content relating to Benny be shared in an email.

It was Oscar's turn to speak. "Good. I wish I had made similar progress. I spoke to Scott Simon. His off-the-cuff prognosis is that we can't be held liable for anything that may be the downstream effect of Benny's actions if we followed procedure, which assumes our procedures have no gaps due to an unanticipated event. Right now, I don't think that's the case. But, that does not mean we won't be dragged into litigation due to the firm's perceived deep pockets in this type of scenario.

"Scott thinks we should at least prepare to be deposed. He strongly cautioned us not to mention anything we don't know personally to be a fact with the police. He understands that a character like Benny overtly attracted attention and neighborhood gossip within the exchange community. We need to avoid the risk of a nuisance suit for defaming his or possibly even his family's reputation or inadvertently directing the police to pursue a false lead or defaming a party the police pursued as a result of something we said. Instructions are not to over-share even seemingly benign information. Given what Jeff Davies described as their line of reasoning, we shouldn't be too interesting to the police for much longer."

On cue, Latesha buzzed Oscar's office. He picked up the phone, nodded, and said Billy and I should return to the conference room. He explained to us that the police wanted to speak to us again, and he wanted to contain their presence to the conference room. I wondered what Paul Stein could have wanted and what he told the police and wondered what happened to him. I hoped our future participation would be limited to turning over account statements but was not optimistic.

As we walked down the hall and into the reception area, I could feel the entire office watching us. Oscar opened the conference room door and stepped back for us to enter first. Billy elected to stand by the window ledge again, I sat in the middle of the table across from the two detectives, and Oscar resumed his seat at the head of the table. The two policemen remained sitting and were finishing up a conversation. It looked like Detective Guzman was checking his notes as they spoke. They both changed their expressions and body language to exude friendliness after we took our places.

Billy spoke first. "What happened to Paul Stein? I sort of expected him to want to speak to one of us before he left."

"I can't speak to that. He was told he could leave after we finished our discussion. He seemed more interested in leaving than sticking around." Since nobody commented, he resumed. "We have a few more questions and are hoping to elicit your help. First, Ms. Daye, you mentioned that Mr. Stein had trading or other kinds of banking accounts. Do you know where or what type of business he conducted with them? You specifically mentioned an IB account. What's that?" Detective Williams asked.

Oscar responded first. "If I may suggest, you'll find this vein of inquiry more productive by talking to the family and referring to his tax returns. We aren't privy to Mr. Stein's activities outside the scope of his trading account with us. We want to avoid the risk of giving you inaccurate or incomplete information, even if it's done on a good-faith basis."

"What's your position on giving us his trading account statements from here, emails, phone records, and anything else he may have kept on his computer here?" Detective Guzman asked.

Oscar nodded. "Good question. We'll need to be subpoenaed with each item you wish being specifically noted. Please don't consider this an indication that we aren't committed to fully cooperating with your investigation. We need to protect the firm from any recourse should his estate be involved in litigation. I'm sure you have seen that these types of situations can take on a life of their own and take years to resolve. However, I have an idea that may suit both of our purposes if you can get the state attorney assigned to this investigation to work with our attorney."

"We're listening," Detective Guzman interjected. Both seemed to anticipate pushback from at least Oscar. They still seemed friendly but didn't look like they had much patience for legal protocols.

With a twinkle in his eye and an arched brow, Oscar leaned forward. "Lane already ordered most of what we anticipate you desire to be produced. It will probably be ready by tomorrow morning. Therefore, you won't be subject to any delay if you can get a subpoena here by tomorrow morning.

I'll even extend to you the courtesy of Ms. Daye's time to give you a list of what she requested after I have a chance to look it over. You can have it by this afternoon to use to draft your document submission request. The firm will even agree to extend up to a mutually agreed-upon number of hours of Ms. Daye's time to review Mr. Stein's financial records, help you interpret his tax returns and probable location of other assets... IF the state's attorney works out an arrangement with our attorney to totally indemnify Lough Key and its staff. Specifically, not to misconstrue the education that Ms. Daye provides as anything other than providing you with sufficient background to conduct the investigation and render your own independent conclusions.

"We wish to avoid being a material witness or even an expert witness. We'll need an agreement that nothing that transpires due to your and other police and state attorney staff resulting in an arrest, allocation, or determination of asset ownership or any other potential legal action under your control or influence is the result of any assistance provided by Ms. Daye."

"So, what you're saying is that you'll help us, as is your legal obligation, but you want to be immune to the extent you may have contributed, aided, or otherwise abetted Mr. Stein's murder or otherwise may have violated any laws that the investigation discovers?" Detective Williams was almost laughing when he asked the question. He wasn't combative but let Oscar know he understood his insinuations.

Oscar continued twinkling and smiling. "Not quite. I'm protecting my firm from the possibility of judicial malfeasance or incompetence as well as the problematic nature of laws that promote nuisance lawsuits motivated by the economics of settling them because it's cheaper than the cost of defense. In return, I'm offering the assistance of one of the best forensic accountants in the business. I'm not sure the police and state attorney's office have people with comparable qualifications, but they must be a limited resource. Ms. Daye's assistance will also prepare the state attorney's office for any defense strategies based on the economics of Mr. Stein's recent activities. As far as indemnifying Lough Key, we not just adhere to but establish industry best practices. I'm not worried about any culpability on the firm's or staff's part in his murder or Lough Key violating any regulation. What I'm proposing fosters the ability for Lough Key to fully cooperate with your investigation while limiting its liability in future litigation that can't be determined at this time. From my experience, every good deed does not go unpunished. I really think it's in the best interest of justice for your state attorney assigned to this case to contact our attorney."

The two detectives were looking at each other and deciding how to respond. Billy took the moment as an opportunity to speak. "I request that we put on the table that you add on the deliverables for your side that you disclose what potential interested parties in the liquidation of Benny's account tell you. If I may, an act to demonstrate equal cooperation on your side would be to let us know what Paul Stein wants. So far, there have been two parties claiming they have some sort of rights to Benny's account, and who knows how many more are to come? Our risk is how we handle them. Any intel you can share would be appreciated."

Detective Williams smiled and nodded to the grinning Detective Guzman. "I think I read you and am good with your proposal. Do you have a card or otherwise with the contact info for your attorney?"

Oscar extracted two business cards from his shirt breast pocket. "Here is my card and that of our attorney, Scott Simon. I'll notify him to expect a call on this matter. Please contact me directly prior to a formal arrangement being established for any further information you require from Lough Key and its staff." That imperial statement indicated Oscar decreed the meeting over.

"How about one more question, and it should be interesting to you, Bill? Do you or what do you know about a Susan Desmond? Paul Stein thinks she may also put a claim on

Mr. Stein's account and other assets," Detective Guzman injected before he stood up.

Billy said he didn't know anybody by that name and asked why Paul thought she would have a claim on his estate. I sat dreading the answer.

"He said Susan Desmond is a long-term girlfriend and may want to claim some sort of common-law wife status. Do you know how to contact her?" Detective Guzman questioned.

"Is she the girlfriend you mentioned earlier?" Detective Guzman asked, looking at me.

Oscar didn't say anything, and he seemed torn on whether to keep me from answering. Billy clearly was interested. "Billy, that's Dizzy or DZY."

"You know her?" Detective Guzman asked.

"Not really. You have to think about the Board of Trade building and trading floor a few years back as a very small town, no, like a high school. Everybody either knows you or knows something about you like who you hang out with. I never spoke to her personally, but she stood out as one of the few women in the currency pits. I think she filled paper, which means she executed orders on the trading floor. Returning to Oscar's point, I'm reluctant to comment because I don't know anything for a personal fact. I used to see her wearing a Jackson Partners' floor jacket, but they shut down a year ago. The exchange's membership department would be a good bet to get at least an old address and employment history on her."

Oscar liked that answer.

"Fair enough. We'll do that. Why did you call her Dizzy?" Detective Williams responded.

"All traders and floor brokers get assigned a three-letter acronym by the exchange. It's associated with them as their identifier on trades, membership fees, and obligations, anything to do with their activity on the exchange trading floor. Her acronym was D, Z, Y, and people called her Dizzy. I assumed it was a take on her last name, but never really thought about it. The acronyms are big and worn on every member's trading floor jacket. After a while, some of the traders and brokers are more frequently referred to by their acronym than their legal name."

"Was she Benjamin Stein's girlfriend for a long time?" Detective Guzman picked up again.

I didn't say anything and looked at Oscar. He stood up and mentioned it was a pleasure to meet them and to be sure to have the state attorney contact our lawyer. He walked to the door and opened it, making it clear we were done. Detective Guzman handed me his and Detective William's card as he walked out and mentioned he checks his emails regularly but would like a call or text when we are ready to send the list of documents we discussed. Nobody shook hands or exchanged any typical end-of-meeting pleasantries. I have no idea if that is normal, but it disturbed me.

After they left, Oscar sat down again.

"Was that idea of cooperation in return for indemnification Scott's idea? You looked like you were inspired on the fly," Billy asked him.

"Remind me when I became a forensic accountant and what training or experience I have," I added. "How am I going to pull that off?"

Oscar chuckled and relaxed the first time all morning. "You're right, it came to me as we were speaking. Scott's advice was to push back and rest on legal procedure, but he likes fighting with people. He's a good lawyer but doesn't live with the consequences of most of his recommendations, nor does he do any cost-benefit analysis. What will we gain making the police go through the bother of subpoenaing us? What grounds would we have to withhold basic email and trading account activity in this situation? I'd rather befriend them and know what they are doing and be able to anticipate how we may be impacted. It's a good strategy. I like it.

"Lane, what's the big deal of being described as a forensic accountant? What do they do other than ask someone like you to pull records and explain trading sheets? You'll do fine. You may even like the change of routine. Please stop by my office no later than lunchtime with the list of documents and files that are being produced. I'll vet which ones to disclose to the police right away.

"The first thing we need to find out is who's the executor of Benny's estate. If anybody else declares an interest in Benny's accounts, inform them that the first step is working with the executor of his estate or trustee should he have formed a trust. Bill, I'm not suggesting you call Paul, but that would be interesting information right now.

"Now both of you, don't answer any more questions should the police or state attorney's office contact you. We need to hold firm on the indemnification. I wouldn't be surprised if either of you are contacted directly, especially Laney, given her newfound expertise with forensic accounting."

Clearly pleased with himself, Oscar left the room leaving the door open. Billy walked over to the seat next to mine, sat down, and leaned close to me to avoid being overheard. "What do you know about DZY? You didn't look so good when she came up?"

"Nothing really, at least not firsthand. You would recognize her if you saw her. She looks like she could be David Bowie's sister... tall, rail thin, pale, short white-blonde hair worn spiked with a lot of gel, and prone to wearing a lot of black and leather. That look is somewhat dated, but I haven't seen her in a long time to know if that's still her fashion preference. I think she was a broker because she used to wear a Jackson Partners' floor jacket, and they only do execution business.

"There were stories about Benny and Dizzy not being discreet with sex. Supposedly, they often were intimate when he had an office with windows facing the atrium. The guys from Redco across the atrium could watch. Most of the stories involve partying like a seventies' rock star. I heard other stories, but I feel like a dirty old lady or weird voyeur even discussing it. I have no idea how much is true versus fun to spread around. I'd think you would have a better idea on that front. I'm not usually in the know on that kind of gossip. Oh, wait, I think I heard that she had some substance abuse issue. I don't recall what, but I think sometime last summer I overheard the guys who make salads in Cellars speaking in Spanish about sending her a card. They seemed to think she is a nice person. One thing I do know is I haven't seen her in a while, and she is hard to miss," I responded, almost in a whisper.

Billy squinted at me, which is a warning sign that he is going to outthink me, or at least thinks he is. "Okay, so what are you saying? What do we care about her or his family if she was just a long-time girlfriend? What business is it of ours?"

"Billy, you're the master of missing the obvious. The firm, you, or I, whoever, couldn't care less until now. You aren't so obtuse or oblivious to her reputation that you don't know she's rumored to be involved with drugs. The stories give the impression of more than a big-time party girl. I get that you didn't connect the dots at first, but now that you've had a minute, it's a waste of your professional bullshit to pretend you don't know more than I do about the stories surrounding both Benny and DZY.

"She must have been a floor broker for Jackson Partners because she had an acronym, and what's their stock-in-trade? Sex, drugs, and rock and roll. The police are sure to figure that out. They had a rocking business from foreign clients in a commoditized business. I saw some of their bills that were submitted to clearing firms carrying the customer accounts. They were getting a minimum of five dollars a contract which is crazy. I saw some bills for ten to twenty-five dollars a contract. That they could command a three hundred percent plus premium over non-professional rates credentials their reputation for something other than providing quality execution services.

"I hope to God she isn't involved with whatever Benny was up to recently. I'm really worried what direction Benny's demise may path the police. I also don't want to be in the middle of a legal dispute over the distribution of his assets.

Right now, I'm so pissed at you, and me, for letting him have an account here and hang out, regardless of his family affiliation. Whatever happened isn't going to go down quietly or without a lot of legal bills."

I stood up and walked out. Ranting at Billy is always a useless exercise. Right then, I had to review the list of documents compiled so far and scope out Benny's trading. It was not a good sign that Billy didn't move or make snide remarks about how I am overreacting as usual.

When I passed Latesha's desk, I asked her to have Raj, Linda, and Kevin in my office in fifteen minutes and for her to join us. Latesha asked if I thought it was safe for Kayreen, the college student who is the receptionist in the mornings, to man the front desk. I nodded yes but wanted instructions for her not to let anybody in who was not staff. I was hoping Benny's recent trading and other activities were as light and benign as I recalled, which would make the task of collating and interpreting his activities here short and inconsequential.

My office is one of the bigger ones in the firm because it has, in addition to my desk and two guest chairs, a wall full of locked cabinets and a table large enough for six people to work. My view is of the federal prison that looks like a big wedge of cheese mislocated a couple of blocks from the Board building. We are high enough that you can see the prisoners playing basketball on the roof, and occasionally waving at people looking their way. Otherwise, my view is of office buildings with a tiny sliver of Lake Michigan.

I have an uncle who is a world-famous and highly acclaimed photographer. His specialty is birds in motion and African landscapes. The artwork in my office is whatever his current passion is. People like coming to my office to see what he is up to and where he has been recently. My walls are usually covered with black and white street scenes from Poland, Russia, China, and American Southwest deserts and ghost towns. I devote one wall to the animals. They contrast the black and white stills with dramatic, color pictures of birds and other animals on the African Serengeti that look so real

45

you get the impression you can touch them. He has a real talent for hues and capturing animals in motion. My favorite is a flock of East African Crowned Cranes taking off in mass over a pond with an orange sunset in the background. It is so delicate and intricate that it resembles a Japanese silkscreen.

Unfortunately, I was not noticing anything that usually gives me comfort and joy. Linda and Kevin from the Compliance Department were already situated at the big table in my office with laptops.

Linda Brokov is in her mid-thirties and looks like every other suburban mom, only she is beautiful and radiates wholesomeness. She usually wears her long, dusty blonde hair in a ponytail or bun, and she takes full advantage of the casual dress code. She works three days a week in the office, but leaves early enough to take a two-thirty train to be home when her three children get out of school. Linda played soccer in college and now coaches her two sons' soccer teams. It is not rare for her to be wearing track pants and a sweatshirt at work so that she can go straight to practice.

Kevin Dohle is in his late twenties and came to us after serving in the reserves and completing two tours in the Middle East. He is from a small town in northern Wisconsin, where I have been going to visit my cousins during summers since I was six years old. He looks like a leading man from a Hallmark movie, specifically one that has a handsome lumberjack or Canadian Mountie.

There are two things that arrest your eyes when first meeting Kevin. He prefers haberdashery and dresses in ensembles, which is in direct contrast to the rumbled, picked-it-up-off-the-floor-this-morning-doesn't-smell-too-bad look of younger prop shop traders or FinTech firms. Dress-up for them is clean jeans and a not-too-wrinkled button-down shirt. Today, he is sporting midnight blue pants with a lilac windowpane design, a lilac shirt, a shiny matching lilac tie, checked socks of midnight blue and lilac with brown shoes. No, he is not gay. I think it is his version of being an urban sophisticate. The other guys don't make fun of him because women of all ages actually sigh when they see him.

The second thing that strikes you is a slight limp when the rest of his movements have an athletic grace. He was wounded during his second tour but never speaks of it. He loves baseball and was quite a player. Now he is an avid coach for an inner-city boys' team and is the company drill sergeant who makes us have an intramural team that actually practices and plays well. He is a perfect coach and compliance officer because he loves rules, practice, and procedure.

My cousins introduced me to Kevin three years ago. He wanted to start a career in a big city, go to law school part-time, but didn't know much else or how to go about it. My cousin told me he needed to be someplace where he would be safe and mentored. I often hear that same request from friends with daughters, to the point where I think I am the first boss of at least fifty women under the age of thirty-five. Now I understand why my cousin asked me to keep an eye out for Kevin. He was an Eagle Scout and still is at heart. He believes that rules serve a useful purpose, all people are basically honest and will abide by rules for the greater good, and he enthusiastically embraces the 'whole team' concept.

After three years in a professional world, he has finally resigned himself that people sign agreements, contracts, leases, etc. with terms they have no intention of keeping, but it still disappoints him. He is baffled why people are overtly usurious and lie and connive while pretending otherwise.

The biggest shock in his life was when a senior executive from a major Canadian bank proved to be a 'non-truth teller' because he was representing the company line and staying on message. Kevin couldn't believe that the bigger and more highly rated international banks have no intention of paying agreed-upon bills for any time less than sixty days and often with deep discounts, which is why we routinely turn down business opportunities with many of them without upfront deposits.

The second biggest shock in his life was when a regulator made allegations that he knew were grossly exaggerated and was counting on us capitulating under the threat of more severe enforcement actions, including personal citations if we challenged them. When we responded in kind, the charges melted away, and he went after more gullible prey, which was bitterly disillusioning for Kevin. I like Kevin, anyway.

Linda and Kevin are an odd but ideal team. She has good instincts and grew up around the exchange-trading business. She can sense if something isn't right and can articulate why. Kevin will do the research to confirm the specific rules, regulatory interpretations, and enforcement actions. Linda is the more formidable foe to pit against a trader or contra party, but Kevin's military training and speech habits with his strong sense of procedure is amazingly effective with regulators who want to strong-arm a case without doing their homework first. Linda is a good soft coach for teaching Kevin street smarts in situations where nobody cares about rules and will abuse power. It has been valuable training in his personal life too, especially with a landlord and a paperwork mishap at law school that could have cost him thousands.

I put on a fleece I keep in the office when I get cold and sat down at the table. "You heard the news. Have you had enough time to render any conclusions or spot any potential cow piles?"

Kevin looked puzzled. "There was no aberrant activity. Actually, he has been pretty tame and not just for him. No Fantasy Football, political comments, off-color remarks, nothing about the market or his trading. Emails that he initiates and websites he has accessed are things like conferences, confirming social and business meetings, exchange sites, and a lot of research on foreign currency markets and economic conditions.

"But there's something noteworthy given that his brother was here. There're a lot of emails going back for over a year about money. Apparently, Benny pays a lot of bills for his mother and sister, and Paul Stein needs some sort of short-term loan. They are all initiated by Paul Stein, and he sends emails to Benny's work email because Benny is ignoring his calls and didn't give him a personal email address. Benny has not responded to one, at least on company email.

"I made a point of checking for anything to or from Larry Katz and didn't see anything. Here is a list of email addresses that he has corresponded with during the past two years. Some of them have exotic names, but that isn't unusual given how he was researching foreign currency markets and looking into international trade shows, research firms, and other professional resources on the subject. Many of them are from URLs of large banks. It will take some time to drill down, but none of them provoked an alert on our AML software that filters for names listed with the Department of Treasury as reportable persons or persons to avoid.

"One thing, though, that surfaced a few months ago. His internet activity zoomed in on a lot of articles about Asian housewives trading currency futures. There were many about Japanese and South Korean housewives trading currency futures during the day that turn into a family side business and their most popular strategies. He was also researching the gaming laws applying to China and India pertaining to currency derivatives and the same sort of anecdotal evidence of average retail traders in Asia hitting it big in currency futures. Around November, he started researching cryptocurrencies which was how he spent most of his time online at Lough Key."

Relieved, I looked at Linda. She looked up from her laptop. "I went on his social media that I can find and was disclosed. Nothing. He doesn't have a Facebook page, has no LinkedIn profile, and no blogs or Twitter account. I used to see him all the time typing into his phone and on his tablet. I don't know if he was smart enough to use an alias, but that doesn't seem like him. He didn't strike me as somebody who didn't understand social media or its technology or was shy about attracting notoriety. I checked the electronic communication monitoring logs and saw the same lack of content that Kevin described. He hasn't even been on the firm's chat except to vote for what pizza to have on Wednesdays and his order on Thai food Fridays."

Raj stepped in with his laptop. He is a tall, thin Indian who is very Americanized. He grew up around the Detroit area and went to college at Michigan State. Yet, his speech still has an elegant, slightly British lilt. Raj favors nice jeans and classic pullover sweaters. He wears glasses with trendy designer frames and the pointy, caramel brown shoes that are so popular with style conscious, younger men. He is by far the most well-traveled, read, and culturally attuned person in the office. He is revered as a god, even by the development team because he can fix anything involving technology as if by magic. I never see Raj alone, even on the street. His open friendliness, patience, and understandable explanations on almost every subject are generally regarded as better than anything posted on Wikipedia.

"Did you notice anything of interest?" he asked Linda and Kevin. Kevin recapped his observations concerning Benny's emails and research on currency trading and the lack of anything otherwise to note. Raj nodded. "That's consistent with my findings. Lane, I double-checked, and he does not have any company devices other than the computer at his workstation. He also never asked any of the Help Desk team for any support, even casual questions regarding his personal cell phone, tablet, or any other tech equipment. It looks like he doesn't retrieve company emails offsite, and he didn't access his trading account, even account statements after hours and never off-site. Not only that, but there's nothing in his directory on our server other than a small number of intracompany emails plus a few saved articles and websites for what's probably future reference. That ties in with Kevin's observations. Not one spreadsheet or filed internal memo. It looks like he was overtly avoiding any sort of footprint on our network."

Latesha had slipped in during Raj's recap. I turned to her.

"You notice everything about everybody. Did you ever notice Benny with a laptop?"

"No, but he always had his cell and iPad on him."

Raj straightened up. "Wait... he asked me a while ago my opinion of using Apple products for business. He seemed more interested in their security than functionality and performance. I remember him asking a lot of questions about how easy it must be to circumvent the various password and access conventions since so many get stolen and resold. He liked my explanation on the ease of restoring them to the original factory settings didn't mean personal information could be compromised if a few basic security protocols were followed. He came back another time asking about encrypted content on Apple devices and seemed impressed by a news story where Apple wouldn't help the government retrieve cell content from a terrorist."

"Did you find out why he was so interested in the risk of tech devices being compromised?" I asked.

Raj shrugged. "No. At the time, I thought he was being careful and asking good questions. Honestly, it's more surprising how careless most people are. I knew Benny liked having the latest in tech, and he was confirming his conclusions with me. I didn't consider it more than office small talk and almost forgot about it."

"Okay, Raj, we have a company policy that no personal computers can be used in the office. This way we can track if anything is sent outside of our network. How much of that is a relevant safeguard for tablets?"

"It should be sufficient. We don't have any guest or open WiFi here. Nobody can get on our network with a personal device that hasn't been configured and certified by us. We don't have CPUs at most workstations, and he didn't have one at his. He only had a monitor and keyboard. Therefore, there should be no way for him to download something off of our network to save on a personal device or cloud account. We elected not to prevent people from turning their cell phones into hot spots or people using their own data plans on tablets in the office. You recall when we had those meetings, and it was determined that staff could retain those functionalities for personal use?"

"I'm liking these answers, but it's going to look as odd to the police and whoever will come calling for his accounts as it does to us. One more thing, how frequently was he signing on to his account, and did it ever look like somebody else may have been given his password?"

"He signed on once most mornings before the opening, and that was it. No other activity," Raj replied.

"Okay. Linda, Kevin, play Devil's Advocate for me. He must have been keeping some sort of side-bar trading tally. He always knew to the penny how much he made and what all of his expenses totaled. He could easily recreate that info manually on a tablet spreadsheet application because he wasn't trading any size. What's our vulnerability on a lookback basis?"

Linda paused. "On a lookback basis he appears to be a waste of time. It doesn't make sense, and Benny wasn't an old-school guy who didn't use or understand technology. However, nothing happened on our watch... literally nothing. It's pretty common now for people to walk around with two cell phones so they can keep their personal content free from firm oversight. That isn't a problem as long as he wasn't conducting firm business on his phone. Since he wasn't doing much of any business, I think we're okay. Kevin, was he trading in his personal accounts that you saw? That's the only other touch point I can see because for some of our guys, we also have to monitor their personal investment accounts."

"No. He wasn't trading SEC exchange regulated products or a member of any SEC exchange for a few years. Nothing he did would require us to be given duplicate copies of his statements at other firms. I checked with Membership this morning, and he's not registered or otherwise affiliated with any other clearing firm or member organization even as an owner. One thing, though, Lane, do we have any written policies anywhere or a pattern of requiring some sort of minimums to have an account here? I didn't see anything in our client agreement forms," Kevin stated.

"Good point, Kevin. No, we don't have any formal standards. What usually happens when a trader or group is down on their luck or not trading sufficiently for us to cover our minimum expenses is their client service rep will talk to them. The result is usually a tactful hint to wind down and close the account or to establish a timeline with performance benchmarks to maintain the status quo. Benny qualified for a carve-out due to his history with us. The 2.4 million-dollar deposit certainly rendered the appearance that he was about to resume trading to his former levels. No, I don't see anything there. Kevin, it would make me feel a lot better if you would check the guidance pertaining to our AML due diligence. I noted in his file what I did, which I recall you reviewed yourself. I still don't see what we could or should have done otherwise, but I have a bad feeling we're going to get sucked into something we aren't prepared for.

"Latesha, please make notes of this discussion and file them in Benny's folder you started this morning. It's a safe bet we'll be asked to demonstrate our actions regarding anything pertaining to Benny."

"Thanks, guys. Let me know if you think of something else but remember to ask me in person."

I motioned for Latesha to wait until the others left. "Latesha, when you go downstairs in a few minutes to cash a check for some petty cash, you may want to share with Joel or whoever is the bank manager today the gossip about Benny. You may even feel compelled to complain about how crazy I'm making everybody by double-checking anything to do with Benny lately, including the AML due diligence in January."

She smirked her comprehension. "Lane, how about I pick you up a salad or something when I go downstairs? Today is Prison Chicken day."

"Oh no, it would be today. Please, I'd like some normal soup, anything not cream based. Thank you for doing this."

Latesha left with purpose. I followed suit and went to my

office to shut the door. Like a lot of trading and FinTech companies, we provide lunch in the office. It used to be a necessity due to the hectic nature of trading and its support. Market conditions and current technology have eliminated the logistical need to keep people shackled at or near trading desks or on trading floors during the day, but it does add to the camaraderie of our firm besides being a nice perk. Food is very important to our culture. Wednesdays are always pizza, and there is always a huge disagreement from where. Friday is usually something a little more festive and often Thai. The rest of the days are generally sandwiches, salads, and typical takeout. On days with major sporting events or Fridays before Sunday home Bear football games, the menu is a ten-year-old boy's birthday dream come true.

Prison chicken is the smelliest fried chicken and comes with ample servings of sides like baked beans in glop and mac-n-cheese made with something resembling glue. I don't think anybody knows the actual name of the restaurant. It is across the street from the federal corrections facility that is nearby, hence the nickname. The second favorite, reserved for Bear and Cub in-office tailgate lunches, is Portillos, a local franchise famous for its hotdogs, Italian beef sandwiches, and chocolate cake made with real mayonnaise. It is as disgusting as it sounds, but amazingly popular. It still astonishes me how long the line of highly compensated grown men is for hotdogs and how many cheat by trying to work the line in reverse to make sure they get at least one piece of chocolate cake.

I must have looked pitiful. It goes against every grain in Latesha's DNA to get lunch for someone like me. She does not do 'fetch-and-go' even when the payoff is free tickets to sporting events and concerts. She considers all of us as grateful subjects of her realm, and to a practical extent, we are.

My priority now is to check out Benny's trading accounts. There was almost nothing to look at the past year or so. He maintained a balance of about two hundred thousand dollars, which was more than enough to fund the little trading he was doing. He seemed to be looking for a new product grouping after he closed out his treasury and Eurodollar positions not quite two years ago. His balance got near four hundred thousand dollars about four times, which is when he would take out the excess over two hundred thousand dollars. He was dabbling in soft agricultural commodities such as coffee and sugar, a little gold, and some corn. He hit it big with what looked like a delivery arbitrage on different exchanges in orange juice. He tried energy contracts for about a month but without success. In November of last year, he started trading foreign currencies, but I couldn't tell what his strategy was. Recently, he was trading mostly option spreads. He wasn't going home flat at night like a typical futures trader, but he wasn't trading size or assuming much risk either.

I was curious why he would attempt to trade currencies at all, especially after his failure with energies. Those products are traded worldwide by the best capitalized, fastest electronic eyes and trading systems in the world. It reinforced the supposition that he had expectations for something other than a great pricing model to compete with the high-frequency trading business that dominated currency trading. It also explained why he was interested in the trading prowess of Japanese housewives.

He never took out money from his trading accounts for personal expenses until February. When he was flush, he withdrew significant sums around when quarterly estimated tax payments are due. Typical of most traders like him, those withdrawals paid for several months of expenses plus his taxes. There were two exceptions, one for one hundred fifty thousand dollars and one for three hundred fifty thousand dollars when he was still trading fixed income options and futures and doing well. In February and the first day in March, he withdrew twenty thousand dollars, which I assumed was for his rent and other expenses we quarreled about. He withdrew fifty thousand dollars at the end of January. I had no clue what it was for but didn't need to inquire at the time because it was his money, or so I thought, and his balance greatly exceeded his margin requirements.

Relieved that any forensic accounting deliverables based on Benny's trading accounts with Lough Key were not going to be a challenge, I gladly submitted to the mind-numbing task of filing copies of his trading statements in his newly established Compliance directory.

Billy walked in with a takeout soup container from Cellars, the cafeteria in the basement of the Board of Trade building. "Latesha said you wanted this. I think it's vegetable and not the beef barley. Find anything interesting?" he asked as he sat down in one of the guest chairs in front of my desk.

I gave him a recap of my observations. I added my uncredentialed theories. Benny didn't stick to orange juice futures because it required trading on a European exchange, and it must be a strategy that is only popular once or twice a year timed around the growing and harvest cycles of oranges. My guess was that he toyed with energies because they are a sector that was heavily promoted in Chicago by the Chicago Mercantile Exchange after it bought and took over the NYMEX, the New York futures exchange that lists energy futures and options. His interest in the trading habits of retail currency speculators was probably linked to the Bitcoin business, but it didn't look like anything official had commenced.

"You mean other than a 2.4 million dollar deposit. How sure are you it was all Benny's money?"

"I have no idea one way or another. Linda, Kevin, and I met this morning, and they agree that at the time, there was no reason not to take him and his bank at face value. Kevin is researching regulatory enforcement actions and interpretative guidance to see if anything pops up that has a similar backstory. The anonymous bankers and Paul don't make me second-guess myself, but Larry Katz's pronouncement this morning does. It also makes my mommy-spidey senses tingle with suspicion at his total lack of any content footprint on our network. Even on a lookback basis, what could we do or say? Hey, Benny, why aren't you messing around more on the chat or why aren't you working harder and leaving your stuff on our server? He wasn't an employee or even a backed trader, so he didn't answer to us on how he spent his time. Regardless, if I were the police, I'd want to follow that thread somehow."

"I agree, Lane. Benny took his iPad everywhere and was someone who loved having the latest gen tech gadgets. He seemed self-sufficient. Now you can do almost anything on a better tablet that you can do on a laptop, and everything can be stored on a cloud account somewhere. So, the only thing he'd need a more advanced computer for would be to use a full-fledged trading system. I'm hoping we dodged a bullet. We can't be held accountable for anything that didn't transpire on our system, especially since he wasn't our employee."

"On another note," Billy continued after shifting to a slouch in the chair, "I spoke to Paul Stein a few minutes ago. He's desperate to get a hold of some cash from Benny's account. I reminded him that as a lawyer, he knows the drill. We need to be presented with the will or trust that indicates the executor or trustee is empowered and in what capacity over Benny's assets. He was literally screaming that we're to prevent anyone from taking any withdrawals and to contact him should anybody try. He wasn't happy when I told him all of that would be dictated by whatever legal document is presented to us stipulating how Benny's assets will be handled upon his demise. If there should arise conflicting documents or instructions, we'll let the interested parties duke it out in court and will do nothing until a decision is rendered."

"Why do you think he's in such a rush? Does he need financial assistance that badly or does he just want to prevent someone from getting to Benny's accounts first? Never mind, don't answer that. The less said, the better. I sense it's very likely we're going to get dragged into a legal dispute over Benny's account."

"Agreed. Before I go, Connie wants to confirm you're on for the symphony this Thursday. I have Blackhawks' tickets that night, and it would get me out of the doghouse if you went with her."

"Liar, as if you ever went to the symphony. You and Connie aren't subtle about trying to keep me busy. However, I'll gladly go to the symphony this Thursday because it's one of its jazz programs. It will be nice to catch up with Connie, too, which we'll do over an expensive dinner you're paying for."

Billy chuckled. "Glad to. I thought you were going to pull the not-liking-to-drive-at-night card. You won't be taking the train at that hour?"

"No, it's not worth the hassle and worry of sticking to a schedule for the commuter line and too late for the 'L.' If I reserve a car, I can be picked up outside the Symphony Hall at the end of the CSO program and home well within a half hour at that time of night during the week. We should be out before the Blackhawks' game is over and traffic builds up on the Ike. Are you picking up Connie?"

"No, lucky for me, the Bransons, who live down the street, are CSO season ticket holders and are going Thursday. Connie can drive down with Judy. Richard will meet Judy for dinner and take them home after the concert. The last time Connie and I tried to coordinate me picking her up on the same night I was at a Blackhawks' game, the game went into overtime, and I had to miss it. I'll leave you be."

"Yeah, I have to get this list of documents to Oscar in time to turn over to the police this afternoon. I'm almost done, and, thankfully, it's no big deal."

About an hour later, and after the Prison Chicken lunch and its lingering smells were removed, I stopped by the office shared by Linda and Kevin. I wanted to check there was nothing else to note. After getting a negative response from them, I asked the same question to Raj with similar success. The only thing Raj added was that Benny asked one of the network engineers about the expense and specs of setting up to trade on Asian and European exchanges. He seemed focused on cryptocurrencies, and his questions were general background information and nothing specific.

When I stepped into Oscar's office, he and Billy were in a deep conversation over the Blackhawks' lineup tonight. The entire town is caught up with the Blackhawks and has high hopes for them winning the Stanley Cup this season. Ordinarily, I don't pay too much attention to sports, but I have to admit that Blackhawks Fever is infectious and prevails a feeling of neighborly goodwill throughout the Chicagoland area.

As I was sitting down, I slipped a copy of the documents gathered and ready for submission for when we are served with a subpoena on Oscar's desk. He looked at it, nodded, and looked up at me with the implied question of whether there was anything of note. I gave him my recap, and Billy concurred. I told Oscar I sent him this same list in an email before I walked in, which should make it easy for him to forward to the police.

Just when I was feeling a little better, Latesha walked in and closed the door. Honestly, this type of behavior is rare for her. She looked stunned. "You all won't believe this, but Susan Desmond is here asking for Lane. I put her in the conference room because I don't think you would want her to wait in the reception area. Before you ask, I don't know what she wants because she wouldn't say. She only said she doesn't have an appointment."

"Nicely done, Latesha," said Oscar. "Lane, go see what she wants. I'll call Detective Williams to ask how they prefer us to respond. It will give me an opportunity to reinforce our request to have the state attorney work with Scott Simon."

I was angry. "Latesha, we have to find out how people are getting all the way up and past the security desk in the lobby. Larry Katz probably has building access, but that doesn't explain Paul Stein or DZY. I'm sorry to snap at you, but there might as well be a parade going through our office. Oscar, wait a second before you call the police. Latesha, did Joel say anything when you stopped down earlier?"

"No, other than to thank you, and he'll let us know anything he can share. It didn't sound like he even knew Benny was dead and the police are involved."

With that, Oscar picked up the phone, and Billy walked with me to the conference room with Latesha trailing behind. Once we got to the door of the reception area, Latesha asked us to wait.

"Kayreen mentioned a man called asking for Lane this morning and wouldn't leave his name. Starz informed me just now that a man and a woman called on her shift asking for you. Neither gave their name, but the man was pretty aggressive about wanting to know if you're in. Starz checked your voice messages, and you have three calls where the caller hung up without saying anything. She doesn't think it's typical cold-calling because salesmen usually leave contact information. I told them not to pick up your line anymore, and all your calls are to go straight to voicemail, which I'll monitor."

"Thanks, I really don't know what to make of this. The next thing I want to find out is how DZY heard of me and how she got up here."

Chapter 3

Whatever I was expecting was not what met us when we stepped into the conference room. This Susan Desmond could be taken for a sickly teenager at first glance. She was so pale and wearing no makeup that she resembled an albino, except for her wide blue-gray eyes. Her hair was a natural towhead blonde cut short, parted on the left, and combed to the right in the same style almost every man and boy wore in the late fifties, with more length to her bangs and back. She was wearing a navy-blue GAP zip-up hoodie with a white t-shirt underneath, well-worn skinny Levi blue jeans, and white Keds with no socks. She was about one hundred pounds and shorter than I recalled, only about five-foot-five inches, but that may be due to not wearing heels. She was clearly on her last leg and not the feisty, loud, laughing DZY who was a familiar face strutting around the exchanges.

When we walked in, she looked like a rabbit fighting the flight instinct. I stepped in further, introduced Billy and myself, sat down, and invited her to also take a seat. Billy had second thoughts about the usefulness of him sticking around. He shook hands, offered his condolences, and left. She nodded and mumbled her thanks as she sat down. She seemed to be trying to shrink into herself and was hunched over with her arms crossed right below her rib cage.

Her response when I offered to get her anything was to ask if she could smoke. In spite of being a smoke-free building by local ordinance, we store a couple of smokeless ashtrays in the conference room credenza for our European and Asian guests. It is less bother and cheaper than paying fines for when they sneak smokes in the men's washroom and set off the smoke detectors. I also retrieved a bottle of room temperature water and a Styrofoam cup that are part of the standard conference room supplies and set them near her on the table.

Her body relaxed. She remained silent as she pulled out a pack, lit up, and inhaled deeply. She opened the bottle of water and took a sip before returning her gaze to me. Taking that as my opening, I asked her why she was here and asked for me.

"I don't know where to start or what to do now. Benny always said you're one of the few nice people in this business. He told me about your meeting with the guys from EuroCredit Bank and thought you were pretty cool. I know there's a lot of money in his trading account here, so I know that you can find out who's in charge of his estate. That's all I want to know, and I don't have anybody else I can ask."

That was a lot for me to process. I was a little alarmed by her use of the word 'always,' which implied I was referred to more than once by Benny. I was also not sure what I could do or say. I opted for delay.

"I think the police are looking for you. Have they contacted you?"

"No, but I'm not surprised."

"Do you want me to give you a card from one of the detectives that were here earlier?"

She shrugged. "Might as well."

She seemed okay with lapses of silence while I thought and was watching me warily. I saw no reason why I had to be circumspect, so I took it as an opportunity to call Oscar from the conference room to get his input. He was expecting my call, informed me the police had not returned his, liked that I had informed DZY of their interest in her and was giving her one of their cards, and told me to use my best judgment. That is Oscar-speak for treat anything I say as on some official record to be referred to in the future. She smoked and sipped water while listening to my side of the discussion.

I handed her one of the two cards I still had in my pocket from this morning. "Well, the first thing we should get out of the way is your contact information. What's your cell number?"

It was her turn to pause while processing my request. She finally gave me her number. "I'd appreciate it if you only used it to contact me and don't give it to Benny's family. I'll call this Detective Williams today."

"Okay, here is where we are. We have not been given any such documents yet evidencing who's Benny's executor or trustee. So, I really don't know at this point who is authorized to liquidate and distribute Benny's assets. It isn't unusual for that to take a while because normally the first course of business are things like funeral arrangements. Since you're here, I take it isn't you who has any legal authority in this situation, and you don't know if Benny has a will or living trust. I also take it you aren't on good terms with his family."

"Right. His family hates me, and it's mutual. I don't want to give you the wrong impression to make you uptight. I don't want the cash or whatever else he had. I only want the house in Florida that he bought for us last year. I know Benny supports his mother and sister. I have no reason to interfere with those arrangements."

"All right, that gives us something to start with. Did you sign anything when he bought the house? If you did, this may be a moot point because your name would be on the title."

"I'm not sure. I think I did, but I was so high at the time. I do remember Benny saying it was where we were going to start over, and we were going to be a normal, legit couple and not live in a crummy apartment anymore. We were going to have a real place."

I moved over to where the conference room laptop was situated on the conference table. After I logged in and did a bit of Google searching, I asked her for the address of the house. I found the website for the county clerk's office for Dade County, Florida, and did a quick search for the owners of that property.

"Well, you're in luck. The property is titled in the names of Benjamin R. Stein and Susan M. Desmond, jointly with right of survivorship. The house is yours other than any mortgage that may be outstanding."

"Does Benny's family have any claim to it? Can they try to take it away or make me sell it?"

"I'm not a lawyer, but I don't think so. If they did, it would be very difficult and expensive to pursue, especially in another state. I don't think it would be worth the money for a long shot unless there's something else in his personal documents that could complicate matters. You really have to wait and see what instructions he left in a will or trust. Do you know if he even made out a will? If not, probate can take years, but it shouldn't affect your ownership rights to that property."

Susan settled back in her chair, raised one knee, and put a foot on the rim of the chair. She leaned her head back and exhaled, facing the ceiling. After a long ten seconds, she faced me again and was almost smiling. "Thanks. I'm sorry to barge in and bother you like this. Benny told me a story once about how you can ferret out any facts and are better than those investigative reporters on the news."

I didn't have time to wonder how my name came up in Benny's conversation a second time. My cell started buzzing with a simultaneous call and text. The text was from Latesha letting me know that Larry Katz had returned and was raising hell outside the doorway again. She had called the building's security, the police, and Oscar to notify the detectives. There was a pause, and the next text said she was having Joe step into the reception area. The number calling my phone was the reception number. I called it back, and Starz gave me the same warning as Latesha did. She added that Larry was yelling he knew DZY was here and other things she could not follow.

Susan was watching me but didn't give any indication she knew what was up but could hear the commotion, even though it was muted by two doors and some distance. Billy came in with a grim, alarmed expression across his face.

"I don't know where the hell Detectives Williams and Guzman are, but they aren't picking up. We've left three messages for each now."

He turned to Susan. "How well do you know Larry Katz?"

"Just well enough to know to stay far away from him. Why? Is that him yelling outside?"

"Uh-huh. He knows you're here. How is that possible? Did you contact him?"

She sat straight up. "God, no!"

I was fed up and done. "I'm going home. I've had it with today and am in no mood for more melodrama."

"You can't do that now," Billy said, half-laughing. I knew he meant because Susan was here, and we were waiting for the police. By now, Susan was becoming agitated.

"Yes, I can and will. Susan, where are you staying if I may ask?"

After another long, ten-second pause, she stared at me. "Nowhere," she whispered.

"Fine, you're welcome to come stay with me. We probably have some obligation not to let you leave until the police have a chance to speak to you. We can inform them where you are, and they can contact you or me to set up an appointment. Billy, I'm grabbing my bag and will be back in a minute. Please run interference so that Susan and I can escape without being followed by Larry. We can't leave this room without being seen through the glass doors of the reception area. I suggest having Joe throw him down the garbage shoot. Susan, where are your bags?"

Billy looked at me like I was nuts. I am not nuts, just impulsive and creeped out. Susan leaned down and pulled a mid-size navy-blue duffle bag up from under the table. She indicated that was all her luggage. Billy told me to return to the conference room, and he would let me know when Larry left. He and Joe would walk us to my car parked in the garage across the street, which is usually a safer bet than parking in the basement of the building.

I called Detective Guzman on my cell and got him. I explained the situation, multiple attempts to contact them, and how I was leaving. I gave him Susan's cell and informed him she would be staying with me. He asked to speak to her. I handed the phone to Susan. She nodded, said okay, and handed my phone back with Detective Guzman still on the line. He asked that I call him when we get to my place to set up a time and location to meet tomorrow. I agreed and was hoping it would not take place in Lough Key's office.

Billy nodded. "We need to talk. Call me as soon as you're finished with Guzman when you get home. Go ahead and get your bag. I'll see what's up in the hallway. Meet me back here."

It took me about twenty minutes to return to the conference room. I noticed the reception area was empty besides Starz. The door was open, and I could see Oscar had joined Billy and Susan in the conference room. When I stepped in, Latesha was handing Susan a cup of tea, and Oscar was chatting comfortably with her.

"So, what happened to Larry?" I asked.

"It was all anti-climactic. I told him his threats and theatrics aren't helping his cause, and a more productive approach would be to explain the foundation of his claim on Benny's trading accounts with us, with the caveat that they may not be substantial. He told me some BS about Benny using his intellectual property for a trading strategy. I repeated what I told Paul about requiring documents, etc. I told him that his claim has to be taken up with whoever is authorized to handle Benny's estate. When the time comes, it would be best for him to submit his contract or invoices or whatever he has to the executor of Benny's estate. It was almost comical when I told him he knew this, and it wasn't one of his better performances. I added never being impressed by his antics and will have him restricted from the building entirely, and I may file a restraining order if he comes back or bothers any of us outside of this office.

"Larry calmed down immediately, which is suspicious. He didn't apologize but offered an explanation that he needs to establish his stake in the ground and make a statement to Benny's family that he'll be dealt with. That's a direct quote. I take it that today's performance was for the benefit of Paul or whoever is in charge of Benny's assets now. Now that his point has been made that he won't be ignored and prone to outrageous behavior, he'll probably go away. He knows we can't be disbursing anything to him from Benny's account. I think he got our message, which was reinforced by Joe standing behind me. We owe the Eurodollar Desk a couple of rounds for Joe assuming office bouncer duty."

"Does anybody know how he knew that Susan was here?" I asked.

"Hector, the security guard down in the lobby, told me Larry was hanging out near the security desk and the turnstiles in front of the elevator banks. Hector said Larry was watching people all day. Larry does have a building pass, which they are in the process of verifying if it's because he's a tenant or if some friend or firm signed him on with the building. They will cancel it if he isn't at least an employee of a paying tenant," Latesha answered.

"Susan, how did you get up here? You weren't signed in by anybody from this office, were you?" I continued.

"I walked in with Maureen from Alquant. Anybody can swipe their building card twice or more to let their guest in without going to get a pass from security. Hasn't it always been that way? It wasn't planned or anything. I bumped into her when I came down the 'L' stairs in front."

"Well, I guess that's a fight to take up another day. Billy, are you and Joe still walking us downstairs?" As an afterthought, I took the other smokeless ashtray from the credenza and dropped into my bag to take home.

As the four of us were in the elevator, Joe asked me why I didn't park in the building and used the unheated lot across the street. I explained that I didn't trust the building security to be able to keep outsiders out. Even in a secure building, I don't like walking to my car when there aren't a lot of people around. I prefer the valet service provided by the parking lot attendants across the street. They will have my car downstairs and warmed up if I give them notice when I will be picking it up. Those guys have been working there for years, and we know each other. I feel safer with them and not because I tip.

Our building has more turnover, and the garage staff seems to be more interested in trying to sell expensive detail services than shuttling my car to the entrance for a few dollars a day.

When we crossed the plaza and got to the lot with my car, Virgil was just climbing out of it. True to form, he had retrieved my gold 2005 Mercedes Benz Series E station wagon and had it waiting for me, all set to drive straight out of the driveway. I thanked him, waved to the other two attendants, slipped the tip into Virgil's hand as he held my door open with another. Joe was laughing as he watched while he assisted Susan into the passenger's seat and dropped her bag in the back seat. Virgil looked twice at Susan but didn't say anything. She didn't seem to notice.

"Nice car, did you pick the color?" she asked after we were rolling on the Eisenhower.

Taken aback, I laughed. "Sort of. I bought it a few years ago from a neighbor who was the proverbial little old lady who hardly drove it anywhere other than church and the Butterfield Country Club to play golf. She moved to Florida and didn't want to bother selling it to a dealer. Champagne, or whatever this color is called, wouldn't have been my first choice, but I grew to like it. I have two kids whose schedules and logistics made it necessary to permit them to drive it. The color eliminates any status of driving a Benz, and the color is so unique that my kids knew almost anywhere they went in the neighborhood they would be spotted by someone I know."

Susan smirked, but I sensed my explanation restored her good impression of me. She decided to continue her round-about interview of me. "Do you always take strays home with you?"

"Yep, until recently, there was a veritable circus going on in my house. Most often, I host friends of my children who may as well be orphans, closely followed by South African, South Korean, and Italian family members of business associates of my husband. Things have tapered off since my youngest went to DC for college. So how about you? Do you have an affinity for strangers like me? Do you have any definite plans during your stay here?"

"No. A friend texted me last night with the news that Benny is probably dead. I made reservations last night to hop on the first plane I could. This morning she confirmed the gory details of his murder. To say I'm in a state of shock is an understatement. I figured I might as well stick with the plan to come here in case Benny's family lets me go to his service. The idea to come to your office was Divine inspiration that just came to me when I landed. To answer the obvious question, you're so tactfully avoiding, I'm in recovery. I have tried it, I don't know, four to six times before. This time I need it to stick. I don't trust myself left to my own devices. Right now, I don't think it's safe for me to stay at a hotel by myself or with most of the people I know well enough to crash at their place. Thanks, really. I know this is a lot to ask from a stranger."

It's only about a fifteen-minute drive in the middle of the afternoon from the parking garage right on the corner of the Congress feeder to the Eisenhower and my exit, Harlem Avenue. From that point, it isn't ten minutes to my door, mostly due to stoplights in Oak Park's business district.

"I have to warn you about my dog, Fred. He's over two hundred pounds and very loud. He'll be positively jubilant to see me this early. When he gets around to noticing you, the worst that will happen is he'll slobber all over you. Frequent guests are used to him and don't seem to be bothered enough to stop coming over or to stop encouraging him," I said as I pulled into my side of the garage.

I live in a 1920s three-story greystone with three separate flats that has a small yard facing a busy alley. I have been told their limestone facades, many with Beaux-Art decorative trim, are unique to Chicago. Back in the day when most families only had, at most, one car and could street park it at night in Oak Park, the outdoor parking spaces immediately outside the fence between the building and alley were sufficient for the tenants who kept cars. The first improvement made when I bought the building was to have built a four-car garage that could be accessed from the building yard without stepping around to the alley. There are still a lot of people in the Chicago area who don't have indoor parking. I don't consider it a luxury but a necessity with our winters.

Susan wisely suggested I go in first to greet Fred and take him into the yard. She preferred to stay behind to have a cigarette. My flat is the bottom one, which is lucky because it is more convenient for letting dogs out. Fred heard me approach and started barking his welcome. He would jump on me if he could, but his heavy frame and center of weight being his deep chest only let him hop, which is oddly cute on such a large beast.

After giving me a slobbery welcome, he charged down the one flight of stairs to the yard. Usually, he growls like a lion when he sees a stranger, especially anybody who smells like smoke or pot. His reaction to Susan was to stand in front of her and observe. She was doing the same to him. Both were making up their minds about the other.

"God, you're big. Um, hi? I guess it's too late to ask if he's friendly?" she questioned, looking at me.

That was enough encouragement for Fred. He walked around her so that he was facing in the same direction and hockey checked her gently with his shoulder. He barked, what for him was a friendly welcome, and then went to the corner of the yard to do his business. When he returned, he was pulling at my sleeve for attention and to return to the house. He played his favorite game of waiting for me to take the first two steps so that he can charge up from behind me to race me to the door, and then block me from opening it with his huge rear end. After pushing him aside and making him move into the house, there was room for Susan to proceed up the backstairs to the three-season porch that is the back entrance to my place before opening up to a more substantial door to my kitchen.

The renovations we made to this flat were completed about three years ago with the intent of making this unit more appealing to renters who are younger than seventy. Except for a dishwasher, everything used to be pretty much the same since the original construction. The apartments in this building all have maple wood floors, lots of built-in hutches including a china cabinet with beveled glass and other woodwork trim in beautiful condition.

The floor plan is typical of the era. There is what my grandmother used to call a sunroom, which is a small area in the front of the apartment framed by large bay windows facing the street. It leads to a living room large enough for a piano, fireplace, entertainment hutch, and plenty of seating for ten. The front door leading to the building lobby area and staircase is off the living room, right before the small hallway to the dining room, which is big enough for huge formal, sit-down dinners served on a massive dining room set. Off to the left of the dining room, there is a hallway with what was originally two bedrooms with an old-fashion bathroom between them. The bedroom toward the back of the flat had annexed a small, narrow room that was either a bedroom for a person who didn't need anything other than a twin bed and nightstand or a large storage unit. The three closets in the entire unit were minuscule compared to modern standards. A good-size kitchen flanked the rear of the apartment and led out to the three-season porch.

I blew out the back wall between the rear of the apartment and the porch and rearranged the floorplan to create a third bedroom where the storage closet was by incorporating space from the porch, added a bathroom with a shower, upgraded the kitchen, and repurposed some of the square footage of the dining room and kitchen to make a small nook for a computer workstation and elliptical machine. The back porch now has HVAC, trellis windows, a collapsible awning, and a café table with seating for four. It isn't huge, but more useful as a nice place to visit with my neighbors without inviting them all the way into my home.

Susan seemed to be having second thoughts as she followed me in. I escorted her to the back bedroom, which is the guest room now that Cahill, my son, seldom comes home. When we moved, I placed most of his childhood memorabilia in storage. My thinking is people may feel they are intruding if they stay in what is clearly a person's private bedroom. The décor is gender neutral with a Madras plaid quilt in primary colors and an Americana oak dresser and desk. The walls and curtains are a sunny yellow because that room doesn't get much natural light. The artwork is huge, panoramic, black and white landscape photographs my uncle took of the American Southwest. They display his penchant for ghost towns, abandoned mines, and empty canyons with a soulful component.

"It isn't the Ritz but quiet with your own bathroom. The TV on the desk has a DVD player in its base. You can watch cable TV, but you may prefer my kids' library of DVDs that are shelved on the porch. To paraphrase Bruce Springsteen, we have not fifty-seven but probably five hundred stations and nothing to watch. There must be at least a thousand videos of all genres out there. Towels are in the bathroom vanity and help yourself to any personal care products.

"I'm going to take Fred for a walk around the block and then go run a couple miles. I'm not in the mood to go out. We have the best takeout variety in this neighborhood. Relax, and when I come back, we can discuss where to order. Oh, yeah, smoking is okay as long as you use this." I placed the smokeless ashtray on the desk.

She did another one of her ten-second pauses. "Can I cook? Is there a grocery store nearby? Really, I'd like to. Cooking is my new thing, and it's no fun if it is just for me. It really is the least I can do for you, and to sound totally ungrateful, it would give me something to do and think about. I'm not great, but adequate and have been doing okay with chicken and pasta dishes. I excel at salads."

Her offer almost broke my heart. "Sure, I'd love that. It would be a treat for me. Thank you. There isn't anything within walking distance from here. However, I went to the store yesterday and am unusually fully stocked. I have chicken breasts, at least two kinds of fish, and loads of salad items and other vegetables. Pasta, rice, and spices are in the pantry to the left of the fridge. Help yourself. If you feel adventurous, I leave my keys on a hook next to the back door. You can Google the Trader Joe's not too far from here which is probably your best bet. *But...* first, we have to call the police. You have no idea how strange that sounds."

We walked into my dining room, pulled out Detective Guzman's card from my bag I dropped on the table, and called him. It was about three o'clock in the afternoon. I told him our plans and asked what time he would want Susan to meet him at where I was assuming his office or station or whatever the term was. Instead, he enthusiastically offered coming to my apartment and could be there before four thirty. I copied Susan's ten-second pause to think. Clearly, he was interested in meeting her, and possibly me, without Oscar or other lawyers supervising the discussion and where we may feel comfortable enough to let our guard down. I didn't care. I wanted this over and didn't want any more drama or gossip due to the police being in our office. Plus, he didn't know about Fred. I also considered that Susan should be spared hanging out at the police station at 17th and State, which is where I guessed he was stationed. It was either that or where a lot of *Hills Street Blues* was filmed on the 900 south block of Maxwell Street. Neither were pleasant places to spend a few hours. I asked Susan her preference, and she opted for them coming here.

"Do you have a lawyer?"

"No, but why would I need one? I can easily prove I was in Florida when he died."

"We need to go over Oscar's rules of having these types of conversations. I'm hardly an expert, but you need to protect yourself from anything you say that may have a detrimental effect on another party or them indicting you for another crime. I'm worried about a money-laundering investigation that would be a separate matter from his murder.

"I shouldn't be telling you that, but I wouldn't have invited you here if I believed you to have criminal tendencies, which is based solely on my first impression due to our short association. My best guess is the police won't be your problem. The way events are unfolding, you could get dragged into litigation regarding ownership of Benny's assets.

"I have seen some crazy things like an ex-wife trying to get money from her ex's partners because she claims she was entitled to more, and the business profits and expenses weren't split equitably. I know of a case where a creditor claimed that real estate purchased by the debtor and titled in another party's name should be liquidated to pay off his debts. Those scenarios are nothing if you get sucked into a money-laundering investigation and have to pay big legal fees to prove your innocence. The money-laundering laws are structured around you being guilty until you prove otherwise.

"We may not have time to prep when I get back. The first thing you must say is that you don't give permission for the conversation to be recorded and what you describe may or may not be included in your written statement. You state you're distraught and not thinking clearly but want to cooperate to the best of your abilities. Tell them you're sorry but can't be much help now but will try. Don't say anything you don't know to be a fact and can explain why. Otherwise, say you aren't sure. Also, don't get nervous if they wait for you to speak or don't immediately respond to you.

"A favorite trick during investigative interviews is to use pregnant pauses to make the subject nervous and to start babbling to fill the silence or to be more convincing. Don't talk to them without another witness or me. The big thing to remember is not to say anything that can be taken out of context if written down. After the interview, you can decide whether to hire an attorney for whatever will go on the official record. I'm sorry, but I really need to clear my head and walk Fred before they get here." Susan nodded her understanding and said she was going to check out the pantry and start dinner.

There wasn't enough time to change and go for a run. Fred hates exercise but loves to socialize. Walking around Field Park is doable for a mastiff. It won't count as a substitute for a run, but we will be outside for almost an hour, which is a half hour more than it takes me with my cousin's lab to cover the same ground. Fred likes the attention from the kids at the playground and can be enticed to walk around the parameter but not without stopping for multiple breaks and to complain.

It is a good thing I opted for a walk and was back right before four o'clock because the two policemen rang my doorbell about ten minutes later. I kept Fred on a leash because it has a magic quality of calming him down and making him behave. He was doing his best fierce-dog barking and growling from behind me when I opened the door. To say they were impressed is an understatement. Detective Williams was definitely scared while Detective Guzman was wary. I pay extra for that.

I explained that I was going to keep Fred on the leash, but he does not like strange men to be where he cannot see them. We were all going to the dining room to conduct the interview. Susan was standing in the dining room watching us and walked to the kitchen to retrieve the smokeless ashtray before taking a seat at the table.

Detectives Williams and Guzman understood they were to walk in front of Fred and me, sat down, and were visibly unhappy. Ignoring their discomfort, I offered them water or a soda, which they did not accept. Susan leaned back in her chair and assumed her favorite position of leaning back with her right leg raised with her heel on the ridge of the seat of the chair and her left arm wrapped around her stomach with her right hand holding a cigarette. She was enjoying the fact that the police did not have the upper hand.

"If I had known you had that kind of dog, we would have

conducted this interview at the station," opened Detective Williams.

"Why, what difference does it make? He's a big favorite in the neighborhood, gets invited to children's birthday parties, and we just came from the park where two mothers took his picture with their toddlers. He's harmless as long as you're polite, which I don't see as an issue." I might have pulled off a more convincing aura of innocence if Susan didn't snort.

The two detectives settled at the side of the table closest to the living room, Susan was opposite, and I was at the end of the table with Fred sitting attentively at my elbow watching. "How big is he?" Detective Williams opened.

"Fred is supposedly the biggest dog in the state. I registered him at a DuPage County dog park that requires dog permits when he was about four and then weighed about fifteen pounds more than he does now, which is somewhere around 210-215 pounds. Every year they delight in telling me they still have the record for the largest registered dog in the state, but I don't think they ever got around to adjusting his weight down. He's an English Mastiff who takes his job guarding seriously. Just be nice and don't raise your voice or do anything that isn't polite, and you'll be fine. He hasn't bit anyone and probably won't bite you either. The most vicious thing he has done is push to the ground a couple of miscreants and sat on their chests. One was throwing firecrackers at small toddlers and pregnant women in the park. The other was a pothead delivery man who entered my house when he was told to wait on the porch. Those were reasonable responses to being provoked, and pretty much the entire neighborhood agrees."

Detective Williams was not comforted. Detective Guzman was looking at Fred like a circus show freak. "How can you have such a big dog in an apartment? How much does he eat?"

I get those questions along with suggestions to put a saddle on him almost daily. "He doesn't eat as much as labs and golden retrievers. Mastiffs don't need much exercise and are happy sitting in the sun or under the table all day and usually won't even bother to get up when they bark unless a person enters the house. My first two really were like live stuffed animals when my kids were young. He is my third one, and by far, the most dominant personality, which for my current stage in life, is perfect. I do a lot of community service and always bring him. I frequently work at an overnight homeless shelter with families. They love it when I come with Fred because it makes them all feel safer. We get frequent requests from a battered women's shelter to hang out and stay the night." Having made my point, I waited for them to proceed with their agenda.

Detective Williams turned to Susan. "Can you please confirm your name and relationship with Benjamin Stein?"

"Susan Desmond, long-time friend or girlfriend. We didn't have an official status." She did an excellent job of spacing out her words and pausing to take a long drag.

Both of the detectives figured out that they would have to play Twenty Questions to get anything out of Susan.

"Okay, good. What can you tell us about Mr. Stein's activities the last few days? How often did you speak?" Detective Williams continued.

"Usually twice a day. I'm in recovery, and he called me in the mornings and evenings, mostly to check in and make sure I was okay and sticking with the program. He didn't really talk about work or what he was up to other than generalities like what he had for dinner, if he worked out, if he went to a Blackhawks' game. Small talk, really."

"How long have you two been in a relationship?"

"I can't say. I'm not even sure where a relationship begins. I've known him for so long I can't remember starting when. Maybe fifteen years. Look, I'm not feeling well and am really doing all I can to hold it together. I want to cooperate with the police. None of this is official, right? No recordings and this isn't on the record or an official statement or whatever the term is, right? Just ask me what you really need to know or care about and no setting-the-stage bullshit, okay?"

Detective Williams gave me a droll look. "This isn't an official statement, just some preliminary background information. Anything official legally must be reviewed and signed by you. There's no need for you to be worried. We know you were in Florida last night. What we don't know or have is a motive or a lead. Do you have any ideas that can put us on the right track?"

"No. I really mean it, no. There's no reason for Benny to die like that." Susan ended the statement in a whisper, and there could be no doubt of her sincerity.

"Okay," said Detective Guzman quietly. "Let's start with basic background information. We'll start with his routine, and maybe you can fill in some gaps with his family and friends. Do you want to start or, do you want us to ask you questions? We want you to be comfortable."

Susan looked at me, and I indicate no, they should ask questions. She clearly understood.

"I don't know how to start or how not to ramble, and I really don't feel good. Why don't you ask me specific questions to make sure I'm getting what you're after?"

I got another look from Detective Williams, who assumed the lead. "Where do you live? Did the two of you share a residence? I understand you're up from Florida. Did you maintain separate residences here or in Florida?"

"We own a house together in Coral Gables, Florida, for a little less than two years. I have been living there pretty much for the past six months or so."

"What about in Chicago?"

"I own a studio condo at 1100 N. Lake Shore Drive. I rent it out and have been for about two years. Before I moved to Florida, I was more or less living with Benny at his place and camping out at the corporate condo Jackson Partners owns or rents at Presidential Towers. Jackson Partners was my employer for I think fifteen years, and they let me stay when it isn't used."

Detective Guzman jumped with the connection. "Is that on

the same floor where Mr. Stein's apartment was, where he died?"

"Yes." Susan wasn't inclined to volunteer more on the topic, which puzzled the police. I wanted to give Susan kudos for following instructions but had to admit that her shutting down could be construed that there was something more interesting afoot.

Detective Williams considered the situation and decided to change their strategy. "Why were you living out of a suitcase if you owned a nice place?"

"Benny was good at managing money, including mine. Don't look at me like that. I made good money for a long time, on my own. Benny taught me it's stupid to own anything that can't generate rental income, which is why I bought that place. After the real estate crash, rents went crazy high. I own my place, free and clear. I knew Jackson Partners had a furnished corporate unit with maid service but was frustrated with the management company of that property at Presidential Towers. They weren't really supervising it, and there were a lot of complaints about clients getting out of hand, staying too long, and lots of resulting fines. The building threatened to kick them out. Benny came up with the idea of renting out his place, too, and taking an apartment on the same floor as the Jackson Partners' unit. The deal was that we would keep an eye on the clients who used the apartment and make sure employees weren't trashing it. In return, they paid the rent on Benny's apartment. Benny thought this would force us into making a permanent decision on what to do since the trading floors were dying."

"If there were so many problems, why did your employer maintain the apartment? Why not sell it or terminate the lease?"

Susan exhaled. "I don't really know. You'll have to ask them. All I can tell you is it's common for exchange firms to have a place where operations staff employees can crash when they have to work long hours due to hectic markets or system overhauls. It's cheaper to have three in an apartment for five or more nights a month that rents for three thousand dollars a month than pay Loop hotel rates for a room for each. It's even a bigger money saver if it is used by foreign clients visiting for extended periods of time."

She noticed the police were not following her explanation. "Jackson Partners offers classes in hedging with futures and options that take anywhere from one to four weeks. We earn a lot of goodwill and business from those classes. Also, a lot of Europeans take long vacations, especially in the summer. They can make part of their trip count as business. But, they have weird rules about expenses. A lot of them get a per diem or can spend a fixed amount without turning in receipts. They can keep or spend it as they wish. A lot of the European clients elect not to spend their per diem on hotels and eating out for every meal.

"For example, guys from Sweden come with suitcases filled with canned meat and fish, packaged cheeses, crackers, and other food that doesn't need to be refrigerated or cooked. The first thing they do when they hit town is buy cartons of cigarettes and booze 'cuz it's so much cheaper here. They sit in the apartment, eat their suitcase rations, and almost get sick on American liquor and cigarettes. Their goal is to eat out of their suitcases to save on the per diem they get from their bank.

"They shop like crazy at the discount malls and are in heaven if they find a Walmart. They load up on jeans, athletic shoes, personal care products, anything relating to contacts, and almost anything with a designer label, which they take home in their empty suitcases, all largely subsidized by the per diem they didn't spend. Any savings a brokerage firm can provide by providing housing goes straight to their party money or souvenir budget. It doesn't cost a firm anything extra if it can let clients use a corporate apartment not otherwise in use, and it doesn't violate any other laws or tax rules or whatever is the deal."

"Is this for real? It really is common?" Detective Guzman asked me.

"Sort of. Most clearing firms do have leases on corporate apartments, some of them are monthly, to provide housing for operations staff during crunch times. Mind you, any time we have a system upgrade or other change, the installation and testing must be done outside of market hours. Some firms have discounts at hotels or downtown business club memberships that include rooms to stay the night.

"The big advantage an apartment has over even a discounted hotel is you can guarantee it will be available every night during the lease period and know what the cost will be. You can't get that surety during the holidays or when a big trade show or other major event is in town. It isn't unheard of for firms to let clients stay at those apartments, but it's mostly due to accommodating an unusual situation where a last-minute visitor can't get into a hotel, and it's typically for a night or two.

"However, to Susan's point, my firm does take out suites at the LaSalle Club in our building during the holidays and make them available for out-of-town clients to visit Chicago with their families or to otherwise conduct business in town."

Detective Williams was unsettled by this revelation. I wasn't surprised. "Aren't there rules against that? Isn't it like paying under the table to direct business your way?" he followed.

"Look, let's focus on what's relevant to the investigation, shall we? I don't mean to play lawyer, but seriously, what difference does it make to you? However, to answer your question, yes, there are rules. It depends on who the regulator is and the purpose of the accommodation. In my firm's case, we get a discounted rate, which we pass on to the client. I'm sure Jackson Partners is abiding by all rules and regs, and it's clear that Susan doesn't have a full grasp of how the entire arrangement is managed.

"It's a common practice in lots of industries to entertain and otherwise host key clients. It's not big news that downtown Chicago's economic viability is heavily reliant on corporate entertaining. I almost stopped Susan from elaborating but didn't want to render the impression we aren't cooperating fully, especially over such a useless data point. And by the way, I can't take seriously ethical criticisms from any city employee, especially Chicago's Finest on something like this."

Detective Guzman smirked, which I took to mean he agreed with me. Detective Williams didn't like being verbally slapped into place, and he really didn't like Fred standing up while rumbling a low growl.

"What's your next question?" volunteered Susan.

"You have nothing to fear from Fred. He's just making a point. I agree with Susan, let's move on," I added.

Detective Guzman decided to help out. "What do you know about Mr. Stein's finances?" he asked Susan.

"Nothing specific. I know he owns a three-flat brownstone in Lincoln Square as an investment. He has a condo at 400 E. Randolph, where he used to live until he moved into Presidential Towers. He rents it out now, too. He never showed me anything like a tax return or bank statement, but he always had enough cash for whatever he wanted. We took nice trips, he had nice cars... I don't know what else to say."

"Do you know if he ever borrowed money or took investors into his trading company?"

"I don't know if he borrowed money from a bank or something equally normal, like for a mortgage or car loan. He hated credit cards and didn't believe in running up credit card debt. I assume he borrowed money like most traders do from their clearing firm. I doubt he ever took in any outside money. Like I said, I don't know anything specific, and I'm sure you can get better answers from his tax returns and her," Susan said and pointed to me for emphasis.

Detective Guzman had taken over the role of being the lead. "Did you ever meet any bankers or investors who were interested in hiring, or whatever is the term, Mr. Stein to trade foreign currencies or Bitcoins?"

Susan arched her eyebrows and took a long drag. "You know about Bitcoins?"

"No, but we heard Mr. Stein was interested in them and appeared to be conducting extensive research on them and related topics. We pulled his internet activity."

I smelled bullshit, and my bet was Susan did too.

Her answer confirmed it. "I doubt that. Benny was paranoid. The only internet activity you could have found by now is whatever was at Lough Key, and I doubt it was much. Just ask me a straight-out question, okay? No fishing or innuendos."

Detective Williams was annoyed. "We did. What do you know about three men who may or may not be bankers or from a hedge fund that came to Ms. Daye's office to open a trading account to trade currency futures?"

"Nothing."

The softness and curtness of her answer took both of them aback. Detective Guzman was the closest to playing 'Good Cop.' "Ms. Daye here and other people from her office concur that Mr. Stein introduced them to three people who were interested in becoming some sort of partner with Mr. Stein to trade currency futures. He never mentioned anything about them?" Detective Guzman volleyed back.

"No. That must have been when I was in rehab. He never said anything about them to me."

"I'm sorry, I should have inquired earlier. How long were you in rehab?" Detective Guzman asked.

"I still am, but I was in sort of a residential program for four months. I'm still working on transitioning to living independently in the real world."

"Okay, let's try it another way," continued Detective Guzman. "To what extent did you socialize with Benny's friends and business associates?"

I noticed Benny was not referred to as 'Mr. Stein' and was wondering why.

"I used to more frequently. We had reason to back in those days because Benny could network with Jackson Partners' clients and sometimes got great market intel. We had the same sort of hang-out friends who worked around the exchanges, but that's kind of like being in a neighborhood, and those people weren't necessarily his friends or mine. I'm not as social as Benny and don't like the club and bar scene. Do you know the names or have a description of the people you asked me about?"

Both policemen looked at me. "Benny brought them into my office on New Year's Eve. One was tall, well dressed, dark with a foreign accent that sounded like he was taught English in the UK. I don't remember his name, but I think it was something like Nivar. One was small, looked Swedish, or some sort of fair European and dressed like a euro hipster. The third was a wanna-be Wall Street type, and it wasn't clear where he was from either. The name he gave was John William Henry Carrington III. He was the one who did the most talking," I responded.

Susan was nodding and thinking. "Before I left for Florida, Benny met a couple of men who could be who you're talking about. It was at the annual Futures and Options FIA trade show. I only remember them because the small, blond one and I smoked a blunt outside, if he's the same guy. He didn't seem to have anything to do with trading or FinTech and was glad to get away. I think his first name was Ericsson like the Swedish telecom company, but he went by Eric. When we went back inside, there was a tall man who matches your description. He was a real creep. I got the vibe he was interested in finding a girlfriend for the night. I left. That was the night of the charity steak dinner. I didn't have to do more than make an appearance and drop off a couple of clients. I went out with some friends in town from Singapore. I don't know anything else about them."

Detective Guzman tried again. "What do you know about Benny's recent business activities? Anything you can tell us can be helpful. What was he trading, do you know if he was making money?"

By now, we were all conditioned to Susan answering questions after she smoked and exhaled. "I don't know what I can add that his clearing firm can't tell you with more of a factual base. I didn't pay any attention, and for the past year, I was mostly high until I went into recovery. He complained for years, like everybody from the floors did, about everything going electronic and the unfair competition of the big firms and banks. I always thought he was doing more than okay. That really is it."

"Did he have any partners or outside investors?"

"If he did, he'd have followed the rules and would have to disclose or report it or whatever. Ask his clearing firm or the exchange membership department. I'd think that information can also be figured out from his tax return." Her tone and body language sent the message that she genuinely could not add anything more regarding Benny's business affairs.

Detective Guzman switched gears accordingly. "What was Benny's relationship with his family?"

"I don't know how to answer that. I guess the same as anybody. Did you speak to any of them?"

The way Detective Guzman looked at me next made me suspect he was trying to case-out whether I would volunteer that I knew Paul Stein had met with them in the morning. He decided not to risk it. "We had a conversation with his brother, Paul, earlier."

"Then if you asked him similar types of questions and if he answered completely, you know that his family hates me, and that Benny doesn't or didn't see much of them. I don't see a point in describing any family drama. Suffice it to say I doubt I have an economic or other motive to have any contact with them."

"Do you know how they are situated financially?"

"All I know for a fact is they give the appearance of having and spending a lot of money. I don't know anything else because I never cared."

"Were they close? Can you provide any color on how often Benny spoke to his family or typical interaction?"

Susan stiffened a little bit but did respond. "Whenever they needed money. At least that was what it sounded like to me. Benny didn't like talking about it. My impression is based mostly from overhearing his side of telephone conversations. He went to big events like weddings and funerals, but otherwise didn't see them in person much."

"What did they need money for, how frequently was it?"

"It sounded like it was mostly to pay for big-ticket items for his mother and sister, Sharon's expenses. She got hurt real bad a long time ago and never recovered. She still runs up a lot of medical expenses. I'm not sure of the facts. I think their father died relatively young and didn't leave a lot of money. Those conversations seem to ebb and flow around whatever is going on with Sharon and their mother. There was no set routine."

"Why don't they like you?" ventured Detective Guzman.

This provoked a longer pause for Susan to consider how to answer. "They refer to me as the 'Coke Head Slut' instead of by my name. They didn't like me before they knew about my habits. I never did anything to deserve that. I think Sharon likes me, and she was crazy about Benny. My guess is that Benny and I didn't conform to their North Shore, Jewish, suburban gentry standards. Look, I'm not a shrink qualified to theorize, and I was pretty good at avoiding them. There really isn't anything more I can tell you about his family."

Detective Guzman seemed satisfied with her answer. "Do you know if he had a will or the name of an attorney or accountant he used?"

"I think his brother did a lot of his legal work, but I'm not certain. His accountant is Tommy O'Doole. Tommy is also a lawyer, and I know he worked on some of Benny's personal matters. When we started being serious about moving away, Benny had me sign a lot of papers. I think I'm some kind of backup to make sure that his brother doesn't get his hands on any of Benny's money. Benny wanted to make sure Sharon would always be okay. Tommy has an office kitty-corner from the Board and across the street from the CBOE on Van Buren. He does my taxes, too, and a lot of people from the exchanges go to him."

That answer was a turning point for the two policemen. Detective Guzman asked if she knew where Benny kept his personal papers. She didn't, nor did she know if he kept a bank lockbox. Her best guess was that he probably maintained digital files on a cloud account. She repeated that she was largely ignorant of what she signed and suggested the obvious solution of contacting O'Doole. Susan had his contact information in her phone and gave it to them.

Detective Williams was now antsy and frustrated. "Do you know where his computer and cell phone may be? We didn't find either at his apartment or at his clearing firm. Actually, it would be nice if you could confirm his phone number and that he only had one."

That surprised Susan. "Really? He never went anywhere without his phone, like even to the bathroom. He had a laptop and a tablet. He loved the tablet and took it almost everywhere with him. That's really odd. He had two numbers. The first is his cell phone and the second is the house phone for our house in Florida that he used as his official business number. I don't think he used it much."

"You wouldn't know any of his passwords or password conventions?"

"I know he didn't trust apps that organized passwords 'cuz he wasn't convinced they were secure. He maintained a spreadsheet with his passwords, and he followed the advice of using multiple passwords and changing them often. I know his devices were all Apple. Maybe Apple support can help you?"

"Any other ideas? He never maintained a hardcopy somewhere, like in a notebook? He sounds like he always had a Plan B. What would he do if he had problems with his hard drive or his phone got lost?" Detective Williams tried again.

"Wait. You're right... he had a fob on his key chain that I think had that information or maybe it was a thumb drive. I'm not sure which, but I remember him saying he kept his passwords on it."

"Do you know if his security was limited to passwords, or did he use encryption?"

"No, I don't know, but like I told you, Benny was paranoid. I know he had multiple passwords and changed them around periodically. He liked the convenience and the cheapness of storing documents and pictures on the cloud and really liked online banking for paying bills. He never kept personal data on any of his devices. He had a separate bank account strictly for bills, and that was the one tied to anything he paid for online if he didn't use a credit card. He said it was stupid to have one bank account because if it were compromised, there would be nothing you could do to get your money back. He'd never use a debit card for the same reason. He paid for a lot in cash and only used credit cards for e-commerce or if there was a big enough reward incentive."

"Do you know if he was paranoid about anything in particular? Why was he so careful?"

"He wasn't a government conspiracy nut if that's what you mean. He read a lot about hackers from Russia and Africa being more prone to theft like bank fraud while the Chinese were experts on corporate espionage and spying. He was alarmed how easy it is to steal someone's identity. He bought internet security software years ago. It had a name like Guard Dog. He set it to the highest level and showed me how frequently attempts were made to hack into his computer. I don't think he considered himself a specific target. He described it as cyber trolling, looking for anybody careless enough to leave an open door to their personal information.

"He was really spooked about using public WiFi networks. Supposedly, some trader was using the WiFi at Ceres, the restaurant in the Board of Trade building, over breakfast. The story goes that by the time he stepped off the grains floor after one o'clock that same day, his personal information was infiltrated, and sixty thousand dollars was stolen from his bank account. He kept his financial information on a computer where he never used the internet, and he'd never file his taxes electronically. Benny had lots of stories about people he knew who had tax refunds jacked and the mess it was to clean up."

I am not sure what the detectives were expecting. My hunch is a more illuminating source of information about Benny's personal affairs and a path to find Benny's digital footprint.

"Not to be rude or disrespectful, but we need to ask if he was involved with drugs,"

Detective Guzman soldiered on.

"No. Benny hated pot and coke. Those are my vices. He was a social drinker and didn't smoke except cigars when he was out. I don't think he really liked them. Look, there's no way this has anything to do with drugs in case you think this was a buy gone wrong. He didn't associate with people who dealt with them and tried to avoid users, other than me."

"Where did you buy, get your drugs?" Detective Williams grimly asked.

Susan stared at him for a full three seconds. "Really? You're a Chicago cop. I think we both know it would be more efficient for me to give you the four places in this entire city where it's not possible to easily procure drugs. I told you before, my habits have nothing to do with Benny."

Detective Williams did not like being shut down. "It's not your call to make right now. Right now, you're to answer our questions completely. Who sold to you?"

That was a strategic mistake. Susan smiled sweetly. "Mostly from cops. Cops are less likely to cut or lace their junk, and they usually offer better prices."

"You're full of shit," Detective Guzman remarked before Detective Williams could respond.

"Am I?"

"Yeah. Cops don't sell retail. Just end this and answer the question, please."

Susan chuckled. "Fair enough. I was an impulsive, on-the-spot buyer. I only bought enough for my immediate consumption. That's true. It's also true that small amounts of coke and pot can be openly bought from any parking valet, doorman, and at any city bar. You can get high on most days walking past the loading docks of big office buildings, and there's usually somebody selling one-lot blunts. Then there're the guys who hang out in the white van in the plaza with the horse next to the CBOE. Oh yeah, the twenty-year-old perpetual high school students supposedly selling chocolate bars for their basketball team during school hours outside office buildings have a nice assortment of illegal wares underneath the cardboard layer holding the candy. I was never meeting nefarious people in alleys, and it isn't a sort of commodity that requires a specific relationship. Drugs are easier to buy than beer. No ID required. You know all this. Again, I didn't involve or need Benny."

Detective Guzman wisely changed gears. "Okay, let's try a little deductive reasoning. You're gone for months, it sounds like Benny was social and liked being around people, so who was he eating dinner with? You said something about Blackhawks' tickets. Did he have season tickets with somebody? Who would he go with? Did he have a favorite bar? Did he hang out with people from his gym?" Detective Guzman was patient, and he wasn't buying that Susan had no idea what Benny was up to and with whom.

That question inspired Susan to fully engage. She put both feet on the floor, hunched over the dining room table, leaning on both elbows while placing her hands on both sides of her head to hold it up. "You're right. Okay, he went to the East Bank Club to workout most days after the close, unless he was trading grains because they have a late start. He knew a lot of people there, but he wasn't especially close to anyone. He liked hanging out afterward at places that cater to traders, like South Branch or Rivers near the Merc, especially during the summer because they have outdoor seating. He used to go to Cactus and Tuttos a lot more, but I don't think he liked that crowd as much anymore. He was spending more time around the Mart, partly because it's close to his gym and because a number of trading firms moved into that building. He never drove if he was drinking. Have you found his driver? He'd know more about what Benny was doing at night.

"He was close with Scott Elderman. Scott is big into electronic trading systems and strategies. He owns Red Sky and has an office in a building in Evanston that's a few blocks from the Metra train station. Benny was thinking of taking out an office there, too. He mentioned that building is a hub for a lot of traders since it isn't necessary to come downtown anymore. He said those groups tended to be older and legit traders. He thought a lot of the younger guys didn't understand trading principals and just know how to work a system given to them.

"Lately, it sounded like he was spending a lot of time with Gregg Krajusky. He is or was a High-Frequency currency trader with the Amston Group. He left over some bonus dispute and has to sit out a year because of a non-compete. I don't know where they met or how frequently.

"Benny has season tickets to the Blackhawks but sold a lot of them 'cuz he thought we would be in Florida full-time by now. He didn't want to give them up entirely because he wanted playoff tickets. He'd go a lot with Danny Glazier, a friend since high school, but Benny used those tickets mostly to take people out who he thought he could learn something from."

The two policemen let Susan finish her uncharacteristic roll without interruption. Both were taking notes. Susan shut down entirely once she stopped and looked down at the table. She really didn't look good. Fred moved next to her and placed his nose between her elbow and chest and nodded his head up and down, making her shake and laugh. He then sat down and put his paw on her lap. I was a little surprised by his empathy. He usually only takes to kids that quickly.

The doorbell buzzed, and since it didn't let up, I knew it was my top floor neighbors, the Metzkers. Fred did too and raced to the door, which I let him do by dropping his leash. As I got up and walked to the front door, I explained to the group the pleasure they were about to have.

"Is everything okay with you? Why is a police car outside for so long?" Leah pounced once inside. She moves Fred with a swat of her hand and largely ignores him. I should have expected them earlier. Leah is eighty-something and keeps fit by spending hours on her Exercycle watching television and the street from her sunroom windows.

Walter was right behind her and equally adept at maneuvering around Fred, who was tugging at his sweater. "We came down to make sure you're still coming to dinner tonight," he said, which was a bald-faced lie. He at least has the social graces to pretend he isn't watching every move all of us living on our block make.

I had enough of the interview, and Susan was exhausted. So, I invited the Metzkers into the dining room.

"Leah and Walter Metzker own this building and live on the top floor. Mr. and Mrs. M, this is Susan, a friend of mine visiting from Florida. The two gentlemen are police detectives, Mr. Williams and Mr. Guzman. I'm sorry, I don't recall your first names. They are here making a courtesy call because of something that happened at my office today. Everything is fine. I'll tell you about it later after the police leave. I'm sorry, I forgot about dinner tonight with all the commotion."

"But, you're still coming, yes? Bring Susan. I made my Greek lemon chicken and have the honey-almond cookies you like," insisted Mrs. M.

"Ah, sure. Six thirty, as usual? Oh, are you making a Jewel run? I forgot to get Susan something to drink. Susan, what do you want to drink?" I asked carefully keeping my face deadpan.

Satisfied I did not have any malicious intent of disclosing the true nature of her chicken or lack of prior dinner plans, she offered, "Yes. I still need to pick up a few things. Susan, dear, what do you like to drink?" she asked.

Mondays are cheap chicken days at Jewel when they are a whole dollar off. Mr. M loves Jewel fried chicken, and Ms. M's Greek lemon chicken recipe is Jewel's broasted chicken reheated with canned chicken stock, rosemary, and slices of lemon on top. She compliments the veneer of authenticity with a box of Rice-a-Roni pilaf and a bag of frozen green beans almondine. Mr. M will go along with the charade if she lets him have the Jewel deli potato wedges with his dinner.

"Any kind of unsweetened iced tea would be nice. Thank you."

By now, Fred was sniffing at Mr. M's sweater pocket and half-growling and almost canine talking. Clearly, Mr. M was giving him treats that he carried in that pocket, and he wanted to escape before I busted him. "Come, Leah, let them finish their business. We need to get ready in time."

The Metzkers usually linger, and I typically have to almost force them out. This was way too easy, especially with the policemen and a visitor to interrogate, so he must really be spoiling Fred. Mr. M comes to my place daily to let Fred out and to keep him company, especially when the Cubs are playing. He likes having a TV by himself without Leah's constant stream of conversation. The irony is Fred really, really likes his naps during the day to be uninterrupted and is fine waiting to go out if I stick to my normal schedule. My guess is that Mr. M is one of those old men who yell and talk to the TV, which explains why Fred is sometimes grumpy when I get home. If I ever make the mistake of getting a recliner, I think Mr. M will try to move in with me. He loves Leah, but isn't into Real Housewives of Wherever and is tired of her sister's daily drama.

The conversation stalled until I returned to the dining room with Fred. He resumed his position next to Susan while sitting up so that he could watch the policemen. By now, Detective Guzman learned to ignore him, but Detective Williams was still unsettled by the dog's staring.

Detective Guzman resumed. "Okay. We're almost done for today. Did you have a chance to look at Benny's account statements?" he asked me.

"Yes, but I can't turn them over or discuss them in any detail until we get the indemnification, and our attorney has to sign off on it. I think it's okay to tell you that for the past two years I didn't see anything noteworthy."

"Like I said before, we're still looking for his computers and cell. Is there any place like a shared office where he had a desk with records or a laptop? He didn't keep one at the house in Florida, did he?" Detective Guzman asked, looking at Susan.

"No. As far as I know, he had the three devices, and they should have been with him in his apartment."

"Do you mind going over to his apartment with us tomorrow to see if anything strikes you as not normal?"

Susan took an unusually long pause where it was obvious she was mulling over the request. "If you think it would help, but I really don't want to. How long will his stuff stay there?"

"We can't say. Now it's dependent on the length of time to determine who's in charge of his estate and after-death wishes, which we won't know until we find a will or trust document. We'll talk to the accountant you mentioned and maybe have better luck tomorrow."

"Can Laney go, too?"

I was shocked by that request. I had no interest in participating. To me, it would be an intrusion on the privacy of a family I didn't know well, nor did I wish to improve the acquaintance. I really did not like the hopeful glances I was getting from the two detectives. My heart softened looking at Susan staring at the table. She looked about to cry and reverted back to leaning over while crossing her arms across the lower part of her rib cage.

"My mornings are pretty booked. Anyway, I first need the green light from our attorney, and you two don't seem to have a hard ETA of when to expect the indemnification from your side, which is the first step."

"How about we talk around ten o'clock tomorrow and see how things are progressing? It will probably be more efficient to first find out what we can from O'Doole. There's no need to rush over to the apartment first thing," Detective Williams suggested.

I took that as a compromise from him, which I suspected was motivated by him wanting to get away from Fred. Fred had figured out that Detective Williams was not a fan, so naturally Fred had to maintain his vigilant staring at the detective reinforced by a periodic, low half growl, half whine. They got up to leave, gave us another set of business cards, and confirmed Susan's and my cell numbers. I noticed for the second time there was no customary hand-shaking and end-of-meeting pleasantries.

After Fred and I escorted the two policemen to the front door, I let him off the leash, and we returned to the dining room. Susan appeared exhausted. She didn't look up to a friendly interrogation and dinner at the Metzkers.

"You don't look like you feel well. How about I make you some scrambled eggs and toast, and you take a hot shower and go to bed?"

Susan was visibly relieved. "You don't mind? I didn't mean for this. Talking to the police was harder than I thought."

I reassured her it was all right and good for me too because I could leave sooner without her. She kept me company in the kitchen while I regaled her with the details of Mrs. M's Greek chicken and a typical Monday night dinner. I made a pot of hot tea and joined her in a cup while she ate her scrambled eggs and Greek toast with grape jelly. She couldn't stomach the microwave bacon, so I used that as a treat to top Fred's dinner.

While eating, she asked what time I left for the office. I took that as a hint to find out when she had to leave. I told her she could stay, warned her not to let Fred out of the yard because he is not trustworthy, and to expect the Metzkers to check on her.

I explained I didn't think the odds were good that the paperwork would be executed between the state attorney's office and our firm's lawyer. Even though the Cubs' season hadn't started yet, Mr. M would come down to watch TV, probably the History channel or old westerns on MeTV, which he is fine watching himself. He'd let Fred out, so she didn't have to bother.

I warned her to expect a pot of chicken and rice soup, which would be made with the leftovers of Mrs. M's Greek chicken augmented by a can of chicken stock and water. It would be okay to tell her she isn't hungry and will save it for dinner because it smells so good. I'll use the chicken to dress Fred's dinner and toss the rest. That made Susan laugh, and she looked a little better after eating.

"I should be going now and will tell them you're beat from a long day. Mr. M notices everything but is too polite to overtly ask questions. Mrs. M will feel it's her moral obligation to find out your story, but she's very kind and will back off if you tell her you don't feel well."

"Okay. I won't mind. I didn't have a plan and am not sure what I'd do if you didn't take me in. Thanks."

Fred had taken to Susan and was nudging her elbow to be petted.

"I know this sounds crazy, but I think what would do you good is a hot shower and sleep. On the coffee table are two books, *If You Give a Moose a Muffin* and *If You Give a Mouse a Cookie*. Fred loves being read those stories, only change the word 'mouse' to 'Fred.' He also loves being able to climb on a bed, which I don't allow him to do. You'll be his best friend if you let him lie next to you and read him those stories. He'll get off when you're done. I'll put a sheet on top of the duvet so that he doesn't make the whole bed hairy and smell like dog. Drop it on the floor when he gets off."

"You're not serious... you read to him?"

"It started by accident. I bring a stack of books to read to the kids at the shelter. Some of them have a hard time settling down. He doesn't understand the words but likes the rhythm of the words. A few of the older kids are embarrassed by being read to, so I started reading to Fred, and he lets the smaller ones cuddle around him. You look like you need help shutting down to sleep. It works for them, so why not try it? Only one thing, he snores like Fred Flintstone. The kids don't mind, but if it bothers you, poke him, and he'll move to his spot in the living room to wait for me."

Susan was laughing when I left.

Chapter 4

Pär was bored and frustrated. The events last night convinced him that he was personally cursed by God. He didn't view him getting to Benny's building before the police shut off access to Benny's apartment as good fortune. The last thing he needed was the police looking into him and asking questions, but that wasn't the point. The point was that he was again thwarted from finding out if Nivar's bank released ten million dollars into a bank account, and if it was deposited into an account Benny controlled. God, he didn't need much. All he wanted was the one million dollars Nivar promised him, and he was down to his last few euros. Selling drugs to get by is easy in Europe but not here. That trade was controlled by black gangs. He couldn't understand their English. They looked like they were predisposed to kill someone like him and certainly would not give him credit to buy product to resell. He couldn't exchange Bitcoins like he did last time he was in the States without access to Nivar's constantly changing passwords to the Netherland bank account.

The original plan was simple. Get here a day before Nivar, tell Benny some story why he needs his cut now, and leave. Pär counted on Benny not caring whether one million dollars was taken off the top as his commission, especially if more was coming. All bullshit, of course, which is why Pär wanted his before it could be lost trading. That idiot, Benny, actually was going to use the money to seed trading FX futures. What a blowhard. It made no sense to Pär that someone who was supposedly such a great trader and well-connected would be interested in their deal. Pär never thought Benny was as gullible as Nivar did. Instead, Pär thought Benny would keep the ten million dollars, knowing they had no legal recourse to compel him to share any of it. The only thing that did make sense is that Benny preferred trading with bank money over his.

It was pure inspiration that he decided to try to see the woman at the trading firm Benny introduced them to. He was smoking in a plaza outside the building trying to think up a plausible story when he saw Dizzy walk in with another woman. He almost didn't recognize Dizzy, but he was sure he was right after watching her. He entered the building a few steps behind and noticed the other woman let Dizzy in, and she entered the same elevator bank as Benny's trading company.

Pär returned to a bench in the plaza to think. The woman Benny introduced them to months ago in that building didn't seem cooperative at the time. Pär inwardly chuckled remembering how she tossed them out. What was funny at the time was how insulted Nivar was that any woman didn't buy his bullshit and how annoyed she was by his debonair act. That clown pretending to be a lawyer looking for alternative investments didn't help. Another idiot. At least he wasn't in the picture anymore. Not that it mattered now, anyway.

He saw two men park a sedan on the side street of the building where parking was clearly not allowed and leave it there. They must be cops to do that, and they looked like plain-clothes police do everywhere. Only here, they weren't white. One was black, and one looked Latin, probably Mexican. He also followed them into the building and noticed they entered the same elevator bank as Dizzy. Great. It can't be a coincidence.

Pär decided to sit on his bench and watch to see what any of them did next. After an hour or so, the cops returned to their car and drove off. It didn't seem like a good idea to follow them. What would be the point, and he didn't want to attract attention. A half hour later, Dizzy left the building from a side door with the same woman Benny introduced them to. Two men were with them—one was huge, and the other was a normal-looking professional man better dressed than most of the men coming in and out of the building. All four walked to the parking lot across the street from the building, the big man carried the duffle bag he saw Dizzy with previously.

Now what? He saw a goldish Benz station wagon pull into the entrance of the parking lot, and the two men were opening its doors to let the women in, and the big guy dropped the bag in the back seat. He would try to follow them, but how? A cab passed but going in the opposite direction of where the wagon was pointed. A woman got out right across from the parking lot. Pär got in and told the driver to follow the gold car that just turned west on the expressway. The cab driver made a quick U-turn in the garage driveway. He asked Pär if he was for real, which Pär took to mean he wondered why he was following a car. Pär told him his friends left without him, and he was not from around here and couldn't give him an address. He also told him he had not set up a phone service plan for the US yet, and it was not possible for him to call them with a European cell plan when the cab driver asked him why he didn't call his friends.

Maybe his luck was changing. What were the odds he would see Dizzy and that she met up with that woman, whatever her name is. It was also lucky their car is an odd color because it was easy to follow. He didn't dare smoke in the cab and wondered how long the trip would be and what he would do next. They drove past some blighted neighborhoods. He hoped wherever they were headed was where he would not stand out so much. Usually, being white made it easier to go unnoticed. The cab driver didn't attempt any small talk. Okay, that was lucky too.

The destination of the Benz was an old neighborhood not too far from the downtown area. Pär was relieved by the older, well-maintained houses that were bigger than the norm in Europe on streets with lots of mature trees. The Benz was about to pull into an alley. Pär told the cab driver to stop and paid him, making a point of tipping a couple of dollars and hoping it was in line with the norm for Americans. Stupid Americans tip everybody and too much, but he didn't want the cab driver not to buy his story by acting desperate for cash.

Pär entered the alley and took full advantage of the detached garages to provide cover. He still could not think of a plausible reason to approach them. He was wondering how he would figure out which residence they entered, which turned out to be easily resolved. He heard female voices close by, and shortly afterward, the world's largest dog rushed down the stairs of the building two garages away. Holy shit. The beast looked like it was half lion and half dog and was overtly attached to the dark-haired woman. Pär wasn't the sort to threaten or use strong-arm tactics, anyway. The dog made him dismiss the idea of approaching them at the dark-haired woman's home. He decided to walk around the neighborhood to find a place where he could sit, think, and smoke without being conspicuous.

He found a park about four blocks away near a school and a children's playground. It had a large walking path where he found a bench away from the playground and soccer field. Pär was aware that he didn't blend into this neighborhood and didn't want anybody thinking he was a pervert watching children.

His first idea was to pretend to be a friend of Benny's. However, he could not approach them at the dark-haired woman's house. How would he explain his appearance at her home? Okay, that meant he had to make his approach from the dark-haired woman's office, which would be logical since he met her there before and was introduced by Benny. She had to remember the encounter. The wild card was the extent Dizzy remembered him. They only met once outside a trade show. He was impressed how quickly she could score a joint and her nonchalance at smoking it in a public place. She didn't strike Pär as the type who would believe Nivar's bullshit, and he didn't know if she would associate him with Nivar. She probably would if she were friends with the dark-haired woman because of the spectacle the three of them made. It had to come up in conversation.

While mulling, he noticed the dark-haired woman in the park with the beast. It looked even bigger as they approached. She didn't notice him. Her attention was on all the people who came up to pet the dog. In spite of being a neighborhood regular and friendly to small children, it didn't look wise to alarm her with that dog. He never left her side, nor did he pull or yank on the leash, which was evidence that he is well-trained besides being devoted to her. He was friendly to kids but was always zoned in on the woman. For lack of a better idea, Pär followed them back to her apartment building. He didn't want to stick around long because it was strictly residential, and he would stand out as loitering. The walk wasn't wasted because he entered her address on his phone for future reference.

The plain sedan pulled up in front of her building, and the same two men he saw earlier got out and walked up its steps. Pär decided that being outside buildings immediately before the police entered was more than a coincidence and maybe was a perverse form of luck. While evaluating his options, he noticed an older woman staring at him from the top floor. It was time to go. He made a big show of looking at his watch, walking up to a couple of doors and appearing confused or lost and walking back toward the busy street a couple of blocks down. He thought he saw a bus and hoped it would take him to whatever train he saw that ran parallel to the expressway originating from downtown. Nobody would think it odd that someone with a strong accent was lost and needed help returning to the city.

He was staying at a cheap Holiday Inn near the Greyhound bus station downtown. The one thing he didn't have to worry about was paying for hotels and airfare, thanks to Nivar. Pär had a bank corporate credit card. Nivar explained the rules and limitations. EuroCredit Bank credit cards had default restrictions on cash advances, most retail store purchases, and, as far as Pär could recollect, anything other than international chain hotels and economy airfares. Executives like Nivar could charge expensive meals and stay at five-star hotels. Pär's credit card had the same privileges as line utility staff like internal auditors and tech support staff, which had limitations on how much could be spent daily based on location. He wasn't going to risk charging any meals that weren't hotel breakfasts and room service, and he was savvy only to order the cheapest items on the menu. His reasoning was there was no way a cheap Holiday Inn didn't conform to whatever was the daily per diem limit for Chicago, and he didn't want to attract attention by charges from restaurants and hotels not already on some approved list.

He would return to his room and think up a plausible story to visit the dark-haired woman at her office the next day. He was glad that he had three passports because she mentioned requiring a passport to conduct business when they were in her office. He had to be careful about what name he used, but all of that was workable coupled with a compelling story. First, he had to figure out what his goal should be. It was too much to hope for that she would release any funds to him, regardless of his stated reason. Therefore, he had to be satisfied with information but useful information that would lead him to a path for his share, assuming it was where he could find it.

He needed to eat and smoke a joint before he could think more. He would be careful not to drink alcohol because that clouded his judgment.

Chapter 5

I instructed Jason to have Latesha see me when she got in. He had a ringside seat for yesterday's drama and was wide-eyed for more today. To mollify him, I mentioned the police might be back today, but I wasn't sure. It was a vague comment he could interpret as he wished. I knew better than attempting to control the ripple effect of gossip under the circumstances. My nonchalance was rewarded by his eyes almost popping out of his sockets like in a cartoon.

At about six forty-five, Latesha entered my office with her morning cup of fragrant, hibiscus green tea. "Jason won't be hating his week watching the front desk. He may even volunteer next week. He asked me who Honey is because three people called and left messages for her already today. He nearly died when I told him it was you, and that's what the older floor ops staff call you. I didn't explain why. He asked me if I thought you were all right and to expect the police again this morning."

Billy walked into my office in time to hear Latesha. "Are they really coming back today, here, at our office? Why?"

I recapped for both of them the interview between Susan, the two policemen, and me. They appreciated the comic relief provided by Fred and the Metzkers. Billy agreed with me that we should consult with Oscar this morning before any of us have another discussion with the police.

"Why are you getting so many calls from the floor this morning? Is today Eddy Gallway's birthday?" Billy asked.

"Tomorrow is. They want to make sure the cake and his corsage are ordered. I got an especially large and purple one this year because it's a landmark birthday, and I think one of his daughters may come down."

Ed Gallway is a boisterously cheerful floor broker whose floor acronym is EKG, which is why he describes himself as the 'Heart Throb Broker for the Stars.' He keeps a black book with everybody's birthday and makes sure each person gets a very loud, personalized shout out before the opening on their birthday. Years ago, I ordered him a flower corsage, a color banner, and a cake for his big day. It remains a tradition but not nearly as fun as when there were lots of cheers and whistles from the people and bustle on the trading floors. Even the cake isn't as good as when the floor officials used to levy a fine for having food on the floor, regardless of the fact they all got a piece too.

Oscar had joined the three of us and was curious about my evening with Susan. I gave a shortened version of the recap, skipping the Fred and Metzker highlights. When I concluded, I asked Latesha if she got any results from Joel from the Lake Shore Bank about its double-check of the anti-money laundering due diligence they did on the 2.4 million dollars. She said that Joel would share their report before eleven but didn't think anything interesting would surface. They use Chase, their correspondent relationship with the Fed system, and rely on it for AML compliance. Joel mentioned to be careful about fully disclosing Benny's affidavit, and Chase knew the bank of origin for the wire. Joel was glad that we gave him a heads-up to get the affidavit because nothing provoked filing a Suspicious Activity Report [SAR].

"Based on your read of the players last night, what's your best guess on where we may be vulnerable?" Oscar asked.

"AML," I answered. "And I don't think the state or whatever attorney has jurisdiction of the murder case can give us an indemnification. I have no proof or any hard evidence other than my 'spidey senses.' That's an issue for Scott to wrangle. The cops aren't stupid. My read is they have a hodge-podge of data they would like help connecting the dots. Susan isn't what they expected on many fronts. She isn't a gold digger, which is how she likely was portrayed by Paul or whatever family they have interviewed. She was totally candid because she doesn't care and not aware of any repercussions. She also has an irrefutable alibi that she was in Florida when he was murdered and no motive.

"Susan mentioned that she knew Benny arranged to take care of his sister, Sharon, and that she was a contingent form of a trustee should Benny die to make sure Paul didn't have control over Benny's money. Paul's rush to claim entitlement reinforces that theory. From Susan's physical demonstrations of grief and the questions she is asking, it doesn't seem that she has any interest in herself being Benny's beneficiary other than wanting to know her stake in the house they bought in Florida. I think she'd comply with Benny's wishes regarding Sharon and his mother.

"My other read is that the police have no line on a motive other than the origins of the 2.4 million dollars deposited with us, and that's a consequence of Larry Katz's showmanship yesterday and my big mouth about the three mystery bankers on New Year's Eve. Therefore, my inner Sherlock tells me the ownership of the money is now their primary focus. I have no idea what Paul's standing is with them. It sounds like he frequently borrows from Benny and was trying to get another loan out of him, but I don't see him as so cold-blooded as to shoot his own brother from close range.

"So, to circle back to your question, if they have to engage another law enforcement agency to help trace the origins of the 2.4 million dollars, it's de facto opening up a regulatory inquiry as an unintended consequence and outside the scope of the Chicago police. Besides getting Scott's input, what's your opinion today about fulfilling your offer for me to help? They asked me to join them with Susan to look over his apartment. They haven't found his cell or any computers or tablets and want Susan to let them know if anything else is missing. They already asked me to comment on his trading activity here."

Oscar was standing with his left arm crossed, his right elbow resting in the cup of his left hand, and his right hand stroking his chin. He was processing every word in multiple ways.

"I'm predisposed to extending the offer of your continual assistance. You know that whole keep-your-friends-close-but-your-enemies-closer thing. Yes, especially because I share your AML concerns. We need Scott to get us an indemnification and see if we can insert broad language. We need to ask him how binding it would be with other law enforcement agencies. For now, my inclination is for you to play nice but don't tell them much, just enough to stick close to them. Bill?" Oscar said, thinking out loud.

"I first want to hear what Scott says. I'm not crazy about Laney being on the frontlines of whatever is the discovery process. If something comes from it, she can be dragged into years of depositions, court testimony, and God knows what. I get your point of advance notice of any directional change coming at us. The other risk is whatever she discovers or renders an opinion on can mean she's stuck in a family legal feud over his estate. I'm voting against her doing more than what she is legally compelled to do. I'll be even more adamant if Larry or Paul resurface here," Billy commented.

Oscar turned to me. "Laney?"

"I'm not loving this. I can't describe the sensation. It's like I'm in somebody else's dream. Everything about yesterday was unsettling. Granted, I exacerbated it by inviting Susan to stay with me. I feel like I have to be on guard reading body language, every word they say, or what I say because it may be used against us or me. Whatever. You get my point."

Billy perked up. "Speaking of Susan, how long are you two roomies?"

"Not sure. I have to admit, I get a kick out of her. I don't feel sorry for her, and she wouldn't want that. She's totally honest and accepting of consequences. Susan's like talking to an overly observant and honest teenager. She said she wants to go back to Florida once Benny has his Shiva or funeral. I wouldn't be surprised if she reconsiders the whole Florida idea without Benny. I'll deal with that after we hear from

Scott, and I figure out what to do with the police."

"What's she doing today?" Billy asked.

"Hanging out with Fred. She said she wanted to clean my apartment because it's good therapy for her. I haven't decided if I should be insulted or grateful. Mr. M will drop down in the afternoon to watch TV, and Mrs. M will convert her leftover faux Greek chicken into chicken soup for lunch and invite her up for a long chat. The police asked her to go to Benny's apartment today to see if anything is amiss. She didn't want to, which is how I got invited to that party. She looks like she should sleep, watch junk TV, and eat normal food. The Metzkers and Fred will be good company for her and give them somebody to bother and fuss over. She'll be all right."

Billy frowned. "How does she get along with Fred? He's hard to control."

"Only for men. He's a big softy to kids, damsels in distress, and anybody who'll let him on the bed and read *When You Give a Moose a Muffin*. Mr. M lets him out, and I told Susan not to be tempted to take him for a walk or out of the yard."

Both men laughed at me, and Billy told me I was a nut case. I retorted that Fred is a pioneer in the art of being a comfort dog. We agreed to reconvene after Oscar spoke to Scott and found out where we stand on the indemnification. All of us had work to do.

At ten fifteen, Susan called me and said the police were insistent that she join them at Benny's apartment and were hoping she could be there by noon. I told her I would call her back shortly. When I checked with Oscar, he informed me that Scott had two conversations with the state attorney on the case, but we were nowhere near an indemnification. The two attorneys were going to battle over every detail. The state attorney didn't want to budge. He didn't think my help was essential and didn't appear to have any regard for the opinion of the two detectives, or so it was represented to our attorney. Oscar said he didn't think this was Scott looking for a fight or insisting on legal purity. He was worried. We decided I would join Susan at Benny's apartment to lend moral support to Susan but not opine on anything. Oscar hoped we would have the best-case-scenario of me being able to observe them without having to contribute to the conversation. I told Susan I would meet her at the McDonald's in the building at eleven forty-five to go over today's set of Oscar rules for the occasion.

Susan was sitting in the back of the McDonald's near the door, smoking with a large cup of untouched coffee. She was using the lid for an ashtray. The other patrons and staff didn't seem to notice the infraction to the non-smoking ordinance.

I sat down next to her. "Here's the deal, and we don't have much time. According to our outside attorney, the police can lie, make any kind of insinuation or implied guarantee during an interview, especially when no charges have been filed, and nobody is under formal arrest. It's apparently part of the game of gleaning information and perhaps a confession or slip-up of a material witness or person of interest or whatever is the label.

"My firm's attorney says we should listen and give up no information that isn't rock-solid verifiable and of no consequence if they have it. Our attorney is interested in being able to gauge how our firm and I can be dragged into litigation or another form of legal proceeding. You should know that our interests may not be aligned with yours. Both lawyers suggest you hire your own attorney, and they will make recommendations for a lawyer who has no conflict with our firm and with a specialty in criminal law.

"Our attorney is worried that the opening position from the state attorney's office is to offer no indemnifications. I have no idea if that's standard for them. Our attorney is concerned enough to consult with a lawyer who has a criminal law practice. I am sharing this with you not to scare you but to reinforce that we really have to be on our guard.

"The police can't make you cooperate without a subpoena, court order, or something more official than hauling your butt into a police station. They can question you, but you don't have to answer. They can make you uncomfortable and deny you things like water, restroom breaks, and cigarettes, but after no more than twenty-four hours, you have a right to be let go unless you're charged or legally defined as a material witness, at which time you can opt to get a lawyer. Neither of the lawyers think it's wise to antagonize or otherwise not cooperate at this point. We're both cautioned against taking anything they say at face value and not to be gulled into thinking they can or will be sympathetic to your or my situation.

"Personally, I'm not liking this one bit. I have no intention of being dragged into a supporting role of a family legal dispute that may include business associates."

Susan looked pretty grim. "I've known since I was ten not to trust the police, even well-intentioned ones. The system takes over."

Not tempted to inquire why, I got up, and Susan followed me into the lobby of Presidential Towers.

The complex is in the middle of massive renovations. It is located a few blocks from the Chicago Mercantile Exchange in the area west of the Loop behind the Ogilvie Transportation Center, which houses a major commuter train line. I am not sure how old it is, but it has been part of the exchange community since at least the eighties.

To my knowledge, a large number of tenants are local companies wanting furnished, corporate apartments with flexible leasing terms ranging from a week to years. The individual tenants appear to be young professionals just starting their careers in the downtown Chicago area, many of whom work at exchanges and trading firms. They also draw a lot of professional graduate students going to law or other downtown professional schools.

The few times I have stepped foot in the place, it reminded me of a mostly male dorm at an expensive college in an urban area. It has all the modern amenities but also the aesthetic challenges of a young, partying, transitory clientele. The spacious lobby is entirely paneled with teak-colored wood with a matching security desk console which looked nicer than my last visit a couple of years ago, and there is actual security staff at the desk and main door now.

Escalators were to the right of the revolving door, which is where Detective Williams was waiting for us. He indicated to the desk security staff we were with him and escorted us to the elevator bank of Benny's apartment. He seemed in a better mood and nicer today. He chatted about the weather, inquired how things were going for each of us, and promised our visit would not take too long. We were equally cordial but not as chatty.

The door to Benny's former apartment was open, and there was a policeman in the hall. Yellow tape was around the door like on TV crime scenes. Detective Guzman was in the apartment standing over a desk and checking his notebook. He brightened when he saw us, smiled, and asked if we wanted to take a seat while he ran a few things past us from his notes. Both policemen were more relaxed than yesterday. I prayed that was a sign they figured out neither of us were going to have much to offer. We declined the offer to sit and stood near the galley kitchen across from the desk. The mess on the carpet next to it indicated that is where Benny died.

Detective Guzman asked Susan to confirm this was Benny's apartment, her living arrangement in it, the location of the Jackson Partners' apartment, and if she knew who the other floor tenants were. She confirmed the first two data points and said she didn't know the identities of the other tenants, but that she did not recall any individual staying for any extended period, so she assumed they were employees or guests of firms that leased them out. She added that from what she noticed of the décor, they all had basically the same furnishings and concluded all were corporate apartments furnished by the same company at about the same time.

Detective Guzman commenced his discussion. "There isn't the usual amount of personal effects, things like pictures, books, and even clothes. Benny wasn't a kid just out of college with a few boxes and a bicycle. Where's the rest of his personal property?"

"What he didn't take to Florida with us, he sold. He didn't have much here. I imagine he had gear at his gym, but that would be the sum total of it."

"He didn't have an office or conduct business somewhere else where he may have had a computer?"

"No, I don't think so. He'd have no need because he has an office or at least a desk at her firm. Did you speak to his accountant?"

"Yes, he was very helpful. Thanks. But I want to confirm, did Benny have a computer or any records in Florida? Should we be making arrangements to have them shipped here?"

Susan had lit a cigarette and looked straight at Detective Guzman. "No. Like I told you yesterday, he kept everything on his laptop and liked the idea of storing files on a cloud account. He didn't bother with paper and hadn't in years. He seldom went anywhere without his cell and tablet, and the laptop was always there, on the desk. The only thing I can tell you that can be helpful is, like I said before, all of his personal tech gadgets were Apple products. I suppose Apple Support can help. I know he had the apps to find lost or stolen devices, and they were activated."

Detective Williams nodded. "Fair enough. Part of the reason why we go over covered ground again is to make sure we didn't miss a detail. Thanks, this was helpful because I didn't think to ask about the tracking apps. Can you please do a walk-through and check out the closet, bathroom, drawers, kitchen, everything? Really to see if anything looks out of place or missing."

I didn't think it was possible for Susan to pale further, but she did. "Okay, but I really don't want to go near the desk." She got up and walked into the bedroom with Detective Guzman following her. Detective Williams opened the drawers of the desk and moved the contents to the kitchen bar. It was pretty stark—a few pens from banks and other businesses, some menus, notepads—nothing outside of typical desk clutter. Certainly, nothing personal. I had to agree with the police, it was odd that there wasn't an invitation, a business card, or even a receipt.

They returned to the living room. Susan obediently checked the contents of the fridge, kitchen cabinets, and drawers. She then observed the desk contents on the bar. She pulled out a cigarette and the smokeless ashtray from her bag and lit up.

"Okay, it doesn't look right. First, it's too clean. Benny wasn't dirty, but he was a slob and had clutter everywhere. There are no newspapers or magazines, and he didn't read those online. The bathroom is immaculate, and he has no laundry piles or shoes by the door. The cleaning lady must have come the day he died. He used the building's cleaning service. The really strange thing is the monthly calendar taped on the fridge is missing. Benny was hooked on technology for almost everything, but he still liked a big calendar with his schedule on the fridge. He liked looking at it first thing when he got up. He didn't have a set-enough routine, especially lately, and he liked a visual reminder for things like when he was going to the gym. A lot of clothes are missing, but they could be at the cleaners. His big suitcase isn't in the closet."

Detective Williams pointed to the piles on the breakfast bar. "Anything strike you as out of the ordinary or missing?"

Susan glanced at the various items and shook her head. "No, he wasn't that kind of a packrat."

"Where would he keep his mail? Did he have a PO Box or have things sent to the office?"

Susan said he paid everything online, and she never bothered to notice where he had his mail delivered.

Detective Williams was bothered by that. "Where did you get your mail? Where did personal mail like Christmas cards get delivered?"

"I didn't get that much after I moved out of my condo. I arranged for pretty much everything to be e-billed and paid. Personal stuff that went to my building, I'd pick up because a doorman would call me. I stopped by about once a month and know all the doormen. They knew I was good for a tip besides being nice guys. Now everything that isn't electronic gets sent to our place in Florida."

He turned to me. "Did he get any mail sent to the office?"

"I don't know but can ask. My guess is the usual industry junk mail of magazines and solicitations targeted toward traders. Some people have Amazon and the like delivered to the office. I don't think it's typical to have all personal mail coming to the office. I have a question for you. Didn't you find sufficient content for whatever you typically look for in his email account? I thought that was like phone records, and you can get them from the vendor."

The two police looked at each other briefly. "We didn't find much which makes us wonder if he had multiple accounts. We were going to ask you if you know what ISP he used," Detective Williams responded.

"I know he had one email address for personal stuff and one for buying things, making dinner reservations, and whatever else he was doing online. I don't know if that was the same one where he paid bills. I wouldn't be surprised if he had another for his online banking and credit cards. He hated spam, and I told you yesterday he didn't trust the internet. I already suggested contacting Apple Support for help. I think I gave you the one address I have, which was his personal one," Susan replied.

They were done with what could be accomplished with Susan at this point. Detective Guzman asked me if I could share any specific intel from Benny's trading sheets. I responded that I couldn't without the indemnification we discussed, which didn't sound like was ever coming from what our attorney said this morning. We also would be in violation of our client account agreements and were not interested in being in the middle of any legal disputes should there be any over control and ownership of Benny's assets. The best I could offer is to get a subpoena. The past two years of Benny's trading account records were already on a disk and thumb drive waiting to be turned over. I told them that I thought they would have better luck with his accountant and personal bank statements.

The two shared another look between them, which I didn't like. They thanked us for our time, and we all walked out together. In the hallway, Detective Williams asked Susan if she was aware that there were no security cameras in this hallway.

"No, I thought every place in America had some kind of video surveillance. It doesn't surprise me, though."

"Why?" asked Detective Guzman.

"For the same reason they aren't in college dorms. I have a nephew at ISU, and pulling fire alarms is a regular prank, especially around finals. We think the administration doesn't install video surveillance because they would have to do something about all the other illegal activities like smoking pot in the halls and underage drinking. It may be the same thing here. It's just a guess that makes sense since I assume they are in the lobby and other public places in the complex. Maybe the building management is just cheap."

That was a mistake. Detective Guzman interpreted the comment as an invitation to explore other avenues. "Why would a building like this or its tenants have any hesitancy about video surveillance in the halls? Would you and Benny care, and why would it matter for your firm's clients? Wouldn't they all feel safer?"

Susan snorted. "Nice try, boy scout. You're cops, and you know the reputation of every block and building in the city. No, Benny and I wouldn't especially care. I can't answer for the other tenants, but I can tell you things have calmed down in the past couple of years. Not so many young guys living with twice the number of allowable tenants and clients coming for extended stays. Although, that isn't the case with people from Korea, India, and I think China, but they usually have some kind of chaperone or official panderer, which will keep things under control. I'm sure you can get a better recap from your logs or whatever you call it when the police are called or by consulting building management and security staff. By the way, why are you asking me? How could I be remotely credible compared to the building management on this subject?"

Detective Guzman didn't laugh, but his eyes did. Detective Williams sighed, which conceded Susan's point. "Look, we're trying to explore all avenues. You shouldn't be worried, we know you were in Florida and have no financial motive. We're just trying to fill in the gaps of what he was up to lately. It would be helpful to see who was coming in and out of his apartment lately and believe it or not, your backdrop explanation is helpful. You're the closest person to the victim, and the only one who knew what was going on with him personally and professionally. Incidentally, we expect you to be available and not leave town."

Another big mistake. The standard line set Susan off. "Okay, then I request one of those indemnifications her firm is looking for. That shouldn't be an issue if I'm not considered a person of interest or whatever the term is for a potential suspect, right?" she snapped back.

Touché, Susan. Detective Guzman's eyes revealed he thought the same thing, and Detective Williams' sigh confirmed he did too.

"Do you two want a ride anywhere?" asked Detective Guzman. We both responded no.

"I don't know when we'll be in touch next. Sorry, but standard procedure is for us to instruct neither of you to leave town."

"How long does standard procedure usually take to wrap up whatever is the process for a person like me, a non-suspect? You know I live in Florida and can't afford to stay here indefinitely," sassed Susan. Her turnaround was impressive. This was the Susan I recall, not the feeble, quiet mouse she had been lately. Her newfound spunkiness was funny under the circumstances.

Both of the detectives noticed the transformation too, but only Detective Guzman appreciated it. His eyebrows raised, and he half-smiled. Detective Williams was annoyed and not going to tolerate challenges to his authority. "We can force compliance. For now, let's consider this a formal request that includes being notified of your whereabouts."

Susan stiffened further and glared. "I'll notify you when I return to Florida and if I stay any place other than Lane's. I don't believe you can order me to stay without cause or something more official for an extended period. The one thing I know about cops is they never request anything if they can order it, and I won't be f-ing pushed around!"

The optic was comical. Detective Williams was at least three times Susan's size and literally leaning over her because she took a step closer to glower up at him. It looked like Tinkerbell and Goliath facing off for a smack-down, and the smart money would be on her. This was the DZY from the Chicago trading pits and a demonstration of why she was successful.

Detective Guzman was enjoying the show. He did chime in, albeit a little late. "Easy, little sister, no need to get excited. We're good if we can count on reaching you by cell for now."

He turned to me. "We'll check on the status of the subpoena for his account statements. It should have been processed by this morning. Do we give it to you or one of your lawyers?"

"Oscar will be the final word. If it makes things easier on you, send it to me, and I'll turn it over to him. Fair warning, though, he'll probably ask our outside counsel to vet it first."

All parties were mollified to some degree by the time we entered the elevator. We proceeded in silence out of the building and parted at the front door. The police parked their car in front. Susan and I caught a cab at the stand down the block. I texted Billy to expect us shortly. He texted immediately, "Bring DZY!"

We got to the office in time for lunch, which was a Mexican buffet from a restaurant in the insurance exchange building. An alternative of salads with or without chicken was also available if you placed your order in time. We went into the conference room where Billy was working on his salad while he waited for us. Latesha ordered soup for me, which I offered to Susan. She accepted it, but all she did with it is hold it for warmth. All of us noticed she looked small and sick, and even Billy looked concerned.

Oscar stepped in and asked how it went. I provided a short recap of the circumstances and Susan's observations. I concluded with a sensation they have seen something that is bothering them, but they don't want to show their hand by disclosing what it is. Some of the questions they asked were odd and not because they were fishing. I did mention that Susan called them out on a couple of them. I can't believe in modern times that the Chicago Police Department can't obtain phone and internet records without a person's personal device. They are clearly bothered they can't find Benny's. My sense is they aren't buying that Benny had no paper records, a desk, or other space for such items and are unsettled by the lack of personal clutter, especially mail and such in his apartment. His apartment was sterile with little evidence of a longer-term tenant, which can largely be explained away by him relocating to Florida.

Susan decided to join the conversation. "They like me too much. They think I'm the common thread of his life, which was true until over six months ago. I agree with Lane, they want to know something specific but won't come out and ask it directly. They act dumb on things they already know the answer, and I don't get why."

"Which reminds me..." I said. "Has anybody checked with Tommy O'Doole to find out if he has Benny's will or if he knows who the executor of Benny's estate is? The police said they spoke to him this morning but didn't share anything else."

"I called him after you left. I wanted to find out the same thing because it would make matters a lot easier on our end if there were a document that authorized a person to take over the account. Tommy was pretty coy, which he should be as an attorney until I mentioned Susan was staying with you," Billy said and nodded at Susan. "He said he'd appreciate it if you would call him to set up a time to discuss a few matters but didn't elaborate further," he continued.

Susan looked like she was going to get sick.

"How about I draft a limited power of attorney for you to sign, giving us the ability to act on your behalf for a month? That way, we can access whatever O'Doole has and look it over for you. It will be only for a month, and you can terminate it at any time. You may want to have your own attorney do that. Do you want us to recommend one?" Oscar asked.

Susan was smoking again. She turned her head to evaluate Oscar and his proposal. DZY from the trading pits returned. Susan arched an eyebrow, straightened up, and looked at Oscar with animal cunning.

"Maybe, but not right away. Let's say I'm the executor of Benny's estate or some kind of trustee. Why do I care how fast I know that and have to act on it? Maybe I don't want that honor. I'm not sure it's a good idea for me, and it could put me in the middle of the legal mess you're clearly avoiding. What if I'm willing to abdicate and walk away? Give me one good reason why I should meet with O'Doole if I have no vested interest in the outcome and only want to be left alone? I think you want to see what Benny's will says, and you want to dump the decisions and legal consequences on to anybody but you."

Oscar walked to a chair across the table from Susan, sat down, and leaned over to address her. "That's very perceptive and a reasonable theory, except for two things... AML and taxes.

"You want to be the driver in any AML investigation to make sure the government doesn't take your house or whatever assets you may have that they link to Benny. To do that, you need to see the same financial records they have. The AML laws are very broad and have not yet had boundaries tested in the courts. You're a little fish that's in a local pond, not some drug lord in a foreign country with millions of assets and corresponding legal defenses and international banking laws to buffer you. This scenario is too appealing to a mid-level bureaucrat wanting to jumpstart a career with headlines about catching a flashy floor trader and his drug-addicted girlfriend. You know yourself that once a story is spun in the press, you can't correct it or infuse any sort of context or perspective. They can allege almost anything without much of a foundation, and you'll have to spend a lot of money defending even superfluous allegations. To put this into context, think Elliot Spitzer. At the end of the day, the most egregious sanction against him was money laundering because he was trying to mask the true nature of payments made to prostitutes, which were compounded by a pile-on of interstate banking laws. The AML laws aren't limited to drug dealing, terrorists, and tax evasion.

"It's my opinion you and, yes, we are vulnerable on this front. We have to affirmatively prove our innocence due to the way the knee-jerk laws were written, which on many levels violate standard due process and constitutional laws. For example, it's a federal offense for a bank to notify a client should the bank be asked for records pursuant to an AML inquiry. In most other situations, it's common to notify a client should bank records be subpoenaed. In law school, they call it proving a negative. The textbook example is we have to prove we didn't kick a dog, not that they have to prove we did before making that allegation.

"Even if I overstate the pain of an AML inquiry, you and his estate have a potential problem with the IRS..." Oscar emphasized, "... not this firm. You have the problem of demonstrating the source of the 2.4 million dollars coming from an offshore bank account and when taxes were paid. Even if the funds were legally earned outside the US, when repatriated, they are subject to US taxes. If he didn't disclose foreign bank accounts and the like on his tax returns and does not have a verifiable history of paying taxes on non-US assets, it can provoke an extensive audit going back for years. Any assets he may have purchased with you, such as your house in Florida, could be seized. You, and you alone, are further vulnerable to have your personal financial history audited since your co-habitation with him is of an undefined nature. Therefore, to some degree, which I cannot calibrate, your personal assets are at risk, which includes the funding of the legal bills for your personal defense. I presume you have limited resources to fund a defense, which is precisely why you are extremely vulnerable.

"You can still abdicate once you see the trust, which is what I assume he established. There's another angle to consider. You can elect your replacement should you wish to withdraw, which is the only way to keep his brother from taking control. You don't strike me as wanting to give Paul the satisfaction or Benny's cash, and, I presume, regardless of your feelings for his family, you would want to honor his wishes. I have offered on multiple occasions to recommend an attorney to avoid a conflict of interest, and there's nothing stopping you from engaging one without our assistance."

Susan visibly processed this information, and Oscar leaned back in the chair and watched her with equal candor.

"All right, so you're not full of shit, but we both know you're entirely self-serving. I'm good with that as long as you don't pretend otherwise. I agree to the following... you write up a letter of authorization or whatever is the precise legal document that's effective for one week. Consent to roll for an additional week has to be evidenced by a signed statement each time. The authorization gives Lane the right to obtain documents and to tell me what they say and to get any additional information a lawyer or accountant has that may be outside of a financial statement or legal document and to answer all of her questions."

Nicely done, Susan, I thought. Billy's smirk indicated the same, although I wasn't pleased to be the appointed middleman. Oscar was a little annoyed but would get over it soon. He got up and asked if she could wait a few minutes for a draft of the letter of authorization and left after he saw Susan nod her consent. Billy took that as his cue to also leave after making a few polite remarks and asked her if we could get her anything.

"What are your plans for the rest of the day?" I asked. "You don't look well. Do you want us to call you a car to take you back to my apartment? I can call Mr. M to expect you and ask him to clear out so you can get some sleep."

Susan exhaled while facing down at the conference room table. "Yes, please. That would be nice. I want to be in a dark room and just go numb. I shouldn't burden you with this. I feel terrible and wish I never came. I want to go home but feel stuck here until I know if there will be a service for Benny."

"A wild thought has occurred to me. What if you have to arrange for Benny's burial? What would you do?"

Susan's head popped up, and she looked at me in shock. "God, no! I thought his family would do that. No, uh-uh. If it's me, I'm going to do whatever is the minimum for a barely practicing Jew. I'm not sure I'd even give his family a chance to do otherwise. There's no way I'm dealing with them, and I am not up for playing the part of the grieving girlfriend."

On that cheery thought, I left to ask Starz, the afternoon receptionist, to call a car for Susan. When I returned, Oscar was sitting next to Susan with a document and speaking in a murmur. She had no fight left in her and was nodding with her head resting on the back of the chair. She took a pen and signed two pages. Latesha was next to Oscar. He handed her both sets of documents, which she stamped with her notary seal. Oscar put one set in an envelope and handed it to her while promising to contact her as soon as we had anything tangible to report. He arched his eyebrow when he looked at me as he exited the room.

I asked Susan if she was okay walking out the side entrance by herself where the car should be waiting by now. She replied she would be okay and took the paper with the name of the car service and license number to look for. Latesha vetoed that plan and had Starz walk Susan out as a precaution. A few minutes later, Latesha, Oscar, Billy, and I were again in the conference room.

Oscar started the discussion. "Latesha, anything further from Benny's bank?"

"No, other than being mad. Joel said that he got a grilling. They were not happy with his explanation that as a bank with no international business and not a member of the Fed, why it isn't just reasonable, but legal, for it to rely on the bank that actually received the wire. He added his bank took the precaution of asking for an affidavit Benny signed stating that the source of the money was from a bank account in his name. The clearing bank verified that the overseas bank account with the funds was in Benny's name alone.

"It sounds like Benny's foreign bank is strictly electronic, no brick and mortar, and no personal interaction, which isn't considered sketchy in many countries. It also won't answer any questions from the police and told them they have to file forms or something with the Treasury Department and FinCen, and that's the legal authority that they will interact with on this matter. I wasn't sure of a lot of what Joel was saying, but that's what I understood."

"Well, that makes his tax returns for the past two or three years all the more interesting," said Billy. "I just called over to O'Doole and told him to expect a fax of the Letter of Authorization. I'm guessing that nothing on them reflected any foreign-held assets. That's probably why the police are still probing into his ISP provider and fishing for other email addresses. I can see why they want his devices and why that only fuels their frustration. But, for Susan's sake, let's hope there's something definitive in the trust documents. If O'Doole were involved, he'd recommend establishing a trust over a will to avoid probate."

"What's going on in your head?" Latesha asked me.

"I don't know Susan. Before yesterday, my entire acquaintanceship was seeing her around and nodding if she were standing next to somebody I know. I'm curious if her present incapacitated state is due to grief, a side effect of staying clean, or something else. I don't think she's afraid of Benny's family or that any one person can scare her, but there's an undercurrent that she is fearful of something. She's cagey around the police, and I don't think it's because we warned her to be circumspect. She could just be one of those people who don't like cops, which wouldn't be unusual for a long-term user of illegal substances."

"Any guesses?" asked Oscar.

"My intuition is she doesn't want to know something rather than she's withholding information. And, no, Billy, I don't know why."

We left with Latesha calling our runner to give him instructions to pick up an envelope addressed to me and to bring it right back. Sammy, our runner, is a fifty-something-year-old man with special needs. I don't remember who he is related to. He is one of the last runners in the city.

Back when I started working at the exchanges, there were two kinds of runners. The first were career runners—little old men in mismatched, usually stained, plaid polyester sport coats and pants with briefcases chained to their wrists. That was in the day when a lot of stock and bond transactions were settled by the physical delivery of the certificate and executed stock powers to the Cage, which is the name for the cashier of every brokerage firm on LaSalle Street. In return, the runner would be given a certified check or a receipt of delivery for payment, and every once in a while, cash. They would spend the day walking around the Loop, which is why the handcuffed cases were necessary, and not because of the risk of theft. Most of the runners succumbed to the temptation for a quick draft beer, or two, okay, probably three, at the Ticker Tape bar on Adams right off LaSalle or at one of the skid-row dives on Van Buren. The only one left now is the Sky-Ride Tab, which has since rebranded its image from dime beers, fifty-cent hotdogs, sticky floors, and never asking for an ID, even from high school kids. It's now a hipster place because celebrities like Keanu Reeves hang out after filming when they want to drink in a legit neighborhood Chicago joint.

The second type of runner was a clerking role on a trading floor. Like the title implied, he, rarely she, took order tickets to and from the booths fringing the floor where they were taken to the trading pit that the contract traded for execution. Runners took tickets for filled orders back to the booths to be reported to the client. A lot of traders and brokers started their careers as runners. It was a way to learn the business and find out who's who. The typical career progression was to start out as a runner, move up to a clerk, and hope to get a mentor or grubstake to be a pit trader or broker. Runner jobs, as well as most other floor and trading support jobs, mostly don't exist anymore. Ten years ago, we accounted for over twenty percent of the employment in the Chicago Loop. Now we represent around eight percent, but it feels worse due to the emptiness of the exchanges and nearby buildings compounded by the lack of bustle from people on the streets around them. I don't think the official statistics reflect the loss of all the self-employed people who made up a significant backbone of the trading community workforce.

However, a handful of traditional trading and clearing firms, a.k.a. not banks or New York firms, still employ runners to run errands. The runners are usually related to someone with business clout or have another legacy consideration. They fetch sporting-event tickets, pick up lunches and breakfasts, dry cleaning, and run legal documents between law firms, banks, and exchanges because they are cheaper than a same-day delivery service. They are also called upon to run over to Cal's for an after-the-close beer on Fridays and sundries from the local drug stores, Radio Shack, and Ace Hardware. It's a steady paycheck with benefits augmented by free food and tips for running personal errands.

Latesha makes sure anybody who asks Sammy to run a personal errand pays her his tip. She sends an envelope to his mother at least twice a month with the cash. It affords them a few extras and prevents Sammy from spending it on booze or being conned into extending loans to the professional beggars who frequent our neighborhood that will never be repaid.

Sammy is about five foot eight, on the heavy side, and not a fast mover. He is hard to miss with the way-too-big floor jacket he wears with pride. He is a sunny, trusting soul and thinks everybody is his friend. Most people in the immediate buildings know who he is, or at least recognize the jacket as being associated with Lough Key.

He was visibly agitated when he returned from his short errand across the street to Tommy O'Doole's office and was hugging the envelope across his chest with both arms. He rushed straight to Latesha, crying. It took her a few minutes to calm him down with some tea and a cookie. When I saw them, Latesha had her arm around him and was cooing that he did good, and she was proud of him. She was going to call his mother and tell her how brave he is and what a great job he did.

She called the security office of the Board and asked for Lou, the head security guard. She arranged for one of Lou's men to escort Sammy home in a car she would order. The guard could have the option of coming back to the Board building or be driven home at our expense. She then called Sammy's mother and explained that he had some 'excitement' getting an envelope today because somebody tried to take it from him. She complimented Sammy profusely and recommended that he go straight home. It is okay for him to be leaving early and to let us know if he doesn't want to come in tomorrow. Latesha explained that we were sending him home in a car with pizza money because he did such a fine job. They agreed that we would figure out how to get Sammy to and from work if he needed an escort. Sammy heard all of it, but Latesha repeated it to him and made sure he knew we didn't want him to be afraid and reinforced what a good job he did. She slipped me a Post-It Note to call the police as she walked out with Sammy.

I did call Detective Guzman and then Oscar and Billy and also asked Starz for sodas and water in the conference room.

"Holy shit, what happened to Sammy?" Billy entered with. Billy and I have seen several market crashes, and the world supposedly close to ending three times. I have never seen him lose his good nature until today. Oscar was right behind him and didn't look any better.

I told them what little I knew, and that we had to wait for Latesha. Oscar asked if I knew if the envelope was taken. He followed that if not, we had to warn O'Doole because he had the originals. I left for Latesha's office to see if it was in her office and found it on her desk.

When I returned to the conference room with it, Billy called O'Doole's office to let him know what happened. O'Doole is in a vintage building on Van Buren kitty-corner from the Board and across the street from the CBOE. Its elevators, telecom, sprinkler systems, plumbing, and security have not been upgraded in decades. There usually is a non-uniform person sitting at a desk in the dark lobby with a sign-in book. The only people who register are those who ask for directions. It sounded like Billy was cautioning O'Doole to be more vigilant and that we would let him know if we thought he was otherwise at risk.

As I opened the envelope, Latesha returned. Oscar pounced on the documents and split them into piles on the conference room table. I mentioned that the two detectives made it sound like they would be arriving any minute. Latesha was shaken as she related what she pieced together. The revolving door to O'Doole's building faces a side street that is about thirty feet away from the corner. That section of the short block has little foot or other traffic. Latesha thinks Sammy said a man approached him and wanted the envelope. Whatever transpired spooked Sammy, and he started yelling. Hector, a security guard in our building, told Latesha that the *StreetWise* vendor who works the plaza on the other side of the CBOE building happened to be walking by on Van Buren, heard Sammy, and saw him sitting on the sidewalk hunched forward over the envelope. There was a skinny, white dude trying to grab the envelope, but he couldn't get it since

Sammy was so close to the ground. The *StreetWise* vendor yelled Sammy's name and started to run the few feet toward them. The white dude left by running in the opposite direction toward Congress. The *StreetWise* vendor helped Sammy up and walked him into our building over to Hector, who brought him upstairs.

Oscar had finished sorting documents by then. Billy asked him what they were. Oscar answered that O'Doole had prepared a living trust, will, and established another trust for his sister. It would take at least a half hour to figure out who is authorized to do what with Benny's account with us. I took it that Oscar didn't care about anything else concerning the management of Benny's estate.

The two detectives entered in a flurry with Detective Williams looking concerned. Dismissing any preliminary pleasantries, they wanted to know why we called. Latesha repeated her description of events while Oscar restacked the documents and walked out. Both policemen were good at masking their thoughts and appearing sympathetic. The giveaway was they would not have arrived so soon if they didn't think this was significant in some way to Benny's murder.

Latesha finished. "Why did you call us? What makes you think this has something to do with our investigation?" Detective Williams asked.

"Everybody around knows Sammy, and he never has anything of any cash value. He didn't have a cell or briefcase that could hold a computer, and anybody looking at him could tell he wasn't affluent. Sammy was pretty upset. He can be hard to understand, but he was insistent that the white guy wanted the envelope. It doesn't sound like a random snatch for a wallet. Oscar told us before he left the room, the envelope contained Benny's will and those kinds of papers."

Oscar returned with even more paper, which he put into three stacks on the table in front of his seat at the head.

Detective Williams asked about the *StreetWise* vendor. We could all describe him and his normal routine, but none of us knew his name. I chimed in that he is very nice and not pushy and often helps me when I am carrying heavy things to my car. He is polite, well-spoken, clean, and is not a street bum or beggar. We thought Hector would be the better bet to get more information. Latesha was firm that she didn't want them asking Sammy any questions until he was calmed down and felt secure again. They agreed and also consented to Latesha participating in the interview and could ask him the questions.

Detective Guzman hadn't said a word and appeared to be mulling. "One thing bothers me. How would anybody know Sammy was going to retrieve something to do with Benny? Let's go with this theory. How many people here knew where Sammy was going?"

Latesha and I looked at each other and came up blank. "Nobody except the people here. I don't think Starz heard, and I didn't notice anybody in the reception area," she said.

"Why are you ruling out Starz? What's her story?" continued Detective Guzman.

"Three college students job share being the lobby receptionist. Starz's shift is usually in the afternoon, which is pretty busy with cleaning up lunch and organizing the mail and delivery services. She's a sweet girl and does a good job. She's the kind with big eyes and a smile for the guys and likes mixing it up with them. She usually doesn't pay any mind to the four of us unless we're asking her to do something. Besides, for her to hear where we asked Sammy to go, she'd have to leave the front desk, and I'd have noticed. We ask Sammy to fetch and go all day long. There would be no reason for her to think anything special about his last errand. It being a nice day is another reason for her not to pay any attention to him. He likes to slip out a bit in the afternoon and cut up with the crew around the delivery dock or with the security guards at the Board." Latesha stopped and was thinking.

"If it were me, I'd ask the *StreetWise* man if he noticed anybody outside of the neighborhood hanging around lately. Check the parking lot attendants across the street on

Financial Place, too. They spend almost every day around the plaza, and between them, they cover the entire block around this building and the CBOE," Latesha explained.

"I'd take along a picture of Larry Katz. Ask the membership departments of the CBOE and CBOT. They may have an old picture from when he was on a badge. He's a skinny, white man, and I wouldn't put it past him to bully Sammy, and this is the type of stunt he'd pull," I added.

This being my fourth encounter with the two policemen, I was starting to view them as people. Detective Williams was again wearing a polyblend navy-blue suit. His uniform was completed with a button-down blue shirt, a red tie with small blue and white stripes, and black, crepe-soled shoes. He always looks world-weary and disappointed when his poor expectations of people are met. Outside of work, he is probably a nice man and a fantastic grandfather and next-door neighbor. Regardless, I would be afraid to tick him off because he seems to have a simmering fuse. I also noticed his cell is a basic model, and he carries a small, spiral notebook. The majority of his observations must be stored in his head because he only jots down short notes. His role is not the good or friendly cop of the pair.

Detective Guzman is the one to watch out for. He is always observing and will cultivate a dialogue versus asking questions and expecting direct answers. He is around thirty-five and more contemporary in his dress and use of technology. He has a Droid smartphone and seems to prefer taking notes on a tablet. His manner is friendly with a sincere quality that could even be genuine. I have no idea if they are partnered every day or how long they have worked together. I can't imagine the two of them being drinking buddies, but they are synced to communicate without words. It seemed that something was bothering them, but neither was giving a hint of what.

"I have another suggestion. How about the Board security guards that work the Jackson entrance in the mornings? They are friendly with the beat cops. Two of them stop by most mornings and hang out around when the stock market opens. They seem to be the same policemen for at least ten years. The Board's security staff doesn't have much turnover either. From the way you're looking at me, you probably already thought of this and checking out Larry. Did they say anything?"

Detective Guzman smiled. "Thanks for the tip. We didn't think of getting a picture from an exchange. We did pull his driver's license picture, but another one won't hurt. We haven't finished canvassing the neighborhood around this building. Mr. Marquis, did you have a chance to review the trust documents?"

"Don't you have copies?" Oscar volleyed back.

"Not yet. They may have been delivered this morning while we were out. We had to get a subpoena first. What are your next steps?"

Oscar noticed information sharing was to be one-sided. "Well, they have been in our custody for only about a half hour. Standard protocol is to wait for the executor of the estate to give us instructions. We have copies due to our limited capacity as Ms. Desmond's authorized agent. Our instructions are to read them and inform her of their content. As of this minute, I can't say with any degree of surety who's authorized to act on behalf of the estate, and I don't see anything time-sensitive to compel any expedited action."

We seemed to be at a polite Mexican standoff.

"Hold on, I almost forgot," said Latesha. "Kayreen mentioned yesterday that a man called three times asking for Lane and hung up without leaving a message. We don't have a name. We didn't pay much mind to it then. We told you yesterday that all messages went straight to voicemail. Do you have a way of tracing phone numbers if you know the time of a call?"

"That may be a lead. We'll need to know the precise time of the call or at least narrow down which calls it's not. When we go back, we'll coordinate that with your phone carrier.

Someone from here will have to go over the record of incoming calls. That may take a day or two, depending on the number of calls. Thanks," Detective Williams conceded.

"We don't get many at the front desk. It's mostly sales cold calling. The only frequent calls up there are deliveries and the security desk downstairs signing in a guest," Latesha responded.

With nothing further to say, they got up to leave. The lack of polite exit social rituals was a mutual habit by now, and they left without an escort.

"What about tax returns?" Billy asked Oscar when they were in the hallway of the building.

Oscar shook his head no. "I agree they are more compelling to us than his trust documents and end-of-life directives. Can you call O'Doole and ask for them? I thought our initial document request was clear, but maybe he didn't have enough time, and this is a rolling submission."

"I'll come over now and make copies. This is driving me nuts. We need to see the source documents, too," I said.

"Any consensus on the police?" Billy asked.

"As I said before, there's something they are holding back that bothers them. Oscar, you were very PC by not commenting on how they have everything from O'Doole's by now. I gotta say that your warnings are spot-on. Anything we say or do will be held against us."

Billy was thinking. "That isn't the big take away from this meeting. They have a point. How would anybody know that Sammy was going across the street to get an envelope that pertains to Benny? Who was paying attention, and how would he know this wasn't a routine errand for something like forms or a check? Latesha, Laney, you two need to ask the security guards and the garage attendants what the police asked them and how they answered. Who do we know who smokes all the time in the horse plaza that can ask the same questions to the *StreetWise* man? It can't be one of us, but we'll contribute to a lifetime subscription or other tip."

"Deena from the Help Desk still smokes and takes breaks all the time. She's always popping up volunteering to make a Starbucks run for any of the trading desks because she can sneak a smoke on the way. It wouldn't surprise me if she and the *StreetWise* man were already friendly. By now, everybody knows what happened, so it would be a natural topic of conversation. I can ask her like I want to hear personally. I really don't like this, and it doesn't feel right. I can't believe anybody would do Sammy any harm, and it's worse if he was singled out for an envelope. I have second thoughts about asking Deena and don't want to put her in harm's way. No, we just won't do that. I'll ask Hector to introduce me, and I'll ask the *StreetWise* man myself," Latesha answered.

Billy was shaken by Latesha and paused. "You're right. I'm sorry, I didn't think it through. I'll ask him. You shouldn't be in harm's way yourself. I flatter myself that whoever it is won't find me an easy target, especially if it turns out to be Larry. God, what a mess." He stepped over and gave Latesha a one-arm half-hug, which was out of character. He usually avoids overt signs of affection or concern. She nodded acknowledgment and was teary.

Billy and I went to his office to call O'Doole. He agreed that both of us could walk over to his office and promised refreshments, which for Irish males means scotch and shooting the breeze, or in this case, comparing notes on Benny's murder.

Oscar walked in, looking grim. "Latesha is right. This isn't a TV who-done-it where private citizens play detective or consult with the police, and nobody but the murder victim in the first scene gets hurt. Sammy's assault puts a different spin on the situation. I have a friend who owns a security company, and all his associates are former law enforcement officers. What do you think about hiring his firm to ask around the neighborhood?"

"My reflex response is they won't get as much as Latesha or me. I'm friendly with the garage guys, and I know way too much of the personal details of the security guards of both buildings. Latesha was laughing at me last week because I knew all about Lou's glaucoma surgery. She told me that was too much, even for me. I don't think they would think anything is funny if I chatted them up on the subject, and they are probably hoping I will. In my best professional, amateur sleuth opinion, it's better to have the conversation framed as gossip than we're spooked by anything in particular," I responded.

"All right, but we need to be smart and stay safe. This has a surreal quality due to the over-the-top dramatics besides Benny being murdered. Let's give some thought on how we can heighten the security of everyone without unduly alarming people. Let me know ASAP what Benny's tax returns reflect regarding foreign bank or brokerage accounts. I pray they do," Oscar said after a few seconds.

Chapter 6

Billy and I agreed to meet in an hour before we walked across the street to O'Doole's. We needed to close out the day and knew that drinking scotch effectively ended the day for both of us, even though I was bringing a bottle of iced tea from our fridge and had no intention of imbibing. I am not opposed to drinking, especially a good single malt scotch, but I had to drive home, and drinking early gives me a headache. I also had Susan and Fred to attend to when I got home.

Thomas O'Doole started his career with a bang as an IRS agent while he went to law school. I think his undergraduate degree was in accounting, but I don't think he ever took the CPA exam. Let's just say he is amazing. He worked at a major accounting firm in their tax practice division and was slated to become a partner. However, that isn't Tommy's thing. He is a non-descript, good-looking man in his fifties with a low-key personality and a quiet chuckle. His professional downfall is he resists the temptation to make any situation a major undertaking warranting huge fees. He likes working with people he considers friends and frequently turns away business from people he doesn't like. Nobody is better at taxes, and he is well-regarded by the IRS. He has a niche specialization with proprietary trading firms and hedge funds. If you are his client, there is no danger of your tax return being ready until October, which is when all extensions have expired. He is not at all interested in expanding his firm's practice to include audits with their set-in-stone deadlines. The thing I like and respect about him is he knows how to handle high-maintenance traders and is not fazed by floor tactics. But then, he is the best.

The last time I was in his office, he was working on the faint green, twenty-four column accounting paper that I didn't know was still available for sale with the modern-day proliferation of Excel and QuickBooks. It is a mistake to underestimate him. He has many blue-blood clients in the prop shop and hedge fund space, and some are featured in books and the press. He also has clients that are large-scale enterprise financial service companies and has steered several large figure M&A transactions. His low-key working MO is because he is a tax wonk that just doesn't like to be bothered. His office is cluttered with lots of old-fashion golfing pictures, statuettes, and desk accessories. Bonita, his admin, works when she feels like it, and she never feels like taking messages. He is a power user of many financial software applications, but that is because they interest him, unlike the mundane office software and technology products that are office standards.

About two years ago, he fully mastered email, voicemail, and OMG texting! That's because after his two daughters graduated from college and married, he and his wife relocated half the year to a condo in Florida on a golf course. His incentive is to be able to telecommute from Florida. Since he figured out those tools, he has totally converted because it means less actual in-person contact.

Billy and I were making a point of noticing details as we walked across the street and down the block to O'Doole's office. The lobby is old-fashion, dark, and lined with beautiful woodwork. Immediately to the right is a bar that changes owners every few years. Across the spacious lobby is a grand piano, and I never figured out why. There is a door connecting the sandwich shop residing in the corner of the building to the lobby. The desk is about twenty paces in and is frequently staffed but not now. We walked to the elevator bank that has six elevators, and you can count on four working on any given day. I recall reading in a local review that they are the slowest elevators in the Loop. O'Doole's office is on the eighth floor, which is why it is a toss-up to walk or bother with the wait.

We elected to wait.

We both noticed the bar was quiet and didn't have anybody near the door. We concluded the bartenders and waitresses must be getting ready in the back for when all the markets are closed. They never seem to have a big crowd unless it is an event or a Friday. It's a favorite spot of mine for an after-work drink because the service is good, they have a nice wine list, and the setting facilitates conversation. It doesn't cater to the rowdy crowd looking for cheap and strong well drinks that Ceres attracts or the sports bar or local dive theme of most of the other neighborhood bars.

The building has an atrium effect because the offices are laid out in a square donut around a large open area in the middle of the building. O'Doole's is the first office on the left, which is shared with several other lawyers and accountants who run their own businesses. His is the first office behind the unmanned reception desk, probably because Bonita had something going on with her kids this afternoon.

He was positively beaming when we stepped in. "Welcome. It's been so long."

Billy noticed the unopened bottle of Glenmorangie and raised an eyebrow. "Whoa, what are we celebrating?"

O'Doole chuckled. "Just got it now from KPE&Y and just got rid of the last of the deliverables for all the audits that were due on Monday. I'm taking the rest of the afternoon off!"

"What happened? That bottle sells for around a grand. I thought you hated working with all the Big Four accounting firms, especially the audit teams?" Billy inquired.

O'Doole shrugged. "I do. I especially don't like babysitting their junior staff, who usually have a condescending attitude. Let's just say this is as close as I'll ever get to a thank you or an apology."

Tommy O'Doole and I have been comrades-in-arms on many occasions throughout the years. We share a similar frustration with the audit teams from the larger accounting firms. Because my firm and his clients represent a low level of audit risk, we tend to get the newly minted college grads and first-time audit managers and seldom get any of the same people assigned to our firms two years in a row. There just isn't enough bandwidth for the more senior accountants and partners to spend much time in the field with them. Most financial service firms, including proprietary trading firms and hedge funds, have their audits due March 1 or April 30. The workload crunch has gotten worse the past couple of years due to the additional statements and disclosures that are required thanks to Enron and Bernie Madoff.

The auditors assigned to us are smart, overachievers, and eager to advance in their profession. They tend to fall into one of two groups.

The first group is crestfallen not to be assigned to a big bank or brokerage firm and are bitterly disappointed by being assigned to us. Tommy has staff that performs many of the routine accounting functions for many of his clients. He has two hedge funds with small operations that consistently produce double and often triple-digit returns. Their clients are entities like a French pension fund and family offices of billionaires. Many of the younger auditors view Tommy and his operation as not more advanced than Bob Cratchit, and consequently, are convinced his books are fodder for financial malfeasance.

The second type, which is more typical with my firm, is the trader groupies. They have a hard time concentrating on their task at hand once they see some of the trader splits, typical bonuses, free lunches, and other office amenities. They stray out of scope with many of their questions, try to befriend some of the finance team and traders, and usually make a point of leaving their resume behind or at least asking if I will give them a reference.

Tommy got out three glasses and seemed almost offended when I told him none for me. I explained that I only ate half a bagel at around seven that morning. The scotch would go straight to my head. I probably wouldn't feel good and certainly shouldn't drive even if I had a small one.

"So, tell me what's going on?" Tommy asked after pouring two glasses of scotch.

Billy took a slow, appreciating sip before he recapped the highlights of the last two days. He's a born storyteller and was relishing the scotch with an audience. "The detectives don't share much. What did you tell them?"

Tommy listened intently to Billy. He mentioned thinking it was very interesting and filled in some gaps with his narrative. The same two detectives arrived at his office this morning at about nine thirty armed with subpoenas. They asked a lot of background questions. Because O'Doole never encountered Larry Katz or the three mysterious bankers, the police focused on Benny's family. He described how Benny had lent Paul around a million dollars over the past several years. Benny asked last year how he could write the loans off, which is why O'Doole concluded that Paul didn't intend to repay them. At first, Benny didn't like the answer that Paul would have to pay income taxes on the defaulted loans for Benny to get a deduction. Benny seemed to change his mind and thought it might encourage Paul to repay at least a portion of the loans. The logic was that Paul would have to come up with about a third to pay the taxes, and Benny would rather have a third than nothing, and Benny could elect to report the gifts or not.

Benny had established a trust over three years ago for his sister, and he knew the tax limitations on the amount of cash a person can gift to another. He was angry that some of the money he gave to his mother to pay for Sharon's expenses went to luxuries. O'Doole recalled an example of Benny not objecting to buying his mother and Sharon a new car but didn't think they needed the top-of-the-line BMW. The turning point was when his mother traded Paul's wife the BMW for her older Jag that was always in the shop, and Sharon's wheelchair didn't fit into it. He also suspected his mother paid for Paul's family cruise.

The trust is for the exclusive benefit of Sharon, and it is very specific on the types of expenses it will cover. Any requests for money have to be justified by a letter from a doctor or a receipt or other evidence of how the money is to be spent. O'Doole thinks that stymied the steady stream of cash requests from Benny's family.

Paul was the initial successor trustee in the event of Benny's demise, but Benny changed that over a year ago and made Susan Desmond the backup when he updated his will and trust. Benny also put Susan on his bank accounts and gave her all the requisite authorities should something happen to him. O'Doole didn't think Benny was concerned about anything in particular at the time. His take was Benny was going through some major lifestyle changes when he bought and sold several pieces of real estate. It was convenient to take care of his legal housekeeping at the same time. O'Doole assumed Susan and Benny were planning to marry.

The interesting take away was that the police asked if Paul knew Susan replaced him as the successor trustee and is the executor of his estate. O'Doole didn't think so because Benny specifically asked if Paul had to be notified and seemed relieved to find out otherwise.

When it came to Susan, O'Doole told them he had no idea she did drugs or how they were financed. He was stoic in his assertions that for years all of Susan's mid-six-figure compensation was from her job and documented with a W-2. Her other income was all properly documented from her brokerage statements with the limited exception of the recent rental income from her condo. No, he didn't find it surprising that she was highly compensated and doubted there was anything underhanded. Everything about her financials was in line with his other successful pit broker clients. He knew she was well regarded professionally and was attributed to having a substantial roster of clients with a fierce reputation in the pits.

Because they seemed to be fixated on her earnings, he felt compelled to ask them if they were asking so many questions because she is a woman. Detective Williams didn't like that and asked if he didn't think it was odd she could be so effective in that line of work when she admitted to being a heavy coke user. O'Doole retorted back that he found it no more unusual than the myriad of doctors, nurses, lawyers—especially lawyers from the big Wall Street firms—and several police officers he knows who are good at their jobs and use coke to cope or manage the erratic hours and intensity of their jobs. That was not an answer either anticipated coming from his mouth.

They switched gears to ask a lot of questions about foreign investments and bank accounts Benny had. O'Doole thought Detective Williams got a little excited when Tommy told him that none were declared or otherwise disclosed on his tax returns for the past few years. He acknowledged that Benny seemed interested in European tax havens around the end of the year, but to his knowledge, nothing indicated Benny established a non-US bank account. However, he also admitted that he encouraged his clients only to contact him for essentials the first quarter of every year. General questions and exploring new strategies could be discussed starting in May.

Detective Guzman fished for gossip and more subjective information such as if he ever heard about Larry Katz or what kind of reputation he has and if he was well known around the exchanges. O'Doole chuckled in his story when he related his response that he couldn't tell them anything about Larry Katz other than his reputation for smelling funny. He said that he didn't think Susan was aware or ever interested in Benny's estate value, but thought she could be trusted to honor his wishes to take care of Sharon.

He got serious when he ended that they asked questions about Lough Key and us individually. He strongly vouched for our personal integrity, great reputation of the firm, and its long history of being one of the industry-standard bearers. His impression was that at least Detective Williams hoped for something juicy. They left with electronic and paper copies of three years of tax returns and all of Benny's personal and trust documents that O'Doole prepared, including those involving recent real estate transactions. Nothing that would lead them to the three bankers I met or the source of the 2.4 million dollars he deposited with us.

He concluded that Detective Williams developed a hostile attitude toward him. He accused O'Doole of not doing his due diligence to circumvent reporting Benny's foreign bank account on Benny's tax returns, and he was sure there would be professional repercussions. His attitude didn't improve when O'Doole informed him that, by their own statements, the account wasn't disclosed and possibly opened until this year. Further, there is no obligation to file anything until April 15, which is more than a month from now, and only for the first quarter estimated payments. Depending on the nature of Benny's foreign investment, there may be nothing more than a disclosure requirement on next year's filing. O'Doole's take was that Detective Williams was more frustrated than serious about pursuing anything against him.

Billy expressed his concern about there being a tie into Benny's murder and the attempt to grab the envelope with Benny's trust documents from Sammy. O'Doole had nothing to say on that front but mentioned he would take the unusual measure, for him, of locking his office. He handed me a box that was about four inches thick containing all of the documents making up Benny's tax returns for the past three years. He added he doubted they would provide any insight. I tucked the box into my satchel bag, and we left with assurances we would keep each other informed of any updates.

From O'Doole's building, it is convenient to walk through the CBOE building and out the opposite side to the doors facing the plaza with the Ludovico de Luigi sculpture of the striding horse on top of a water fountain to where I park my car. Billy walked with me as we shared observations about O'Doole's revelations. Everything felt normal and was like our routine of closing out the day until Larry Katz appeared as we crossed the plaza directly across from the parking garage. We weren't paying attention to outsiders and were both surprised.

He made some demands that I can't recall now, but whatever he said made me mad. I kicked him in the shin with all my might with my Borg wooden clogs, and when he started to fall forward, I swung my fully loaded satchel bag with both hands and clocked him in the face, forcing him to fall backward.

I usually don't have a problem with anger management. This is the third time I have experienced a white rage to the point where I almost black out. The first was when I was in college and worked a long night at a bar where I was assigned the back room with a huge number of one-hit-wonder band members and its entourage. I was a new waitress, and it looked like they were trying to stiff me for the bill, for which I would be docked, besides being out any tip. The drummer was leaning back on his chair and made some snarky remark while he pinched my boob. Provoked past my breaking point, I backhanded him with my tray for all I was worth causing him to fall flat on his back. That, fortunately, was considered hilarious and resulted in me being promoted to a bartender and the check paid with a nice tip.

The next time was years later. I was picking up my daughter at a park playground where she had a play date with friends. I recall a ten-year-old-looking boy pushing down a chubby, smaller boy with obvious special needs and making horribly cruel comments while kicking him. The mothers at the playground were making ineffectual clucking noises but couldn't do more than call the police and wait. The bully had the support of a bulked-up young man who seemed to be in his twenties, laughing, and said that the boy who was pushed down had to 'toughen up.' I rushed behind the young man to push him down, then I kicked him in the butt with the riding boots I was wearing at the time. The sniveling snot actually had the nerve to threaten me with an assault complaint. I told him to go ahead. The literal ass-kicking he got from a mommy would ruin his street cred. Neither were seen in the neighborhood again.

Clocking Larry had the cathartic effect of defusing my anger. I was reeling from the impotent rage of feeling helpless besides being convinced he hurt Sammy. Billy held me in a bear hug from behind. He yelled at Virgil to call 911. Billy and I counted to ten, and he released me. Virgil and the two other garage attendants surrounded Larry, who decided to stage a theatrical performance of exaggerated harm.

I recall the next few minutes of the situation in a blur. A squad car came, and two police jumped out with Larry in a fetal position screaming his head off. Everyone around me stated that he attacked me, and I reacted in self-defense. By this time, I had calmed down and regained my wits. I gave the patrolmen Detective Guzman's card and reported that Larry was a person of interest in a murder case, and he was wanted for questioning. The words rolled off my tongue with a calm dignity as if they were actually technically correct versus me repeating TV cop show lingo.

Virgil had my car waiting for me. I told Billy I was okay and needed to go. He agreed but wanted the box of documents from O'Doole's office to put in an office safe. I also thanked the guys from the garage and insisted I was fine to drive, just a little angry and over it. Against his better judgment, Billy didn't fight me, and I got in my car and left. There was no way I was waiting for another police interview. I really was okay. I just needed to be by myself. Good thing I didn't have a drink. This was bad enough.

Virgil was worried and told me to text him when I got home. In almost twenty years in the worst of weather and late nights, he never did that. His gesture of kindness upset me more in the aftershock than realizing what happened. I turned on the classical music station and counted my blessings going home. I really was fine. Driving where I had to concentrate without any real pressure due to light rush-hour traffic was good for me. I stopped for Thai takeout and rebelled by not informing either the Metzkers or Susan of my progress and dinner plans in advance.

Susan was smoking on my porch when I arrived with Fred at her feet. I entered the porch, dropped off my satchel and Thai food bag on the café table, and let Fred out. He didn't have any business to take care of but liked prancing around the yard playing his growling game while he nipped at my sleeves. After a few minutes, we went up the stairs. Fred had to be in front of me so that he could hip check me on the banister. All good, clean fun and he made me laugh.

I explained to Susan that I had a taste for Thai. Susan responded with a nod of her head. My dining room table was set for takeout along with a bottle of my favorite chardonnay with a glass by one place and a big bottle of non-sweetened iced tea by the other. Her insight and kindness reminded me to text Virgil. He responded in two seconds 'good to hear' and to check in with him tomorrow. I really can't explain how these simple gestures touched me, except that I hate to cry.

After I pulled myself together, I asked Susan if having wine around was a trigger for her.

"Not really, liquor isn't my preferred vice. My demons are coke and pot. Besides, I have to get used to people socializing around me with a drink. My problem with wine isn't that I crave it. It's once I start drinking, my resolve goes, and I want a hit of coke." She squinted her eyes and grinned. "I heard about your knock-down with Larry Katz. God, I wish I saw it!" she said.

"It happened an hour ago. How'd you hear so fast?"

"Darnell from the parking lot told me. Virgil saw me get into your car yesterday. Now I feel like a jerk not saying hi, but he was cool I wasn't up to social pleasantries. Count on your phone blowing up all day tomorrow. You're a hero! Anybody who's met him wishes they punched him."

I poured some wine. "You didn't tell the Metzkers, did you?"

"No. He was down here this afternoon right after it happened to let Fred out. I told him you had to work late tonight, and I have to help. I don't think he believed me. He said it was good you have a nice girlfriend to keep you company. I borrowed one of the bikes I saw in the basement to go to the liquor store. I was planning on offering to get dinner when you got back."

"Thanks, but I couldn't wait. I'm so amped up and haven't eaten since early this morning." I opened the bag and took out the various cartons and plastic containers of food.

Once we had full plates, we settled in. "Why did you hit Larry? That seems out of character for you," Susan asked.

I described what happened to Sammy coupled with Larry's appearance and demands at our office. I explained how he matches the description of Sammy's assailant. Larry also mentioned Susan by name during his second visit, and the security guards saw him hanging out in the lobby. It must be Larry. He is a skinny white dude, mean enough to hurt Sammy, and wouldn't think twice of seizing the opportunity to pull that sort of coup over us.

Susan didn't eat a bite during my explanation. "God, I feel terrible. I'm sorry I ever thought it was funny. I had no idea."

I sighed. "Wait, it gets worse for you because Benny put you on his bank accounts and named you the successor trustee for Sharon. You're also the executor of his estate. That's what was in the envelope, Benny's documents."

Susan lost any appetite she may have had and asked if she could smoke. "What does that mean? Does his family have any rights or obligations?" she asked and lit up a cigarette.

"I don't know. I think you may want Oscar to recommend a lawyer to give you advice."

"Well, that certainly puts an interesting spin on my conversation with Sharon this afternoon. I called her to ask if they were planning any kind of ceremony. She said she didn't know. All Paul and his mother seem to care about is Benny's money and who controls it. She said she wanted to give me a heads-up they are talking smack about me and planning on putting up a fight. Paul consulted with a lawyer in his office. They are mad at Bill and Oscar and think you guys should respect their wishes. They already know they can't get their hands on her trust and are already anticipating spending money from his estate. I always liked Sharon and will do what I can to make sure she's all right. I really don't want to see the rest of them again or be dragged into their drama. This is just crazy. I can't believe any of this."

I ate a small mountain of pad Thai because I would get a headache if I didn't eat. Susan offered to clean up, and I let her. I thought walking Fred to the park before it got too dark would be good for both of us. The walk was rejuvenating. Fred and I like watching the kids practice soccer, and we ran into several neighbors.

When I got back to the apartment, the unsettled feeling I had returned. "Susan, I'm moving upstairs for the night. I don't know why, but nothing feels safe or right. I have a better chance of getting sleep on the second floor where an intruder would have to go through more work to get in. Otherwise, I'll be awake all night listening for something. My security system is Fred, who sleeps like the dead and wakes up groggy. You're more than welcome to join me, or you can have this place to yourself."

"Doesn't someone live up there? You can't have two apartments?"

"No. Mrs. Brown rents the middle apartment. She winters in Florida and hasn't returned yet. She must be ninety, and I'm a little concerned that her health has been failing. When the Metzkers last spoke to her, it sounded like she may move into the same assisted-living complex as her sister down there. I know she won't mind. She used to like hosting any overflow from my house. You can have the guest room, and I'll take a sleeping bag, blankets, and a pillow for on top of her bed."

Susan opted to join me. We packed up and took the wine, iced tea, and Fred with us. When we settled down in Mrs. Brown's front room, I suggested Susan call the police to find out how to go about getting possession of Benny's remains and who to contact. They must know when his body can be released for burial. She agreed and thought that would be the pivotal date in making her plans. She also thought consulting a lawyer was wise and wondered if the lawyer could also find out what to do regarding Benny's body.

My cell rang. It was Connie confirming the symphony Thursday night with an invitation for Susan to join us. Apparently, the husband of her friend has tickets to the Blackhawk game and would rather attend a playoff hockey game than the symphony. I told Connie I would call her in fifteen minutes with an answer.

Susan was initially apprehensive. "Why is she asking me?"

"A combination of two reasons. She's genuinely a good person. She and Billy think it's their duty to watch over me, and she is otherwise probably a little curious about you. If you come, you can plan on a fabulous dinner as the guest of Billy, during which you'll be surreptitiously interviewed. You won't be able to resist telling her your life story and will be charmed and enchanted. The symphony has a jazz program tomorrow that will get out at about eleven. We may be leaving a little early because I ordered a car, and I want to be past the United Center exits on the Eisenhower before the game gets out. Her neighbor, who's also going, is a very nice lady who writes and illustrates children's books. A lot of them have to do with children in difficult situations and how they conquer their challenges. Actually, she really is interesting."

"So, what's your story? Why does everybody hover around you, and why is it so nice you have a girlfriend to keep you company?"

"I have no story, or at least I didn't until recently. My husband has been MIA for about two years. He's a highly trained chemical and petroleum engineer and paid for a lot of his education from scholarships by joining the US Army. When he got out, he never lost the bug for being in the military and couldn't stand office jobs. His most recent job was with a big defense contracting firm that had something to do with refurbishing the Iraqi oil fields to make them profitable again. Nobody can tell me what happened to him. I'm sorry, but I can't stand talking about it. It makes me physically sick and anxious whenever I do. Oscar and Billy are always calling senators and congressmen, and I know they have spent a lot of money hiring people to find out what happened to him. The only thing they tell me is there's some high-level security issue, and whatever that is means I can't find out for sure if he died or is alive somewhere.

"My kids are in college. My son attends grad school in Scotland, and my daughter is a freshman at Georgetown. Ellie Rose almost didn't go because she was worried about me. Fortunately, everybody around convinced her to go and take full advantage of the opportunity. I talk to her pretty much every day and Skype with Cahill at least weekly. I have trouble sleeping, so Fred and I volunteer a lot in the evenings at a shelter for battered women and at a PADS facility for the homeless in addition to Saturday's at the neighborhood food pantry.

"Billy is my first cousin, and we've been close since we were kids. Connie tends to swoop anybody up with troubles. Hence, I am fully absorbed into their family and social life.

"So, have I made Thursday night sound irresistible?"

Susan laughed and agreed to go. Both of us were exhausted and went to bed even though it wasn't ten yet.

Chapter 7

Pär was back in his hotel room. He could not imagine how the day could suck more. Besides making stupid mistakes his luck just sucks. He disgusted himself. He can't even steal an envelope from a retard. The tall black dude that hangs out around the exchange buildings selling magazines saw him well enough to give a description. Pär wasn't confident the precautions he took of changing clothes during the day rendered him invisible to that guy. The black dude looked everybody in the eye when he hawked his magazines. He also seemed to be on friendly terms with all the neighborhood regulars.

Pär spent the day moving around the two plazas that bordered the exchange buildings. He figured out the rhythm of the neighborhood routines. To make him less noticeable he walked around a lot and changed his shirt, jacket and wore different baseball caps that he stashed in a backpack. Besides blending in better using a backpack than his satchel case, he bought a pair of ubiquitous khakis and white athletic shoes and got a haircut. He avoided all contact and was sorry he smoked a joint with the guys working the loading dock of the pinkish exchange building yesterday.

The risk he took prior to his failed attempt at theft was chatting up a girl wearing the same kind of colored smock as he noticed people did that worked at Lough Key. She was in the horse plaza almost every hour to get coffees and smoke a cigarette. He noticed yesterday that she was friendly and liked conversation while she smoked. Pär approached her under the pretense of needing a light. He used an old pickpocket trick of pretending to trip and dropping his full cup of coffee near her feet. While she was distracted, he lifted her building security badge from the large, floppy pockets of her jacket. She looked the type that routinely lost things and hoped no one would think it was unusual. However, if asked, she could probably give an accurate description of him.

Pär thought his luck changed for the better when people in the pinkish buildings were leaving in mass around 4:00 he saw the dark haired woman backhand with her briefcase a small blondish man. She was mad as hell. It didn't look like the little man did anything more than say something to her. The black guys that work the garage jumped to her rescue and police were there within minutes. The general physical resemblance between himself and the man she hit caused Pär to hope the other man was identified as the culprit that tried to steal the envelope from the retard. Pär came close to praying that guy didn't have an alibi.

Unfortunately, that was the highlight of his day. Pär returned to the horse plaza wearing a blue, button down work shirt and khakis shortly after 6:30. He followed a bunch of younger men entering the building to the turnstiles and used his stolen pass to access the elevator banks. He punched the floor where Lough Key was located. When he got off he found the custodian closet things looked promising when the custodian closet was unlocked and had a ladder with assorted maintenance items, including light bulbs.

Pär put on a Blackhawk baseball hat he had in his backpack. He noticed almost every male in town was wearing one. Pär recalled the general office layout from his visit three months ago. The girl's badge opened the front door the empty reception area. There was a conference room to the right and a glass door that led to a hallway. A kitchen was past the glass doors to the right with two younger men talking in it. The dark haired woman's office was up the stairs in front of the kitchen in a section of offices that overlooked the trading floor that occupied the main floor. The main floor had an open floor plan with at least two dozen pods that had workstations configured for multiple people. Some were almost complete circles with a work table in the middle, while others were arcs with seats for around six people. There were a handful of men on the open main floor that seemed to be concentrated in three workstation pods and a few others scattered among other pods. Pär was relieved nobody was in the upstairs level that had offices and cubicles.

He recalled where the dark haired woman's office was and noticed the name plate next to the door matched with what he thought her name should be. Not surprising her door was locked. Like office buildings in Europe, the ceiling tiles in this building were about two square feet and removable by lifting a hand and pushing them up. Pär opened his ladder next to her door, climbed up and started moving ceiling tiles to make a gap big enough for him to climb over the top of the drywall that bordered the ceiling tiles. If someone were to notice him, he would explain he was changing light bulbs and something was not connected properly with the light fixtures. He doubted anybody would pay attention to a custodian and was counting on that type of maintenance to be performed after normal office hours.

Pär was willing to chance the eight foot drop. However that was not necessary because there was a sturdy credenza next to her office door. Nobody seemed to notice the loud noise he made when he landed or the following racket from items falling off the top. Pär was hoping copies of the documents he attempted to steal earlier would be on top of her desk or someplace equally obvious. There was a manila file with " Benjamin Stein" in large black letters, but it didn't contain anything remotely like a financial statement. It was just a bunch of legal documents and no mention of where or how much Benny's assets were. He took the file to study later. Her computer monitor was dark and required a password when he pressed the space bar on her keyboard. Pär knew it was not likely for copies of Benny's bank statements to be conveniently displayed, but was hoping for something more illuminating.

Frustrated, Pär opened the door to her office, closed his ladder and walked out without encountering anyone. There was no point in reassembling her credenza if he wasn't going to reinstall the ceiling tiles or replace the file on her desk. He returned the ladder to the custodian closet with the two lightbulbs he took and closed the door. Pär was pleased with himself that he wore hospital plastic gloves during his burglary. With the bill of his cap pulled down low, he waved at the security guard and kept walking out the revolving doors when asked to sign a book.

He noticed earlier that the security guards were in a booth behind a counter in the corner of the building right next to the doors. There was no way they could stop anybody quickly because they would have to go to the back of the booth and out the door. Where ever that door was, it did not open in the lobby of the building. At the time he thought the set up was stupid. It was not possible for the security guard to do anything other than yell at a miscreant or call the cops. Both were ineffective if the person just left quickly, which is what he did.

Pär walked from the exchange building to his hotel. It was a nice night and the 45 minute walk was refreshing. Besides he could smoke outside, which facilitated thinking. He purchased a Subway sandwich meal and went up to his room.

Nothing his whole life came easy. He often thought he was destined to be close to wealth and success, but never have them. Just like his mother. His mother was a beautiful girl from a poor village in Russia. Her father and uncle pimped her out by selling her to Russian mobsters that sold drugs and stolen American muscle cars in Sweden along with black market gasoline, liquor and cigarettes. He was sent to be raised by his aunt and grandmother when he was born. He didn't meet his mother until he was ten. She returned home consumed by various STDs and probably died of AIDS. Her homecoming was being beaten by her various male relatives due to her lack of earning potential. He recalled his mother telling his aunt she was the lucky one because she was plain enough to get to stay home.

Before she died she gave him a sealed letter that was to be given to his birth father when he was old enough to go to university. She explained to Pär that his father was Swedish and a successful businessman that loved her and knew he had fathered a child with her. She told him to go by the name Pär Ericsson even though his last name was Rybokav. He was fair enough to pass for being a Swede and had the same cornflower blue eyes as his father. She picked Ericsson for his middle name because it was his father's surname. She told him to go to Sweden when he finished what schooling there was in their village and cautioned him against using his Russian surname because people look down on Russians and think they are all gangsters and whores. The one thing his mother stressed and practiced with him was to improve his English so that he spoke more like a Swede than a Russian. She didn't have long and told him to practice. Many Swedes speak English with American or British accents, which is a sign of being educated. She made him read best seller books in English to get used to English speech. He especially liked Steven King, but he read her Nora Jones novels too.

She also gave him a woman's diamond and emerald ring and told him to hide it for all he was worth. His uncle and grandfather would steal it from him and she took great care to hide it from them because that was all the legacy she could provide for him. She instructed him to show it to his father when they meet because he gave it to her and would recognize it.

From a total lack of other prospects, seven years later Pär did as his mother instructed. It didn't take long to find his father. What was difficult was getting to see him. He worked in a highly secure building, had people answer his phone and lived in a building with a doorman. Pär observed he lived with a woman that must be his wife, and they were often joined by a girl and man in their late twenties. The meeting was arranged due to Pär leaving several letters with his father's doorman stating that he had a letter from Petra. After a week the doorman gave Pär a note with directions and a time to meet at a restaurant for dinner.

Pär was too worldly to expect a warm welcoming, but he was hopeful besides being curious. The restaurant was a large friendly place that catered to informal gatherings. The other customers looked like families and people who were friends as opposed to business colleagues. It was easy for Pär to identify his father because he had not changed much from his mother's description. He was a large, bearish man with a pink complexion, ash white hair cut like bowl around his head and the same eyes as Pär's.

His father did not rise when Pär approached the table and didn't say anything when Pär introduced himself. He sipped a beer and was watching with friendly candor. Pär was invited to sit with a hand gesture and a nod. Out of discomfort and not knowing what otherwise to say, Pär handed him his mother's letter. Pär had read it at least a hundred times and knew it was a request for his father to fund Pär's education. She ended with the plea that she was sorry things ended the way they did and that she really did love him and knew he cared for her.

"So, what do you want?", his father asked, what was the obvious question.

Pär prepared for that question for the past two years. He didn't want to blow his one opportunity by asking for too much. "Nothing more than help in establishing myself. I know I have no claim on you as family. I would truly appreciate any assistance you could provide. I don't know if you know my circumstances, but there is no path to economic prosperity where I come from. That is why my mother wrote the letter. I think that is why my mother wound up here. She was a good, moral person that cared. She just didn't have choices."

Pär played the situation perfectly. The problem was that his father had limited cash that he could spend without his company or wife knowing. He was relieved to hear that Pär didn't like school and was hoping for something other than higher education. Looking back at the situation, Pär should have opted for university. At the time he had no idea what that entailed or what professions college graduates pursued other than being doctors.

His father got him a job clerking in a store front office of a bank that exchanged currency for tourists. At first Pär loved the job and his life. Everything was clean and Stockholm was beautiful. He relished long walks along the miles of water front with boats in the summer and people ice skating in the winter. Pär became a regular patron of the many bars and restaurants staffed by pretty, friendly girls. He worked in the older section near the opera house, palace and large, ornate buildings on wide streets with flowers and seasonal decorations. He marveled at all the bridges and large walk ways connecting the city and the cleanliness of Lake Malaren. Even his modest room, in what was basically a youth hostel, was clean, freshly painted and equipped with indoor plumbing with plenty of hot water. Compared to his home town everything was festive and the people jubilant and welcoming.

Sweden's open, tolerant culture embraces a free life style. Heavy drinking, recreational drugs and serial monogamy without commitment are accepted without censure. The Swedes could outdrink anybody he knew in Russia and were fun. Russians tend to be sloppy and hostile drunks that turn violent if they don't pass out first. Pär easily fit in and was considered good company, but he never made any real friends. He was leery of anybody discovering his background and quickly appreciated the wisdom of his mother's advice to not let on he was actually Russian. When asked, he claimed to be half Swedish and half Polish.

He met several waitresses from Russia and former Soviet Block countries. They complained about their passports being taken away from them and only being paid a portion of their promised wages. They lived mostly off of their tips. Regardless, they were grateful to be in Sweden and not relegated to prostitution. Most of them fancied a better life was possible if they married right and were optimistic about their prospects of doing so. Pär was careful to resist the temptation of admitting he was Russian and became adapt at speaking only Swedish and English. He avoided contact with

Russians because they were depressing and always on the make. Swedes and tourists from Australia, Canada and America were better company. Germans were the most rowdy and more likely to stand him a drink.

Pär's problem in Stockholm was a chronic lack of funds. Everything was so expensive. It wasn't like in Russia where everything was expensive, but didn't matter because there wasn't much to buy in his village. Everybody in his town wore clothes previously owned by multiple people. Only people in the bigger cities knew or cared about style. Russian food was basic peasant fare with little variety or freshness. The only plentiful commodities at home were Samogon, which is homemade vodka and Cheap White cigarettes, which are god awful.

Pär's lack of funds didn't make him an outcaste because so many of the younger Swedes he met also struggled with poor paying jobs. Many thought he was lucky because he had a permanent, full time job. He met a lot of people that were always looking for work, but couldn't land anything better than short term, freelance gigs. The difference was they had family they could live with or childhood friends to share an apartment. He had been invited to share housing, but just couldn't. He treasured the privacy of being a single occupant, even in a tiny room that had the commode and shower down the hall and no real sound proofing between the rooms. He could relax and not worry about being judged or beaten. Those were true luxuries. He also didn't want to worry about safeguarding the few possessions he had from roommates or their friends.

It wasn't bad in the summer months because of the street scene filled with outdoor kiosks serving food and bars with outdoor seating. The days were long and sunny plus there was more to do that didn't require much cash. Summer in Stockholm had theatre and movies in the parks and neighborhoods with free music and art shows. Summer was also the peak tourist season with business for him during the day where he could meet up with people from multiple nationalities to show them the town, all willing to pay for drinks and maybe a meal for some local color and guidance.

Pär hated the cold and the dark. He also hated not having warm clothes and no money for better boots or a car. In the summer a car or taxis being out of his price range didn't matter. He dreaded another winter on foot with worn out shoes and not being able to afford the nice sweaters and other clothing layers to keep warm. Summer clothes didn't require style. Not being able to afford basic winter clothes in good condition made a person a social outcaste in the bars. Last winter he spent many nights alone in his room without eating because he couldn't afford to go out. Pär did not want to repeat the experience.

Pär learned how to leveraged his income from working at a legitimate currency exchange by introducing customers coming in to obtain larger quantities of cash to his new friends that could sell them drugs and other forms of contraband. He was adept at spotting people who wanted cash for illicit activities. Pär offered a form of legitimacy to his vendor partners besides expanding their business pipeline. He also became useful in laundering sums less than 1,000 Euros.

That's how he met Nivar. It was in October and winter had set in when they met. Nivar is dark and expensively dressed with an odd accent, which prevented him from blending into the lower belly of Stockholm society. He stopped into Pär's store to get money to ostensibly pay for parking because where he wanted to park would not accept credit cards. It turned out he really wanted to buy cocaine and needed cash. He also had a taste for hard core, professional women. Pär quickly ascertained Nivar's true intentions and cash resources. Pär offered to broker for Nivar and correctly guessed that promising anonymity would appeal to Nivar.

And f@#$%, Nivar was here in Chicago! Nivar just texted from O'Hare airport wanting to know if Pär was in Chicago yet. Pär responded that he was but had a stop to make tonight and not sure when it would be done. Nivar told him to meet at the Swiss Hotel on Wacker tomorrow morning at

7:30 for a breakfast meeting. That was oddly lucky. Usually Nivar needed Pär to scrounge up female companionship and score some coke if he was unchaperoned by another bank officer. Ten minutes later Nivar wanted Pär to meet him at the Swiss Hotel once his stop was complete and to give him notice when to expect him.

Time for Plan B. Pär left his room and walked to the nearby Enterprise car rental store. He got there at 8:40, twenty minutes before closing and just before the desk staff closed the door. Pär rented a mid-size car that turned out to be a dark blue Ford Taurus with his bank credit card. He showed them his Swedish passport and international driver's license with his real name. It was an easy drive to get on the expressway out to the dark haired woman's flat. This would be his third trip to her neighborhood and he had no more of an idea what he was going to do on this trip than he had on the first two. He decided to postpone his drive west of the city until after he ran Nivar's errand.

Pär's first mission was to acquire cocaine for Nivar. One of the terms of Pär's nebulous bank employment was to keep Nivar readily supplied. At 10:00 Pär drove to a steak house he remembered from his last trip to Chicago. It was just north of the downtown business center that catered to businessmen with big expense accounts. He pulled up for valet parking, spotted a likely source and stepped out of the car to ask if the valet knew where he could buy some blow. Pär spoke in a highly exaggerated accent and insinuated a lack of knowledge of what the transaction should cost. The valet was a skinny, younger black man with a design shaved in his closely cropped hair. He stared at Pär for a full minute, noted the rental car plates and then instructed Pär to get in the car and the valet would drive to someone who could help him. They drove to restaurant's valet parking lot. The black guy got out and sold Pär a bag of enough cocaine to keep Nivar sated for at least three days. Pär was not happy about dipping into his cash reserves, but pleased and surprised by how much the price of blow had come down since his last visit. Everything is so much cheaper in America.

Pär drove to the parking lot of a large grocery store that was still open. He parked away from the store and pulled out one of his FDX envelopes he always carried for these types of drop offs. He carefully wrapped the plastic bag with several layers of clear, mailing tape and put the contents into a large inter-company office envelope. He taped a blank white label the size of an index card on the sealed FDX envelop with Nivar's name and room number at the Swiss Hotel. He texted Nivar informing him he could stop by to drop off the intercompany envelop Nivar was expecting, and wanted to know if Nivar was coming down to doorman station or if he preferred the envelop to be given to the front desk. Pär guessed right that Nivar would meet him and was pissed. Pär texted back he had a good reason and to work with him. He also wanted 500 Euros in cash, which would be a nice profit for Pär.

Pär drove the Taurus up the circular drive of the hotel's front entrance. He explained to the doorman he was only dropping off an envelope to a business colleague that just got in from the airport. The doorman told him he had to be gone in ten minutes and to leave the keys in the car. Nivar was waiting for him in the busy lobby about 100 feet from the reception desk. Pär trotted over to reinforce a sense of urgency and said he would explain it all at breakfast. Pär only added that he hoped to have some information on how to access Benny's trading account or to find out where he banked. Nivar was satisfied, and probably craving his coke, so he dismissed Pär without a word, but nodded his consent. God bless Nivar, he is a pompous jerk, but he did give Pär an envelope with 500 Euros.

By 10:30 he was on the expressway just south of the downtown financial district heading west. Pär was careful to drive only five above the speed limit. He made it to the dark haired woman's neighborhood in about a half hour. During the easy drive he had time to think. He considered that he should not be spotted around her block and the car could be traced back to him. Pär noticed that few cars were parked on the street, unlike the city neighborhoods. He guessed only non-residents parked on the street. He found a house that had several cars parked in front that was two blocks away from his destination. Pär parked behind them betting he would be gone before anybody noticed another strange car.

He approached her flat by the alley and hoped it was late enough that nobody would be taking their garbage out or returning home. He was also hoping that the woman retired early and had already let her dog out for the evening. Pär's idea was similar to his earlier office break in. All he needed to know was where Benny banked or where he had the, hopefully $10 million EuroCredit invested with him to fund the bogus trading account. It would be a bonus to find any corporate documents regarding the trading venture which were supposed to be ready for Nivar's signature. Since Benny died, it was up to Nivar to spin some official banking bullshit about why an officer of EuroCredit was legally able to control those funds.

Pär slipped into the yard of the three flat and was careful to stay away from the various street and building lights. He was relieved there didn't appear to be a motion detector to further light up the area. He walked around the sides and noticed no sounds or lights on the ground floor apartment, but there were lights on in similar rooms in the top two units. His plan was risky and not likely to succeed. Pär was determined to try because he had nothing to lose. All he had to do was stay away from the dog and to run away before anybody could call the police.

Almost holding his breath he tip toed up the stairs and stopped on the landing in front of the woman's apartment. There were no lights on in the porch or in what was probably the kitchen. The porch door was cheap aluminum with sufficient space between the track of the door and the wooden door frame for a credit card. Pär was in within a minute. Pär paused before treading soundlessly to the back door to the apartment. This door was more substantial and had a good lock. Lucky for Pär, it also had a glass pane window located about a foot higher than the lock.

Yesterday Pär bought a glass cutter, putty, Duck Tape and other sundry items for burglary at the Ace hardware store that was walking distance south of the exchange buildings in an area south of the Loop. He cut a round hole big enough for his arm in the glass pane and removed it with the putty and Duck Tape. It was easy to then reach in and unlock the door. He waited for a few minutes to make sure there was no noise or evidence of anybody, especially the dog being awake. He couldn't hear the dog snore. Pär wondered if the dog was locked up in a crate like he thought people did to dogs in finer homes.

Pär finally braved entering and turned on his flashlight. The flat felt empty. It was bigger than typical apartments in Stockholm, but not so big for him to not sense any occupancy. From the kitchen he could see a dining room and larger sitting room. From changing his vantage point in the kitchen he could see a doorway that must lead to bedrooms. That meant Pär should stick to the kitchen and dining room.

He swept his light over the kitchen table and was grateful there was a wooden caddy with compartments that held mail. Pär noted routine bills and one bank statement with a man's name on it in addition the woman's with almost $2,000. In another compartment was mail from two universities. Pär took pictures with his phone of the envelopes, but did not open them. He also took pictures of any statements that were not in envelopes. He noticed a large bulletin board with dozens of pictures of older children and younger adults in various academic and sport activities. Most of them featured a tall, dark haired male and a younger girl with brown, curly hair. From the pictures, both graduated from some level of higher education.

Pär crept to the doorway of the dining room and listened. There was nothing to indicate the dog was around. The dog mustn't be much of a watch dog, but Pär wasn't going to chance waking him. His flashlight revealed another doorway to a room opposite from the bedrooms. He took his time to approach it. Great! It was an office. It was also out of the line of vision should somebody wake up. The woman's briefcase bag was on the desk. Pär pulled out the contents and found no paper documents of interest, but he did find a disk in a clear envelope with Benny's name on it and dates with a range going back two years. Pär took it and decided to make a hasty exit. He replaced the contents into her bag as well as he could and quietly retraced his steps without the benefit of any light other than what came in from the dining room and kitchen windows.

Pär dismissed the idea of trying to reset the glass. Instead, he took the glass pane he cut and all of the other materials he brought. He did lock the kitchen door as a precaution to give him more time in case somebody woke up in the next few minutes. It might slow them down for a few seconds. When he turned on his car he was surprised the whole operation didn't take a half hour. It felt to Pär that it took hours and he was relieved to breath freely again. He was tempted to calm his nerves with a smoke, but didn't dare incurring the cleaning fine on the rental car nor did he want that fee to attract any unwarranted attention to him by making him notable. He did, however, smoke a joint walking from the parking garage to the general area of the hotel.

He inserted the disk in his laptop and thanked God it wasn't password protected. It looked like some kind of statement. Slam! He saw a $2.4 million US dollar deposit, the most recent account balance had what looked like a free cash balance of over $2 million US dollars. He couldn't figure out what was going on with the other activity and didn't care what prior balances or history were. There weren't any statements from other financial institutions. The name of the bank from where the deposited funds came was not noted on the statement.

Hoping for inspiration Pär looked at the pictures of the mail he took on his phone. Three names were on many of the documents. Pär noticed that the mail from the universities were bills or account statements for tuition. He Googled the names he saw and discovered that a girl with the same last name was going to Georgetown and won a scholarship. Pär figured out Georgetown is a prestigious school since her high school prominently mentioned it on its website newsletter. The dark haired guy had the same last name too and was going to graduate school in Edinburgh, Scotland. From the looks of the billing statements the dark haired woman must be very wealthy if she was paying their tuition. Pär wasn't sure how any of this information would be useful, but he committed the names of the students and their universities to memory just in case.

The day ended on a good note. He came two days earlier than Nivar to end run him for some portion of the money. There was no point in being disappointed that wasn't possible. He took some comfort that the last couple of days and this evening at least resulted in tangible information Nivar may be able to use. Pär was an optimist and had experienced many occasions when odd fragments of information turned a profit.

Before turning in, Pär put most of the items he purchased from the hardware store in the brown bag they were placed at the time of purchase along with the rubber gloves he wore and the glass pane from the apartment window. He first found the receipt in the bottom of the bag and flushed it. Placing the bag in his satchel he left the hotel and dumped the bag into a garbage can in an alley two blocks away. He wanted to avoid his midnight errand being recorded on the hotel's video surveillance. Pär took as much time as he dared being a small, white male that was more prosperous than the mostly black vagrants roaming the neighborhood streets at night. He wanted to give the impression he took a short stroll to smoke and walked more casually once he was on the same block as the hotel. By the time he got back to his hotel room he was coming down from the adrenaline high. He slept soundly and actually needed the alarm to wake him in time to meet Nivar.

Nivar was in his typical imperious and bad mood at breakfast. It didn't get better when Pär informed him of Benny's murder, Benny's girlfriend being friends with the dark haired woman and a lot of police around the office and Benny's apartment building and two of them visiting the woman at her apartment. Pär also shared his observations that indicated many people in the area were somehow involved or at least aware of Benny's death and business relationship with Lough Key. Pär didn't mention his failed mugging attempt, but did explain what measures he took to garner the information he collected.

The data point that most interested Nivar was the $2.4 million US dollar deposit in January. Pär expected that and brought his laptop where he copied on his desktop Benny's January and February statements. Pär took the occasion to give Nivar the press clippings on Benny's murder he saved from two local papers.

"Do you have any idea where the rest is?", asked Nivar.

"No, and I don't know if anybody else does", answered Pär. That told Pär there for sure is more. He knew Nivar well enough to know that his question didn't mean Nivar may not know what happened to the rest.

Nivar studied the account statement and pointed to wires being sent to a bank from the trading account. He asked if Pär knew what that were for.

"No, I didn't get this until last night. I think that is a bank in the Board of Trade building. I didn't see any statements or even marketing mail from any other bank." Pär then described how when he got to Benny's apartment early in the afternoon two days ago, the door was open and Benny was dead on the floor. Pär didn't want to be a found there and took only a second to scoop up what mail and letters were on the top of the desk. He didn't see a computer or tablet and wasn't going to risk sticking around looking for a cell or other devices. The mail was all junk from local businesses, nothing personal.

Pär continued with his observations that a clerk type person from Lough Key went to a next door building to what Pär thinks is a lawyer's office, how a man looking a lot like him tried to snatch it and how that same man was also hanging around watching people without purpose Monday and Tuesday. Nivar stopped eating during Pär's description of how Elaine Daye hit him with her briefcase when he approached her and how fast the police came to arrest him. (By this time Pär was sure of Elaine's name and decided to count on the police attributing the botched theft of the envelop on the other man). Pär concluded with he didn't know for certain that the other man was looking for the same information and that his conclusions are deductions and not facts.

Nivar narrowed his eyes while he sipped coffee. "Not bad, Pär. It seems there would be no value had I arrived earlier. Do the police have any idea of who it is that killed our Mr. Stein?"

"I don't think so. I follow the story on all the local on-line news services. I don't know how open police are here with that type of information. They wouldn't be in Sweden. I have a personal reason to be concerned. I am as nervous as hell that I show up on video surveillance as being in the building before he was discovered. Benny's murder is a big topic around the exchange building, and from what I overheard, everybody is asking the same question."

Nivar asked, "How likely do you think that will occur?"

"If you mean placing me in the building, I hope not bloody likely. It is a busy building even in the middle of the day. When I left the apartment I checked for cameras in the hall and elevators and didn't see any. I don't think I would attract notice from surveillance in the lobby or around that building. I kept my head down and stared at my phone like I was engrossed with it to avoid a clear picture of my face. I wasn't wearing unique clothes and wasn't carrying my case. As you can see, I have since shaved and had my hair cut drastically shorter to blend in with the typical fashions here."

"Suggestions?"

"Not really, I was hoping you would be inspired. I don't think the woman we met in December liked you, and she might hit you with her case if you make her mad." Nivar didn't see the humor in that comment. Pär continued, "I looked up Lough Key and its CEO is William Keegan and they have a lawyer that seems to be in a senior position. He is Oscar Marquee. You may have better luck approaching them, but you will have to come up with a good tact. The fundamental challenge is inventing a reason giving you legal status to inquire."

Pär then dropped the file he stole from Elaine's desk with the legal documents. "These are the only documents I found concerning Benny. My English isn't as good as yours and you are better skilled at American legal terms. I don't think these have anything to do with his business. I think they are a will and different documents stipulating how his money should be distributed and managed. It looks like all the money goes to a sister and managed by the girl friend."

"Agreed. I need to do some research. Right now I think we may take the approach that Mr. Stein committed theft or fraud. I shall see if anything in that file provides another avenue." Nivar had finished his meal and signed the check. He got up, took the file and instructed Pär to join him at 9:45 in the lobby.

Pär gladly left. He wanted a cigarette with his morning coffee. He would get a takeout cup and walk around the wide sidewalks with seating near the Chicago River and enjoy the scenery in peace. He enjoyed the view of the Tribune Tower and the Wrigley Building. One thing he decided, he wasn't joining Nivar in Lough Key's offices. He didn't want to be recognized by the girl he chatted up to steal her building pass or any of the other building regulars. He hoped it would be easy to convince Nivar his absence would have no positive impact and could jeopardize their cause.

Chapter 8

Wednesday was going to be busy. I got up at four forty-five, which is plenty of time to make it to the office by six. All the margin, banking, and cash settlement obligations had to be processed before I went to the floor for Ed Gallway's birthday celebration scheduled for eight that morning. I was looking forward to the festive silliness and had gotten used to the time change, so I was in a better mood.

I left my bedding on Mrs. Brown's bed and roused Fred. We went down the hallway stairs to enter my apartment from the front door. Our usual routine is for Fred to have time to wake up while I shower, and I let him out right before I leave for the day. He was lumbering through my place half awake. He uncharacteristically perked up and started growling. He then ran barking into the kitchen. Annoyed, I proceeded to my bedroom to get ready to shower. When he didn't settle down, I went into the kitchen and turned on the light but still didn't see anything to cause alarm. And then I felt it.

There was a draft coming from my back door, which was closed. Confused, I walked toward the door and had to force Fred to let me proceed. I was about two feet away before I saw a roundish hole cut into the windowpane of my kitchen door. My cell was in the pocket of my hoody because I had used it as my alarm. I called 911 and reported a break-in. I could barely hear the instructions to leave the premises with Fred barking. I ignored the instructions to stay on the line and took Fred by the collar and ran out my front door and through the entrance vestibule. Once outside, I called Detective Guzman's number and left a garbled message.

It wasn't two minutes later when a squad car arrived with its lights blinking. A female police officer got out first and walked over to me. She stopped about five feet away from Fred and me. By this time, he stopped barking but was still agitated. Officer Razik was tall, young with dark hair parted in the middle and pulled back into a bun. After introducing herself, Fred decided she could approach us. I didn't have his leash and was sitting on the building stairs holding his collar.

Officer Penner was about five feet ten, stocky, with dishwater blond hair and a round, boyish face. He looked like he would be everybody's favorite high school coach if he weren't a policeman. I suggested he stay on the sidewalk until I could figure out what to do with Fred, and he gladly complied.

Officer Razik asked me what happened, and I described the hole cut in my backdoor window. I answered the follow-up questions that I didn't think anybody was in my apartment, and I didn't stick around after my discovery to notice if anything was missing or vandalized. We decided that I move Fred off the stairs and on to the lawn, which would permit Officer Razik to get past us to check out my apartment. Fred didn't look like he was going to warm up to Officer Penner, so he elected to search the back yard and porch.

They were both back in about ten minutes. By that time, the Metzkers joined me attired in their pajamas and bathrobes. The officers reported that nobody was in my apartment, the stairwell connecting the units, or the backyard. Officer Razik requested that I join her to walk through my flat to see if I noticed anything out of place. She mentioned that it didn't look to her like anything had been disturbed. That news was more alarming to me than if something had been stolen. The hairs on the back of my neck tingled, and my stomach lurched.

There was no way Fred was going to stay outside if I left, even if I had his leash to hand to Mr. Metzker. Officer Penner remained outside, and Officer Razik walked into my flat ahead of Fred and me. Once inside, I let go of his collar. He ran back to the kitchen growling. Following Officer Razik's instructions, we walked around my front rooms, bedrooms, and bathrooms, making a point to confirm that the medicine cabinets were intact. Fred decided to join us when we got to the dining room and became very agitated in the office. Officer Razik noted that my tote bag and all my office equipment didn't appear touched. She had me check that my wallet was in my bag with all of its contents. Nothing in the kitchen or porch looked different other than the hole. I unlocked the back door, and she walked around my porch and noted no broken glass or other remains of the break-in were left behind. Fred was quiet but not calm.

I grabbed Fred's leash, and we returned outside. Officer Razik shared her observations with Officer Penner, who was completing a police report form mounted on a clipboard. My cell rang just when she finished informing me that I had twenty-four hours to report anything missing if I noticed it later. She also said to be prepared to provide serial numbers or other means to identify the items because the insurance company would want them noted on the police report if I were going to file a claim.

I noticed the call was Detective Guzman and asked them to wait a minute. I thought I calmly and succinctly described the situation, after which he asked to speak with one of the officers. I handed the phone to Officer Razik, who said they would wait on the scene. Clearly puzzled, she informed us that my apartment was to be treated as a crime scene, and technicians were on their way. She and Officer Penner were to secure my front and back door to not let anyone in, including me.

All the air left my body, and I plopped down on the stairs. Gathering myself, I pulled out my cell and called Latesha. She picked up immediately and asked if I was okay, which is not typical for her.

"I'm fine, but I don't know when I'll be getting in. Please ask Billy to go over the morning wires. My place was broken into last night, and the police want me to wait around. Oh wait, can you sign for Ed's cake and tell the floor guys to start without me? Not that they would wait. Have Sammy get the corsage from the drink fridge and bring it down."

"Laney, your office was broken into last night. Police are here now. Girl, are you sure you're okay? How did anybody get past Fred, and where was Susan?"

"We spent the night upstairs in Mrs. Brown's apartment. Susan was with me. It's a long story. I'll tell you later."

Billy was next on the phone, and I had to repeat everything to him. He too was interested in Susan's whereabouts. He answered my questions to the extent he knew describing how someone entered my office from the ceiling, and nothing looked touched except for the items on the top of my credenza. The police were looking into how the building and our office were breached. Building security was called to interview the night desk person and to obtain the lobby surveillance videos.

A white SUV with blue letters on its side identifying it as a Chicago Police Department vehicle pulled up, and two nondescript men wearing blue windbreakers with 'POLICE' written on the back got out. They walked over to the police officers to confer with them. I wanted to hear, so I told Billy I would call later. It was the opinion of the Oak Park police officers that, while strange, no further action seemed warranted. A theory was that the intruder may have been scared away and might not have even entered my apartment. The crime-scene technicians disappeared into my building with some large cases.

By this time, it was somewhere between seven and seven thirty. The patrol car and white Chicago Police Department van with the Metzkers and me out front in our PJs were attracting the attention of our neighbors and a few morning joggers. Susan came outside and walked over to the Metzkers, who were too upset to enjoy the limelight and excitement. Once she heard the news, she lit up and came to sit by me with a question on her face. Fred let her pet him but was still on guard.

To pass the time, Officer Razik asked me the typical questions of how much Fred eats, how much he weighs, and if he is usually friendly. She mentioned that she had heard of him and asked if he is the dog that sometimes spends the night at the women's shelter. Mrs. Metzker came up and requested to return to her apartment to make coffee. Both Metzkers went upstairs with promises to return with coffee for the group. Once the Metzkers were upstairs, I informed Susan that my office downtown had been broken into last night. I asked her not to mention it to the Metzkers. She looked like she was trying not to get physically ill.

I never did get the names of the technicians. The older one with a shaved head came out and asked me to join him without the dog. I explained it wasn't safe to leave him with anybody he didn't know well under the circumstances, and he will stay by me. He isn't vicious and won't bite anybody. Not happy, the technician agreed for Fred to escort me back into my apartment. The other technician was on the phone with Detective Guzman, and my tote bag was on a white cloth spread out on my dining room table. When Fred and I got close to the officer, he started growling again, and the hair on his back went up when we approached my tote bag. The bald one asked me to review the contents of my tote bag and to carefully consider if anything was missing. He took the items out one by one. It took thirty seconds for me to notice the disk was gone. Shocked, I sat down on one of my chairs and hugged Fred hard.

I explained what was missing and its significance. I wasn't allowed to touch anything but was requested to note if anything may have been tampered with in my desk drawers or cabinets. I left Fred in the dining room, and with the technician moving the articles, inspected my office contents. Nothing looked different or touched as far as I could tell.

I asked if Susan could have her duffle bag and if I could get some clothes and toiletries. Susan was then escorted in to confirm that nothing was amiss with her duffle bag. She said it didn't look like it had been opened since she left it. I couldn't touch any surfaces but could get clothes from my closet. The technician gave me gloves to open my dresser and bathroom cabinets so I could shower and dress upstairs. Everybody seemed pleased to have Fred and me leave. Susan took her bag and joined us. Once Fred was in Mrs. Brown's flat, I ran outside to inform the Metzkers. It was then I was told Detective Williams was en route by Officer Razik.

Susan agreed to wait for Detective Williams so that I could hop into the shower. When I was through, I returned to Mrs. Brown's dining room, and Susan went into the bathroom. While waiting, I called Billy and gave him an update.

"Hey, Lane, did you keep anything on your desk or unlocked drawer?"

"No, other than pencils and the like in the catch-all caddy on my desk. Oh, wait. Oh, no. I think I put the file I made of Benny's wills and trusts on my desk, and it had a big label with his name on it. I forgot to take it home, probably a consequence of all the recent excitement. I made a copy just before we left to give to Susan for when she consulted an attorney. I really don't remember."

"Well, it ties in with the disk being stolen from your place. It wasn't on your desk, so unless you dropped it into a drawer, it's been taken by our intruder."

"Billy, how did they get into the office? It can't be that easy."

"The security logs that track every time a person uses their building pass show Deena's being used at around six thirty last night. The security videos are being checked this morning, and Latesha was invited to look at them to identify everybody she can. One thing did surface, though. Deena lost her badge yesterday afternoon. She didn't report it because she hoped it would turn up and didn't want to pay to replace it. This would be her third badge she misplaced. The key chain it was on also had her ladies' room key and exchange access badges. Latesha told her we were done paying for replacements, and if it happened again, we would charge her the hundred-dollar fee for new ones."

"How could anybody get hers? Does she remember when she last saw it?"

"Right now, she's a hot mess. Lots of tears, apologies, and not making any sense other than not wanting to get fired, and she loves her job. Latesha told the cops to wait an hour for her to settle down, and she'll talk to Deena with them. By that time, we'll have the video surveillance starting at six last night."

"I feel awful about leaving that file on my desk. It's against policy, but I really didn't consider it firm property, and I meant to take it home. What happened to the box with the tax returns you took back?"

"I gave them to Kevin in Compliance to look over. He's been helping in new account due diligence lately, and he gets a kick out of looking over other people's tax returns. He locked the box up, but it didn't look like the intruder was interested in any spot other than your office. It may be a stroke of luck you didn't lock up the file. It links the dots between the two break-ins, and maybe it satisfied the intruder enough to keep from rooting around more last night."

"Billy, what use can that information be to anybody other than Susan and Benny's family? It's not worth all the risk and work."

"I've been thinking about that all morning. I agree with you. The only thing that makes sense is our intruders are hoping it leads to where Benny kept significant funds, and they want at it first. They also may not have known what the specific contents were when they stole the file and disk."

"Billy, I have to go. Detective Williams is here. I'll text when I'm en route."

"Wait, Lane. One more thing. Beverly and Paul both called this morning wanting Susan's contact information. They were demanding they meet with her and us this week. Because they were so rude and aggressive to Starz, Latesha instructed the girls up front to simply take a message, and if they don't hang up, to put them on hold until they do. You may want to give Susan a heads-up."

"Really? Susan spoke to Sharon yesterday. You would think they would just ask Sharon. I'll tell her, but I don't think their demands are a priority with Susan now, and they certainly are low on my list." I looked up and noticed that Susan had entered the room.

"I hear you. Just sharing. Remember to call when you leave."

Mrs. Brown's apartment is decorated in relic, gentile old lady. The dining room is furnished in large, overly ornate carved, dark wood furniture that overwhelms even her large dining room. Besides the table with lion claw legs that can seat fourteen people when it is fully extended, there is a buffet, a sidebar, and china cabinet with four shelves of displayed china and crystal. That is in addition to the built-in hutch and decorative shelving containing Lladró, Belleek, and Waterford figurines. Her artwork is mostly dead relatives or floral still life paintings. The furniture in her living room includes wing chairs and a matching couch with Queen Anne legs in a swirled autumn leaf design upholstery. It is overstocked with various types of decorative tables loaded with bric-a-brac with lace doily protectors. Her TV is a console set from the eighties that barely works and only gets the major network stations. There is a stereo-radio console from the sixties in her bay window area with a reading chair and ottoman. She has an extensive collection of swing band era original recordings that she enjoys listening to and likes that her old stereo permits six records to be stacked on top of each other for her listening convenience.

Detective Williams arrived and asked if he could talk to us in Mrs. Brown's dining room, and if we would kindly put Fred somewhere else. Susan snickered and took him upstairs to the Metzkers. Fred went but under protest with lots of moans and whines. By the time she returned with a carafe of coffee and three cups, I had finished retelling my version of the morning's events.

Detective Williams was trying to be nicer today. "Once more, why did you spend the night here?"

"I have no tangible reason. I know I sound neurotic. I've had a creepy feeling that I can't describe since Monday. Probably Sammy getting jumped and Larry Katz coming at me reinforced my anxiety. My reasoning at the time was that I felt vulnerable in a first-floor flat, and I'd be awake all night listening for noises."

"With that dog?"

"Yeah. What can Fred do against a gun, and Benny was murdered! I have no idea what he, or even if it's a she, is about, and clearly, some number of people are violating my personal space."

He seemed sorry and changed topics. "I hear you have no security cameras on this block. If your sensation of being watched is valid, and somebody is observing you around your building, they risk being seen. Who's the best bet to notice anybody not typical on this street?"

"Mrs. Metzker, but only for anything that happens in the front. She exercises looking out her front window and hangs out there a lot watching her shows during the day. She can't observe much in the back yard and alley."

"So, where we are, what was stolen is exactly the contents of what we already have from Benny's accountant or lawyer, Mr. O'Doole, right?"

"Yes."

"What good does that do anybody?"

"Probably nothing. Billy and I think someone is seeking a trail to where Benny kept assets. We don't know what kind or where. The thought occurred to me that the person who killed Benny may not be my home invader. The murderer may have that information. But, the person who took the files may not know what's in them or how useless they would be."

Detective Williams paused and reviewed his notes. "You have any ideas of what the killer or your intruder will do next?"

"Yeah, but I'm not sharing and am taking pre-emptive measures without notifying you first. I'm not trying to be antagonistic, but you give me no choice. Your lawyers won't give us any form of indemnification, and I'm not sure how binding they would be, anyway. I have never been involved in a law enforcement investigation, but I gotta figure the process is the same with civil litigation and regulators. The way it works with regulators is once an investigation is more than a routine, garden-variety potential violation, it gets escalated to a specialist group or other agency. There's then a regulatory pile-on alleging hundreds of rule violations, many of which are exaggerated or flat out not true, to entice the defendant to settle. Sometimes the motive is to grab headlines or otherwise boost the career of a mid-level regulator. Lawyers initiating lawsuits use the same strategy because it costs more to defend baloney claims than allege them. The goal is to maneuver toward a settlement without going to court by making the cost of defense so expensive.

"Here is how I interpret the situation. Benny is dead, so there won't be any glory for whoever has jurisdiction into potential money laundering. A dead man can't be charged or fined. We don't know where the trail of money leads or when it started. I'm not worried about Lough Key or any of our staff violating any rules. However, if it's alleged, mind you not close to proven, people like Susan can be dragged into the mess, and his estate can be in dispute. That can lead to hundreds of wasted hours of Lough Key staff and big legal bills in our capacity as a witness and last custodian of a sizable amount of his cash. A common enforcement action for financial crimes is disgorgement of the ill-gotten gains. Whoever is leading the charge will not be the local Chicago police. You'll be long gone should this play out the way I think it can."

A very tired Detective Williams sighed. He was unimpressed by my logic. "I can't comment on whatever is frustrating you. I don't really follow your thinking. It must bother you that your intruder is still at large and can strike again. From what you say, you feel vulnerable and will

177

continue to be vulnerable until we find Benny's murderer. I don't see how it's helping your cause to shut down communication with us."

"Is communication two-way, and you share with us?" Detective Williams was too tired to engage in banter. His response was to raise his left eyebrow and glare at me.

"I don't have a specific suggestion now and want to speak to our lawyers first. I'll call you this afternoon. That really is the best I can do for now."

"Fair enough. Have the technicians taken your fingerprints yet?"

Susan and I both nodded no. "Is that really necessary? Both of us have been fingerprinted because we work for exchange members. Can't you use those?"

"I guess, but it would speed things up if we can eliminate what prints are yours today. Do you really care?"

Susan and I agreed to be fingerprinted and were directed to return to my apartment and ask for one of the police crime-scene techs. We were told we could leave the building, and I was asked to check in with Detective Williams after I spoke to counsel. Susan elected to go downtown with me in the hopes of meeting Oscar to get a referral for an attorney and help making an appointment. She thought she might walk to Macy's on State Street for more clothes since her return to Florida was likely to be delayed.

In the car, I relayed the messages from Beverly and Paul Stein. She muttered the f-bomb under her breath. After a few seconds, she voiced that she would rather get it over with and initiated a call on her cell. I noticed she had the number already and wondered again if the calls to my firm looking for Susan were a ploy. For what, I couldn't guess.

It was Paul she called, and he picked up immediately. I couldn't hear what he was saying, but he was loud. Susan hung up without saying more than hello after about fifteen seconds. Her phone immediately rang again. She looked at it and hit what my daughter calls the 'FU' button to disconnect the call. She let the phone ring two more times and repeated the process.

With a big sigh and another muttered f-bomb, she selected a number and made another call. "Hey, Sharon, it's me, Susan. How are you doing?" I couldn't hear what Sharon said, but Susan didn't look any happier. "I don't want to make any trouble for you. This must be hard. I'll text your asshole brother to remind him I won't take his crap. If he wants to speak to me, it's on my terms, the first one being that he has to mind his manners with me. No, I don't want to speak to your mother. Just let me know if there's going to be a memorial or funeral, okay? Yeah, I think it's wise to go on pretending you don't have my number but call if you want to talk or meet or something. Take care."

"I wish I could smoke. Don't worry, that wasn't a hint," she said and then sent a text.

Her phone rang again. She looked at the number and snorted. Susan is a great snorter.

"Hello, how are you? This is a prompt, and you say you're fine and ask how I am. Otherwise, I hang up, and you can go to hell. Got it?"

"Fine, thank you. Everything aside, I'm sorry and hope your family and mom are doing okay. I am not going to ask if there's anything I can do. You're calling because you heard that I control Benny's estate and Sharon's trust. Don't bother pitching or threatening me. I had no idea and still don't know what that means. I'm going to meet a lawyer to find out. Just shut up. I didn't want this, and I don't know what it means other than I'm responsible for Sharon. To make sure we're clear, I'm responsible for making sure Sharon is taken care of, not you, your wife, or mother. Screaming at me isn't a good strategy for you. It's not like we ever gave a shit about each other. You not speaking to me again is my goal. I suggest we remain civil and finalize the funeral arrangements. I don't know much about your traditions, but I'm willing to honor your family's wishes. I only ask to know when the service will be. I won't try to take the place of a family member."

I heard loud screeching over the phone. Susan hung up. "Once an asshole, always an asshole."

"What did he say?"

Susan shrugged. "He was yelling and saying trash, I don't really know. I can't be bothered. God, I hope Oscar comes up with a lawyer who will deal with them. I'm done with this shit."

At this time of the day, I can make it downtown to my parking garage in less than a half hour. We were almost there, which was good because Susan needed a smoke.

The news of my office break-in had spread like proverbial wildfire. Virgil came up to the car when I pulled into the lot. He looked genuinely concerned and instructed Susan and me to make sure we text him when in the area and to let him know if he should come get us. I got teary again. One of the things that I love about working at the exchanges is that we really do have a community, but I never expected this level of kindness from someone I considered a neighborhood acquaintance. We assured him we were okay and thanked him. Susan stayed behind to smoke with some company.

The building security desk is a small office constructed like a booth with a counter to the right of the revolving doors nearest the horse statue. In the morning, Angelina is usually manning the post and is the person who registers guests. Clayton, the maintenance man, was walking over to me. For some reason, she and Clayton call me Lois as in Lois Lane. I've learned to ignore it and presume it is a form of a compliment. They also wanted assurance I was okay. After I instructed Angelina to permit Susan upstairs, Clayton laid a bombshell on me.

"I'm real sorry if I messed up, Lois. Never thought I had to double-check that the supply closets are locked."

"Sorry, Clay, but I missed a beat. What are you talking about?"

"Dude that broke in got past by pretending to be maintenance is the cops' guess. A ladder was used to get over the wall into your office. The supply closet was messed up this morning. Somebody was messing around with light bulbs and the ladder last night."

Clayton is a tall African American with kind eyes and always has something nice to say. He wears a navy-blue uniform and usually is toting a vacuum cleaner. This is his day job. At night he plays blues guitar at various clubs, and his band is always selected to play at the building's annual tenant picnic in the summer. This is the first time I ever saw his essence of cool rattled.

"Whoa. Actually, that makes me feel better. It's less creepy if it seems like someone didn't have superpowers or wasn't a professional thief to get in. The real question is how did he get in the building and into our general offices. No worries, Clay, this isn't on you, nobody got hurt, and nothing of value was taken."

Angelina and Clayton looked somewhat relieved but still concerned.

"Hector was on shift last night and worried this will be on him. He did see someone leave last night after seven. The guy walked real fast out of the building and didn't go to sign out, even after Hector called out to him. There wasn't anything Hector could do once he left the building. You know the building security also answers the phone for the LaSalle Club and takes some calls for the Everest Room, and we are in this closet. It's not like we can run out to stop anyone. Hector was on the phone at the time and didn't think it really mattered. It didn't look like he had any equipment or anything on him like a case to take things out of the building. Lots of guys leave and don't like taking the time to sign out. If we know them, we enter their name and time on the log ourselves," Angelina said.

"Could he describe him?"

"Hector said he was a skinny, little white guy. He looked like most of the tenants here, you know... white, khakis, golf shirt, and Blackhawks' cap. Cops are all over him 'cuz he can't say for sure if he's the same little dude you thumped on yesterday," Clayton answered.

It was now close to ten in the morning. In my world, half the trading day was over, and the more crucial tasks of the day were done. The only thing that kept me from resisting the temptation to go home was that the police were probably still there. I also knew I had to face Billy and Oscar. I just wasn't up for more people I knew to be anxious about me. Leaving, I thanked Angelina and Clayton. Both made sure I had their numbers, and I was instructed to call or text should anything be wrong. It made me feel terrible. Sure, I bring them hot chocolate and coffee when they are working in the winter near the doors, I order extra pizza for the building staff on pizza Wednesdays, and do other small tokens of thanks. That doesn't compare to putting yourself out for my type of situation.

Susan had entered the building and joined me for the short elevator ride to the Lough Key offices. I quickly shared what Angelina and Clayton told me. Susan added that Virgil was still working at seven last night and hanging out around the front of the parking lot across from the plaza. He didn't see anybody out of the ordinary but probably wouldn't think twice if a white man dressed as Clayton described walked out of the building.

Starz was at the front desk and greeted me with a huge smile. "I'm so glad you're okay. We heard your place got busted into last night. Some crazy shit, right? Oops, sorry, I mean crazy stuff. Can I do anything for you? Today is pizza day, do you want me to order you a salad or something? Raj made the fancy tea you like and said for you to stop by."

Starz is an amazing girl from blighted conditions. Her story would break your heart. She was introduced to us by one of the groups Lough Key works with to provide education and career opportunities for inner-city kids. She's come a long way in getting used to office manners but has retained her natural charm and essence of fun. I am a big fan of hers. Her favorite color is purple, which she tends to accent with bright pink. She really likes neon-blue nail polish with silver star designs. Starz attends Robert Morris College and is working on an Associate Degree in Business Administration. Latesha has her almost talked into getting a four-year degree in Human Resource Management and thinks she is a natural in that field.

However, Starz is a sponge for gossip and tends to dramatize events—typical traits of any young girl working in an office with a boring job. She is one of the part-time receptionists, but she usually is on shift to qualify for the glamour job of putting away the Pea Pod food deliveries in the kitchen. At first, she hated it. Now she loves it because the guys come in to see what was delivered and to have first dibs on the Dorito Ranch-flavored chips or to conspire for her to hide the Mountain Dew where only they can find it. They also try to coax her into ordering Red Bull and Monster drinks because Latesha won't. Latesha says they aren't healthy and will mess up a body's system.

I took advantage of Starz's offer to order me a salad, especially since it may be past the cutoff time. As an afterthought, I offered Susan one, which she accepted. I asked Susan to wait in my office while I found Oscar and Billy. She understood that I wanted to speak to them without her and picked up that morning's *Wall Street Journal* from the reception table near the guest chairs.

After I walked Susan to my office, I went back downstairs to the tech area with my teacup. Raj and I are tea aficionados and bring in our own tea. He has a Capresso electric tea kettle at his desk that brews tea. True to his word, he saved me some of the smoky, white oolong tea he made that morning. Sammy caught up with me by then and handed me a carefully wrapped piece of cake with a squashed frosted flower from EKG's birthday celebration. Some of the clerks on the floor helped him take pictures and a video of EKG's birthday toast on Sammy's phone. The Help Desk crew joined us watching the video of Ed doing his best impersonations, mugging with his corsage, and offering the few remaining women on the floor a big wet smooch with promises of avoiding smashing flowers. The highlight is EKG announcing he "has a body of an eighteen-year-old, with a long pause... in my basement. BOOM!" Definitely not politically correct but harmless and silly fun.

I'm not sure when I got to Oscar's office. Billy and Latesha were there too. Billy was explaining how his reporter friend found out that the police still don't have the weapon but discovered that Benny bought a Glock a couple of years ago, and they think it is now registered as being owned by Paul.

"Good, I'm glad you and Susan are here. I'm supposed to go downstairs to the security office with Deena to look at the security videos. I said we would be there at ten thirty. Check this out, Deena said she let a small, white man with a funny accent light her cigarette yesterday afternoon. Bill thinks it was a setup. For some reason, she spilled her drink, and he helped her. She didn't have her building badge when she tried to re-enter the building after that.

"The *StreetWise* man told Martinez that the police found it interesting when they finally got around to talking to him that he saw two small, white, blondish men hanging around the building and plaza these past two days. He saw Sammy right after he was pushed down and saw the guy who did it run away. He was wearing a hat, and his back was turned 'cuz he was running toward Congress. *StreetWise* man doesn't think it was Larry 'cuz he's too mean of a cuss. If it were him, Sammy would have broken knee caps, and the envelope would be gone. It sounds like after Deena and I view the videos, the police will want to ask *StreetWise* man if he can spot either of the men on the videos."

I didn't have time to absorb the information because my cell was ringing. I noticed it was Angelina.

"Good morning, Ms. Lois. I hate to disturb you this morning, but there's a Mr. Nivar Amirmoez. He's here to see Mr. Keegan or Mr. Marquis. I explained to him that you handle their calls, and we're to obtain access permission from you for those two gentlemen. He is an officer of EuroCredit Bank and insists he flew into town to meet with them on a time-sensitive matter." She carefully and slowly tried to pronounce his name.

"Angel, is he tall, dark, and handsome with a killer suit?"

"Yes, ma'am, that would be correct. I'll hold."

I put my cell on mute and informed the room. We decided to permit him upstairs and call the police. "Angel, please inform Mr. Amirmoez that he can come up, and I'll try to arrange for a meeting with at least one of the gentlemen. However, he's to wait until I send someone down to escort him up. Oh, wait! Get a copy of his driver's license or passport if you can. Make something up about him not being registered with the building and tightening security because of recent break-ins. A passport is best."

"I understand. It won't be necessary to hold up your guest further for an escort. Lou is here, and he offered to take the gentleman up."

"Nicely done, Angel. Thanks."

While I texted Detective Williams and Detective Guzman, Latesha warned Starz what to expect and instructed her to get a cold bottle of water and newspaper and put both in the conference room where our guest is to wait. Detective Williams texted back to hold him here. Detective Guzman texted they would be here in about thirty minutes. When I finished texting, Latesha suggested we get Jason to help Starz out.

"Won't he mind?" Billy asked.

She chuckled. "Are you kidding. He's having a great time being in front with all the excitement. He may even volunteer for phone duty next week. Starz is a good girl but young. This isn't fair to her. What's she going to do if he tries to bolt? You know what else? I'm going to ask Lou to hang in our lobby area and make sure the doors are locked once our guest is in the conference room."

When Latesha walked out, I walked over to the chair she vacated and collapsed. Oscar asked me if I was okay, and I could see he was noticing I was dressed in jeans and a hoody sweatshirt. My office uniform is dress slacks, usually black, a button-down shirt with a collar or a cardigan sweater. I may wear a jacket or accessorize with a scarf. Today, I was going for clean. I didn't even bother blow-drying my hair and just swept it back in a sort of bun with a hair clip. I explained how the events of the morning didn't give me a chance to do more than grab a few things, and I had to shower in Mrs. Brown's apartment because mine was being treated as a crime scene.

"We have more news to process before the police get here. Remember our old friends from Merrill who moved over to JP Morgan Chase? Chase is the correspondent bank Lake Shore Bank uses for wires, especially anything overseas. Jennifer called me this morning to give me a heads-up that their AML office was asking about Lough Key. That wire from Benny's bank branch in the Netherland Antilles was funded by a wire from Gibraltar," Billy advised.

"Gibraltar, as in the drug gateway to Europe and money-laundering haven of the world?" I questioned.

"Uh-huh. I asked if there was anything left in the Chase account, and she said she can't tell me and probably shouldn't be sharing what she did. Her excuse for contacting me will be a follow-up due diligence on their end. The only additional data point she shared is that the Gibraltar bank is part of HSBC, and that bank is in hot water for facilitating almost every type of money laundering... Mexican drug lords, terrorists, arms dealers to the point where it's hard to believe they could be so flagrant. Because of it, Chase is supposed to put an additional review layer on anything coming from there. I get a feeling there's more behind that curtain, but she can't disclose it."

"Great, my worst-case fears are realized. I need to find out from Scott if there's any way we can avoid or subvert attempts to drag us into this. I have a call into him already to confirm the extent we can sidestep the Stein family feud that appears to be brewing." Oscar sighed.

"Susan! I forgot about Susan," I said. She's in my office and hopes you have a legal referral for her to deal with Benny's family." I told them what I overheard in the car. I asked if they knew why there was such a sense of urgency emanating from Paul. There has to be more to it than they don't like Susan and want control over Benny's estate. It sounded like this was a higher priority than Benny's funeral arrangements. Oscar asked me to have Susan join us in his office, which is when Nivar arrived.

Starz buzzed Oscar's phone and announced our visitor. She said he was invited to wait in the conference room, and she could not confirm how long it would be before he could meet with either of them. Nivar was not going for that and was being assertive. Jason stepped in and told Nivar he would wait in the conference room and like it. Lou heard the commotion and mentioned that it would be a good idea if Nivar complied with our request. Oscar asked to speak to Jason and confirmed that the front door cannot be opened without Starz or him buzzing a person in or out.

"I bumped into Peter Gardner from Gardner, Loeb & Wilson yesterday at a fundraiser at the Union League Club. I asked him if he had a sense of the state of affairs of Paul Stein's firm and practice. They both do a lot of commercial real estate and development work. He said there are rumors that things are in a complete meltdown. Paul's firm initiated the same strategy as some of the legal firms in Silicon Valley pursued in the height of the dot.com era. They negotiated a sizable reduction of their regular billing fees in return for equity in the start-ups. Paul and his group are working with a couple of highly leveraged real estate investment trusts commonly referred to as REIT. Paul invested personal funds in addition to foregoing a significant portion of legal fees. The idea was to load up and heavily borrow, and flip or whatever, the properties, many of which are resort or luxury condos in Naples, Florida. His problem is that real estate values have plummeted, and some comparable properties in the same area are in foreclosure, which has provoked the banks to make what sounds like a margin call for some portion of the debt to be repaid. Paul and his syndicate have to come up with more capital, or their bank will foreclose, too."

"Well, that solves the mystery of why Benny wasn't answering Paul's emails and calls, and it explains why they are so aggressive with us and hostile to Susan. What a mess," said Billy.

I left to get Susan. When we returned to Oscar's office, the two police detectives were being escorted in by Starz. After salutations, Oscar took over. He gave them the update on the gossip concerning Paul's finances. He alluded to having information from non-US sources that may interest them, should their search encompass more parties than Paul, who we understand has a gun matching the possible murder weapon registered to him. Oscar continued that none of his information was probably news to the police. He suggested that Billy join the police in speaking with Mr. Amirmoez, Lough Key's guest, in the firm's conference room since Billy was more conversant in banking and finance matters than he suspected the two detectives were.

Detective Williams wasn't going for the idea and didn't like Oscar's attitude. He made a half-serious comment about obstruction. Oscar waved his hand in dismissal. Detective Guzman was watching the show. Oscar responded that if that was their position, then they were to please remove Mr. Amirmoez from our office immediately and conduct their business elsewhere. A compromise was reached, resulting in Oscar getting his way. Billy left with the two detectives to interview our guest. I was glad to be exempt.

Oscar and Susan discussed the attorney he recommended from our law firm. Elizabeth Baird specializes in family law and has high-net-worth families who have struggled through legacy disputes and dissolutions of estates. He told Susan that he had taken the liberty of forwarding to Elizabeth the documents and account statements we have, said she could walk over with hard copies of Benny's last tax returns, and gave her a short list of things to consider first. The first things to consider were how fast she could get access to funds to close Benny's affairs for things like his funeral and the extent his estate would or should cover her legal fees, and lastly, if she could represent Susan in dealing with the police to retrieve Benny's body and negotiate in her stead with the family. He repeated the news about Paul and what some form of regulatory body may want to do regarding any of Benny's cash that they attribute as having been derived from an overseas bank account. She should inquire if her assets are at risk.

Susan appeared unfazed and was following the points Oscar was making. "God, what a nightmare! I can't believe this is for real. Do you think there will be anything left for Sharon?"

"Anything I say is pure speculation. I suggest you find out from Elizabeth, who may need to consult with another attorney with a banking practice, the extent you need to be shielded from any liability. I think you have reasonable defenses such as you maintained your own household and were employed and supported yourself. You weren't filing joint tax returns which is also in your favor. I'm not an expert in these matters to render an opinion. Just be careful and take her advice," Oscar advised.

Susan turned to me. "Do you mind if I crash in your office a bit longer to make a few phone calls?" I said it was okay, and she should find her salad in the kitchen and eat there too. She thanked me and left, saying she could find the kitchen and her way back without me.

"Lane, how about we stroll down the street and get sushi today?" offered Oscar. He looked tired and deflated, not like the usual Oscar, even though he was dressed neat as a pin in a soft gray cashmere V-neck sweater, gray slacks, a light-yellow shirt, and gray silk tie with yellow diagonal stripes. "I think the office can get by without us for an hour, and it looks like a nice day for a short stroll."

"Love to. I can't concentrate anyway and won't be able to get much done until I hear what happened in the conference room. I have this sensation like I'm awake, but in a dream, watching myself. These past couple of days had too many weird things happen with no reason, just like dreams where odd things happen that don't make sense and can't be controlled. I feel worse than when I pull a night shift at the shelter. I feel like my head and body are made of cement."

I didn't bother going back to my office to retrieve my bag. On the way out, we stopped by the security desk where Angelina, Clayton, and Martinez, one of the daytime security guards, were congregated around the lobby security booth. I walked over to them. "Hey, Angel, nice going. Thanks for calling me and play-acting with our guest. It gave us time to prepare and call the police."

"No worries, Lois. I remembered him from before. That guy stands out with his fancy talk and high manners. Latesha has everybody in your office trained pretty well to call in advance to register visitors, not like most of the tenants. No way was he from around here and somebody just forgot to call down. What's his story? Who is he? Is the reason the two cops ran up to your office?"

I did owe the three of them the latest installment of our adventure but didn't have much to offer. I shook my head. "I really don't know, but I'll give you his timing is interesting. All I know about him is he works for a European bank and came a few months ago as a friend or business associate of Benny Stein. The police are with him now. I'll fill you in later. Hopefully, they will all be gone when we get back."

"Lois?" Oscar questioned as we walked away.

"Uh-huh, and I don't know why. I just roll with it."

The short stroll down LaSalle Street and west on Adams to the sushi place right before Franklin felt good. The air was crisp, we had a blue sky, and there was no bite to the wind. We had turned the corner from winter and could hope for a nice spring. In Chicago, we usually go from winter to a drab gray, mostly wet and chilly spring to summer, which is why spring is my least favorite season. Everything is dirty, and it is usually too cold to want to be outside. On the way, we chatted about normal things like how excited Oscar was to have tickets for tomorrow's Blackhawks' game and my plans for a girls' night out to the Chicago Symphony. Once we got to the restaurant and sat, Oscar asked me for my take on Susan.

"Not what I expected, not that I gave her and Benny much thought before. She's not wild and frantic like before. Every once in a while, the old Dizzy surfaces, but it's when she is pushed, and she's not the type to take it. That must be the consequence of giving up cocaine. She strikes me as alone. I get the impression she and Benny were both estranged from their families, but I don't know the full story as to why, especially for her. Benny's alter-ego wasn't such a goof. Maybe that was the real Benny. According to Susan, he was thoughtful, shrewd, and his bluster was an act, and, get this, they were planning on marrying and settling down in Florida to get away from their lifestyle here. She gets along well with my neighbors and Fred but is detached like she's grateful to have a sanctuary. I'll give it to her, there isn't an ounce of bullshit in her. She is equally candid about herself as are her cutting observations about others."

Oscar thought the recap was interesting but not as interesting as finding out Susan was going to the symphony too. "Who would have thought?" was his comment.

Chapter 9

When we returned to the office, Kayreen was the receptionist on duty. She is majoring in accounting at DePaul and has been with us for years. She is a tiny, soft-spoken woman, and my guess is she is close to thirty, which makes her older than the regular receptionists. She wears plain, black-framed glasses, pulls her hair back in a severe bun, and is always dressed in a dark pants suit with a white or blue button-down shirt. I never get what her schedule is. She has a little boy named Michael, and she likes working with us because she can get a forty-hour week with benefits and a flexible schedule. Most of the time when she is at the office, she is working with the finance and accounting team. She'll help out at the front desk during pockets when the two or three part-time front desk staff aren't around. Lately, I have seen her with a couple of the younger traders huddled over a book in a conference room after treasuries and Eurodollar futures markets close. They are tutoring her through calculus. Latesha says Kayreen doesn't mind working the front desk because she can do homework and get paid.

"Kayreen, anything noteworthy while we were gone?" asked Oscar.

Kayreen didn't look up all the way from her textbook but looked over the rims of her glasses with an expression that implied he must be kidding. "Um, the man in the fancy suit didn't leave looking too happy. He was making threats to Mr. Keegan about lawsuits. You just missed him. Mr. Keegan is still in the conference room with the police."

"Always something," Oscar muttered as we walked to the conference room. The detectives looked grim, and Detective Guzman was writing on his tablet. Billy was somber. He raised both eyebrows quickly at us when we entered. Susan was sitting at a corner seat and rolled her eyes. Not a good sign.

"Well?" asked Oscar.

"Good. You're back. Lane, do you have time to answer a few more questions?" asked Detective Guzman. My guard was definitely going up by the second. I nodded my consent and took a seat across from them. Oscar sat next to me.

"The gentleman who just left, did you see him? He's one of the foreign bankers you mentioned yesterday, right?" stated Detective Williams.

"I didn't actually see him today, but the security staff remembers him as my visitor, and the description fits what I recall. What did he say? Did you get a card? I never did."

"His version of your meeting is kind of interesting," Detective Williams continued with a pause. "He says he came with just one associate."

"What!" I blurted.

"Yeah, or it was so long ago, and he's so overly scheduled globetrotting, he can't remember. He sure as hell doesn't know any John William Henry Carrington III. He admits to having a business associate who matches the description you gave of a third man wearing jeans with longer hair. Said his name is Pär Ericsson, who he describes as his personal concierge. He made a big show of checking his phone calendar and claiming there's nothing indicating another party was with him when he met with you and Mr. Stein."

"There's no way he doesn't remember the third man. He did most of the talking. Wait, did you call him out by pointing out the building would have a record?"

"We didn't mention the security log. Next thing I'm doing is asking for it to see the names they signed in under. He's very assured. He can retract by saying he didn't remember the particulars of the meeting, but denying an association with one of the parties is interesting."

"They were just asking Susan if she ever saw him with Benny. Susan was asked to sit in the reception to see Nivar leaving," Bill injected.

"And?" prompted Oscar.

"I think so. I didn't join them for any meetings or socialize. I only saw him at the FIA trade show, and thousands were there from all over. He does match how Benny described the head guy of his bank deal. The name Pär or Ericsson sounds like he could be the guy I smoked with outside. It stands out because I remember thinking he was Swedish. Can you check with the passport agency to confirm if they were in town then?"

Detective Guzman's eyes laughed. "Yeah, now that we have his business card and copy of his passport. Having a name of the one associate helps, and they might have traveled on the same plane."

Oscar was on a mission. "What did Nivar say transpired at his meeting with Lane?"

"He says Benjamin Stein committed bank fraud, stole millions, and Ms. Daye here aided and abetted the crime," Detective Williams responded deliberately.

"Holy shit!" came from Susan.

"It gets better. He's demanding we immediately wire all funds in Benny's accounts here and assist with the investigation of the crime's perpetration. We're to expect bank lawyers to be contacting us eminently. Our cooperation may influence the extent the bank initiates legal proceedings, including filing a claim with assorted banking authorities alleging bank fraud that includes money laundering," continued Billy.

When you read books describing a character's stunned reaction to outlandish accusations, it's nothing like the real thing. The feeling of watching myself in a dream returned.

"You left out the best part," continued Detective Williams. "Mr. Amirmoez insists we conduct a thorough investigation on you, Ms. Daye, to make sure you didn't instigate and otherwise facilitate the burglary of your office. His lawyers will be asking for some formal confirmation of the investigation being initiated and taken seriously."

Turning to Oscar. "Now what?" I whispered.

"We have to notify Scott of this development. This is too absurd to comment on."

Detective Guzman asked softly, "Hold on. Lane, think. Is there any way that putting a different spin on your encounter with those men can be construed as you being more involved than what you related to us?"

I shook my head no, leaned back, and closed my eyes. "Damn. Nobody from our side was at that meeting." I straightened up. "I had only the one encounter, and it was so short that nothing significant could have been discussed. I hope to God the security team keeps logs that far back. Although I don't think most visitors sign out," I answered.

"Listen, Lane, this is important. Is there any way your relationship or discussions with Benny can be portrayed differently?" asked Detective Guzman. "Did you ever meet with just him, ever out of the office?"

"No! I told you our conversations lately were mostly stupid and him trying to get a rise out of me."

Oscar's body language went on high alert. Billy straightened and then got up to stand by the window with his arms crossed.

"Gentlemen, where are we going with this? It sounds like you're focusing on Lane. We may want to postpone further discussions until we engage counsel to participate," Oscar questioned.

Detectives Williams and Guzman shared a look that meant something. Detective Williams moved to a chair to be on my side of the table. He faced me, leaned over so that his forearms were on his thighs, and folded his hands. His manner indicated he was about to give me really bad news.

"Ms. Daye, get rid of that attitude you all have that you're doing us a favor by cooperating. Think about what you said this morning, about how banking fraud and money laundering can take this matter out of our hands. We're there now. My partner and I don't like you for the murder, but you're profiling real good as a person of interest for whatever the deceased was up to that may have led to his murder."

He looked at Oscar. "Wait a minute, hear me out before you go jumping on us and getting your lawyer. You want to hear this before you call him. Look at the facts. Mr. Stein and his banker associates come to meet with just you, Ms. Daye, on a day when no other executive is in the office to discuss opening an account. You claim to have only a slight acquaintance with the deceased, but he appeared to hold you in some regard. You also claimed to have no previous acquaintance with Ms. Desmond, your houseguest. I saw your dog with her. They don't seem like strangers. Then there's the point of, for no reason other than a premonition, you, Ms. Desmond here, and your dog don't spend the night in your apartment on the night of the break-in. This is in spite of the fact you have the world's largest dog, and it's a safe bet he scares people blocks away. Very coincidental, and on the same night that only your office is broken into. Add to that long list of coincidences is the file you left on your desk, contrary to firm policies, with Mr. Stein's name on it and the disk supposedly lifted from your purse wasn't password protected, and you all have copies of its contents here in a location other than your office. We also have you being authorized to act on Ms. Desmond's behalf in some capacities as the executor of Mr. Stein's estate. Interesting since you weren't friends until two days ago, and both Mr. Stein and Ms. Desmond are well known and liked around here and probably have a lot of friends."

It felt like I was physically punched and the wind knocked out of me. I am a boring, nice person. I work hard, take care of good kids, and except for the issue of my husband being MIA, my life is entirely void of anything noteworthy. I am now a character in a thriller story and don't see a way out. I could tell what the next bombshell would be, and I was right.

"Ms. Daye, where's your husband? Our search reflects you're married, but he doesn't seem to be living with you or part of your current life," inquired Detective Guzman.

"Lane is done answering questions for today. We can take this up tomorrow. I sincerely want to thank you for sharing your perspective. We need to process. Should we set up a time tomorrow? In anticipation, what else should we prepare for you to make this more efficient?" I have never seen Oscar look resigned before. Not good.

Detective Williams understood he had the high ground now but wasn't going to get us to budge without a lawyer. "Okay, let's try again here tomorrow morning at nine. Your coffee is better here than at the station," he said with a smile. It made me feel a little better. I don't recall the ending pleasantries.

I needed to go for a walk. Billy wasn't letting me out of his sight and told me to wait. Oscar sat down with Susan to discuss her appointment with Elizabeth Baird that was scheduled within the hour. We agreed Susan would return to the office and drive me in my car back to Oak Park. I decided to ignore for now the insinuation that I wasn't fit to drive.

Once we hit the street, we decided to hike east on Van Buren toward the lake and Buckingham Fountain. It hadn't been turned on yet, but it was a nice walk, and we can be back in a little over a half hour.

Billy was being nice to me, which I hate. He only does that when he is worried or feels sorry for me. "Where do we start? I honestly can't think, Billy."

"Well, first, we have to assume they know about Mark and that he's off the grid in the Middle East, last seen in Iraq. We don't know if that adds to the shadiness of your profile. Crap, Laney, this is the worst example of no good deed going unpunished. No way could anybody anticipate how it would look to the police. At the time, I thought it was a stroke of luck. We could keep Susan close, help her out, and you would have some company. Sorry, but it's true. You've had a short fuse this year, and not all of it is due to year-end closing of the books and taxes."

"I know," I whispered. "I can't sleep or concentrate anymore. That's why I volunteer so much at night, to avoid thinking about Mark. At first, I thought it was worse because Ellie Rose is gone, and the house is empty. That's not why anymore. I think he's alive and somewhere in pain and maybe even tortured." Looking at Billy, I see his skeptical look. "If he were dead, he'd be found by now, and we would be notified. I know you and Oscar made calls to people of real influence in Washington. Mark's brother works for SCIA, the big defense contracting firm that's doing billions of business in Afghanistan and Iraq. They have a lot of contractors in the Green Zone. His company is offering a sizable reward for information about Mark and an even bigger one if he comes back alive or if his body is retrieved. After all this time, somebody would have stepped up if he were dead.

"I keep thinking of a story my dad told me years ago after he retired from the military. He had a contract with a firm that sold night vision equipment for military purposes. He had to go to Saudi Arabia for a meeting with the buyer. On the flight, he met an Asian woman, I think from Korea, who was some nuclear engineer. My dad found out she wasn't married and didn't come from a family with resources. He flipped out when she told him it was an assignment between just her and the Saudis. He was suspicious at the time that it may not be with Saudi Arabia, the government. Everybody knew Iran was gearing up its nuclear capabilities, and it didn't sound right for that type of mission to be engaged by the Saudis.

"He set up a system with the woman for them to speak or email at least every other day, and under no circumstances less than once a week. They had a code to ensure emails were really from her and some keyword to indicate she was in danger. Well, he was right. Two months into it, she went dark. He had friends in the press and a wide network of arms dealers. He made it known he was going to blast her name all over the press in some scandalous way implicating the Saudi government for assisting Iran in circumventing the embargoes. She sent an email, but he spotted it wasn't from her since she didn't follow the code. He ran with that, and she got lucky. She was allowed to return to the US a week later. She had a tale of being kept in a locked dorm adjacent to a lab where she was assigned to work on a nuclear power plant that she thought was really an arsenal of nuclear weapons. She had no idea of the location, or even if she were really in

Saudi Arabia. There were two other foreign, extremely educated people on the same project that weren't allowed to leave either. They were Russian Jews, and I don't remember their story. Billy, if something happened like that ten to fifteen years ago, it can still happen today."

We walked for a bit in silence. "Sorry, Lane, I can't say you're wrong, but I don't think he's alive. Nobody knows what to do. We're all on eggshells around you. Not that you're going to take my advice, but maybe see a therapist and explore getting meds for you to sleep."

"You're right. I came to that decision myself lately. I even made a couple of calls. It's easy to find someone specializing in substance abuse, eating disorders, depression, and other normal maladies for women. I didn't find anybody who sounded like they had any prior experience with my type of situation. I was referred to someone who works with many vets who have PTSD, which isn't my issue either. I just don't feel like telling my story again to someone on the phone. I sound like a crazy person, and I sense the person taking the call finds my story too incredible to be true. It makes my impotent rage worse."

"How about if Connie calls her friend, who's the President of Northwestern? I think that hospital association has a wide psych network, and Connie can do the initial fieldwork."

"That's a good idea. I should have thought of it myself. Thanks. But now, what are we going to do to keep me out of jail?" I sighed. "Looking back, I don't think I'd have done anything differently other than not forgetting the file on my desk. You know how I scorn all the execs from banks and exchanges who always seem to have an entourage. I've never attended a meeting with the Merc with less than five people. Banks usually come with at least three. I see the wisdom in that now. All that aside, the police have a point. I'm the lynch-pin to something, and it does look dodgy the way Detective Williams described recent events. What sucks now is I probably can't leave town. I was hoping to join Ellie Rose during her spring break. I bought tickets to see Cahill at school in Edinburgh and a few days in London with the two of them."

"Lane, you're scaring me. You lost all the fight in you. Stay with us? It might relax you, and you can hole out in the guest suite. Bring Fred. Connie will ply you with wine, old movies, and set you up with a spa date."

"No thanks. It's against my nature to curl up in a ball and hide in a dark basement. I'll be okay. I just have to get past the shock and to think. Like for starters, why would I be staging break-ins for items I have when I could just make copies for an accomplice? Second, who would want Benny's tax returns and trust docs and why? They might not have known what they were and just grabbed what was immediately visible with Benny's name on them. That must be the ticket."

"Well... if I were the suspicious type, I'd counter that you staged the break-ins of useless documents to deflect attention away from you."

"But the opposite occurred. I'm now under more scrutiny from the police than if the break-ins never happened."

"You either miscalibrated or are desperate because Benny's death meant whatever crimes transpired to result in the 2.4 million dollars coming over would be discovered."

"Damn, your take does make sense. All right, next tactic, which sounds like I'm desperate or paranoid. I feel like someone is watching me. It's probably because of the break-ins. If this were a TV cop show, we would hire a detective to review the various security cameras. I have no idea how many are around the exchange buildings and my parking garage. I don't think there are any on my block because Detective Williams told me so this morning."

"Not a bad idea. Let's start by asking Lou to let us see the videos from our building and the CBOE and see if he can get access to the BOTs and some of the local businesses. Problem with that is if the police are ahead of us and took them. If we're lucky, they keep them for at least a week and are digital, so the police won't have the only copy."

"I like that idea. It gives me something to do, and we can get started on it now." We were back in front of the CBOE exchange entrance and about to walk through the atrium to the office tower attached. We decided that Latesha is the better choice to ask the security staff of both buildings. She has a better business relationship with them, plus she may have some intel from watching the tapes with Deena earlier to know better what to ask for.

Latesha texted us during the walk to find her when we returned. She had news. The guy that Deena spoke to before she noticed her building access badge was missing was in several frames throughout the day loitering in various spots near building entrance doors of the plaza. There were no good shots of his face because he had a baseball cap pulled low over his face. The most interesting thing about the discovery is he is a short, small-boned, white man like Larry Katz. Only he wasn't Larry. Larry was also spotted in several frames in the office tower lobby and the horse plaza to the west of the building. He couldn't be confused because he wasn't wearing a cap and wore his bright orange U of I sweatshirt. Being a chronic pot smoker, regardless of location and time, Larry is well known by everybody who frequents the plaza.

Latesha said that *StreetWise* man was also called to view the videos, and he said that the unknown man was not only hanging around all day Monday and most of Tuesday but would periodically change his baseball hat. *StreetWise* man thinks he could be the guy who pushed Sammy and has been making a point to look out for and watch him. He added that he's not sure but thinks that guy got a haircut and wore clothes more like everybody else on Tuesday.

The police gave Latesha a screenshot of the unknown man and told me to call them if I recognize him, which I didn't because I could not see much of his head. Hector and the parking garage crew were being asked if they recognized him. They were in the process of reviewing videos from the building lobby between five thirty and seven thirty. They had to wait for Hector to come in for his shift. Susan would also be asked if she recognized the same man and Larry.

The big find was the tape from Monday from the video camcorder located by the garage entrance to the One Financial Place building across the street from where I park. It shows a small blond man getting into a cab, and the cab making a U-turn in the parking lot driveway and going in the same direction as my car not a minute after I pulled out and hit Congress on my way home with Susan. Because the cab driver partially pulled into the parking lot, there is a good shot of the cab's license plate and the man's profile. The police already initiated contact with the cab company to find the driver.

Billy looked hard at what could be viewed of the passenger. Joe already did, and neither recalled seeing the man or noticing any cab in particular when they escorted Susan and me to my car. They were both too focused on watching for Larry. Cabs frequent that block because it is a common drop-off point for the Metra train station next door and a good spot to pick up fares getting out of the exchanges and office buildings nearby. A lot of people cab it to the other two Metra stations, especially to the one that is about a mile away. There would be no reason to think twice about the cab picking someone up, turning around, and hitting the expressway.

I found it hard to believe that someone would actually follow me like on TV and in the movies. Even if it were only remotely possible, Oscar thought we needed to call our lawyers. He wanted someone with a relationship or experience investigating criminal cases to interview the cab driver. Oscar was concerned about the legal boundary of obstructing a case from my rights of obtaining information for a defense before being charged. He was also interested in learning how we could find out if Pär Ericsson was in Chicago or at least the US. He thought the best ploy was to entice the police to share that information but was not optimistic about the chances. He thought a law firm that had investigators for insurance fraud or a high-end criminal law practice might have the appropriate resources and hoped Scott could recommend one.

For lack of any other inspiration, I asked if the profile and better pictures of the small, blond man could be made for me to show the Metzkers. They would notice someone hanging around the building.

The phone in the conference room buzzed, and Oscar picked it up. He sighed and said we would come right over. After hanging up, he turned to me. "As if this day couldn't get any stranger. That was Elizabeth Baird. She contacted Paul Stein to inform him she is engaged by Susan to represent Benny's estate and the trust. Paul dropped a bombshell that she is to expect a substantial invoice to be paid immediately for consulting services rendered by Larry Katz. After hearing Susan's recap of the discussion with the police this morning, Elizabeth would like us to meet with her and Susan."

I was not surprised and half-expected this type of move. Billy thought it was hilarious and laughed. "Talk about strange bedfellows. Paul must be really desperate to go into cahoots with Larry. Larry's hard-earned reputation for creative, but ethically flawed business practices implies it's a safe bet that whatever they come up with is a partnership to get at Benny's assets. Larry's favorite form of negotiation is threatening to sue, bad publicity, or the like, which gives me an idea. What time is it? I want to make a few calls to London. We may need to use some of the same strategies," Billy announced.

Billy left for his office, chuckling. Oscar and I left the building and walked the few blocks to Elizabeth's office in the Sears Tower. Her firm occupies several floors near the top of the building. It has gorgeous views of Lake Michigan and a great cityscape of the various buildings going north. Elizabeth is a partner at a marquee firm with a clientele of old-money families, and, lately, former wives and girlfriends of various professional athletes. She is considered the best for family partnerships, trusts, and endowment funds. Divorce lawyers on the other side of the table like working with her. She devises solutions on the most tax-advantaged basis for all parties and labels her recommendations as 'wealth preservation,' which pushes the focus away from just financially screwing the contra party of her client. Benny's combined assets are below par for her client base, so she must be doing this as a favor for Oscar.

When we walked into her office, the first thing that struck me was that it is like being in the movies. Her office is fairly large, beautifully finished with several large vases of fresh-cut flowers and dozens of pictures of her with celebrities. Elizabeth is somewhere around sixty with perfectly coiffed light brown hair pushed back behind her ears to showcase her exquisite diamond earrings. I don't know much about high fashion, but I would not be surprised if her navy-blue knit suit and canary-yellow blouse with matching scarf were from designer boutiques like Chanel. She exudes warmth and has a twinkle in her sharp, blue eyes.

Susan was sitting in a chair around the small table that had a tea and coffee service laid out in what I guessed were Italian ceramic cups and service pieces. She looked ill, but it may be due to nicotine withdrawal. Elizabeth met us at the door to her office and pointed for us to join Susan at the table, and she followed. Susan shook her head, indicating bad news.

Oscar caught it and looked to Elizabeth. "I take it things aren't going without a hitch. What could have happened so quickly?"

Elizabeth paused. "We have had quite a few interesting developments. First, let me recap. Before I met Susan, I reviewed the various documents prepared by O'Doole. They are quite good and solid, but, as would be typical, didn't anticipate encroaching business obligations. Mr. Stein's trusts, living will, and other documents are all consistent that Susan is to be the executor of his estate and the trustee of his trust and legacy assets. Mr. Stein's real estate holdings go to Susan, and all residual assets are to be liquidated and contributed to the trust that has previously been established for the exclusive benefit of his sister.

"The trust is explicit on the types of expenses and living allowance that are to be available to Sharon Stein, how the trust assets are to be invested, what are allowable expenses for Susan, the tax accountant, and any legal services. Whoever drafted the agreement was anticipating some risk of pilfery because the trust is equally explicit that pre-approval from Susan is necessary, and receipts are to be provided to Susan to turn over to the tax accountant. Should Susan deem it appropriate to award Sharon a living allowance, it's clear what the conditions are and that the cash should go into a checking account in the name of her trust with no affiliated debit or credit cards. At the onset, the maximum monthly allowance is three thousand dollars to be paid in monthly increments and for no advances to be available unless Susan warrants an exception."

"So, he intentionally engineered his estate and trust to cut out the rest of his family. Three thousand dollars a month isn't enough for business loans to Paul or expensive luxuries," I said. "Is Paul Stein, Benny's brother, aware of this?"

Susan's snort confirmed he does. She was looking a little better with a malicious grin.

Elizabeth paused again. I notice lawyers all like the pregnant-pause thing when explaining something. "Yes, although he has not seen any of the documents. His information was based on what I discussed with him over the phone. He was most insistent on being given copies of the various documents. I was clear there's no legal compulsion for Susan to comply with that demand." She paused again. "But Paul seemed remarkably well-prepared for this news. He asserts that his brother owes a partnership around five million dollars for consulting services and intellectual property rights. He asserts that anything outside the scope of the existing trust for Sharon be liquidated to pay down that business debt. He further asserts that those expenses are personal liabilities of Benny, and therefore, must be paid before any of his assets can be allocated pursuant to the instructions of his various legacy documents."

205

"Okay, how safe of a bet is it that he or Larry Katz are behind the partnership? This is unbelievable! Do you know the name of this business? Is he prepared to submit proof of that claim?" I blurted.

Elizabeth turned to Oscar. "Susan gave me a vivid description of Paul Stein and the recent antics of Larry Katz." She nodded to Susan. "It was Susan's recommendation to invite you two here. Susan has concerns that these claims can't be summarily dismissed."

Now it was Oscar's turn to pause. "It may be productive to first provide some of the backdrop story. Mind you, much of this is anecdotal. Larry Katz is a local legend for legal malfeasance. He supposedly is trained as a lawyer and may have even practiced but now is disbarred. I don't know how much is true or a self-perpetuated urban myth. He has never been associated with any situation in a positive light." Oscar repeated the same stories we told the police two days earlier about some of Larry's business dealings.

"It seems that his working MO is to do much of his own legal work because the state laws only preclude him from providing legal services for compensation to other parties but not from him representing himself. This nuance is his most potent weapon. He has mastered the technique of filing substantial amounts of superfluous claims, at no cost to him, that require a significant investment in time and cash to deflect.

"One other thing. He'll run to the bar association to file an ethics complaint against an opposing attorney. I hear this is his most confounding strategy. I never heard any of them resulting in an unfavorable decision against the attorney, but it costs time and money to defend. This strategy has been effective in discouraging lawyers from taking cases that oppose him. I apologize if we inflicted this risk on you. I had no idea."

Elizabeth laughed with a gleam in her eyes. "Well, I haven't had a good challenge or an adversary I love to hate in a long time. It sounds like this bug needs to be squashed. I know a trick or two about encumbering assets and their forced liquidation. I can put the tricks I learned from celebrity divorce attorneys to good use."

"One more thing. Larry likes to threaten personal bodily harm, and I have heard stories about people who cross him having their cars vandalized. There's also a story about a clerk of his committing suicide that a lot of people think is pretty suspicious," I added.

"What?" asked Oscar.

"Yeah, I heard that, too. Larry had a clerk who was working in my crowd. I was in treasuries at the time. I always thought he was really a runner selling drugs. It was around when the Feds put some undercover guys in the pits, and they were coming down hard on asking people about what trades were legit versus prearranged to inflate trading account profits. There was a lot of attention on Larry. The day before the Feds were to interview his clerk, he jumped off his balcony. A lot of people think he was too drunk and stoned to climb over a four-foot railing by himself. They think Larry got him hammered and somehow picked him up and tossed him over to prevent him from testifying," Susan answered.

"How plausible is this story?" Oscar asked.

"I don't know, but I recall the clerk's parents not accepting the suicide theory, and a lot of people who knew him were skeptical that he had suicidal inclinations. It was well-circulated that the Feds were giving immunity to the first people who testified and putting a lot of pressure on the smaller players to cooperate." I turned to Elizabeth. "He's a little squirt, not bigger than I am. On his own, he's not much of a threat, but he does imply he knows people in organized crime, and he makes no attempt to curb his constant drug use during work hours. The combination does make people wonder."

Elizabeth's laugh sounded like a tinkling bell. "Well then, I'm going to have to invite him in on a day that BadAzz is here with his posse and introduce them."

"You know BadAzz, the rapper!" asked Susan. I was equally taken aback.

"Oh, yes. He has been a client for a long time. There's nothing he enjoys more than an opportunity to give a rich, white man a scare, especially those who think they are some sort of societal menace. He usually arranges it to be done in public like a club where a reporter also just happens to be. He has helped me out in similar situations. It helps foster his self-created reputation and stage name. Now then, before games, let's get down to business. How does Lough Key fit in, and how independent is Sharon?"

Susan perked up and sat upright in her chair. "Thanks, I'm not sure what I could do by myself. Sharon has neck and back pain that limits her mobility, but she can walk, go to school, and otherwise engage in a normal life as long as she doesn't overexert herself. Sharon would love to move out and have a place of her own. Sharon isn't a fan of Paul and his family and is tired of her mother. I don't know if she can drive. I think taxis and public transportation are a viable option, especially if she had money."

Elizabeth prodded for more. "Has she attended college, ever held a job, even done some volunteer work? That's important to paper a case that Sharon can function without support from her mother."

Susan nodded. "Oh, sure. Sharon is accepted at DePaul and wants a degree in some kind of art and psychology. It might take her longer than four years to get it, but I don't think too much longer. I know she's interested in going to grad school to be some kind of counselor. Benny offered to pay the tuition but straight to the school, and he'd decide what extras there would be like for books and stuff. He was really pissed the last time his mother spent money on a cruise when it was supposed to be for Sharon. He thought that Sharon moving on would prevent them from asking him for money to pad their lifestyle and force them to let Sharon grow up. They claim she can't take care of herself or move around much in the winter, but she does okay. She needs a little help when it's snowy or really icy, but so do lots of people with mobility challenges."

"Susan, would you be willing to have her live with you? It's the obvious question. Sharon is old enough to make that election," asked Elizabeth.

Susan sat straight up and stared. "I guess, I don't know. I never thought about it. I mean we're friendly but not close. There would be a lot to talk about first with Sharon. Wouldn't they say I'm not qualified being a recovering addict and all?"

"Not if she's an adult with full mental capacities. Her physical issues aren't life-threatening, and it sounds like she can manage them. From what you have described, Mrs. Stein and her other son's family have compromised their case to be a better steward of Sharon and her assets. It will be hard to argue that case since Benny took great pains to make you the trustee and to circumvent them from controlling the money. You have on your side that you were a highly-paid professional for many years with enough investments and other assets earned and managed by you to be able to retire early. They can't prove you have an addiction problem or when it commenced. All they can point to is that you took it upon yourself to seek treatment for a condition that was brought upon by excessive strain from your work. That's hardly tabloid news or anything shocking now. In fact, you may even appear more responsible given how you have managed your life lately."

"Really?" asked Susan.

"Yes. What you're being treated for is a confidential medical record. The facts as I know them don't warrant a court order to confirm otherwise."

Susan clearly liked that answer. "Well, let's say I'd consider speaking to Sharon about cohabitating. Maybe not roomies, but in the same building and seeing her daily and being available on a regular basis for whatever support she needs."

Elizabeth nodded. "Good answer. Part of your position is to stage Sharon to function independently as an adult, and you would facilitate that by bridging her toward that goal. You would obviously follow the recommendations of her doctors. All right, now that we have that settled, Oscar, what's Lough Key's position in this?"

Oscar shook his head. "It's a mess. We're sitting on about 2.4 million dollars in cash that passed the AML scrub of a major money center bank and the regulatory compliance due diligence standards. There doesn't appear to be any missed steps on the part of his accountant for failing to report a foreign bank account on tax returns, either. However, that doesn't deflect our vulnerability. The cash was wired from a bank account in Benny's name at an HSBC bank located in Gibraltar, which is a reputed money-laundering cesspool. We have no information on how or when Benny received those funds."

Oscar continued with a recap of the past two days' events, including the various threats made by Nivar. "Frankly, I'm very concerned about potential regulatory or criminal charges pursued against Lane or the firm. I am not worried about the claims Paul, and I suspect, Larry Katz have on the 2.4 million dollars. That can easily be addressed by putting the money in an escrow account under your direction, Elizabeth, until a court renders a decision. Our attorney referred us to a London firm with a New York office that has a specialized practice in foreign banking and money-laundering laws. We're also getting a recommendation for an attorney here who can represent us on any criminal charges that may be levied. The most unsettling aspect is there's no path for us to obtain information directly. The police have access to more information, but that means the matter has escalated to federal law enforcement agencies. There's no requirement for them to share information with us until charges have been filed. By that time, it's too late to deflect full-blown indictments complete with regulatory disclosures and probably a fair amount of press in the financial newspapers. I'm confident we'll be found not complicit in any type of wrongdoing, but that can still take years and at great cost."

"I have a question," said Susan. "Can they stop me from selling Benny's other assets or taking money from his other bank accounts for Sharon? What about the house he and I own in Florida, is that up for grabs, too? Lane looked it up, and the county clerk has it registered in both of our names."

I jumped in and added how the house in Florida is registered with the Dade County Clerk. Because it is joint in its entirety, and my understanding is nobody can put a lien on it unless both Susan and Benny had a liability to the same party. I hoped I was right.

Elizabeth went to her desk and looked up the same website I did from the Dade County Clerk's Office and confirmed that the house in Florida was Susan's free and clear and safe from former claimants of Benny's. She asked Susan what the addresses were of Benny's other real estate, and after a few minutes of frustration, informed us that Benny had titled his two rental properties in Chicago the same way. She said that a lot of what otherwise could be held up are assets in Benny's name. Nobody knew the extent to which Sharon's trust was already funded, but that would be off-limits to any third-party claims.

Elizabeth frowned and looked to Susan. "The timing is interesting. He commissioned his last trust and will and changed the title of his Chicago properties the same month, which was about three months before you moved down to Florida with him and bought a house there. People aren't usually that diligent unless they have something like a serious illness or a pending divorce. Was he worried about something? You never gave any indication you knew this."

Susan sat quietly and finally blurted. "I'm sorry, but I need to smoke. I have one of those smokeless ashtrays. Do you mind if I sit in the chair against the wall away from everybody?"

Elizabeth told her it was okay, and Susan moved. "Benny didn't seem worried about dying but about change. None of us thought about Sharon as ever being an adult. What centered around her at the house was school stuff plus taking care of her rehab. There was never any discussion of what Sharon's life would be like as an adult and after she graduated. It hit Benny last summer how they were all babying her, and she was angry. Sharon wanted to dance and have a few drinks at some wedding. She did the radical thing of not sitting at the family table and hung out with people her own age. Sharon's mom was really pissed. I heard Benny yelling at her on the phone that her real problem was that she'd lose her martyr status at her temple and in the neighborhood. Benny thought that Beverly keeping Sharon at home and dependent on her not only justified stringing Benny along for cash infusions but gave her a face-saving way not to be able to afford the lifestyle of her friends.

"Then there was the floor basically shutting down for everybody but brokers. That took away the foundation of his routine. After the last crash, so many of us left the business entirely or moved to places like Idaho and Colorado to trade remotely. Benny and I both did very well during the last quarter of 2008 and the first bit of 2009, but a lot of people lost their jobs or tapped out. We know a bunch of guys who filed for disability claims from insurance companies and can't go near the floor or the business to retain those benefits. There aren't too many people left to joke around with or watch each other's back during trading. Late last year, Paul started calling at least weekly begging and sometimes even demanding money for something to do with real estate. His mother was even more obnoxious with her daily dialing for dollars.

"My coke habit got worse, and I wasn't maintaining anymore. He said we had to get out because there was no reason to stay in Chicago. It was a bad environment for both of us. In his mind, there was no reason to stay. When Benny decides something, he acts on it, and he is... or was a very good business manager."

"Were Benny and Sharon close? What was the dynamic of their relationship?" asked Elizabeth.

"No, they weren't close. Sharon is twenty years younger. Benny's mother insisted it was all Benny's fault she got hurt. Paul was at Lake Geneva the same day with his snobby friends trying to fit in with the people who have real money. Benny didn't go because it wasn't his scene. Beverly insists that Benny should have gone to chaperone Sharon since he knew some of the people she was with because their fathers traded on the Board. For some reason, Paul gets a pass. Benny knew it was all bullshit. She can't really think Benny should have spent his weekend with a bunch of teenagers he didn't know, on their boat, and without an invitation. As time went on, it got worse. It was a way to guilt Benny into giving them money. Benny did like and care about Sharon, he just couldn't stand being near his other relatives and having the same whiny conversations."

Susan looked like she had said all she could.

"Okay. This is useful to set the stage. Oscar, I think your suggestion of putting the cash from Benny's trading account with you in escrow in an account our firm controls. I think it would be wise to do that today. Can you do it now into an account with our firm? We can transfer the funds later into a bank account in the estate's name. It may be possible to have our bank set up an account by tomorrow morning. Susan, we have bank resolutions and signature cards here in the office. You need to sign a couple of forms, and we can be on our way," Elizabeth instructed.

"It can be done that fast?" I asked.

"Uh-huh. We have lots of experience moving cash out of joint accounts within a moment's notice and have a process all set up with our bank. I can't guarantee it will secure that cash from other claims, but there's that possession-is-nine-tenths-of-the-law thing going for us, plus it insulates you from an injunction if the money isn't in your custody. One of the reasons why I think it's imperative to do it now is that your firm has not been charged with anything or given reason to believe there's anything other than an ongoing murder investigation. It sounds like you don't know if that may change

213

or when. Doing this now under my advice provides you some protection.

"The next thing we have to do is catalog the trust's and Benny's assets. I'll have an associate start on that today. We should be able to make pretty good progress from referencing the source documents of his tax returns. Last question. Is there any reason why Sharon may need a cash disbursement in the immediate future? That may complicate things."

Susan said she didn't know and couldn't think of a reason why Sharon would need a significant sum shortly.

While I called the office and spoke to Billy to initiate moving all 2.4 million dollars out, Oscar and Elizabeth continued the discussion. They agreed, insisting that Paul first produce a stack of documents to substantiate his claim would be an effective postponement ploy. She felt that the date of the formation of the legal entity with the alleged claims would be as interesting as the invoices and consulting agreements they would have to submit. My take is that if Sharon was not in dire need of cash, Elizabeth was all for stringing this along for years to the point where Paul, and possibly Larry, run out of steam.

Elizabeth buzzed her admin to bring the standard new bank account forms for Susan to complete and had Susan hand over her driver's license to be copied. The three of us left her office around three o'clock just in time to get back after the stock options market close. Pretty much all of the markets had closed, and the trading community was getting ready to finish the day's processing and shut down for the day. It felt so strange to be isolated from my old routine.

Chapter 10

The three of us walked back to the office. Susan was in a better mood, but Oscar was pensive and preoccupied. In the lobby of the Board of Trade building, several people came up to Susan to offer condolences. Most addressed her as DZY or Dizzy. It occurred to me that I don't think of her that way anymore. Oscar and I went ahead to the office and left Susan with a group of three traders.

Kayreen was still manning the front desk with a book opened. She informed us that Billy asked us to go straight to his office and said that Latesha said she could leave if we didn't need her. Oscar wished her luck on her test and told her it was okay to go. I went to the kitchen to get bottles of water and joined the two of them in Billy's office.

Billy's office is blandly furnished with traditional wood furniture. His back is to the window, and he faces the door. His desk is L-shaped with the section to the side covered in monitors of screens tracking various news services and market data. He has another on the front of his desk he uses for emails and the like and is the one that flashes alerts for extreme market movements or an account in trouble. Billy and his family are avid skiers. His office walls are adorned by family photos at various ski resorts and a large travel posture of people skiing down a mountain in Chili.

Oscar gave Billy the highlights of our meeting with Elizabeth. He ended by saying he wanted to get the law firm handling the potential AML problems to give their opinion on moving the money into an escrow account. His concern was that if those funds were determined to be illegally obtained, they could be subject to a claw-back and have to be returned even if many years later. Billy wasn't concerned and liked the idea of moving the money out of our firm and off our books. He did want some sort of letter of instructions from Elizabeth and nodded when Oscar told him it should already be here via an email. By this time, Susan had joined us.

Billy waited for her to sit down and light up. "Well, group, I struck paydirt. I caught Melvin Bunter in London before he left for dinner. He sounded like he already had a couple of pints in him and was loving an opportunity to tell one of his endless stories. He's crossed paths with Nivar and thinks he's one of the less reputable banker types of his acquaintances, which is saying a lot given who Bunky knows."

Susan shot up. "Wait, Bunky, as in the guy who has the lock on almost all the good paper out of London? The South African guy who's always drunk?"

Billy leaned forward. "The one and the same." It struck me that Bunky wasn't the only one who was going to indulge in telling long stories this afternoon.

"Okay, I bite, who's Bunky? I have a headache. Can we keep it short and get to what he knows about Nivar?" I asked to move it along.

"Well, it turns out Nivar and Bunky are kindred spirits of sorts. Only Bunky has amazing good luck and is an adventurer while Nivar sounds like he keeps missing his grasp on the proverbial brass ring."

"Billy, get to it," I snapped. The way his eyes were dancing, I was glad nobody had any scotch in the office for Billy to sip while he told this tale.

"This has to be savored to appreciate. Relax, you have to hear the whole story. You'll be glad you did. It turns out they both went to the same university and are bastard sons sired by a wealthy person of nobility. Bunky's father is some sort of fourth son of an English lord who had to make his own fortune, which he did in South Africa. He made a killing in diamonds but also liked playing English lord of the manor on a coffee farm. His wife didn't take to Africa, which left his father free to carry on with a South African woman as a common-law wife. He had children with her, one being Bunky, but never married her because he never divorced his wife. The story goes that Bunky's mother came from a nice family and had no idea he was already married. Don't raise your eyebrow at me, Laney, I'm just sharing what I have heard over the years."

"Whose last name do the poor darlings have?" I asked skeptically.

"An irrelevant detail, dear. In any event, Bunky's father did stake at least the boys to a first-class education in London, and Bunky was smart enough to get accepted into the London School of Economics. The problem was that Bunky could never be on par with the British upper crust and be a member of all the posh clubs of the high-finance elite over there. So, being like his father, he went abroad to seek his fortune. In those days, he was a salesman for oil field equipment. His favorite mode of ingratiation was providing illicit booze and parties in Arab countries. One night, he hosted a huge blow-out at the penthouse suite of a very tall hotel in Kuwait. It was still going strong at four in the morning when he looked out the window and saw armed vehicles approaching the capital city. Assuming they weren't ordered by the Emir, Benny woke up the male members of his family who were passed out at the penthouse. While the men were calling the Kuwaiti army and Air Force to duty, Bunky went to the palace and got the immediate first family out of the country by flying some in his corporate jets and got planes organized for the others. He's the one who called the UK ambassador, his college friends at Goldman, and a couple of the banks that had assets of Emir and his echelon. The story goes that the London bankers were instrumental in notifying the UK and US armed forces of the Iraqi invasion so quickly."

"Which explains why he has the inside track on the best paper coming out of London," said Susan. "It never made sense to any of us why he was always associated with certain types of orders and customers. He doesn't do anything but drink, but everybody has to kiss his ass to get access to his flow."

"Exactly," beamed Billy.

Oscar was listening patiently but was not in the mood for one of Billy's storytelling hours. "So how is this relevant to our situation?"

"Bunky told me today that Nivar Amirmoez is the illegitimate son of a nephew or cousin of the Emir of Kuwait and an Indian servant. He has the double whammy of having a dark complexion and being a bastard. Bunky found this out when they were at university together when Nivar was drunk. Bunky figured out that in spite of Nivar being educated at private boarding schools in the UK, typical of many wealthy sons from oil-rich countries, he wasn't considered a peer. Bunky thought it was odd that Nivar didn't understand how lucky he was that his father's family just didn't send his mother and him packing back to India. Instead, he was bitter about being trained to be nothing more than a highly-trained servant. Nivar considered his education as a means for his family to get cheaper talent managing some of their banking functions. Bunky says Nivar is very smart and a gifted financier but could never get into the upper echelon within the white London bankers or their various Arab clients.

"So instead, Nivar took a high-level job with a small Austrian bank that was acquired by a German one. He and Bunky met up again in Frankfurt. By this time, Nivar had developed a cocaine habit and a taste for other Western vices. Bunky thinks his role initially had something to do with establishing lines of credit for European companies doing business in the Middle East. They went out one night, and Nivar was complaining about not making as much as his peers at the bigger banks and never getting to be a C-Level executive because he is dark and Germans being openly racist. He was also resentful of what he considered the socialistic compensation structure of the bank that was below par for his education and revenue production.

"Which brings us to the present. EuroCredit Bank is in the process of being acquired by the second largest German bank conglomerate. The due diligence for the acquisition is being done now. Bunky heard it's not going well due to EuroCredit

Bank having some sketchy-sounding joint ventures with banks in the Caribbean, Netherland Antilles, and Gibraltar. A lot of them are under Nivar's management. Here's the part you'll like, Laney... Bunky has met the elusive John William Henry Carrington III with Nivar!"

Billy gave me his best ah-hah look and raised his eyebrow during this dramatic pause. Honestly, I love the guy, but I wanted to smack him like when we were kids. "Get on with it, Billy. We're all hooked," I prodded.

"Well, the story continues that John William Whatever's specialization is alternative investments designed to vanish into thin air at a moment's notice. Bunky thinks his clients are mostly the Russian mob and Pacific Basin cyber crooks. Bunky said the one consistent story that floats around is that this guy sets up online gambling sites in the Cayman Islands. The sites offer crazy odds and pay for a while, then once they have access to a critical mass of cash and client credit cards, they disappear. New ones subsequently pop up in different countries. He also sets up legitimate transportation companies with small jets that supposedly move specialty items like organs for transplants and rare art and jewels that their customers want to insulate from the risk of larger carriers. Some of the jets are geared to provide luxury and confidential transportation with personal security for the super-rich and supposedly have a client roster of A-list celebrities and royalty.

"Funny thing is their routes tend to be obscure locations with minimal government oversight like Greek and Caribbean islands. They even have specially equipped jets to land in remote places in Eastern Russia. Bunky heard the planes are some sort of front for moving arms and drugs. These companies also tend to evaporate when under official scrutiny. Every once in a while, a plane gets confiscated, but there's never any cargo, the crew knows nothing, and no other parties of the operation can be found. The occasional bad luck is merely the cost of doing business, and another is formed.

"The genius of these ventures, especially the transportation company, is that on anybody's books, they look legit. The transportation company obtains its jets from hedge funds and private equity investors who buy small shares of a company that makes the purchase. The company pays exorbitant returns and produces very little in terms of financial reporting. Everybody is happy as long as the fat checks keep rolling in. The end result for this guy's clients is perfectly clean money in a legitimate bank. For Nivar, Bunky surmises the other advantage is they must have a way to funnel bank cash in the form of loans at way above-market interest rates. Nivar may be getting some skin on the back-end separate from his bank salary."

"Is there any way Bunky can get a line or contact information for John Carrington that we can turn over to the police?" I asked. "This is too crazy to believe."

"I doubt it. Bunky said that he wasn't sure that's his real name. His last anecdote is that he thinks he saw him at an FX conference for hedge funds in London. There was a group of investment managers from the Dutch public pension fund. You know it's the largest in the world and has a reputation of being able to invest in assets other than traditional stocks, bonds, and real estate. Bunky thinks it was the same person, but he was dressed in grungy jeans and a band t-shirt. He was sporting long hair, didn't have glasses, and was speaking with an Australian accent. Bunky thought he was trying to fit in with the Dutch. They all dress like college kids and love to party. Bunky had to leave and didn't get a chance to confirm his impression."

"All very interesting, but I'm not sure it's useful to our cause. I'll call the New York firm and see if they can do something with this type of intelligence. Frankly, I'm not optimistic that, even if any of it can be verified, it will extract Lane from the investigation of Benny's financial antics," Oscar surmised.

I didn't have time to be disappointed because my cell rang. It was Detective Williams notifying me that they interviewed the cab driver who picked up the blond man we saw in the video. The cab driver said he had an accent but didn't know what kind other than it wasn't Spanish or Asian. The cab driver stated he was told to follow a gold Mercedes station wagon, which he did to Oak Park. He was easy to remember because he claimed to be following friends and didn't know the address of where they were going. The fare said he hadn't yet set up his phone for the US to communicate with them by calling. The cab driver thought the whole situation was odd, including how he dropped the man off at a corner and not in front of a house. The driver didn't remember the corner, but the general location and route are near your building. The man paid cash, which means there is still no way to know who he is.

"Hey, where are you staying tonight?" asked Detective Williams. "Can you stay with friends?"

"I have to think about that. I could stay with Billy and his family, but I don't want to. Can't a policeman be posted at my house?" The others in the room were concerned. I shook my head and held up my hand.

"No, we don't do that unless it's an extreme case, and then we move you to a secure location. You also live in Oak Park, so you wouldn't be on our watch anyway. I'm sure we can arrange for the Oak Park police to make a point of patrolling around your block more, but I think a better idea is to clear out for a few days, at least until we get a positive ID on this guy."

"Um, I have to think about this. This is a lot for me to process. It doesn't seem real. I need to think. Thanks for notifying me."

"Fine, but call me after you make up your mind, no matter what you decide. This is very real, and you should be around lots of people. Pay attention as you go about your business. Avoid being alone, seriously," said Detective Williams.

"I will. Are there any other updates?"

"Not on our end. Why don't I call you tomorrow to check in, okay?" said Detective Williams.

Detective Williams being nice was not comforting. I thanked him and agreed to keep him posted on my whereabouts. When I hung up, I shared the information with the others.

"Unbelievable! Okay, you and Fred are moving in with us. Susan, you're welcome to join. Lane, this isn't something to argue over," Billy ordered.

"I have to agree with Bill. I can't see any valid reason to object. If nothing else, it will let all of us get some sleep if we know you're safe," Oscar confirmed.

"What about your safety? What about the Metzkers? I don't know... I don't see how this is really that much safer. Whoever it is, hasn't tried to contact me in person. In fact, he seems to be avoiding that. I don't want to put anybody else in harm's way if he does decide to approach me. Susan, I'm sorry, but I think you may want to consider going to a hotel."

"Don't worry about me, but I think they are right. You should move in with Bill. I don't mind going to a hotel. I can also stay at your place or the upstairs apartment to keep an eye on the building and your neighbors."

"Lane, this isn't the time to be stubborn. Seriously, what can you do to protect the Metzkers?" challenged Billy. "Besides, you don't know if he'd have made direct contact if you had been alone. You have been either here or with Susan this week."

"I have an idea," said Oscar. "I'll make a call to Elizabeth to see if she can recommend a security company that provides personal protection. I'm hoping she can refer one that her clients use. I'm making the call now." He got up and left the room.

"On a similar note, I'm calling my handyman to have him change your locks and fix your window tonight," said Billy.

"Who?" I asked.

"You know him. Danny. He's the McDermott kid who lives across the street from me. He went to the University of Michigan and majored in the classics or Greek philosophy. His parents weren't going to fund graduate school. For employment, he started a business putting up and taking down Christmas lights and lawn decorations for twenty-five grand a shot and set up a landscaping and handyman business. Connie likes him, and he seems to be doing well. He's got something like three trucks now. Anyway, I'm sure I can get him to drive over to your place tonight and do something about your locks and fix your back window."

"What internet provider do you use?" asked Susan. "Mine has a home security package that's great and pretty cheap. I don't remember how long it took to get it once I ordered it, but it didn't take long. Maybe Danny can take a look to see if you need any hardware. I think you can buy it from them. Sorry to butt in, but it seems like an easy fix, especially if this is going to be a problem for a while."

"Genius idea!" said Billy. "We should have thought of that. Lane, do you know if that's possible?"

It turned out that I have the same ISP as Susan, and she started looking up a description of the home security features on her phone. We were wondering how it would work in a building with three residences and if someone can cut the cables or somehow disable it from the outside.

I agreed to have Danny go over to my house, and while Billy was discussing logistics on the phone, Oscar returned. He explained that Elizabeth's firm has an arrangement with a private security firm. Oscar asked for them to send a person over to my building right away. He thought another could be required at Billy and Connie's house and was to call back if that was what we wanted. I decided to stay at my place and felt better if we got better locks, and I gave in about having a private bodyguard at my house. I didn't want to impose any risk of harm to Billy's family or worry Connie. Oscar wasn't happy but did concede that if we had a bodyguard at my building, it wasn't fair to scare the Metzkers more by me being gone too. Billy didn't participate in that discussion because he was on the phone.

Billy hung up. "Danny's on his way. He can change locks and fix your window. He suggested taking a look at your screen door, too. His thought is that most are easy to open with a credit card or small screwdriver. He can pick up a standard size screen door and secure it with a better lock on his way over. I told him about the idea of your ISP's home security system, and he said it was a good one. He suggested, given our sense of urgency, to go with them for equipment, but he said he'd canvas the building and participate in the discussions with the install team. Sorry, Lane, but I didn't think you would be up for that."

I sighed. "Okay, good. Having a plan makes me feel better, less helpless. I'm going home now. I should call the Metzkers and let them know we're installing a security upgrade, and I'll explain it when I get back. Damn! I'll be stuck having dinner with them. I can't take that tonight."

"Can we order takeout and bring it up to their place. You can duck out, and I'll stay and hang out with them?" offered Susan.

"You wouldn't mind?"

"No, I'd like to. I get a kick out of them. It lets me be useful, and it's not like I'm so busy. I'd like a chance to pay it forward or whatever," Susan shyly responded. She broke my heart. She looked and sounded like a little kid.

We agreed that was the plan once Susan committed to Oscar to stay in Mrs. Brown's unit with me. Oscar insisted she let Fred out and not me, which I pretended not to hear. Susan confirmed contact information with Billy and Oscar while I called the Metzkers to inform them of the plan. It was easy to distract Mr. M from any explanation of why to expect a handyman to fix my door and window when I told him I was bringing his favorite sausage and peppers from Salernos for dinner. I asked him to have Mrs. M make a salad, and tell her we are coming with dinner and wine. He was too elated to ask any questions other than confirming Susan was coming. I was grateful to get him because Mrs. M would not have let me off that easy.

I wasn't in the mood to talk to anybody and damn well wasn't up for questions or sympathy. I ducked out the fire exit door and walked down the stairs to avoid the elevators and general office. Susan and Billy met me in the lobby. Angie and Clayton were by the revolving doors and called us over to ask how things were going. Billy reported that the police found the cab driver and had other snapshots of information but still didn't have a solid ID on the man we presume broke into our office. Angie said she heard that everybody who looked at the security videos said the same thing—there were no shots of his face to get a description of him.

Virgil parked my car on the ground floor near the cashier station. Before he pulled it out, he said essentially the same thing. They could identify a small man hanging around who most thought was blond, but nobody remembered seeing his face. He asked Susan if she was staying with me and seemed to like the answer. I was getting pissed and was not going to turn the wheel over to Susan, not that she gave any indication of wanting to drive. I was taking a stand with Billy and told him to shut up.

Once on the Eisenhower, I asked Susan to call Salernos to place a takeout order for four servings of sausage and peppers, one eggplant parmesan, and one shrimp Alfredo plus whatever she wanted. She opted for eggplant parmesan. I ordered the extra sausage and peppers because I had no idea if Danny and the bodyguard would need to eat.

Susan next called Sharon. That conversation did not go well. Beverly took the phone from Sharon, and I could hear screaming. It didn't stop for at least three minutes. Susan never said a word once Beverly commandeered the phone and elected to hang up rather than speak.

"What was that about?" I asked.

"That was Benny's devoted mother. She seriously needs to be put on meds. Her son is dead, f-ing murdered, and all she cares about is his money. She doesn't give a damn about his funeral. She demanded I turn over to her, like tomorrow, a list of his assets, accounts, and passwords. She said the most vile things to me. I don't get it. She should know by now I can't be pushed around, and she has no say. She really sounds crazy. It makes me wonder what's going on and what her plan would be if Benny didn't die."

"Do you think she's afraid of what would happen if Sharon moved out? It could be that it would be the equivalent of losing two children for her."

"No, she sounds like she's desperate for cash and needs it now. Sharon wasn't mentioned either. It puts a different spin on whether I want to stay in town."

"Why?"

"It's a feeling I have that it would be abandoning Sharon in her family prison. Like she can't take a call without her mother listening. It's not like they knew to expect my call, and this happens almost every time we speak. I can always tell the few times her mother isn't in the room with her because she's whispering."

"What do you think you're going to do? You seem to be doing so well with your recovery down in Florida?"

"Yes and no. I have to rethink everything with Benny being gone. It would be too lonely to be in Florida without him. My problem isn't so much avoiding coke but staying busy. That's what got me in real trouble."

"What do you mean?"

"Well, I guess you could describe me as a functioning coke addict for ten or so years. I wasn't self-medicating or hooked from partying too hard. In fact, I'm like doing great compared to most women I meet in a program. Coke helped me stay sharp and compete on the floor back in the days when that was necessary. I didn't crash until there wasn't an adrenaline rush from the job anymore."

"That sounds counter-intuitive to be able to sustain for so long."

"Not really if you ever tried it. I think it must have the same effect as the drugs they give kids with ADHD that are really prescription speed. Coke helped me hyper-focus. I could see and hear more clearly the entire crowd and keep track of every order in my mind. I miss the physical rush from the top of my scalp surging down my arms and spine when the opening bell rang on the floor. After the close, I'd relax with a blunt. The nicotine and pot brought me down with no jitters. At night, coke let me party without getting sloppy or stupid. Way better than booze. It's hard to describe but food, music... God, everything is better with coke. It's like you're more alive. Everything is exuberant and gives you a rush."

"How do you replace that, or do you? Most people I know who are recovering have a motive like being a good parent. Why did you quit if you don't mind me asking?"

Susan chuckled softly. "No, I never wanted to be a wife and mother with crying babies and a husband wanting some and teed off 'cuz money is tight, and sex isn't fun anymore. I don't know what I'll do. Leaving Chicago seemed like a good idea. Benny and I did everything this town has to offer. We had the best seats to the Bulls' games during the Michael Jordan era, saw any concert we wanted, were regulars at all the clubs and upscale restaurants, and were even members of the zoo and aquarium. Then everything slowed down, and the buzz was lost. I started using more then. It all caught up with me, and I wasn't functioning. Instead of feeling charged, I was in a haze and sick. I don't miss the coke as much as I miss the energy level of my routine. I thought that moving to Florida would force me to find a new lifestyle. We should have picked someplace else. Everybody down there's either one hundred or barely getting by or is big-time involved with drugs."

"Do you think you'll move back here?"

"I'm lucky that I don't have to make a decision right away, now that I know what the deal is with the house and all. I guess I have to see what will happen with Sharon. I don't know."

We had arrived at Salernos, and I got out to pick up our order and to say hello to the bartender, who is an old friend from high school. My grandmother taught several of the original Salernos' kids. My family has been regulars since it was a small pizza joint with Formica tables, plastic molded chairs, and the menu written with magic markers on round cardboard pizza trays tacked on the walls. Now it has printed menus, large dining rooms with oak tables and chairs, and the wait-staff isn't all teenage relatives. They still have tripe on the menu, and it still grosses me out when I see it.

When I returned to the car, Susan and I agreed we would put the food in the oven to stay warm, and she would take Fred outside. She volunteered to go upstairs with Fred to give the Metzkers a heads-up and to attempt to keep them there with the promise we would bring dinner up shortly. I had to assess what I wanted Danny to fix and figure out accommodations for the bodyguard. Elizabeth had texted me during the drive to inform me of his name and sent me a picture. He wouldn't be far behind us. The eerie feeling returned. I should be going for a long walk to get some air and decompress, not rendezvousing with professional bodyguards and having home security systems installed.

After I got organized for my two visitors, I packed a bag and got my mail. I was getting a box packed for Fred when Danny arrived. He is your basic, nice-looking twenty-something-year-old man with baggy jeans, a gray zip-up, and Blackhawks' cap. After saying hello, he asked about my dog and was relieved when I told him he was staying with the upstairs neighbor.

After inspecting my two porch doors, he explained that I might as well not have a lock. He showed me how easy it is to open my exterior door. He told me a couple of stories of home invaders using the same technique of breaking the top window of an otherwise solid wood door and reaching in to unlock the door. He said that someone he knew had a bolt lock with the key nailed to the other side of the door frame, and the intruder found it and still got in. He brought a replacement exterior door and a couple of locks for the interior porch door to my kitchen. The locks were a stop-gap measure since there was no evidence that my keys or locks were compromised. Danny thought a better solution was to replace the interior door with one that has a grated window that he could install tomorrow. He thought that was more practical than fixing the window and changing the locks of the present door. I agreed to his suggestions and left him because my front doorbell rang.

A mountain of a black man dressed in black pants and pullover windbreaker was at my door. His large head was shaved except for the thin beard that formed a triangle border around his mouth. He was way larger than my friend who played defensive line for the Detroit Lions. Jamal Roper introduced himself and showed me his ID. I noticed then that he had two duffel bags with him. I invited him to the dining room to sit down, and as we walked, I told him I never engaged his kind of service before and didn't know what to do. He actually looked friendly and comforting when he smiled, which helped a lot.

Jamal explained that he was going to canvas my building after he asked me questions regarding the tenants. After I gave him the low-down on the Metzkers and Mrs. Brown's middle-unit apartment, I introduced him to Danny. Danny was definitely impressed by Jamal, although I am not sure if it was due to his profession or size. Danny repeated his recommendations for my two back doors, which Jamal thought were good first steps, except for the security system from my ISP. Feeling foolish, I asked Jamal if he could recommend a security system that could be installed quickly and not crazy expensive. I told him I liked the idea of being able to see my house from my phone.

Danny said he did something similar for his house and business building, and it is linked to his smartphone. He pulled his phone out of his pocket and opened the app. I could see the exterior to the alley behind his buildings, and he could zoom in on views of his windows and doors. He showed me how he could elect and change settings from his phone and gets alerts if his building entry points are being tampered.

Jamal was nodding and seemed to concur. He mentioned it is a great solution for most people, and he knows it can be configured for multi-residence buildings such as mine. He ended commenting that solution is great for normal break-and-entry protection but not if a professional wants to inflict harm. He also said the fundamental flaw is it is reliant on a working internet connection. We resolved Jamal would spec out my building and have the tech team from his company make a recommendation. Danny would participate in the setup and teaching me how to use it.

Danny went to his truck to retrieve my new storm door, while Jamal and I went to the dining room to confer on my situation. I explained the events of the past couple of days and what provoked his engagement. Jamal listened intently, but I got the impression he was trying to gauge my mental state more than following the details of my narrative. When I finished, he asked to walk around the building. I finished packing Fred's box and checked on Danny, who was getting off his phone.

"That was my mom. She said Mrs. Keagan asked me to make sure you don't need me to stay the night. I told her about Jamal, but she said to check with you anyway."

I sighed. "No, I don't see there's anything more for you to do besides helping me with the new security system and replacing my doors. In fact, it would make me more anxious if you did hang around. Thanks, though. I got takeout of the world's best sausage with peppers pasta. You can have it here or take it with you unless you want to come upstairs and join my geriatric neighbors and my dog for dinner. I understand if you want to take a hard pass on the later."

He laughed. "No, thanks anyway. I'll take you up on your offer of taking dinner with me to go. I should be done in an hour, and I'm hoping the worst of the traffic will be over by then. I want to hit Menards by me before it closes to buy your door. I called, and they have something that's a good stop-gap measure until one like we discussed can be ordered and delivered."

Jamal rounded the building and walked up my backyard steps. "Well, this won't be too bad, and I don't think we need to have anybody else here watch the place. We can secure the front door to the building lobby, your front and back doors with a simple door alarm for each, which are fine for now. They are about twenty dollars at most home improvement stores."

Jamal explained further they are like car alarms that emit a loud noise when a door is opened. He thought that would be sufficient until a more encompassing solution is installed, especially given the building is rarely unoccupied, and he is spending the night. We agreed that Jamal would run to the local Ace Hardware to obtain a couple of door alarms while Danny finished working on my back door. He got back as Danny was packing up. They exchanged contact info and made tentative plans for the next day.

Back in the kitchen of my apartment, I opened the fridge and told Jamal to help himself. He was more interested in my coffee maker and my stash of Dunkin' Donuts coffee but really perked up when I started pulling the Salernos' dinners out of the oven. He was surprised and laughed when I told him I ordered two extra sausage and pepper dinners because I wasn't sure how many were coming.

Jamal took my bags up to Mrs. Brown's apartment with me while I had the rest of the Salernos' orders. He then followed me up to the third floor holding the food because we thought it would be a good idea to introduce him to the Metzkers, Susan, and Fred.

I have to say he knew how to handle an awkward and frightening situation. Mrs. M answered the door and was rendered speechless by the enormity of Jamal. Jamal didn't pay any notice, asked where he could set the food down, and if he could check out their back porch and its entrance. He explained it was part of the service package offered to all clients and not because there was a reason for alarm. After introducing himself, he told a funny story about how he was looking forward to this job because his last was watching over the birthday party for some of the Chicago Bulls' children. He kept moving and talking and didn't allow anybody an opportunity to engage in any form of conversation. Fred was fascinated and followed him around from a respectful distance behind Jamal.

231

When Jamal returned to the living room, he sat down and held his hand out for Fred to approach. "That's some dog, good thing he's friendly. He is, right? He can't be much of a guard dog that your place got broke into with a clean getaway."

"Well, you did come in with me smelling of food, but for the most part, you're right about him being friendly. The only thing I can figure as to why he didn't stir last night is, besides him being a very sound sleeper that snores loudly, whoever it was must have taken great care not to make any noise. The police think that's possible. Speaking of the police, I have to call Detective Williams with an update."

Jamal remained until my part of the call concluded. Detective Williams asked to speak to Jamal, and the conversation was mostly one-sided on the part of Detective Williams. After hanging up and giving me back my phone, Jamal said he was going downstairs to install the door alarms. He repeated several times that none of us are to go out the front door tonight, and that he will be walking around the building and up all night if we need anything. He asked if he could show me something downstairs, but that was a ruse to remove me from earshot of the Metzkers because he suggested Susan and I block Mrs. Brown's back door by moving her kitchen table and two chairs in front of it. He said he didn't want to install a door alarm on her or the Metzkers' doors because we may forget about it and have it go off by accident. We also agreed on when we would exchange texts.

Then the fun began.

Mrs. M could not contain herself further and exploded with clucking questions. Mr. M got her to calm down and said we should explain over a nice glass of wine and some dinner. Susan and I removed the contents of the takeout containers on to platters, and Mrs. M finished setting the table with the salad.

I wasn't hungry, but the chianti did warm me up and took some of the edge off what I was feeling. I gave a brief recap of today's events, skipping any mention of my office being vandalized. Mrs. M seemed disappointed something more sinister and dangerous wasn't imminent. She kept mentioning how it was just like some TV mystery series she likes. Once Mr. M had his fill of sausage and peppers, he asked more practical questions about Jamal, what type of home security system was going to be installed in his building, and how long they would be necessary to justify the cost. I told him not to worry that he would be consulted, and my firm would pay for it. He was mollified but not convinced.

Susan took that as her cue to compliment Mrs. M on her chicken soup and offered to help clean up. She also got Mr. M to embark on a lengthy discussion of the merits of Italian food from Chicago. As I was sneaking out under the guise of having to catch up with some work, Susan kept Mrs. M in the kitchen. She shortly followed me with Fred and reminded me that I am not to let Fred out because he is no match for a gun. I didn't bother to point out that neither is she. But it did make sense for her to let him out as long as Jamal was with them.

After checking in with Jamal, I took a long shower and called my daughter. It was difficult to act normal, but she was amped up on being selected for a research internship and didn't notice my lack of participation. I didn't take it all in at the time, but hearing her so excited and happy was a good way to end the day.

Susan returned not long after I hung up with Ellie. She too checked in with Jamal, and they let Fred out through Mrs. Brown's back door. Susan joined me in Mrs. Brown's living room and pulled the smokeless ashtray out to light up.

"So, if you don't mind me asking... what's the deal with Mr. M and the building? I thought you owned it. Mrs. M kept giving you looks, and you clearly weren't expecting to justify the security system with him. Heads up, he's expecting to really take this up with you tomorrow and is giving you a pass tonight since you must be scared and upset."

After swearing, I got up to pour myself a glass of wine and offered to get something for Susan. When I sat down again, I started to explain. "I'm not sure he knows the extent he doesn't know I own the building or if he just doesn't want to acknowledge it. It's another long, sad story. I went to high school with their daughter, Sophie, and we're still close. They had a son who was around five years younger. There was always something that didn't seem quite right about Joe. He is one of those who went to several schools but never graduated. Then he became a self-proclaimed entrepreneur and tried his hand at several business ventures, which all went bust. I suspect he gambled heavily and knew he was into hardcore drugs and drank too much.

"Like a lot of parents in similar situations, the Metzkers were in denial and insisted his misfortunes were due to the misdeeds of others or bad luck. Joe was their golden boy, which drove Sophie nuts. They never paid much attention to her opinions because Joe was male which somehow qualified him to understand business. He convinced his parents to convert the ownership of the building into a limited liability company and had someone who supposedly is a lawyer explain the various tax advantages, especially once the Metzkers passed away. The story goes that this was a way to protect the inheritance of the two siblings. It sounded like the goal was to guarantee some sort of income stream or at least a place to live for each child.

"The Metzkers didn't inform Sophie of the plan. Whatever was executed in the operating agreement made Joe the managing member with full signing authority. The first thing he did was take out a huge home equity loan. The Metzkers didn't find out until the following year when they got a statement from the bank relating to the interest, which is when Sophie found out. Joe had a song-and-dance about opening a pizza parlor that served some of Mr. M's favorite dishes and would be named after the parents. It turns out he bought into a strip joint in Cicero, which is such a house of ill repute, that still has trouble staying open even in Cicero. Not surprising, local gossip says the place is mobbed up, and nobody other than the mob gets a penny out of it. The more popular theory is Joe owed significant gambling or drug debts, and that was how he paid them off.

"There wasn't sufficient income from the two rentals to service the debt. The loan was exorbitant because the appraised value was very high in 2006, in spite of the rental income not going up since sometime in the seventies. The bank started getting aggressive after the real estate market crashed and was going to take steps to foreclose. The Metzkers would have been out on the street with nothing in their pocket from the sale because they hadn't made an upgrade in decades, which is why Sophie came to me for help.

"Mrs. M knows full well that I paid off the loan, including the interest and back taxes. There was a lawyer handpicked by Sophie during the close who took great pains to explain the impact of the transaction to the Metzkers. The deal is they can live in the building rent-free, and I pay a check every month for alleged custodial services to Mrs. M. I make sure only Mrs. M gets the check, and Mr. M sees me do it. We pretend it's for rent. It's really a form of a reverse mortgage that provides the Metzkers with enough cash to live off of but not enough to get into trouble.

"Sophie used this incident as grounds to have her named their legal guardian, so she has the legal authority to make sure they get proper medical attention, which has also been a challenge lately, and not be taken advantage of financially again. She says it's amazing how many con artists target seniors. She wasn't worried about that as much as Joe making a pitch again, which to make a sad story end on a sad note, isn't a problem anymore since he died late last year."

"How?"

"He died in a mysterious car accident with so many drugs and booze in his system that the police credit it with being a self-inflicted death from a DUI. There are many who think he got in hot water again with his problems and was taken out. I like not to think about it or how incredulous it is that those kinds of things still happen."

"God! For real, how awful. How is everybody taking it?"

"Sophie views it as a tragic ending, but for the better because she didn't see things turning around for him."

"What's Sophie's story?"

"She's a midwife, a nurse practitioner. Her husband does medical research for Children's Memorial, and they have two unbelievably cute kids. They live in a fabulous bungalow in Berwyn, so they aren't too far away. They do okay, but I don't think she was prepared to support her parents."

We were silent for a few minutes. Susan perked me up by asking about tomorrow night. She wanted to know what I was wearing. We discussed her plans to go downtown with me to sign whatever papers Elizabeth's office would have ready. She thought afterward she would trek to Macy's on State Street for some clothes shopping and then return to Oak Park for the afternoon. Susan saw no need to hang out downtown all day, and we made plans for her to meet us at Acantos at five thirty because it is a couple of blocks from the Chicago Symphony Orchestra Hall. We agreed she would drive my car back when she returned to my building in the afternoon, which eliminated my problem of getting to work the next morning since I wasn't driving home after the symphony. I then excused myself and went to bed and slept soundly, which I attributed to Jamal and exhaustion.

Chapter 11

Pär was swearing silently to himself as he listened to Nivar's delusional, drug-addled rant. They were sitting in the bar of the Swiss Hotel while Nivar recounted his version of his meetings at Lough Key's office. Pär noticed that Nivar was using more than he was just last month and wasn't sure if it was because product is easier to get in Chicago and so cheap or if Nivar was spiraling down in a panic and trying to maintain.

According to Nivar, he turned the tables regarding Benny's account at Lough Key and now had the upper hand. From what Pär could discern as valid, Nivar claimed that Benny stole an undetermined amount of money from EuroCredit Bank and deposited it into his account at Lough Key. He threatened various types of legal actions and made varied demands on the Chicago police. Pär suspected that Nivar didn't really believe he had anyone scared enough to comply with his demands and was trying to convince himself with expensive scotch and cocaine. What was apparent is he is now known to the local authorities and associated with Benny and the source of his money. The bank wouldn't like that.

Pär picked up an undercurrent of fear emanating from Nivar. In his diatribe, Nivar mentioned a need to inform the bank of the whereabouts of millions of euros to satisfy an accounting audit. It didn't seem Nivar knew where the money was versus pretending he didn't because he had plans to keep it. Pär concluded this did not bode well, and it was time for him to sever his association with Nivar. Pär never doubted that Nivar would try to blame Pär for whatever happened if there were a chance it would be construed as plausible.

While Nivar droned on and not noticing a lack of participation from Pär in the conversation, Pär knew it was time to act. He evaluated the situation from his perspective and concluded the only trail leading to him was his bank credit card and recent car rental and hotel charges. He was hoping they could escape notice because he wasn't traveling with Nivar and hadn't in months, a decision for which he now congratulated himself. He never was introduced to anyone at the bank and wasn't an employee. He was a strategy consultant who got paid when Nivar submitted and approved an invoice for services rendered. He had no contract nor was there any other record of his personal information or arrangement with the bank. It was Nivar who arranged for him to have a bank credit card consistent with the limits of support staff.

His first dilemma in distancing himself was how to get cash. He didn't dare take out a cash advance against the credit card, but he did plan to buy a one-way ticket back to Stockholm tonight on the bank credit card before it was shut down. He reconsidered and thought a ticket to Munich would be less noticeable.

Nivar was getting antsy, and it seemed he consumed already what normally for him is a three-day supply of coke. In a burst of spontaneous inspiration, Pär offered to replenish Nivar's stash plus get him a few joints to relax. He closed with the enticement of a black hooker. Pär suggested purchasing at least double the norm because of the risks of drug transactions in a place where he stood out because of his accent. He also reminded Nivar that the hooker might be more to his liking if she were high. Pär normally tried to avoid setting up Nivar with prostitutes. He felt sorry for them and didn't like being reminded of his mother's fate. He noticed Nivar had developed a preference for what he called 'black beauties' and was wondering if he took out his resentments for his dark complexion on them. Another thought Pär didn't want to explore.

Par knew Nivar carried around thousands in euros and US dollars, so he asked for one thousand dollars. When Nivar balked by raising his eyebrow, Pär volunteered to bring back change but wasn't sure how much things were here and what it would cost to make discreet arrangements. Nivar seemed satisfied by what Pär thought was a dubious explanation given their history, which was another reason Pär thought the end was near for Nivar. Pär took the ten one-hundred-dollar bills, which he noticed depleted Nivar's cash, and walked out the door, hoping never to see him again.

He noticed in his wanderings that State Street had all kinds of retail stores, and it wasn't a far walk from the Swiss Hotel. Pär turned off his cell and ditched it down a sewer entrance. While walking, he decided not to return to the hotel. He concluded that he had only one encounter with its staff when he checked in, and there was no reason to attract attention to himself. He had nothing in his room other than a duffle bag, a few clothing items, and toiletries, which were no great loss and couldn't be traced to him.

Okay, now what? Pär found what seemed to be an emporium that sold every type of sundry item. It was amazing. It had toiletries, liquor, a sushi bar, hair and nail salon, small pets, basic clothing items, and cell phones. He bought a few items, including a gym bag, a few clothing items, basic toiletries, and struck gold with a cheap flip phone that could easily be replenished. He didn't need a smartphone because his bank laptop got WiFi. It was originally issued to Nivar, but he never used it after it became dated and probably didn't remember ever having it. Lucky for Pär, the bank didn't notice.

Pär was inspired to return to Oak Park. He needed to talk to the dark-haired woman apart from all the people he saw her with around her workplace. It was early enough to blend in with the early commuters going home, so he wouldn't be so noticeable walking around her block. Pär had previously discovered a commuter train line with the first stop in Oak Park, which he liked better than the local elevated train that made multiple stops within the city limits and in some very dodgy-looking neighborhoods. The disadvantage of the express commuter line is it had only one station to board, and they didn't run every few minutes. Pär opted for the commuter line. He reasoned that trains must run more frequently in the late afternoon and early evening, and the station was only a half-mile walk from the emporium.

Once on the train, Pär tried to come up with a way to approach the dark-haired woman, but he came up with nothing during the fifteen-minute train ride. He decided to walk to her building instead of taking a bus. He was still uninspired when he got to her block. Pär thought he could walk past her front door without notice if he were hunched over with his new gym bag and laptop bag like he was walking home from work. His best investment was the Blackhawks' hat which covered most of his face and conformed to the local uniform for every man, woman, and child.

Three doors down, he saw the largest man he had ever seen in his life talking to a younger, tall, skinny dude who was also wearing a Blackhawks' hat. They were pointing to windows and then walked around the side of the house. The large man looked like a character in American action movies— he was black, shaved head, and dressed in what looked like an expensive tracksuit. Pär noticed a service van parked in front of a big, shiny, black SUV with tinted windows. The dark-haired woman must have called for professional help to secure her building after his break-in. Pär wondered what her deal was that she surrounded herself with giant people and dogs.

Par proceeded to the nearby park to smoke and think. He decided to view this development as lucky since he saw the two men first and could rethink his non-existent plan. *Okay, what to do now?*

There was no reason to return downtown. Even cheap hotels were expensive, and he wanted to be somewhere safe to walk around at night. He resolved to walk back toward the busy streets that buses travel to get something to eat that had WiFi. After wandering almost an hour, he stopped at what Americans call a hotdog stand. It apparently was very popular, looked cheap, and smelled fantastic. While downing two dogs with everything, fries, and a frothy milkshake, he looked up hotels in the area. His luck continued by finding an old-fashion hotel within a twenty-minute walk for only one hundred dollars.

Once there, he was surprised by the age of the building. It was red brick and built around the early 1900s with old-fashion windows and awnings. He noticed older buildings in this neighborhood but thought all Americans liked more modern buildings for businesses like hotels. The lobby was dated and stark but clean. The one person at the desk was polite but mildly irritated to be diverted from what looked like a school textbook. Pär decided to chance it and use his bank credit card, hoping the insignificant amount wouldn't attract attention. He reasoned he should keep using it until he couldn't to reserve his cash. Like at the downtown Holiday Inn, the desk clerk was satisfied by his credit card and asked for no ID. Pär was again grateful that the US didn't adhere to global practices of requiring a passport or other form of ID and keeping copies of those documents.

His room was clean and furnished much like a European businessman's hotel not frequented by Americans or wealthy clients. It was small but had free cable television with lots of channels, WiFi, and a coffee maker. The worn carpet and two twin beds didn't bother Pär. He could just dump his bags on the other bed and not bother with unpacking. At first, Pär relished the silence. The Holiday Inn had little soundproofing with an eclectic clientele, many being on the seedy side. It was hard to avoid hearing toilets flushing at all hours, rough sex, and loud drunks who need to have their television at full blast.

He needed to think. Pär grabbed his laptop bag and headed out for a coffeehouse or bar. He took the laptop and Blackhawks' cap to blend in. He quickly found a friendly-looking neighborhood pub with club-style chairs and side tables. Perfect. Pär ordered a Guinness and enjoyed himself for the first time in weeks. Pär had to focus on his problem. He had to find a way to entice the dark-haired woman to want to talk to him and to know what to ask for that was feasible.

Pär reviewed the pictures of bills he took from her kitchen. He remembered he stole a business card from her desk and retrieved it from his wallet. For the next two hours, he cyber researched the dark-haired woman, Elaine Daye, and her two children. It was easy getting information on the girl because she had few privacy settings on her Facebook page. The son was at a university in Scotland that disclosed many of his accomplishments as well as his undergraduate college. The business card provided direct contact information for Ms. Daye. She seemed like a big deal in her business. Pär ached for a cigarette but didn't want to break his concentration.

Found it! Pär ordered his fourth Guinness and sat back. This could work, but what should he ask for? He knew he'd be awake all night rehearsing and changing his mind. Instead, he sipped his beer and bought a coach plane ticket to Europe leaving the next day.

Damn, no early morning flights. No matter, there were plenty of choices in the evening. He bought a ticket to Munich for a ten o'clock evening flight because his plan either would work or not. If not, he would have to get out of town fast, and it would not matter if it worked.

Satisfied, Pär strolled back to his hotel, enjoying his beer buzz and cigarettes.

Chapter 12

I woke up before my cell alarm went off at 4:42 a.m. I was restless and wanted the day over with before it even started. What I really wanted was to have a nice and boring routine day. Deviating from my routine, I made coffee before hitting the shower. My first cup is usually from Dunkin' Donuts at the corner of the same block where I park. I made an effort to look nice today and wore a skirt and sweater outfit with jewelry and dressy flats. I topped it off by blow-drying and styling my hair and wearing light makeup, something I haven't done in months. My motivation wasn't just dinner and the symphony tonight, but not to further worry Connie due to my lack of interest in my appearance.

The activity woke Fred up, who naturally had to go out. I paused. Last night Susan let him out under Jamal's watchful eye. I didn't see a reason to wake up Susan and wasn't sure if Jamal was supposed to be up now too. Following orders, I texted Jamal and asked if I could let Fred out and noted Susan wasn't awake. He was because he texted right back and said it was okay, he would meet me in the yard. All the lights on the back stairwell had to be turned on, along with the pole light I installed in the backyard because Fred doesn't see well in the dark, and the moon was still out. I grabbed a jacket but didn't bother leashing Fred. As promised, Jamal was on patrol in the back of the house and seemed pretty cheerful for someone who was up all night.

By this time, Fred was used to Jamal and paid little attention to him as he marched to the back near the alley to do his business. I stood next to Jamal and asked if he got any sleep. He said he didn't but seemed satisfied that the night was uneventful. He explained being up all night is no big thing unless he has to deal with a security breach. I told him I made coffee and asked if he wanted some. Jamal accepted as Fred ambled back. The three of us went up the stairs together while he thanked me again for the best sausage and peppers he ever had and asked for the name of the restaurant where I ordered his dinner.

Once inside Mrs. Brown's kitchen, I invited Jamal to sit down while I got his coffee, which fortunately he took black. We heard the shower go off, which meant Susan was up too. He got down to business by asking what our agenda is for today.

"Well, my best guess is we're going to be slammed today but located mostly in the office. Susan may have to go to her lawyer, which is a short walk away. I don't have reason to leave my office all day until Susan and I meet friends for dinner and go to the symphony. Our plan was for Susan to join me, driving downtown, and take my car back late this morning when her business is finished. She'll get downtown herself again in time to meet us at the restaurant at five thirty. I suppose I should know the answer to this, but what are your instructions? I didn't think about anything other than you watching my building and didn't consider you needing food and possibly a place to sleep. I don't have anything to offer you for breakfast since I never eat it at home."

Jamal smiled. "Thanks, but clients aren't expected to provision us. I'm good but do appreciate the coffee. My firm is sending a security system specialist for multi-family buildings at ten. Your man, Danny, will be here then. Is there a place you don't mind me grabbing some sleep that won't disturb your dog or neighbors? It would be nice to save the time driving to my place."

I took Fred and Jamal down to my place and set him up in my room. I changed the sheets, got out fresh towels while he was explaining that wasn't what he meant or necessary. I mostly ignored him for the next ten minutes until I was done. I walked him to the kitchen and showed him the pantry and fridge and told him to help himself. The problem was Fred. The Metzkers don't usually rise until around seven. We decided we would let him out again, and I'd ask Mr. M in an hour if he could take Fred up to his place or hang out with him in mine.

We returned to Mrs. Brown's apartment to find Susan in the kitchen freshly showered with damp hair, no makeup, and her navy-blue GAP sweatshirt with what was probably a new t-shirt. We discussed the day's itinerary again and made plans to check in with each other no later than eleven this morning for updates. Jamal was up for remaining a fixture at my building for the next few days and would wait to hear if that meant during the day too after the security system was installed. I let Fred out, gave him fresh water in my kitchen, and let him return to my unit with his bed in the sunroom for his morning nap. Susan joined me in my car after a slight delay because she wanted to take some coffee for the morning ride to the Loop.

Susan turned to me and gave me and my clothes a look. With an arched brow, she said, "You look nice... is this the real you, or did you dress up to impress Connie?"

"Ha-ha, very funny. I thought I'd aspire for a higher standard than clean today. But, I have to admit, it made me feel a little better, and I feel more in control. Don't know why and don't want to discuss."

"What's up first today, do you know?" Susan asked.

"Well, my best guess is lots of forms, first. The immediate goal is to get the 2.4 million out of Lough Key's custody and into an account controlled by some combination of Elizabeth and you. I'm not sure of the legalities other than we want it done before the Steins or an enforcement agency put some sort of injunction or claim on the money. That's more of an issue with Whatever-his-name-is from EuroCredit Bank making threats."

Susan was silent. "Is that for my benefit or your firm's?"

"I honestly don't know. That's a question for Elizabeth. I think you have more control, and certainly the Steins and Lenny Katz have more obstacles if the money isn't in an account with us in Benny's name. I have no idea what can happen or if the bank really initiates legal action or if some

Fed agency with AML enforcement powers takes an interest, which is another question you should ask Elizabeth. I'd ask how the account title will be set up so that you can't be construed as culpable if there were an AML violation."

We rode in silence for the next ten minutes until I came to the corner to turn off the Congress and into my parking garage. I left my car and keys and explained to LJ, one of the attendants, it was okay for Susan to take the car early in the day. I walked into the building without Susan, who stayed behind to grab a smoke.

Jason was manning the front desk when I walked in at about six thirty, and we exchanged typical morning pleasantries. Jason made me actually laugh out loud when he asked me if anything unusual was expected today and said I looked nice.

"Thank you for the compliment, and I really don't know but am hoping not. However, I'm expecting the phones to blow up later today, but you'll be off duty here and will miss that fun. Thanks again for helping out. I realize manning the front door for clearing sheets is a pain, and you got thrown in the middle of a crazy sideshow. I appreciate how calm you were. I wish I knew how and when this all will end, but I don't think it will be any time soon."

"I really don't mind. Sorry to admit, but it was kind of fun. Wait... I'm sorry for you and everyone, too," Jason stumbled.

"I understand and know what you mean. How much talk is there around the office?"

"Epic! And not just here... the floors, building, even a lot of bars around here. The *Trib* did a piece and mentioned us, or I mean Lough Key, in the story. I didn't know Benny was ever a big deal. Is it true what the *Trib* printed about him being an Alpha floor trader?"

"That was really printed in the *Chicago Tribune*? I never heard that term before. Well, I guess he was back in his heyday. It's a nice epitaph for Benny. I think he'd like being described that way. Well, I have another big day. I'm hoping for no new installments today or at least not here."

I walked to my office with the purpose of looking online for the article Jason mentioned. I wanted to see the extent I or anyone else was mentioned by name. It was easy to find since I have a digital subscription. In fact, there were a couple of articles. They didn't illuminate anything I didn't know about the circumstances of his death, but the reporter was dedicating a lot of ink to what a prominent figure Benny was a few years back on the trading floors. I wasn't too happy about the statement alleging Benny was the most successful independent trader who cleared through us or that the police were questioning firm executives, but was mollified that the only mention of any of our names was a quote from Billy expressing sorrow for Benny's family. From my perspective, the most important omission was that the break-ins weren't mentioned since they took place in my office and apartment. My phone buzzed with a text from Billy saying he and Oscar are on their way up, he is bringing me a latte, and to bring Susan. He suggested we meet in Oscar's office because it is the least visible to the general office population.

After texting Susan suggesting she check out the *Trib* article, I informed her about Billy and Oscar wanting to meet. I next checked in with the morning crew in charge of balancing, margin, and regulatory capital to confirm it was business as usual. There wasn't really a need to. I just liked the normalcy and was delaying going to Oscar's office. I was the first one, so I texted Latesha to have Raj, Linda, and Kevin meet with us in my office at nine thirty.

Once we all convened except for Billy, Oscar took over.

"Susan, I hope you don't mind I took a few liberties this morning at Elizabeth's office regarding how to title the account for the money from Benny's account here. It can all be changed, which is why I opted not to wait for your input. Bill is having what remains in Benny's account wired out now, as we speak. The sooner it's out of our custody, the harder it is for anybody else to make a claim on it, which I have reason to expect will happen shortly. I can't recommend enough having Elizabeth review your options and the potential ramifications. You need to be confident she's acting in your best interest and to understand all the nuances. She's expecting you in about a half hour. Before you go, I think you need to hear the latest from Bill. You, too, Lane."

On cue, Billy's quick footsteps were heard approaching. He was carrying a cardboard coffee carrier with three paper cups. He handed me one, told Susan hers had black coffee as he gave it to her, tossed the container, and sat down with his cup in a few quick, fluid movements. He commenced by explaining the wire went out, and we paid two hundred dollars to expedite it.

"Susan, the plan was for Oscar to explain why we jump-started this morning without you." He continued after Oscar nodded. "But there's more to the tale. Lane, remember Nickki, the bartender from the Martini Bar across the street? She's now at an obscure watering hole on LaSalle, somewhere a little north of Madison. It turns out that Paul Stein and Larry Katz picked that spot to have a strategy session on getting their hands on Benny's money here. She could hear almost everything since Paul was pretty drunk and agitated. She recalled reading about Benny in the papers, and it has been a popular topic with almost everyone based in the Loop. She also recalls liking you and the name of the firm from all the events we hosted at her old gig. God bless that girl... after they left, she called around until she found someone who knows our night help-desk phone number and left a message for me to call her, which I did."

Billy took a sip of his coffee. "Their master plan is to send various legal missives to the firm, you, and Susan as early as this morning. Larry was to do all the drafting last night, which is how they can move so fast. They will also be filing in court this morning what sounds like documents to hamper our moving the money. She didn't follow everything, but she heard words like 'injunction,' 'liens,' and 'cease-and-desist order.' It sounds like it's the legal nuisance strategy of filing everything and anything, regardless of how applicable because we have to legally rebut whatever they lob over, thus postponing our ability to release funds. It also provides them with insight to the status and nature of Benny's funds."

Susan and I were both stunned into silence. I couldn't imagine what she was thinking, but I would be tempted to cut-and-run if I were her.

"Lane, I suggest you join Susan in Elizabeth's office this morning. The firm can't avoid being served, but you two can at least delay it. Elizabeth will know the protocols and how to protect yourselves. Susan, I'm sorry it has come to this, but I need to preclude Lough Key from being involved in the Stein-family disputes. Since being served some sort of legal document appears imminent, I propose you two walk to the basement garage and down the fire escape stairs now. Go to my car, and I'll drive you to Elizabeth's building where you can't be noticed exiting this building. They have no reason to believe you have legal representation yet or at least with whom, so you have a good chance of arriving at Elizabeth's office undisturbed. However, we have all witnessed a propensity for miscreants waiting and watching you two from the building grounds and even at your residence, Lane. My suggestion may be a little dramatic, but I think it's prudent, given the circumstances," Oscar instructed.

It took me about a minute to process. "Okay, I need to go grab my wallet, so I have an ID to sign into her building. Billy, can you alert Latesha, Raj, Kev, and Linda that our morning recap may be postponed?"

Susan was also processing the latest development. "Wait, shouldn't we call the police or something?"

We all looked at Oscar, who frowned. "I honestly don't know. This may all be out of their purview, but it's a valid question. I'll call our attorney, and you should pose the question to Elizabeth. We may be given different advice."

We all got up to leave. We decided that Oscar would take the elevator. Billy and Joe from the Eurodollar desk would escort Susan and me to the basement garage and down the fire escape stairs. Joe would also ride shotgun and accompany us into Elizabeth's office. On the way down the stairs, Billy gave me a left-handed compliment on how different and nice I looked. I was beginning to take the hint I should put more effort into my morning routine.

We arrived at Elizabeth's office without incident. I thanked Joe, who was very nice. He said it was okay, but he would appreciate being taken out for a beer for the rest of the story. Previously, I felt like I was in an altered reality, now I felt silly.

Elizabeth's admin met us and escorted us through building security, her firm's reception area, and we breezed into Elizabeth's office where she was waiting for us at her desk.

Susan spoke first. "Good morning and thank you. It sounds like you already put in a lot of hours on our behalf, and things have to keep moving fast. I don't fully understand what's going on other than we're trying to stop the Steins and Larry Katz from end-running around Benny's will and trusts. This is so f-ed up! I really need to light up. Please say it's okay with my smokeless ashtray in the corner chair."

Elizabeth nodded and pointed to a chair with a little end table big enough for a lamp in the far corner of her gigantic office. She was beautifully dressed and coifed again this morning in a black suit dress with a lot of pearls. After offering us coffee or water, Elizabeth explained her strategy. She drafted an irrevocable trust putting her in charge as the trustee of the new trust established for Sharon. Elizabeth explained that irrevocable meant Susan or anybody else could not remove Elizabeth, which took Susan out of the loop of any litigation due to potential conflicts of interest, health problems, or whatever the Steins could allege. Elizabeth said once things calmed down, she could relinquish her capacity, but this gives everyone a safe harbor to make long-term plans and makes it harder for anyone to make a claim on the trust funds. Elizabeth ended by asking Susan if she had questions or objections.

Susan sat smoking and looking out the window but was clearly listening and thinking. She took at least two long minutes after Elizabeth finished before responding. "Okay, first, I like this. I haven't decided on whether I want or can handle the responsibility of being in charge of Sharon, and it means I don't have to deal with the rest of them. Honestly, this was never something I envisioned, and I'm not close to Sharon. I get why Sharon needs protection and a buffer from her family, and I want to do that for her, but I don't want to be stuck with them myself.

"So, first question is how much will this cost? The funds have to be invested somewhere in a safe place in investments that make sense for Sharon. You must charge something, and there will be the accounting, tax, bill paying, and God knows what other fees. Two million isn't really that much money if a lot of professional fees are taken first. Let's start with the fact that I don't know what her expenses are or should be or what kind of care and support she needs or even what kind of insurance she has."

Elizabeth took a second, long look at Susan. "All good questions. In fact, I'm impressed. I suggest we first execute these documents to give us time to mutually determine what's best for Sharon without interference from her family. We can come to an agreement after we both understand the realities of the situation. I'm prepared for my status to be a stop-gap measure. We can both explore other resources for what will be involved and their commensurate fees. I hope it will give you some comfort that these documents clearly stipulate I have a fiduciary responsibility to Sharon, which legally binds me to act in her best interests."

Susan nodded. "Thanks. Next, how effective is all this from preventing anyone else staking a claim or initiating a bunch of bullshit lawsuits that are expensive to defend? How am I at risk?"

By now, Elizabeth had concluded that Susan may be a little rough but was very astute. "You're asking all the right questions. Second question first. I view your risk as almost non-existent once you sign the irrevocable trust. You clearly had minimal prior knowledge and are well within your rights to abdicate. You may have to pay some legal fees personally, but they won't be much. You also are fulfilling your obligations as the sole trustee by getting a qualified surrogate. You can even make the argument that recusing yourself is in Sharon's best interest due to the acrimonious nature of your relationship with his mother and brother. Secondly, we can turn the tables on someone pursuing baseless litigation by making it very expensive for them with the present structure, at which I assure you I'm a master.

"The important point to focus on now is for you to sign over your trustee capacity and approve the retitling of the funds pretty much now to avoid a claw-back claim for whatever the brother and his dubious business associate are working on now. It doesn't matter if Benny owed money to another party if it's spent and gone and properly documented. It's just like they can't ask you to repay your share of a trip you went on with him, especially if it were a gift."

"Okay, I'm ready to sign, but I have more questions."

Elizabeth buzzed in a paralegal who was a notary and also her admin to witness the various documents. I was called upon to sign as a witness too.

Once it was just the three of us, Susan had further inquiries. "Oscar says I'm going to be served or subpoenaed. I'm not sure if there's a difference. What do I do if that happens?"

"Now that we executed the various documents well before you had notice of their intent, there's no reason for you to avoid being served. It would have been a problem before you signed over your authorities. Don't sign anything, take the envelope, and turn it over to my office."

"What about notifying the police or someone?"

"You may want to as a courtesy, but I wouldn't recommend it without me being present, which I apologize, but have to make sure you understand, you'll be billed for personally. Remember to look in the file you'll soon be given for the two engagement letters you signed. Representing you with the police can't be billed to Sharon's account. Regardless, I think it would be a wise preventative measure, and I don't recommend you describing the impact of the documents."

"That makes sense. What if someone claims the money was stolen from a bank or was part of an AML scam?"

"The first question is easier to answer. It's too bad and gone, just like my trip example. I can make it very hard and expensive for a bank to try to recoup those funds. They shouldn't try for no reason other than the publicity I'll generate that could cause serious reputational damage. I have no experience with AML but am confident it will take years for a government agency to be able to make a case that the funds were subject to the AML regs. I understand they have to start proving their case with the source of funds originating in two other nations and one with heightened bank secrecy laws. You, personally, aren't at risk from what I can discern, and as you pointed out, two million isn't really that much. Who's to say how much will remain after five years? I don't think the government wants headlines describing it making a handicapped girl provide restitution for her medical expenses. My prediction is we'll be approached, possibly threatened, but nothing further is likely."

Susan was looking better and smiling. "Okay, then, let the games begin."

I, on the other hand, wasn't feeling better. "I know you aren't in charge of my security service. Thanks for the referral. Jamal has been a godsend, but it's time for me to take ownership myself, not Billy or Oscar. From this discussion, I take it I can step out of knowing or being involved further with Benny's account. It sounds like I need to spend time with our attorneys for some risk triage. If it's not a conflict of interest, can you advise what I should do if served with a legal document? Oscar said on the way out that firms can't avoid it."

"I don't think it matters much if it pertains to the dissolution of Benny's estate. I can't respond to anything else. I'm glad Jamal worked out for you. Here's the card of the account manager for my referrals. I hope you won't need them for much longer. What are you two going to do now?" Elizabeth questioned.

"Well, I can't speak for Susan, but I've had it. Jamal is working with people who'll make a security system recommendation and can install it. A family friend will fill me in on how it functions because he can be on-site when they are there, which reminds me, I need to head back to check in with him."

Elizabeth said she had a few more items to discuss with Susan, which relieved me. I wanted the short walk back alone. Susan and I confirmed we would meet early this evening, and she would be returning to my place with my car after finishing her business. She knew to expect Danny and a security install team and to work Fred's outings around them.

I was buoyant knowing I could not care about Benny's money or be accountable for it. I was just concerned about how I could be held accountable for how it got deposited with Lough Key. The more I thought about it, I became mad, really mad, and was done being afraid. In spite of my morning feistiness, I walked around the side of the building and down the driveway to the parking garage returning to the office by way of the fire escape stairs. I didn't need to be the subject of any more neighborhood gossip or pity. Halfway up the first floor, it occurred to me this was supremely stupid. I was alone, and no one could see or hear me. I changed my mind and left the stairwell on the second floor because it had public access with a restaurant and health club located there and texted Billy belatedly informing him I was almost back.

I took the elevator after all but at least avoided the lobby. Second stupid thing I did was how I reacted when the elevator door opened on my floor and was pounced on by Larry Katz jumping up and down, screaming, "there she is, there she is." For an instant, I was tempted to retreat back into the elevator but didn't want to risk being stuck in it with him. I glared and stomped down the hall toward the reception area of my office with Billy, Joe, and Oscar rounding the corner and opening the glass door. Larry started to run toward me, followed by a bigger man wearing a gray sports coat, who was followed by Hector, the security guard. He grabbed my arm and tried to stop me while yelling, "give it to her now!"

I didn't try to force my hand free. Instead, I used a trick I learned in self-defense class. I brought my arm toward me, which pulled Larry closer. With my other hand open and my palm heel jutting out below closed fingers, I slammed Larry in the jaw with all my might fueled by an adrenaline rage. He collapsed to the floor on his back, screaming, which looking back was ridiculous. I couldn't have hurt him badly, I just surprised him. Hector was now standing between the two men and me. Joe used one of his football moves and rushed around all of them so that I could slip past the howling Larry and the guy in the gray jacket who was fumbling and shouting, "which one is she?" Billy rushed behind and propelled me behind the glass doors laughing heartily. So was Oscar, the growing crowd in the reception lobby, and Joe when he entered. So much for avoiding being a subject of gossip and drama.

By now, Larry was standing, red with rage, yelling about being accosted, suing me, the firm, the building, and everyone present if I didn't come out now. Billy regained his composure and shouted he called 911 to report an attempted assault and possible kidnapping and to leave. I walked away into the hallway leading to my office wondering who was crazier, me or the rest of the world?

I sunk into my office chair, not hurt but shocked. I leaned over my desk and raised my hands to cradle my head with my elbows on my desktop. I'm not sure how much later Latesha, Oscar, and Billy poured in. Latesha handed me a cup of tea she said Raj made this morning. Nodding my thanks, I leaned back and drank heavily. I heard lots of clucking sounds asking if I'm all right.

"Yeah, yes, thanks. I'm fine, just processing the shock. Seriously, who lives like this! Okay, I'm fine and just need to calm down. Let's change the subject. What happened out there besides me decking Larry?"

Gingerly, they rearranged themselves into chairs around my office table. Billy shook his head. "Honestly, Lane, we're not sure. It happened so fast. We were on notice to lock the reception area doors. We concluded there was no legal way for a business to avoid being served, but we wanted to postpone it until we were sure the wire hit the new trust account. Larry shows up with that other guy who's a professional process server. Latesha, find out how the hell Larry got past the turnstiles. We never closed that loop the other day. Do you know what happened next?"

"Everything was fine. We're all used to the front doors being locked now. Larry shows up with that other guy not much more than fifteen minutes ago, yelling his fool head off. Can't hear what he's actually saying the way he carries on. I called Hector to come up and told him to call the police. I didn't know anything about being served court papers and just thought he was up to his old tricks. You get off the elevator and know more than me since I couldn't see much past down the hall," Latesha reported.

"By the way, Laney, nicely done."

I glared at Billy and turned to Oscar. "What next? Can we just accept the papers and be done with this? Can we at least file a restraining order? This is the second time he has come after me in a public place."

Oscar also annoyed by Bill's comment, turned to me. "We have an appointment this morning for a call with the AML practice from Scott's firm, with Scott to assess our risks and to plan a preemptive defense. I think it's wise to unlock the front doors and arrange for the desk staff to call Latesha when we are served. It should be soon if I guess right. Lane walking up behind Larry Katz and his server threw them off but won't delay them much.

"Latesha, please call the building to inquire if we can pay an extra fee for the building to have a security guard remain in our reception area to prevent them from wandering into the general office area.

"Bill is right about preventing them from having general building access unless Larry is a tenant. See what can be done to stop him from loitering on our floor and the lobby.

"Lane, you dodged getting served probably because of them not expecting you, but also the server didn't know who you are. I can only conclude he has papers to serve for two women. You might want to call Susan and have her also notify Elizabeth. I think we should call and invite the two detectives for an update for no reason other than to have an official record because it's anyone's guess what will happen next. Lane, are you all right? Should you go home? You look pale."

"No, really, I'm fine. I'm just shaky because I need to consume something other than caffeine."

Billy stood. "Laney, let's get you some eggs at the Buck downstairs. It'll be quiet now."

I agreed, and we both left with the understanding that Latesha would know our whereabouts the entire day. By the time we entered the small dining area of the LaSalle Club, I was famished. I ordered three scrambled eggs, bacon, raisin toast, and a big glass of milk. The milk came first with Billy's coffee. I downed half of my milk in three swallows and asked for water.

"Lane, what gives? Aren't you eating? Didn't you have dinner with your neighbors last night?"

"I think it's nerves. I've never been so high-strung like I may hit the ceiling if a plate is dropped. I thought I slept okay last night, but I haven't really had a deep REM sleep in days. I try to eat, but don't seem to get much down. Billy, I can't take much more of this. I need to regain control of my life. My husband is missing without a trace, and I'm being stalked by persons unknown with the occasional Larry Katz sideshow. On top of that, I may wind up in hot water over an AML look-back violation and sued or worse by whatever bank has a claim on Benny's funds here. Look at me, my hands are shaking. I'm not prone to hysteria, and I hope to God this isn't the new me. Dammit! I may need to take a leave of absence for no other reason than I'm a liability now."

"Hey, it's going to be okay. Maybe you're right and need a break. You just need a resort vacation. Wait, a better idea is visiting Cahill and touring castles and whiskey distilleries, get out of town until this blows over. Connie would love to join you."

"Billy, think... this may be the new normal! There's no end in sight or known milestones to cross. We can't anticipate what's going to happen next or who's at risk, or even why. Running away isn't a solution, not to mention Connie has your children to take care of, other responsibilities, and shouldn't be put in danger. What I want is to hole up in a quiet hotel and sleep for days. I don't dare take something to sleep because self-medicating is never a good idea. Talking this over convinces me I should see someone because I'm a basket case, and I don't know how to live in constant fear."

My breakfast arrived. Billy and I were silent as I inhaled most of it while Billy checked his phone. Breakfast did make an immediate difference—the shaking stopped, and my headache was going away. My phone started to buzz with texts, which I mostly ignored. One did make me laugh, and I responded. Billy looked up from his phone and was clearly curious.

"Everyone around here has heard about my altercation with Larry Katz this morning. I can't figure out how that news spread so fast because it happened on our floor, not in a more public place. The last text was from Nathan Lee, my self-defense instructor."

"I was going to ask later what inspired you and how you knew to do that. I didn't know you took classes."

"Well, I didn't go to class. Nathan gave me a few lessons because he insisted on repaying a favor."

"Who's Nathan?"

"He's young, hasn't been out of school for long. He graduated from MIT and got a job at QAlgos, you know the quant prop shop firm across the river? He's friends with several from our quant team and has come to the office when we host the Algorithmic Trading Society lunches. QAlgos makes all their traders do a stint on a trading floor even though they mostly trade upstairs. He's smaller and very polite, which made him a constant target for minor harassment. He didn't flinch at having pens thrown at his head in the index pits or the elbow jabs and unnecessary pushing. He got moved to the big pit with exchange traded funds last year, which you may recall had a terrible reputation and was performing last against all the other exchanges in its listings. The floor brokers started going to Nathan because he was quoting size and was smarter and faster than most of the traders in that pit and could easily price complex orders. The harassment escalated when he went to sit on his stool, and Jerry Weiss pulled it out beneath him and tried to stomp on his hand when Nathan was down. Nathan jumped up and ninja-like kicked and punched Jerry so fast it was a blur, and Jerry crashed to the floor. Jerry suffered a cracked tail bone among his other injuries.

"I was there with Kevin that day testing the synchronization of the floor clocks. I went with Kevin just to kibitz. We saw the whole thing. It looked to me suspiciously staged, other than Jerry being the one getting hurt. There were just too many people hovering around, including TJM, my least favorite floor official. Kevin and I followed him back to his floor booth and stood on the back stairs where we could see into his booth, which is how we saw people laughing and him paying out cash. It was so well-known what Jerry's plan was that TJM was making book on it with odds, and it turns out several market reg floor officials were in on the fun, too. I naturally had to video it, and so did Kevin from another vantage point."

"Why did you bother? That stuff happens all the time. Why did you care?"

"Because I know Jerry and TJM, and both were mad. Jerry got an ass-kicking from a skinny, little guy that half the floor videoed, and TJM was out a lot of money betting on the wrong guy. TJM initiated a suspension against Nathan for starting a fight on the floor. Remember how aggressive the exchanges became enforcing anti-harassment and decorum rules? Jerry was going to get a pass because he was alleging to be a victim, and Nathan's behavior was described as unprovoked.

"Jerry was making noises about suing Nathan and his firm for a huge amount claiming his injuries were permanently disabling. As I expected, no one stepped up to defend Nathan because his firm was the current Pariah, hated by what remained of the independent traders and small firms. The head of floor ops at Nathan's firm is a friend, and I'm on very good terms with most of the senior floor ops managers at the exchange. Kevin and I were willing to provide a different version of events substantiated by our corresponding videos of TJM being a poor looser with exchange staff looking on. Jerry got suspended, and TJM lost his floor official status. Nathan and the rest of his crowd got stern warnings, and as usual, nothing happened to the exchange staff. Nathan was extremely grateful and wanted to do something in return. I asked him if he could teach me a few tricks to be less vulnerable, but not a martial arts expert like him. And this morning, you saw the results."

Shaking his head, Billy signed the check. Unfortunately, we were spotted at the elevator bank by some client reps from another clearing firm who called me, I think, the Terminator and were hooting about me getting another shot at Larry Katz. I just nodded.

"Some other time," Billy said while pushing me into our elevator. Thankfully, nobody else rode up with us. Before we entered our office, Billy announced he had an idea and asked me join him in his office. He added that he was calling Latesha too.

Starz was at the front desk and started to tell us something. "Sorry, Starz, have something that needs immediate attention. I'll circle back in fifteen," Billy said. Latesha met us in his office. Her soulful brown eyes communicated how concerned she was about me.

Billy directed us to sit in his guest chairs. "It's clear we have a personal safety issue with Laney. Let's start with some simple, common-sense solutions. Let's sync Lane's phone to ours, so we can track her whereabouts like my wife does with our kids." He then called Connie to confirm the best apps and how to do that. I thought it would be in poor form to volunteer I knew how.

"Next, Lane, you're to text us at least once an hour with your location. Say, fifteen minutes past each hour. Let's all set a reminder on our phones to keep track of the time. Lane, no sending one-word shortcuts like 'fine' or 'same.' We need a warning code, too. Say, if you're worried for any reason and can't call us, text the word 'cold.' We can lay off when you're at home with the bodyguard.

"We have to rethink that more, but this is a good start. Lane, you need to be thinking of a schedule. You have to consider your routine outside of work. Maybe you don't want to come in every day. I hate to mention the obvious but maybe step back from your volunteer night shifts at the shelter. We should consult the security service for a recommendation."

Shifting gears, he asked Latesha if she made progress limiting Larry Katz's building access.

She shook her head, indicating no. "He must be using someone else's card because he isn't in the system with an active one, which isn't that hard to do. The other problem is one security person is standing behind a counter in that corner booth by the west side revolving doors. The location limits their view of the lobby much past the first elevator bank. That security guard is also checking people in, which gets busy if you think about all the food deliveries, messengers, service vendors, besides guests. Hector told me that they also answer the phone and sometimes take reservations for the LaSalle Club and Everest Room. The second guard has to frequently back up the first one in the booth. Even if someone were standing by the turnstiles, there's not much they can be expected to do if Larry has a card. Hector thinks Larry got in through the garage today with his card, which is how he got the other man in with him. We all know the security is just enough to stop traveling salesmen who walk into offices selling hot watches and gym bags. It's enough to keep random thefts down, but not much more."

Oscar walked in. "There you are. Larry's process server is back. He's demanding access to serve Lough Key papers and quoting our requirement to accept service. Since they can accomplish the same thing by sending them by certified and simultaneously regular mail, I think he must also want to serve Lane and Susan. Probably Susan because she doesn't have a known address here. I told him to come back at two o'clock. We'll have the opportunity to consult with our lawyers by then. What's going on here?"

It was almost nine thirty after we gave Oscar our update. I went to the Compliance Department office, and Latesha was to see if Raj was free and could join us. Linda and Kevin were surprised to see me and asked the usual questions about my well-being. Linda added she hoped the building has a video of me punching out Larry, but she had the good grace not to joke about it or ask for details. I started when Latesha and Raj joined us.

"Kevin, Billy informed me you have Benny's tax returns going back at least three years and the source documents to prepare last year's return. See anything interesting?"

"Not really. The first thing I checked was for any offshore accounts, and there weren't any noted. I looked at the names of all his accounts, and until recently, they were all in his name or a trust in his name. That changed a little last year with DZY being added to checking accounts. The last two years, he made a lot more money trading in his IB account than he did with us, and he was getting more rental income those years, too. I checked to see what he was trading, and it was all exchange-traded stuff in various asset classes. He consistently traded the eMinis versus SPX, and I wondered why he did that in a customer account. Linda explained that the exchange membership, transaction fees, and things like market data costs take away the cost advantage of one guy trading those contracts, and the margin treatment at IB is almost the same as what upstairs broker dealers get. He has less-active positions that must be longer term or conservative strategies in his trust account. There's nothing to worry about that I can see. His accountant took hardly any travel and entertainment deductions. His biggest non-trading expense was for his health insurance."

"Nice work, Kevin. It's actually comforting. I have a new research project for the two of you. Find out everything you can from cyber searching EuroCredit Bank, the German bank acquiring it, and two guys, Nivar and John William Henry Carrington III. I'm particularly interested in any scuttlebutt on how the acquisition is going and how EuroCredit Bank had a business line of financing alternative investments. I'm not sure who was the lending party or what type of financing. The story I heard was they were financing elaborate private jets for boutique transportation companies. The paper is sold to hedge funds and wealthy private investors because the returns are way above market. There's an insinuation of money laundering and the planes moving drugs. This business line is supposedly hubbed out of the Netherlands Antilles and Gibraltar," I explained.

"This sounds like it could be fun, but why are we doing this research? Shouldn't the police or the Feds? I'm not sure what we can find with our resources since we don't have a Lexus/Nexus subscription or whatever is used in Europe," Kevin asked the obvious question.

"Good points. I agree it's highly unlikely you'll find anything. My interest is in demonstrating how that information, if it's true, wasn't readily available or something that should have been discovered during routine compliance vetting."

Linda asked about updates. I gave them all a brief recap but didn't mention Jamal or the security system being installed today. It was clear they connected the dots the same way as the police and I did—there must be a connection between Benny, my office break-in, and home invasion.

Raj was next on my agenda. I wanted to know about Apple products' security. Now that Benny is dead, is there a way to access whatever he had on the iCloud? Something must be on it if his devices were synced. He explained that it is possible to make content on those devices irretrievable without security access, but those conventions are too inconvenient and sophisticated for most people. He offered to make some calls but would need some starting information like Benny's device serial number or Apple ID. He thought Susan was in a better position to pursue that thread.

"Good. I don't want to know anything more about Benny's finances, and I'm not sure Susan would want to either if it ties her up in litigation. I was curious how far the police could get without Susan because of her being in charge on so many of his end-of-life documents. My take away on your answer is we don't know, but it requires a specialized skill set to try with a legal foundation to compel cooperation."

It was almost ten. I thanked them and ended the meeting with a promise of sharing the highlights from the meeting with our attorneys, which had started prior to my arrival into Oscar's office. Nothing was concluded during the hour-and-a-half meeting with at least four senior partners with various banking practices. The working premises is it will be difficult for any US agency to get information from banks and bank affiliates located in countries with strict secrecy laws. Susan may have better luck if she wants to retrieve assets, but she can't go on a fishing trip. She needs to start out knowing for sure and evidencing that Benny had deposits with the bank.

The firm and I were more vulnerable to being made a case-study example of what can go wrong. We can be sucked into an investigation, but there has to be probable cause of at least a lapse of our policies and procedures, which are assumed to be updated and sufficient. The wild card is AML, which is like postal violations for conspiracy to commit fraud. It's a great add-on to whatever is the core charge. There was also the condescending suggestion not to permit any meetings with only one person from the firm in attendance. I guess I deserved that given how expensive this was going to be for Lough Key. Today's call had to be at least ten thousand dollars.

I left because Danny was texting me regarding the security system install. He and Jamal gave me the rundown of the tech recommendations. They didn't sound too expensive or complicated. I gave the okay and asked Danny if it was okay for him to be my proxy and to charge me for his time.

Billy texted me to return to Oscar's office. They asked me for an update on my house. They liked the idea of a new security system and Danny showing Susan how it worked this afternoon. I told them I was taking tomorrow off, and one of the reasons was Danny agreed to meet me tomorrow for a comprehensive tutorial. I also told them I discontinued the services of Jamal. It was just making me more crazy and tense thinking about it. They didn't like that but didn't argue.

When asked what I missed, Oscar said things weren't so bad. That's Oscar-speak for not good, but not the worst possible. He said the firm's likely worst-case scenario is being dragged into various disputes and having large legal bills to prep and paper our de facto defense of not being involved. He said that whatever agency investigating the source of Benny's money would have a lot of hurdles to thread Lough Key and me as accomplices or even inadvertently aiding and abetting. Again, the worst case is the corresponding legal fees. The bright side is that Nivar's bluster can be ignored. Whatever bank that he is representing has to paper its case, which it will probably be hesitant to do given from where the funds probably originated. Also, someone from the bank had to authorize at least one transfer. That and the amount of money that crossed over to us isn't worth their fees and time to recoup from us what we don't have custody of anymore. We were congratulated for getting the money out of our control before any claims or enforcement authorities surfaced.

265

As if on cue, a second time today, Latesha buzzed and said a gentleman that sounds like our bank visitor yesterday is on the phone demanding to speak to either Oscar or Billy. This was what Starz was trying to notify Billy and me about when we walked in. It was his third attempt this morning. Oscar said to patch him through but to first write down the telephone number of the caller. Oscar put the phone on speaker before he picked up.

The voice was the same silky smooth, urbane voice of the man I met with Benny who started all this trouble. He introduced himself as Nivar Amirmoez, the Managing Director of Global Alternative Investment Strategies for EuroCredit Bank that is now DTB-Franco Bank. He graciously acknowledged getting off to a bad start yesterday and expressed his condolences for the loss of our colleague.

Oscar thanked him for his sympathies and acknowledged that he was joined by Billy and me, referring to us by our formal names and titles. He prompted Nivar by asking the nature of the call. Nivar said he would like to meet to discuss how his bank can repatriate funds that were to capitalize an investment strategy conducted by Mr. Stein, who has unfortunately passed away.

Oscar smirked, which is unusual for him, and responded that we aren't in receipt of or have any type of direct or indirect custody of any assets belonging or being associated with Mr. Stein. He strongly suggests Mr. Amirmoez contact whoever is in charge of Mr. Stein's estate and any business ventures, which may not be the same parties. We are sorry we cannot be of assistance, but Lough Key, like his bank, does not share confidential client information. Oscar disclosed us having no such funds as a courtesy to avoid wasting his time. He suggests contacting an attorney to discover who Nivar may need to approach, but we have no information that is helpful to his cause. Nivar countered with a statement implying Oscar did not understand the severity of the situation and Lough Key not cooperating, at which point Oscar hung up, again smirking.

Oscar asked Latesha if she got the phone number. When she answered affirmatively, Oscar left a message for Detective Williams saying he had some updates that might be interesting.

Chapter 13

Pär slept in until eight thirty. He wished he checked into this hotel when he arrived in Chicago. Besides being clean, it was quiet, thanks to the building's old-fashion plaster walls. The clientele was nicer too. He felt safe and didn't get the feeling he was constantly being watched for a lapse in his guard.

He reconsidered his situation last night. He remained optimistic in the morning and still thought his plan could work. Pär saved most of his earnings from his nefarious consulting services because the bank paid his living expenses whenever he traveled with Nivar. The past two years they traveled ostensively for legitimate reasons, and because Nivar preferred his lifestyle likewise being subsidized by the bank. It just wasn't enough to start a business, which was Pär's goal.

He had a couple thousand euros in addition to his capital nest egg, plus about two thousand dollars in his wallet. Pär silently thanked God for the one thousand dollars he absconded from Nivar two days ago. He chuckled, thinking of Nivar's impotent rage trying to reach him. Two thousand dollars was enough to get somewhere until he could start a new line of work. He was done being a professional panderer and knew he had to distance himself from Nivar. Nivar was on the cusp of self-destruction. His coke habit was now insatiable, and it was obvious the ten million dollars was gone and irretrievable to the bank or Nivar personally. His career was destroyed with jail possibly being imminent. Pär doubted Nivar had the discipline to have any significant investments, and it didn't appear he had any family or school connections with influence. Nivar was finished with only a few weeks left on the bank expense account to abuse.

Pär relished the hot shower, thick towels, and nonsense American television until it was time to check out. He felt free and empowered, which were new sensations. He strolled down to a little commercial area and found a coffee shop with WiFi. The espresso and pastries were good but not like in Europe. Pär whiled away the time rechecking for updates on Benny's murder in the news and streaming Netflix. He wished he had someone to call or email. He was tired of being lonely and of no consequence to anyone. He promised himself to change that too in his new life.

One last time, Pär did an inventory of why he cannot be tied to the missing ten-million-dollar fiasco—he was not an employee, had no authority, no business cards, and Nivar submitted all his invoices, approved all his expenses, and submitted them. Pär could be a phantom that Nivar invented to misappropriate bank expense reimbursement funds. He seldom was acknowledged or introduced in any official meetings. There was no record of him existing in a bank capacity. Even the credit card was arranged by Nivar. While exceedingly convenient now, it all was a wake-up call to Pär on how invisible he was in the world. No one would remember him. He was too insignificant even if someone did. This was like his mother's life, only he was a highly-compensated pimp and a small-time drug dealer. Not anymore.

Pär looked at his watch. It was time. He went outside and found a little parkway with a bench. He needed to smoke while he did this.

He pulled the dark-haired woman's card out of his wallet and composed an email.

Chapter 14

When I returned to my office, I called Susan to update her on Nivar's call and Larry Katz's process server's demands. She didn't say much other than thinking the information should be added to the discussion when she and Elizabeth meet this afternoon at three. I also told her Raj's opinion and suggestion concerning retrieving Benny's information off the cloud and what the lawyers said about needing solid evidence that Benny had an account at a bank before any bank will cooperate with an asset search.

"Seems nuts to try to go after that pot of gold, right? How would that make sense for me to do the work and pay for tracking down whatever may exist in a foreign bank and risk getting in the middle of an expensive lawsuit over its ownership. I have plenty of my own money and am not pissing it away on legal fees. The two million dollars should be enough for Sharon to have a new start in life. I'm taking a hard pass. Benny's family and Larry are more than welcome to it, without my help."

"My guess is Elizabeth would agree with you. Anything new on your end?"

Susan chuckled. "Oh, yeah. Elizabeth called Paul's office, leaving a message. He called, like minutes later, with Larry. God, she's great! They started with threats and demands. She let them go at it for at least twenty minutes. When they finally stopped, she dished back a lot of legal terms about how their claims are baseless and without merit. Best part was when she said she recorded the entire conversation and will use it as evidence to file ethics complaints against Paul and will have him disbarred and lodge a criminal complaint against Larry. She laughed when Paul was so mad he was spitting about not giving his consent to record the conversation. She said she'd see him in court and suggested he reread the rules about initiating superfluous litigation, and in Illinois, only one party of a conversation needs to consent to be recorded. She said she was sending them written notice that all contact with me or anything pertaining to Benny's estate will be in writing and through her office and hung up. It was great."

"So, where we are is nobody but Nivar knows we don't have the money anymore, and nobody knows you don't technically have it either."

"Yep. Elizabeth said we don't have to volunteer it, and it will keep them busy spinning their wheels for months to figure it out. She told me not to engage with them in any manner. She gave me cards with printed instructions for process servers to contact her office. She said to try and video or get someone to witness if they approach me in person."

"I'm so sorry, but I forgot to tell you about my encounter with Larry this morning and how Oscar agreed to accept documents from the process server today at two, which is about now." I then told her about being ambushed and how it sounded like Larry had something drafted for each of us to be served with.

Susan laughed and screamed. "Why didn't you tell me this before? I wish I saw it. Does the building have videos?"

"Probably not, which is probably a good thing. I half-expect Larry to add assault resulting in permanent disabilities to his list of legal grievances."

"Are you doing as well as you sound?"

"I'm good, thanks, just tired of all this. What are you up to next?"

"I'm at O'Doole's office to see if he has any other account statements of Benny's or insurance policies. I'm to take all of Benny's records out of his office, so he doesn't have them to turn over if he gets subpoenaed. I'm supposed to stop by Elizabeth's office again this afternoon to sign more papers. She's hot to get all of Benny's money into bank accounts controlled by her firm before Paul and Larry find them. When I leave here, I meet Danny at your place in about an hour and a half."

"How are you holding up? Are you okay with going to meet Danny?"

"Yeah, it keeps me busy, and I feel useful. I wish we weren't racing around grabbing Benny's money. It's like all that matters is his money now. I haven't got my head around him being gone. There's been no time to grieve or plan a service or really be just... sad. Thanks for asking. I'm fine. I'll see you at five thirty." She hung up.

Chapter 15

The process server showed up at 1:55 p.m. I accepted my documents and Lough Key's as a firm officer. He was angry about Susan not being available to accept hers and my not knowing how to reach her. I recited the speech I was given about it not being the firm's or my legal obligation to assist him in his pursuit. Hector was present, and after giving the guy a minute to grouse and threaten, escorted him out of the building. The whole performance took about five minutes and was almost unnoticeable.

I spent the next hour catching up on emails, which were mostly gossipy inquiries about what was rumored to be occurring with Larry Katz and me, and a few people heard Susan was staying with me.

I almost deleted one email because I didn't recognize who it was from. I didn't because it had the names of my children in the subject. The email opened with he has no intention to harm me. He is the person who broke into my office and home to retrieve information regarding Mr. Stein. He has useful information that is valuable in defending the firm and me from any legal action EuroCredit Bank is planning. He wants to meet with me alone to give it to me because he wants to avoid trouble with the police. He suggests meeting at the restaurant near my building with the train car at four o'clock. He assures me he is harmless, but his colleagues are not, and they know the names of my children, that my daughter attends Georgetown University, and my son is at the University of Edinburgh. He assures me it is in both of our best interests and closes that he will be alone sitting at a back table. He warns me that he is being monitored and to meet him alone.

It took my breath away. I reread the email dozens of times. I don't know the time when Latesha poked her head in my office to remind me to check in. She said something about developing the habit even if it wasn't necessary now. Maybe because I looked stunned or didn't otherwise respond normally, she stepped in and asked if I was okay.

"No. Latesha, close the door, then come around and read this."

Latesha complied with my requests. "Girl, what's wrong with you? You're making me all nervous."

I didn't say anything as I turned my monitor around and pointed. Latesha's reactions were similar to mine—shock, disbelief, and terror. She sat down in one of my guest chairs staring at me. "What are we to do now? Get Bill?"

"No. Don't. Help me think this through first. We don't have much time before four, and I think the police are coming then. Billy will want to storm in and do something violent. Even if he can be prevailed to go in with the police, that doesn't protect my kids. Let's break this down. He hasn't asked for anything but must want something to risk meeting. It can't be anything I'll have with me. It's a public place where he's the outsider and will stand out. He knows it's modern times where every corner has a security camera, and everyone has a smartphone."

"Sounds like you're talking yourself into going alone. Why not at least notify the police?"

"What good will that do Ellie Rose in DC or Cahill in Edinburgh? I know it defies common sense to go by myself. I'm just not liking my choices. But, if I tell him the second I sit down that my phone is synced to two people, and the police are in the office, all on alert for any movement outside the restaurant or the phone being shut off..."

"That's the problem. What happens if your phone is shut down, and we lose you and can't get to you fast enough?"

"Jamal! I'm calling him now. I have fifteen minutes."

Latesha listened while I called Jamal and got no answer. I called the general number of the service and was told to leave a message.

I decided to get out of the office before the police arrived. Latesha joined me. We agreed that I would text 'k' every ten minutes, and she would sit at the bar, which was an anteroom to where my mystery date would be waiting. Her guise for hanging out there as a lone, respectable African American woman was planning an event in the upstairs party room, something we have done several times before. The owner/manager would be swooning with the prospective business and would be attentive to her while manning the hostess stand at the front door. She didn't like the plan and kept telling me how foolish it was. I agreed but reminded her no police anywhere have found a trace of my husband, and I wasn't going to put my kids in danger. We again agreed that the code word for trouble was 'cold.'

We walked in together to the dark interior. The décor was the sixties or seventies neighbored Italian bar and restaurant joint. I am pretty sure the owners are Greek, but the regulars from the exchanges let them maintain the Italian façade. The first room is a bar with captains' tables, dated red carpet, and a large, old-fashion wooden bar. This is where the serious drinkers hang out. The next room is a dining room with something like eight round tables, the restrooms in the back, and the same tired, red carpeting. The room next to it is a repurposed train car soldered to the building with a door cut out in the middle of the side adjacent to the restaurant to provide access into the rest of the restaurant. There are a separate staircase and door to the party room upstairs. Why I agreed to the rendezvous is the door into the bar is the only entrance into the downstairs restaurant, and I could easily be observed by Latesha. Four o'clock is prime happy hour with lots of people in the bar, but not too many in the train room.

Latesha walked in first and mentioned to the owner at the front desk she was here because Lough Key might be needing a party in two weeks that the upstairs party room could accommodate. She apologized for the short notice but said we didn't know until just now. She added she was fine sipping club soda at the bar when he had to seat people. He beamed, escorted her to the bar, and was distracted by running around getting the catering menu while watching for people who needed restaurant seating. I promised myself to at least host a big lunch there.

I easily slipped past the owner and walked through the anteroom to the train car room and saw him. He was sitting at the very most back table, at least four tables past the entrance door huddled in the corner chair. He was part of the trio who came to my office with Benny. His general physical type was the same as Larry Katz. Only this guy was clean, not scruffy looking with a contemporary haircut for his white-blond hair. He was a lot younger too. I pegged him for around twenty-five.

He smiled and stood up when I approached, which threw me off my stride. He held his hand out, pointing for me to sit down. "Miss Daye, I'm happy to meet you and apologize for the situation," he said in accented English. While correct grammar, it hinted that English was not his first language.

"It's nice to meet you also. What's your name?"

"You can call me Eric. Please sit down. Would you like something to eat? Please have a glass of wine or something to drink? What do you suggest is a good house dish?"

It occurred to me he was as uncomfortable as I was. I sat down. "Thank you, maybe in a minute. First, I need you to understand I have several friends watching for me." I pulled my cell out and placed it on the table and texted 'k' to Latesha. "My phone location is synced to two other people, and I'm to text a colleague every ten minutes."

Eric nodded and said I was wise. He asked me again for a recommendation. I gathered the waiter, who I always guessed was a relative of the owners, was lurking, and we were seated in the restaurant section. I told Eric the chicken and fish are all good, and my favorite is the veal salad. I wasn't joining him because I had dinner plans.

He looked sad. "I'm hoping you can join me at least for a drink. I hate eating alone and haven't had a meal with company in some time."

Against my better judgment, I ordered a glass of chianti. Eric ordered chicken parmigiana with a house salad and asked for a bottle of chianti for us to share. I texted Latesha this may take a while but am okay. He watched but didn't comment.

Since he didn't immediately say anything, I opened, asking what he wanted. He had a shy expression when he said all he wanted from me was a letter of reference for him to get a job on a cruise ship and hoped that would be acceptable to me after he explained his story. I stared, laughed, and texted Latesha to join us.

I was still laughing when Latesha and the wine arrived. I was laughing so hard from relief or tension release, I was crying and using the table napkin to wipe my tears. When I composed myself, I introduced them and said Latesha is one of the people watching me. For some reason, I trusted her joining us wasn't going to be an issue with my children's safety. Latesha read Eric as a lost lamb or some such person needing help, and he responded to her eyes.

"Okay, let's start again, Eric. I need to know if my children can be kept safe, then tell us about your associate, Nivar, and what to expect from the bank, and I'll probably agree to write you a recommendation letter but may need some help from you."

Latesha didn't say anything but sent a text to Billy, I assume, and sipped her club soda while sitting across from Eric.

Chewing on his salad, Eric commenced. "Your son and daughter are safe. I made up the danger to get you to meet me."

"How do you know so much about them?"

"I took photos of papers in your kitchen. Some were university invoices with names. I saw pictures on a board above your table in the kitchen. It was easy to look up online, especially your daughter, who has a big presence on Facebook. Google has information on both your son and daughter at university, and the pictures on Facebook made simple that you're their mother. I told no one, and they aren't in any danger from the people I know or me."

I took a gulp of wine. "What were you doing in my house and office?"

Eric said he needed to start his story from the beginning, which was last October when he was in Chicago with Nivar and another person who specialized in capital introductions for high-net-worth people and private equity investors. That was when they met Benny, and the master-mind idea of trading cryptocurrencies was hatched. He said that Benny thought it was to be a legitimate trading business and maybe with other currencies. He knew Nivar and the other man, who apparently has lots of names or aliases, thought it was a way to funnel money from the bank in the form of loans with the intent of incurring losses on the bank's books, but seeding businesses outside the bank's scope. The businesses were often illegal or supporting illegal activity like buying and leasing jets that happened to transport arms and drugs.

By now, the chicken parmigiana arrived. Eric continued his story. The loan funding had to be moved into accounts in the name of the borrower. That was the purpose of the charade at last year's end when they came to my office. Due to EuroCredit Bank being acquired effective January 1 of this year, that was the last day significant sums could be wired out of EuroCredit Bank exempt from the acquiring bank's oversight and controls. Eric suspected Benny knew all along I wasn't going to open an account or take money into a company account not properly papered. Eric thought Benny gambled and won. Ten million dollars was moved into an account in his name in a bank domiciled in Gibraltar because Benny wasn't signing loan papers in his name and wanted the company doing the trading with the loan proceeds to be formed first. Benny was being a stickler for legalities, and Nivar relented because the window was shutting on those types of deals.

I can't describe how entranced I was with Eric's narrative. I knew Benny was shrewd on a short-term basis but had no clue he was cunning and capable of long-term planning. Latesha listened and continued to send periodic texts.

I asked if Eric knew how things were supposed to progress. He said a rift occurred when Benny found out Nivar just wanted him to immediately default on the loan and not deploy the money as trading capital. It had to be a default for an easy windfall for Nivar. Benny wanted to use the money to trade. Nivar wouldn't wait for profits from the enterprise, which is when Benny ceased communications and appeared to have usurped the funds personally. I asked if anyone knew where the ten million dollars was, and Eric said the hope was with Lough Key. All he knew is ten million dollars was left in the bank in Benny's name, and Nivar authorized the wire on the last day of the year.

I paused. "So where do you fit in?"

Eric poured himself some wine. "I don't. I was Nivar's personal assistant. I walked away the other day. His demands were wrong, and I wasn't going to get paid what he promised. Understand I wasn't working for him anymore even if I was paid. I'm sincerely sorry for the problems and worry I caused. I was only trying to find out how much of the ten million dollars was with your company. I was promised one million dollars. I wanted to start an independent life, buy a business. I'm so sorry."

I wasn't buying his act of contrition but was game for getting the police to interview him and believed my children were in no danger. Eric was having none of it. He agreed to sign a letter once he was out of the country, but would not say when he was leaving, which meant soon.

I asked him what he hoped to accomplish by his disclosures. He repeated his hope of me writing a letter of recommendation stating he was a good performing former employee who was trustworthy. He explained he wanted to start in a new profession, and with his skillset of being trilingual and prior experience in customer service banking, he thought he would do well on cruise ships or resorts. The problem is he needs a glowing reference from a recent employer.

Latesha got up to leave and wished Eric well. She told me it would behoove both of us if I showed up at the office quickly and to be in time for my dinner date. She repeatedly mentioned she was giving me fifteen minutes. I knew she was going straight to Billy, Oscar, and that the police were probably still there. I nodded my understanding.

I asked for the check since Eric didn't seem predisposed to pay. I told Eric I would write a letter for him conditional on him writing a statement I can give to the police of what he described. As we were leaving, I asked him if he had any idea who shot Benny. He said no, and he and Nivar assumed it was something that happens in Chicago all the time from what they read in the newspapers. He described how Nivar wasn't in town, and he just arrived when it happened.

We were almost out the train car when a woman in her sixties with a beige rain hat pulled over her eyes and matching trench coat walked in and addressed me as Elaine Daye. When I said yes, she pulled a gun out of her right-hand coat pocket and told Eric and me to shut up and walk in front of her outside. I was too shocked to resist.

Outside on the busy corner of the Congress Expressway and Wells, we stopped. "I trust you know why I'm here," the woman said with a gun pointing at my abdomen.

Eric looked at me, which is when I figured out she was speaking to me. "Um, no, I don't know who you are. I'm sorry, but I don't and can't imagine what you want."

She tensed up, and her arm holding the gun shook. "I'm Beverly Stein, Benjamin's mother and sole heir. I need my money now. You can wire it to me. I'm not waiting for lawyers to settle this."

"Mrs. Stein, we don't have any of Benny's money. It was wired out pursuant to a court order this morning. I'm so sorry..."

"Well, then, you'll have to wire me the same amount, and you can fight with the lawyers to get it back. We're going to your office now. I know where it is. I've been there before. We don't have much time before the banks close."

As stupid as this sounds, in a public place with a witness, when someone clearly unhinged is pointing a gun at close range, you do what they want. It's not like TV where you can wrestle the gun away.

Eric ambled along in front of me, not sure what else to do. Mrs. Stein walked behind me with the gun poking in my side. We walked across the street, across the plaza with the Italian horse statue, and to my building. Naturally, the guard was on the phone with what sounded like a reservation for the hotel or Everest Room, and she waved my two companions and me on. I swiped my building access card three times across the turnstiles to let us all in, and we proceeded to the elevator. We stepped in, and as the door closed, Eric stepped out and jumped to the side. Mrs. Stein wasn't prepared for that but didn't seem to mind. Her eyes remained fixed on me with her gun pointing at me. And the doors closed.

I wasn't panicking, more incredulous. Eric getting off the elevator made sense. I would have given half a chance. My hope was he wanted his recommendation letter enough to call the office. He seemed resourceful enough to figure out how.

Mrs. Stein and I rode in silence during the thirty-second ride. I decided she didn't have a plan and was acting spontaneously and out of desperation. An awful thought occurred to me. She could have killed Benny, her son, over money. It fit. He was shot from someone right in front of him with a gun that might be his. My brain was buzzing with what-if scenarios and stalled when we got off on my office floor. It took another minute or so to get to the office front doors, which we walked in grim silence.

Latesha, and only Latesha, was in the reception area, which was odd. She looked up at me from the reception desk and said, "Good. I was wondering where you went off to. Don't forget you have to meet Susan and Connie downstairs to make your five-thirty reservation."

She then turned to look at Mrs. Stein. "I didn't know you were expecting anyone. Who's this? You going to the symphony, too?" I hoped this meant Latesha knew something big wasn't right.

"Oh, I'm sorry I forgot to tell you. This is Mrs. Stein, Benny's mother. She stopped by for any of his belongings that were left here. We won't be long. I need to grab my fleece before I leave. I'm very cold. I didn't expect being this cold with my sweater and jacket. We're going to my office first."

"Can I bring you something, some tea?"

Mrs. Stein nodded no. "Thanks, but that won't be necessary," I replied.

"Okay, but don't be long. Bill is planning on walking down with you on his way to dinner before the big game tonight."

Praying Latesha's Academy Award-winning performance made Mrs. Stein reconsider the wisdom of using her gun on me, we proceeded to my office with Mrs. Stein remaining behind me. When we finally entered my office, I went to my desk. Mrs. Stein closed the door before walking over to it and sitting in one of my guest chairs. I waited, not because I am brave but at a loss of what else to do.

She pulled from her other coat pocket a piece of paper. "Here's where I need you to wire five million dollars. We can wait here until you get a confirmation it was sent."

"What! You're out of your mind! Wait, I'm sorry and don't mean to be disrespectful, but that's not possible. It's after five o'clock, my bank is closed, and I don't have sole authority to send five-million-dollar wires, anyway. There're several security protocols, and one is a fob that's locked in a safe in another room that I need to activate to get a passcode that changes every minute. You must know this isn't feasible. Why are you doing this?"

"I have been waiting for you all afternoon. I know you can send the money if you really have to. I killed my own son, and

I'll shoot you, too. I don't have anything to lose. You're a smart, international business person, figure something out."

"How do you think you'll get away with this even if I figure out a way to wire you the money? Why do you need to do this?"

"Because the money will be immediately wired or converted where it can't be returned. I doubt an old, desperate woman will spend any serious time in jail. We're in Illinois where even mass murderers get probation, and there's no death penalty. It's my money, and I will have it. Today. You have one minute to get busy. Call your bank in Hong Kong or London. I'm not stupid. Banking is twenty-four hours for big trading firms."

I learned long ago you can't reason with a desperate person. I hoped Latesha and Billy were up to something, and the police had a plan other than barging in on a crazy person with a gun pointed at me.

I started my desktop computer and made a big show of looking up something. I dialed a bunch of random numbers and subtly hung up and dialed Billy's extension. "Hello, this is Elaine Daye from Lough Key. I need to wire five million dollars out to meet a margin call tonight. How do I do that? Yes, I have the firm credentials. No, I don't have the fob. No, neither are here. What can be wired on my own authority?" I recited my office phone number prefaced with the international code for the US and said I would wait for instructions.

The whole act seemed contrived and beyond stupid, but I hoped it bought me some time. Mrs. Stein's eyes were getting glassy and wild-looking, and her hand with the gun was shaking. I tried again.

"Mrs. Stein, why are you doing this?"

"Because my one son is an idiot, and my other is a heartless clown. That coke-head slut isn't going to get my family's money. I can't get it myself. Benny has CIA level protections on his computers. Idiot Paul will take whatever money he can for himself. Being a career idiot, there won't be much left, anyway."

"Why do you need money so desperately and fast? You can't be worried about being homeless. Please, it can't be this bad."

"You're an idiot, too. I killed my son. It was an accident. I meant to scare him into giving me my money. He made me so mad, I just shot and shot him. I found out today that they can trace the location of his phone and computers and will know it was me. I need money to leave or at least have when I get out. I'm serious, nothing matters but me having millions. Not pity money to buy groceries."

She was screaming and shaking more. I now knew how Benny got shot three times in the face, and I was next. BLAM! My door was kicked open, and I dove under the desk. By the grace of God, I didn't get hit by the bullet Mrs. Stein shot. I don't recall the next few minutes or even how many bullets were shot. What I recall is Latesha pulling me up and sitting me in my chair, lots of police, and so much noise it made me dizzy like strobe lights.

Chapter 16

I was admitted to Northwestern Memorial Hospital for shock. I was supposed to stay longer for observation and for the police to interview me. I wouldn't let them put an IV in, which turned out to be good because I could walk out after a couple of hours. I was fine and wasn't waiting for hospital bureaucracy. I think I was sent there because the police didn't know what else to do with me. My guess is they wanted me where they could find me after they established a theory about Mrs. Stein and her gun.

I took an Uber home. Thank goodness for Uber because I had no money or credit cards. I found Susan smoking on the back stairs watching Fred in the yard. She was relieved and pleased to see me. She explained how she tried reaching me by phone, but I wasn't picking up. She figured I would surface back at my flat where she would wait and hang out with Fred. Fred ran up to me and slobbered his welcome all over and leaned into me. I kneeled and hugged him hard. I felt empty and numb.

We went into my kitchen. After noticing Fred was fed and hadn't touched his dinner, I grabbed a bottle of wine, cheese, and crackers and went into the living room where I flopped on my couch with my feet up. It was only eight thirty, and I was exhausted. Susan followed me in with glasses and a bottle opener. After she did the honors, I asked her if she knew what happened.

"Not all of it. I went to Elizabeth's office at three and was done signing papers with enough time to walk to your office. I thought I'd meet you there, and we would go to the restaurant together to meet your friends. I sent you a text but didn't think anything of it when you didn't respond. I figured you would only respond if it wasn't a good plan. The receptionist told me you left with Latesha and didn't know if you were coming back. Then Latesha blew in and raced into the conference room without saying a word to us. It wasn't long before Latesha came out and told the receptionist to go home and leave fast. She noticed me when she was on the office intercom announcing the front door and stairs up to the accounting department are closed for maintenance and to use the fire stairs to leave the building. She pointed to the conference room and just said, "Go." I did but left the door opened, which is when the front desk phone rang, and she grabbed it. Bill, Oscar, and the two police detectives were already there. Latesha yelled that the man she told them about just called from the lobby security desk to warn us you were coming up with Benny's mother holding a gun on you.

"The police jumped up. The big one made Bill and Oscar go to the back of the room and be quiet. The short one was making calls on his phone with lots of police codes. The big one told Latesha she did good and to sit at the reception like what they planned. He asked about locking interior doors and left. The short one closed the conference room door and motioned us to be quiet. I didn't see anything else but heard your voice when you entered. When you were gone for a few minutes, the short one got out, and I could see him with other police in vests with guns coming in a line. He kept signaling to be quiet. In a couple of minutes, there was lots of noise from what must have been a door knocked down, shots, yelling, and a woman screaming like she was in hell. I next heard Latesha running around the office telling people to stay away. I didn't see where Bill and Oscar ran to when they bolted out of the conference room.

"I stayed in the conference room where I could watch. It was orderly chaos for almost an hour, I'm not sure. Paramedics came, but it took them a while. You were wheeled out. God, I thought you were shot. I didn't think you were dead because I could see your head, and I thought you were trying to talk. Then regular police left with Beverly on a gurney. She was totally silent with her eyes closed. My guess is she was sedated. After more time, I got up and walked in past the kitchen where I could see most of the office. Police and your crew were clustered in smaller groups, which is when I decided to leave. I drove your car home and have been hanging out since around seven. Oh, I told the Metzkers I have a headache and bailed on the symphony, but you went ahead with your friends. They didn't think anything of it, but I had to dodge dinner with them and Mr. M's offer to watch the Blackhawks' game with me."

I had nothing to say when she was done. We sat in silence while I processed. Susan smoked and watched me. Fred kept slapping me with his giant paw and putting his head on my stomach. Signs I need to snap out of this. I turned so that my feet were on the ground and fished my phone out. It was now time to face the music and hoped the hospital didn't notify anyone I left. I was counting on the HIIPA medical privacy laws not to alarm anyone. I turned my phone back on and noticed Billy and Latesha were looking for me. Damn, I hoped they didn't go to the hospital. I texted both I was fine and home. Latesha responded in two seconds.

I answered her call and asked where she was. She just got home after leaving the hospital. They would not tell her if I was there or not. She was with Billy and Connie. All they were told was that the police came in with two patients into the ER, and they aren't permitted to share any information. I explained my phone was off, how I left because there is nothing wrong with me that being left alone won't cure, and I wasn't going to hang out waiting for the police to speak to me. I didn't want to do that alone, which mollified her. She said to call Billy fast. He's in the office with Oscar and Connie, and they are blowing up the phones of every person they can think of to get news on me. She sounded tired and relieved when we hung up.

Next was Billy, who called twice when I was speaking with Latesha. I hoped he figured out why I didn't answer. He picked up immediately and started blasting me with questions and yelling at me for being stupid and inconsiderate. Connie managed to snatch the phone away from him and started over, only calmer. I apologized profusely, could offer no excuses other than I wasn't myself, and assured them I was fine but needed some serious alone time and rest. I told her I didn't have the energy to explain what happened and again apologized for worrying them.

The whole time I heard Billy storming and ranting in the background. Connie gave the phone to Oscar, who asked if I was really okay and made me promise to let him know if I needed anything. He liked me being at home and Susan being there to keep an eye on me. The mention of her name provoked Billy to get on again, demanding to speak to Susan. I held it up and out for her with a nonverbal question. She nodded and got up to take the phone. From what I heard, she promised to triple-lock the building, double-check the security system, let Fred out, and not to let me out of her sight. I took the phone and told Billy I needed to sleep and would check in with them in the morning.

"Thank you. I owe you an apology, too. I'm very sorry for all the drama and the pain it must cause you. I'm also sorry about Billy, but he means well."

"Hey, it's nice to have people who care so much."

I bolted up and asked if there was anything in the news that would alert my kids. We both checked and didn't see anything. I called Ellie Rose and was grateful when she didn't answer. She texted, asking if I was at the symphony. I responded positively and just wanted to know a good time to check in tomorrow. Because it was two in the morning in Edinburgh, I decided to call Cahill in the morning.

I sat up. "I'm sorry, but I really need to sleep. Is it okay if I ask you to pick being here or in Mrs. Brown's apartment? I need to be alone and not feel disoriented with sounds from other people. You're truly welcome here. You have been a huge help." I felt like it sounded like a lame invitation. "Wait, I just thought of something. It probably doesn't make sense for you to return to Florida for a while. Why don't you stay at Mrs. Brown's? I know the décor is onerous, but it's convenient and fully furnished, and it would be nice if you were around."

Susan watched me while exhaling. "Isn't she coming back?"

"I don't think so. I told her daughter that it was time to have her somewhere safer. I was catching her do things like falling asleep after her before-dinner drinks so soundly she was leaving the stove on. One time, I went up there because the smell of gas was so strong. I checked on her another time when I heard bathwater running for too long. She fell asleep in the bathtub. Thank goodness I checked because she could have drowned, and the water could have flooded. She was shaky on her feet when sober, which was never past six o'clock, and what would happen if she fell? I didn't want the responsibility, and the Metzkers aren't up for that level of supervision."

"Yeah, thanks, I'd like that. I don't know for how long, though. How much is the rent?"

I got a bad case of the giggles. "Nothing. I've never collected a penny from Mrs. Brown."

"What's so funny about that?"

"She pays Mr. M five hundred and nineteen dollars every month like clockwork on the first day of the month, and he deposits it. The person who'll be upset by the new arrangement is Mr. M. I think that was more than his mad money. It maintained the illusion he still owns the building. We can worry about rent if you're staying a long time and after you change the furniture."

"Five hundred and nineteen dollars a month for her place, for real? Besides being a weird amount, that's free. Why?" Susan asked.

"Some things are just not worth the bother. It's too hard to explain."

"I really appreciate this. I like it here."

"Truly, my pleasure. Besides the hailstorm is about to get worse regarding Sharon. I wager Paul and his wife demand guardianship. And, poor Benny's service still has to be arranged. You shouldn't have to bother with finding a place to stay. I'm sorry, but I need to crash."

"One more thing. Are you staying home tomorrow?"

The question surprised me. "No. I better go in and make an appearance. It will quell the rumors about me if I show up. Good point, though. I'll text Billy, Latesha, and Oscar to let them know I'll be in before lunch."

"Okay, but don't forget, I need to show you how the security system works. It's real easy, but you need to pay attention, or it will go off when you don't mean it to."

I nodded my agreement but couldn't comprehend anything else. I defied orders and let Fred out. Susan took the ashtray and a few items and went upstairs. I immediately fell sound asleep, into the deepest sleep I had in years. So much so that I didn't hear my phone ringing the first time it rang. It was before three in the morning when it started ringing again. I was so disoriented I struggled to remember where I was and finding the phone.

Once I saw it was Cahill, I was sharp and wide awake. "Cahill, Cahill, are you all right?"

"Mom, what the hell is going on? Where are you? In the hospital?"

"No, no, everything is fine. There was an attempted robbery at the office. I'm fine, nothing much came of it. I almost called you, but it was too late for you. Wait, how did you hear? I checked the news."

"Mom, half the guys I went to school with called me. Two of my fraternity brothers clear through Lough Key. How did you not think I'd hear? What's going on? I heard you were attacked twice and shot and sent to the hospital. Something is going on. Are you safe? Should we come home?"

My delayed response wasn't helping. "Look, I'm sorry. I was going to call tomorrow or I mean this morning. I really didn't think something so silly and local would get so much attention."

"Mom, did you really cold-cock some guy by the parking lot? I thought that couldn't be true, but then I heard about your ninja moves when some guy jumped you. Several people sent me texts last night about police with guns rushing your office, and somebody said he saw you getting into an ambulance. None of that sounds minor. You haven't been answering your phone, and neither have the Keagans. What's going on?"

I was sitting cross-legged in bed trying to sound lighthearted and calm. "It's a long story I'll tell you over the weekend. Honestly, it's not that bad, just long and, well, I can't really describe how nonsensical this is. The guy I did knock down was trying to get me to accept legal papers in an office building during business hours. I was never at risk for robbery or bodily harm. I hate to admit it, but I outweigh him by at least fifteen pounds and am the same height. I've known him since before you were born. He's a neighborhood bully who keeps pushing, poking, and trash-talking. The whole situation was nothing worse than something that happens on a playground. Really, just an annoyance."

"And the office robbery with a fully-armed swat team? Did you go to a hospital as a patient?"

"That's more complicated. The unsuccessful robber was a woman in her sixties who was more bark than a real threat. No swat team came. There were a few street-beat cops, and the whole thing was over in a few minutes. That one was scary but not the big deal you heard. I can tell you the play-by-play once I know more."

"Were you in the hospital?"

"For an hour. I took an Uber home. Really, I'm fine."

"Mom, you're full of shit. You gotta appreciate that, well, you know, since Dad didn't come back."

I sighed. "I know, and you're right. That's why I was going to call later today when I'm more coherent. I'm so sorry and am really fine. Tell you what, I have a houseguest, installed a security system, and am being careful. I probably shouldn't have told you that, but the danger wasn't directed at me, and everything is okay now."

"Can I call Aunt Connie?"

"Good idea. Just wait until after she has her morning coffee."

We exchanged pleasantries and hung up with the promise to speak this weekend. He promised not to alarm Ellie Rose, and I promised to come clean with her over the weekend. I was glad I asked Susan to stay upstairs. I was too wired to sleep. I made some herbal tea and played classical piano music. It was nine when I woke up, exhausted, and not sure when I fell asleep.

Chapter 17

Pär looked out the window as the jet took off from O'Hare for a nonstop flight to Stockholm. He splurged for a window seat with a bit more leg room. He easily made his nine-thirty flight and enjoyed the Admirals Club lounge's booze and sandwiches beforehand. The decision to go to Stockholm made more sense. He needed to distance himself from the reach of German authorities because the German bank might want an investigation. He was too insignificant to chase in Sweden, if they found him. He knew Stockholm, and it was getting warmer there. It would be nice and clean and safe for someone like him to walk the streets whenever and wherever he wanted. It was cheap enough and he wouldn't need a car. Yes, a good plan.

He still planned on asking Miss Daye for a letter of recommendation. The only drawback was admitting his name isn't Eric, but that could be explained as his nickname because of his last name. Pär suspected he easily slipped onto this plane because if someone were searching for him, they wouldn't be looking for a Pär from Sweden, but an Eric from Germany. He hoped she wasn't compelled to disclose his real name to the police.

Pär started composing his email to her in his mind. He would have to apologize for leaving her in a hostage situation, but would justify it because he had the security desk call for help. He had nothing to lose, and she seemed nice. She may even laugh again at his request. Yes, another good plan. Pär sipped his beer and toasted silently his reflection in the window.

Chapter 18

I woke up so groggy and disoriented, I changed my routine and went to get coffee instead of first showering. Susan made a fresh pot and left a note saying she let Fred out and took him upstairs to hang out with the Metzkers. I was unnerved how soundly I slept that I didn't notice her moving around with Fred. Her note continued that she left instructions for the Metzkers to let me sleep, and she had to get to Elizabeth's office first thing this morning.

Returning to my room, I recalled speaking to Cahill and his intent to call Connie. When I picked up my phone, I saw three texts from Susan asking me to call her ASAP. I took the phone and my coffee to my reading chair with an ottoman in the sunroom. I figured it had to be significant for Susan to be so persistent.

I was right. The Steins had erupted into a hell storm of chaos. Susan sounded calm and asked if I would mind if she put Elizabeth on speakerphone. What Elizabeth related was that Paul and his wife are demanding immediate custody of Sharon's trust and any other assets of Benny's. They also are going to court as soon as possible to be named Sharon's legal guardian. They physically relocated Sharon to their house and were not permitting her to leave or speak to anyone on the phone without them present. Elizabeth didn't sound like that would be more than a short-term inconvenience for Sharon because their actions were so extreme, and Sharon was over eighteen, of sound mind with only slightly challenged mobility. Elizabeth was preparing a rebuttal and was going to ask for restraining orders to preclude them from approaching Susan or Sharon.

I wasn't connecting the dots to how or why I was involved. Susan explained that she was hoping I was okay with relocating Sharon to Mrs. Brown's apartment to live with her until she could find another housing solution, which she assured me she would do quickly. She couldn't easily kick out the tenants in her condo or Benny's buildings and needed somewhere fast to present to the court. She now sounded exhausted.

"Sure, that will be fine. I'm not sure my place will be to either of your likings, but I'm okay if it buys you some time. Honestly, the biggest concern should be whether you're up for the responsibility and the fight. Nineteen-year-old girls can be a lot to handle. Sharon may have other high-maintenance needs."

Susan exhaled and sounded like she was rubbing her head or was otherwise in pain.

"God, don't I know it. I'm not sure. I don't have any experience with this type of thing, and I'm still working on staying clean. I spoke to Sharon this morning, which is why they took her phone away. From what it sounds like, the only plan left to the Steins crazy nuts financial problems is to control Sharon and her money. It's unreal what she told me. Paul gambled whatever assets he had plus got his mother to take out a huge equity loan on her house for whatever he was doing with real estate. The real estate market tanks, and they have nothing. Paul is in trouble at his firm, too. Things are so bad that Mrs. Stein was pawning jewelry and selling things on eBay. According to Sharon, they were getting desperate because the items that brought in the most cash were the Louis Vuitton luggage sets and designer purses. Sharon was told to sell anything on eBay she could mail, even shoes.

"I'm not ready to be a caretaker for an adult child, but I can't leave her in that hell. I know this is a lot to ask. I promise to stay out of your way and be just a tenant. I just need some time and to show the court Sharon will have a place to stay."

"Okay, then. Do you need to have a lease or a letter from me? Wait, don't answer now. I'm desperate for a shower and need to call the office. My phone is blowing up, and I don't want any more people to worry. Send me a text of what I need to do or sign and when. I'm in."

Thinking how I have to get over my impulse to solve other people's problems, I checked in with Latesha. I told her I would be in within the hour, and the reason I was not responding was I was in a deep sleep. She sounded pleased with that recap and said she would let Virgil and the building know. Damn, I hoped that wasn't still necessary.

Having learned the collateral damage to my reputation caused by my limited concern over my appearance, I put in more of an effort that morning. Virgil hugged me without asking if I was okay. Angela and Clayton called me Lois and said it was good to see me, and no one said I looked "nice today." The extra few minutes to style my hair and put on mascara were worth the effort.

Starz was at the front desk. "Hello, Lois, I mean Miss Lane. Sorry. Mr. Marquis said to ask you to go to his office. The police are here again." I laughed and thanked her.

Detective Williams and Detective Guzman were sitting in Oscar's guest chairs, and Billy was leaning against a windowsill. Latesha came in right behind me and hugged me, which made me feel bad for how much she must have worried. Oscar has a small table that is between two additional guest chairs, which Latesha and I took. I took it we were on good terms with the police since Oscar permitted them into his office.

After assuring everyone I was fine, I pointedly changed the subject of how I left the hospital. By now, I knew most of the story about Benny's murder but didn't know what to expect next. Detective Guzman asked where Susan was. I told them the gist of my conversation with Susan and Elizabeth before leaving for downtown and explained that I am expected back at Elizabeth's office to sign some papers so she can file them in court to spring Sharon. I added that I hoped whatever she was filing would have some sort of restraining orders to keep all of the Steins away. I asked again what was going to happen to Mrs. Stein.

After arresting her at the hospital, where she remains under sedation, the police went back and took another look at the security videos from Presidential Towers. Mrs. Stein was seen entering and leaving around what has been concluded as the time of Benny's death. She was wearing the same beige trench coat and rain hat pulled down over her face and was carrying a tote bag. There was no reason to consider her a person of interest when the video was first viewed because she was an elderly woman, and they couldn't see her face. It was surmised that she was carrying something heavier in the tote bag than when she entered by the way it hung down over her shoulder.

Mrs. Stein's house was searched last night, and they found a gun buried in her garden that was recently shot. It has been sent to the crime lab for confirmation it was the one used to kill Benny. Interestingly, it was not the same gun she pulled on me. They also found the tote bag with Benny's keys, laptop, tablet, and phone hidden under an old cabinet in the garage used to store gardening equipment and miscellaneous household junk. She apparently tried to breach the security protocols and broke the screen of the tablet. A review of her internet activity revealed a lot of time spent trying to open Apple devices without a password or fingerprint. She was not tech-savvy and didn't know to erase her history. One of the last articles was how an iPhone can be found and prior locations tracked remotely if stolen, which is probably what panicked her.

I asked what would probably happen to her. Detective Williams sighed. "Nothing all that bad considering. She's a respectable, suburban, old white lady. Don't need a smart lawyer to argue temporary insanity and other mental problems. Throw in some medical issues, and she'll get life in a skilled nursing place with other old folks all paid for by the state."

I remembered what she said in my office and mentioned how she told me then she needed real money and not just enough for groceries and how she had nothing to lose since nothing would happen to her if she got caught. I next asked about Nivar whatever-his-name-is and the bank.

"Well, that's more interesting. From what we were told, there's a lot of money unaccountable from the bank. So much that an INTERPOL investigation and alert went out on him," Detective Williams said.

"Really? INTERPOL is really a thing?"

"Yes, ma'am. Although I'm not sure what'll come of it, but I'm sure we won't be told. What happened to the skinny little blond man who was last seen having dinner with you? He disappeared without a trace. You ever get his name?"

"No. He told me it was Eric, and he was definitely one of the three who came to my office at year-end. I wouldn't be surprised if that wasn't his real name, and he never told me his last name. He told me he was leaving town, and my bet is he left that night."

"So why the hell did you meet with him?" Billy asked.

Latesha started to come to my defense, but I stepped in. "Because he implied my children could be at risk. Billy, I'm not going to argue with you now. You would have done the same thing. I was never in danger. You and Latesha could track my whereabouts from my phone, and Latesha plus dozens of other people could see us."

Detective Williams asked what he wanted, and if he was the same man who broke into my house and office.

"Yes, he admitted to the break-ins with the hopes of getting information on where ten million dollars was wired from the bank to at least one account in Benny's name." I then told them his version of the story and how he was promised one million dollars but had figured out that it wasn't to be. He said he wasn't working for Nivar anymore and needed to leave town. I started laughing when I told them all he wanted from me was a glowing letter of recommendation for him to start a new career working on cruise ships.

After more comparing notes and commenting how Eric's story matched Bunky's, I learned that Eric did run to the security guards and told them to tell my black-lady friend I was coming up with Benny's mother and she had a gun. So, I guess I do owe him a letter of recommendation.

Before the police left, they informed me I could anticipate being contacted as a victim or witness to Mrs. Stein's attempt to kidnap me and extort funds. They had no idea how long it would take but hoped it would not go to court and be settled with a plea bargain.

I walked out with the police and went to Elizabeth's office. Neither Susan or Elizabeth were there, but a stack of legal forms, a lease, and a letter from me as a character reference for Susan were prepared for my signature. I went straight home afterward. I just wasn't up for all the sympathy and well-wishers hoping to hear a better version of recent events from me.

Home turned out not to be my private sanctuary. I could hear footsteps upstairs, including Fred's. The Metzkers were watching for me because I wasn't past my kitchen when I heard them ringing my front bell inside the entryway. Sighing, I opened the door and stepped out to close the door behind me. I firmly told them I couldn't talk but promised to come upstairs once I checked in with my children. I was insanely compelled to have dinner with them and promised to bring it upstairs. They looked hurt and didn't stop clucking about being worried and so many new people in the building. I didn't respond and locked the door once I re-entered my house.

I fired up my desktop and Skyped to Cahill. He arranged for Ellie Rose to be available too and connected her to the call. We talked for well over an hour. Cahill did speak to Connie, who had a less dramatic update from what he heard from his friends. I recapped the past week and became tired all over. They had lots of questions, for which several I had no answers.

I bolted alive when I was explaining how Eric, my home invader, told me how easy it was to obtain information on them and how he said it was especially easy for Ellie Rose because her Facebook page is accessible to anyone. At another time soon, we need to revisit this. I didn't add that we also have to consider that someone could try to reach us regarding their father, and we needed to leave that door open. They knew. We agreed to talk again together on Sunday. After hanging up, I never felt so sad or lonely in my life.

Time to snap out of it. I went upstairs with Fred's leash and found the front door to Mrs. Brown's apartment open. Inside were the Metzkers, Susan, Fred, and a very thin and frail young woman with long dark hair in a braid down her back dressed in PINK sweatpants and matching top in the living room. The girl was on the floor with Fred rubbing his belly. Susan introduced me to Sharon as the downstairs' neighbor, and her smirk alerted to me that the Metzkers were introduced to Sharon as the landlords.

I asked if there were any requests for dinner and was shocked when Susan told me they already decided on grilled hamburgers. Sharon had a craving for them, so Susan was planning on going to the hardware store to buy a charcoal grill and to the Jewel for the ingredients.

She slyly looked at me and asked Mr. M if it was okay for her to have a little Weber grill in the yard. He graciously allowed it but would need to personally supervise its location and her grilling rituals to make sure it was all safe. I told Susan to take my car and left with Fred for a long-overdue walk. I couldn't decide if I was pissed or bemused by the charade I wasn't the building owner. Then inspiration struck!

After sending Fred to his bed in my sunroom for a late afternoon nap, I went to the Metzkers' unit. Mrs. M greeted me ecstatically and had me sit down in their living room. She was overjoyed I was back, so relieved everyone was safe, and wanted to know if it was true I was almost shot, was thanking God I was alive, etc. Mr. M was sitting in his easy chair listening and engaged but waiting to butt in.

When Mrs. M finally paused for a breath, he gave it his best shot. He liked Susan, and Sharon seemed like a nice girl, but I have no right to be renting out Mrs. Brown's apartment when it's not sure she won't be coming back, and he never approved of Susan or young girls living in the building. I let him yammer for a few minutes and stopped him cold.

"Enough. I apologize we haven't had a chance to talk, and a lot has happened this week. First, Mrs. Brown isn't coming back. I told her daughter she has to make other arrangements because it isn't safe for her anymore. Don't argue with me. You know she almost drowned, and she was passed out every night by the time the six o'clock news was over. She could have burned the building down or caused a flood. Neither of us are equipped to watch her, and God forbid, she fell, and we didn't check on her.

"Secondly, you forget I'm the legal trustee of the building. Out of respect for you, I won't remind you how that came to be. It's my job to do what's best for the building and our mutual safety. Susan moving in with Sharon is a good thing. It's on a probationary basis, no longer than by the end of the summer if it doesn't work out. I don't need your permission. Your job is to make sure the building is properly maintained to your standards and to let me know what needs to be done so that repairs and things like painting get done.

"I apologize again for the stress and needing to have a security system and a bodyguard one night. All that's over, but it's a good idea for the security system. I also apologize for not consulting you, but believe me, things happened so fast, it wasn't possible. I didn't find out about Sharon needing a place to stay until this morning on my way to work. Are we good?" I was standing up with my arms crossed.

He wasn't happy or fooled by my status as the building trustee but accepted the face-saving solution over being outed as not the building's owner. He probably was unsettled by so much change, and that Mrs. Brown leaving was another sad milestone of time taking its toll. Once we were done, Mrs. M was happily fluttering about how wonderful it will be to have Susan and Sharon downstairs and how we need to welcome a young girl from such a sad situation.

Two weeks later, my orbit was calmer but not back to normal. Mrs. Stein was denied bail at first, which was a moot point since she couldn't come up with it. Being a frail, elderly woman who was portrayed as not posing a threat to the general public, she was confined to Paul's house with an ankle bracelet. I objected to the characterization, but the State of Illinois didn't want the bother or expense of incarcerating a little old lady. Sharon's opinion was that jail would be more pleasant.

Susan agreed to permit the police to turn over all of Benny's devices stolen by Mrs. Stein to the FBI with a release they could do whatever they wanted with them, and that Sharon's and her trust had no claim on any assets outside of the IB brokerage and two bank accounts. His real estate holdings were apparently outside the scope of their interest. As of the date of this writing, she has not heard back with any results. As Elizabeth anticipated, no authority or bank tried to reclaim the two million dollars that was wired from Lough Key to Sharon's trust account. She surmised that it would take years for them to confirm the source and build a case, and it wasn't worth the bother or her ire.

Elizabeth sent Larry Katz and Paul Stein restraining orders and cease-and-desist orders. My bet is once they knew Benny's devices were with the FBI, they knew it was a lost cause to try to mine for more of whatever cash Benny may have elsewhere, and they weren't going to intimidate Elizabeth into relinquishing a cent. In fact, she nicely turned the tables on them, and they were in defensive mode. Even Larry was, which was impressive.

It turned out Sharon was enrolled at DePaul University and had successfully passed one online class. She couldn't take more classes because the money Benny gave her for her tuition was usurped for the Steins' living expenses. DePaul has trimesters plus a summer session. The spring trimester starts at the end of March, and Sharon was registered for four classes. She had two girlfriends from high school who were also attending DePaul who were living in a campus-sponsored apartment for four girls. One of the other girls dropped out, and Sharon was slated to take her place.

Susan was in Billy's office when I returned from O'Doole's. Before I could ask why, Billy wanted the scoop on why O'Doole was so frantic for me to stop by.

"You remember Steven Link, acronym LNK? His firm had the big options specialist operation before the banks and New York firms bought them all out. It's the same LNK story that just won't die. I don't think he's as delusional as everybody says, just a pushy egomaniac who wants to be considered in the same league as the real high-profile traders who get a lot of press."

"He hasn't been relevant for ten years, and what's going on that O'Doole is wasting time during tax season on him, and why are you involved?" Billy asked.

"It's beyond stupid. The big industry trade show next month in Florida is recognizing a couple of LNK's peers from back in the day with some sort of industry founder award. Gossip has it that LNK aggressively lobbied to be included in that group and succeeded by paying an exorbitant amount of money to underwrite the conference. I have no idea if that's true, but it sort of makes sense.

"Another story floating around is he's writing his memoirs and wants proof of his P&L exploits. He wants O'Doole to somehow credential old daily P&L daily runs, some pre-date Y2K. O'Doole has told him dozens of times why he can't, but LNK won't let it go. I was asked to stop by to remind LNK of the real nature of those spreadsheets and the source of the firm's biggest paydays."

"Why would you know?"

"I was the lead partner of the audit that was engaged to stage his firm for a sale. LNK kept pestering me about not using GAAP and to reflect the profits on his daily sheets. O'Doole did his taxes then, like now, and used to explain why the tax returns have to sync with the clearing sheets, which LNK liked because he paid less taxes on the clearing sheet reflected P&L. LNK understood his sale price was a function of P&L and wanted to bolster it. He kept explaining to me that his firm made over a one hundred percent return on capital.

"I was in his office one morning when I saw how his daily sheets were run. He had a high school kid from IMSA write a script for a data file that was downloaded daily. One version had all the trading accounts with the normal KPIs. At the bottom of the dashboard was a button labeled 'Make Me LNK Worthy.' Once activated, another version would run without any of the losing accounts because LNK didn't like seeing them in his totals. One of the reasons why a high school kid, albeit a genius, was commissioned to write that program was because no legit programmer would, besides him being too cheap to pay the market prices for development projects."

"So?"

"O'Doole asked me to recount my knowledge of the daily sheets LNK was so hot to credential. He gave up on trying to explain accountants don't sign off on internally run, ancient spreadsheets with no source documents. I also shared my memory of his firm really hitting it big after one of his traders rolled the dice and gambled on the outcome of a trade agreement vote. That was a big problem with the pitch book because the firm didn't have those levels of profits previously. I also reminded him the P&L earned during the Dot.com bubble was mostly lost when it burst and after 911.

"When I was done, O'Doole suggested that I wasn't the only one with a long-term memory from those days, and, perhaps, LNK shouldn't press his luck by provoking any public corrections or amplifications."

"How'd LNK take it?"

"Okay, I guess. He was deflated and frustrated but figured out he wasn't going to prevail. O'Doole hopes LNK realizes he was trying to protect LNK's reputation but only time will tell. Meanwhile, LNK gets his award and is out of O'Doole's office. Enough of that, why are we here?"

Oscar walked in and asked if we were told yet.

Billy shook his head.

"You know Boche Bank that just bought Giro Group? Both are big customers of our prop desks here and in Europe. They called us first with shows and when they are looking for pricing. Boche Bank makes most of its money trading, while the acquired bank has the biggest book of buy-side end-user clients. Only they don't trade options much and are mostly cash with occasional futures hedging.

"Helmet Maer, who's now in charge of Business Development Strategies, remembers his son participated in a workshop taught by our Education Department. He wants to know if we can send people to present two simultaneous workshops at the end of the month over a three-day European-wide bank holiday. One for beginners and one more advanced, but he doesn't want anything too mathematically intense. We don't usually provide that type of service offering and don't have the bandwidth within the Education Department. We'll have internal classes ending then, and one of them has a wife expecting their first child any minute. And then I remembered..."

I hate it when Billy indulges in pregnant pauses for dramatic effect with a twinkle in his eye. It means he agreed to something that he thinks is some combination of clever and hilarious.

I indulged him. "Yes?"

"I spoke to Gail, our bond trader who does this sort of thing freelance. She used to run education and training for another group and speaks something like four languages. She's in if our guys produce the PowerPoint presentation, which they can easily do. She's great for the advanced session. I thought Susan would be great for the beginners. Again, our team will produce the workshop materials."

"Gail, as in GDH, the ski instructor who owns race horses and looks like her sister, the runway fashion model?" Susan asked.

"Yep, and you!"

"Why?"

"I shared my observation with Helmut that Europeans, especially from Catholic backgrounds, aren't going to be excited about working during what's to them a three-and-a half-to-five-day holiday. But, if the instructors look like Gail and you, maybe we can get a little more cooperation. The workshop is scheduled to run Thursday through Saturday morning, so everyone can be home Saturday night. A lot of the participants are Middle Eastern or from more secular European countries like the Dutch. They are the ones who'll benefit the most, anyway. You know Gail, right?"

"Yeah, she's great. I'm not so sure I'm ready. That's going to be one hardcore group of partyers. I like the idea and think it could be fun, but I don't want to risk my sobriety or your workshop."

"Two things..." He was back to pausing and eye twinkling. "Laney and Kevin are joining you, and the whole event will be contained at a hotel where no one should leave the premises."

"What? Why am I going?"

"Helmut also wants advice he describes as actionable on the tax and other considerations of sending people to the US to work and hiring US citizens to work in Europe. He suspects his advisors of over-complicating the issue and knows we have expatriate experience. He's willing to pay for the consulting and to give us a favored-nation status in conducting business under the new regime. All you need to do is give him the high points and point him in the direction of lawyers and tax specialists you think are good. It's only a couple of days, and you can then go see Cahill. Bring Ellie Rose because I recall it's her spring break."

I hated to admit liking the idea but did. "Why is Kevin going?"

"To chaperone?" asked Oscar.

Susan snorted her laugh.

"He needs exposure to European compliance. Helmut will arrange for him to shadow counterparts at the bank. He can develop his professional network and learn business etiquette and protocols. Let's face it, his tours in Afghanistan didn't prepare him for conducting business overseas. Susan, I was hoping you would be his guide."

Within the next two days, plans were settled, and we each prepped for our respective functions. It was fun doing something new and consistent with my actual job at the firm. Billy was right, Ellie Rose could join Cahill and me. Susan hoped going with Gail, Kevin, and me would be enough of a support system and said she had to figure out how not to rely on Benny. It sounded like Gail was already well acquainted with at least half of her workshop group.

I did get an email from Pär Ericsson, otherwise known as Eric, hoping I was well and asking if I would please prepare a letter of recommendation on company letterhead. For my convenience, he attached a draft. It wasn't too bad. It said we were professionally acquainted, and I knew him to be resourceful and honest. He spoke English, Swedish, and Russian fluently and was conversational in German, French, and Italian. He also had excellent social skills and got along well with people from different cultures.

I obliged his request even though the part about him being honest was a stretch. I wished him well and asked that he not contact me again.

THE END

Silent Partners - FAQ

How closely do many of the events in *Silent Partners* resemble actual events and people?

To answer that, I am going to refer to lawandorderfandom.com for its clarification as to the extent *Law & Order* episodes advertised as 'ripped from the headlines' are based on actual events. Like the television show, *Silent Partners* is inspired by actual events, and some of the characters may resemble real people. However, *Silent Partners* is a work of fiction, and its characters are embellishments or totally made up by me. My book is not intended to be a sly 'tell-all' but a fun story staged within the Chicago trading community. Characters who are based on a specific individual have circumstances and encounters that are largely fictional. There is one exception, and that is EKG, the charismatic floor broker. Someone like him really does exist but nothing like the situation where he is featured actually occurred.

Are any parts of *Silent Partners* true?

My father really did tell me about his introduction to a Korean scientist he had to rescue exactly in the manner a similar situation occurs in my book. I actually met a person like the character working on capital introductions for nefarious business dealings making a similar pitch. I was threatened by an insinuation like the main character is by a trader I caught rigging closing marks on his junk bonds.

The elements of the story that are authentic, I hope, are my descriptions of the neighborhoods where the main character works and resides. I tried to portray an accurate reflection of the culture and depict the Chicago Loop trading community post the 2008 market crash. Like the main character, I have enjoyed a varied and rewarding career working at exchanges and trading companies. Like in the story, most of the people I encountered are genuinely kind, care about their families, are hard-working, and active in charities and their communities.

The trading floor culture has changed and is radically different from the mythology. Although, it is true, and a shame that so many CME traders don't know any adverbs or adjectives other than the F-bomb. I try to describe the evolution from the perspective of people who are impacted by the changes.

I hope you enjoy *Silent Partners* and don't spend too much time guessing who may have inspired certain characters. I am working on a sequel. Feel free to contact me at **mtw@aether-analytics.com** if you have a good story that may be inspirational.

Acknowledgments

Big thank you to Chet, my husband who always enjoys a good laugh. I am especially thankful to Nicki Kuzn of Booktique Editing for being patient with a novice writer. Kudos to Kate for designing the jacket and Jodi Welter. Fred is inspired by my beloved English Mastiff, Moose who passed away. It will be lonely writing without him.

About the Author

Financial Services executive with vast experience with derivative proprietary trading companies, options and futures exchanges, hedge funds and financial technology firms. Is an active member of the community in various volunteer capacities for roughly 30 years. Writing mysteries is a new hobby that provides ample opportunities to reminisce with friends about our collective experiences working in the Chicago, New York and San Francisco trading communities. *Silent Partners* is also a fund raiser for The Greenwood Project. The net profits will fund its various programs for minority, college students to pursue careers in financial services and financial technology. Please check out www.greenwoodproject.org for a complete description of this worthwhile organization and its work.

I plan on offering *Silent Partners* to other non-profits that I support. At the time of this writing they include The Naperville Humane Society (**www.napervillehumange.org**) and The Neighborhood Food Pantries affiliated with The Northern Illinois Food Bank. (**www.neighborhoodfp.org**). Feel free to contact me at **mtw@aether-analytics.com** if you are interested in *Silent Partners* being a fund raiser for a charity you wish to support.

Made in the USA
Monee, IL
29 October 2022

16789267R00184